Horace Brown

Academy

DETECTIVE ~~AGENCY~~

RIDDLE OF THE
REDWOODS

Written by Troy Woodginski

Edited by Richelle Braswell and Laurie Shelley

Cover designed by Troy and Jennifer Woodginski

Special thank you to all of the test readers who made this story the best it could be.

ISBN/SKU 9798998608605

This book is dedicated to my wife, Jennifer, who pushed me to take the leap and turn my passion and creativity into something I can be proud of.

To anyone who hasn't found their Jenn yet,
I sincerely hope you do some day.

1

LEO checked his watch as he waited for the red hand to turn to the walking figure. It was only 1:26PM, and he had about four minutes to make it two more blocks to the detective agency.

He considered it a challenge. The moment the light changed, Leo continued to sprint down the sidewalk. He dodged and weaved around tourists, bicycles, and a very angry dog walker.

"Hey!" the man shouted, pumping his fist in the air.

"Sorry!" Leo shouted back at him, looking back to see him tangled up in the leashes.

For anyone not acquainted with the city, the honking of horns and clacking of metal grates in the sidewalks combined with the general stale smell could be overwhelming. New York City could also make a person feel small and insignificant with the size of its buildings and population. It could even be a place for new beginnings. To Leo, it was simply home.

Leo popped his earbud back in, blasting his workout playlist. He began to think about the reason he was running. It all boiled down to one single sentence that kept rolling around in his brain. A statement from the guidance counselor from his high school.

Normally, students with a similar grade point average would choose a different college.

That was enough for Leo to push harder than he had ever before. After the summer, he was going to be a senior. Then, he was determined to attend Adams College, which had the highest transfer ratio for baseball players to move to the big leagues. They also had an incredible scholarship program for athletes, which was something he would need if he wanted to attend *any* college.

As he came up to the next crosswalk, he slowed down and recognized a familiar face.

"Hey, Mr. Kumar!" he greeted, panting between each syllable.

"Leo!" his neighbor responded. "How are you? And your Gran?" Mr. Kumar lived down the hall from them in a building just a few blocks in the other direction.

"Good, good." Leo said, still trying to catch his breath. "And you?"

"Fantastic, thank you for asking. Where are you running off to?"

Leo's thoughts diverted to the true reason he was running. He explained that in just a couple of minutes, he had scheduled an interview with the famous detective, Horace Brown. For the first time ever, he was accepting three interns to share his knowledge with.

"Ah, no baseball this summer then?"

While his words were said innocently, they had felt like a punch to the gut. Every year, Leo's school offered a baseball camp. Every year, Leo attended with his friends.

This year, his final year, he had opted out of it in an attempt to build up his resume with extracurriculars. This was another recommendation that came from his guidance counselor. In her own words, *only if he really wanted it.*

"No, but I'll be back in the Fall," Leo replied, pushing down the feeling that he had disappointed yet another person. First his friends, then his coaches, now his neighbor.

The light changed and the two said their goodbyes. As he ran, he could feel the cool wind on his face. The breeze kept taking his tie, leading him to tuck it into his shirt until he reached his destination. His thoughts fell back to the internship.

It wasn't something he would've ever considered. Leo often listened to true crime podcasts, but he wouldn't think of mystery solving as one of his skills. Not to mention, Horace Brown seemed to be a mystery himself.

Leo had done some research to see what he could find on the detective, but there wasn't much before 1973 when the detective agency opened in New York City. Ever since then, Horace had been bouncing from case to case. Most were high-profile and had some odd circumstances surrounding them.

As the building came into view, Leo saw a crowd of people standing outside. Although there were dozens, maybe even hundreds, of applicants, Leo was determined to be accepted into the internship program. After pushing through the group of people, he pulled the door open with one hand and took the tie out of his shirt with the other, pushing it flat.

He took a deep breath and peaked at his watch. *Right on time.*

ALURA had her ShutterSwift account open on her phone, but she was hardly paying attention to it. There had to be at least 30 people crammed into the tiny office that held 15 comfortably. There were a few unoccupied chairs in the corner, but she wasn't even going to try to move over there to stage an attempt to secure one. She had already checked in and tried to move out of the way for anyone else who may need to let the receptionist know they had arrived.

In a way, Alura felt a little sorry for the woman sitting behind the desk. It was a well-known fact that Horace Brown was the best in the business for years before Alura was born, operating from the same office that was down the street from her aunt's apartment. According to the year on the door, the office had been open for over forty years. Honestly, Alura wouldn't be surprised if this woman had been working here just as long. She seemed a bit overwhelmed with the number of teenagers and some of their parents invading her workspace that was, more than likely, usually incredibly quiet. Overall, though, the receptionist just seemed very surprised that there were so many people here.

Alura was initially intrigued by the internship when she saw someone else posting about it online. She herself was a bit of an online celebrity, with close to fifty thousand subscribers to her ShutterSwift account for her makeup tutorials. When it

4

became available, she submitted her application almost immediately. Alura was hoping that this new experience might be an opportunity to figure out what she wanted to do once she graduated high school.

The idea of working in a detective agency also made her think of the Book Club for Two, a tradition that she shared with her mom before she had passed away. Toward the beginning of the school year, a car accident took the lives of both her mother and father. Small things, like agreeing on a book, reading it, and talking about it each month seemed to mean so much more now. Mysteries were their favorite genre.

She grasped her necklace, a small lump of gold that was molded into a beautiful seashell. It had been her mother's good luck charm. Today had been the first day that Alura had worn it since it had been left to her. It felt like the best day to cash in on all the good fortune that had been stored inside.

Thinking about it all now created a whirlwind of feelings in the pit of her stomach that she pushed down. She shifted focus to the people around her.

"Mom, stop!" a younger boy, probably a freshman, groaned. His mother was helping to get his tie situated.

"Bro, that's weak!" an older boy said, standing in the middle of the room with one of his friends. The two of them were obnoxiously practicing their handshakes, squeezing each other's hands as hard as they possibly could.

A girl near the door was wearing some sort of dress that was borderline inappropriate for a job interview, scrolling through to find the right filter for her selfie.

The rest of the crowd was split between deep-in-thought,

glazed looks and the classic nervous package: the shaking leg, the two hands cupped over the mouth, the darting gaze around the room. Some of the high-strung crowd read through their resumes. Alura avoided the late proofread as there was no way to fix any issues now.

Alura opened the camera on her phone, which was conveniently in selfie mode, and began to double check her makeup. Not too long after, she was happy to move out of the small, overcrowded space. A man came out of the hallway beside the desk, leading out a boy who was looking slightly defeated. The thin man stood tall, with white slicked-back hair accompanied by some unkept facial hair. He was certainly older and moved slowly but had a very distinct determination about him, both in his movements and the look on his face.

The old man wore tan slacks, a white button up shirt, and a bowtie. Alura did her research before she applied for the internship, and there was never a picture of Horace Brown without some kind of bowtie around his neck.

"Next up, I'm looking for Alura," he said deeply, "Alura?"

The room fell silent for a moment, then conversations started back up when the others realized they weren't the ones that were being summoned.

Alura moved toward the desk, making sure to thank the receptionist on her way by for all her help. A smile came across her face, then she turned back to assist the next applicant in line.

"My name is Horace Brown," the man introduced himself, smiling. It was very genuine, as if he hadn't been repeating that statement all day long. He gestured down the hallway, "Right this way."

LIZ entered the small office space, immediately recognizing a Newton's Cradle, a device that demonstrates momentum, that decorated the detective's desk, along with a stack of folders and a pencil cup with some zany-looking pens inside. The small room was also lined with bookshelves. Liz noted his collection, including numerous encyclopedias, history books, and how-to books for new inventors. Some of her favorite mystery authors made an appearance on the shelves as well. Liz had a real urge to organize everything before she sat down, but she fought it with all her might.

She took a seat in the chair opposite the desk at the same time that Horace slowly lowered himself into his office chair with a small grunt. He shuffled some papers around, finding one that he began to look at through small bifocals that perched on the edge of his nose. She recognized it as her resume that had been sent over earlier in the week. With the amount of clutter in this office, she was surprised how quickly he was able to find it. The older man moved the paper back and forth to get it to come into view through his spectacles.

"Elizabeth," Horace said. "Is that right?"

"Yes sir," she replied with the most professional tone she could muster. Liz had been on a few interviews, mainly from local news stations about her science fair projects. "Most people call me Liz, but whichever you prefer."

"Well, which do *you* prefer?" he asked, quizzically.

Liz's face contorted for a moment, the question catching her off guard.

She had never really thought about it before. She supposed that one day someone had called her Liz, just because it was easier, and everyone had assumed that she liked it better than Elizabeth. She shook off the looming existential crisis and tried to piece together an answer.

"Oh, uh, I suppose I prefer Liz," she fumbled out. "I like Elizabeth too, but it's really long. I guess it is just easier for people to call me Liz."

"Alright," Horace replied, shifting in his chair a bit. "Let me ask you something. Why did you apply for this internship?"

Good, an easy question that she had prepared for.

"Well, I am looking forward to my senior year starting in September. I'm going to start applying for colleges, and I'd really like to build up my resume with something as prestigious as working with a world-renowned detective," she explained, just as she had practiced on the bus ride over.

Part of my 27-step plan to become an award-winning biologist, Liz thought to herself. *After building up my application with this internship, I'll definitely be admitted to Olympia University.*

"Why *this* opening though?" he questioned, "It looks like you are certainly interested more in science and mathematics in school. Not to kill any expectations, but detective work is a little different than what you might see in calculus class."

Liz paused for a second, not really expecting a rebuttal from the old man. Although, out of everyone who would push for more details, a famous detective would certainly be toward the top of the list.

"On the contrary," Liz began confidently, "I believe they

take many of the same skills. I love reading mysteries and finding the solution before the final chapter. I really love laying out all the pieces of the puzzle and trying to figure out what exactly happened, taking things away and replacing them with other ideas, similar to a science experiment."

The chair squeaked for mercy as Horace leaned back in it, his cheeks drawn tight as his lips curled into a smile. He shook his head and returned his focus to the paper in front of him.

"I recognized your last name," the man noted, "Your parents, they are doctors, yes?"

"Yes," Liz nodded.

Her parents were semi-famous, known around the world as Doctors From Down the Street, or Doctors Rodney and Martha. Some considered them geniuses, even visionaries, within the field. They had dedicated most of their lives to traveling the world, helping anyone they came across. It was common for teachers and advisors to acknowledge her parents, but she didn't expect the famous detective to know who they were. Liz assumed that they ran in different circles, after all.

"Do you know them?" Liz asked in an attempt to break his concentration on her resume.

"No, no," Horace admitted, "I've never met them. Just know the name is all. You don't want to follow in their footsteps?"

Liz could feel her jaw getting tight. It was a question that she had been asked close to a hundred times. Legacy was very important to her family. Although her three siblings, Junior, Kelly, and Emily, were much too young to understand, their parents pushed them all to be incredible people that could change the world.

She couldn't wait to be recognized as *herself* and not the daughter of her parents.

"Not necessarily," Liz responded after thorough calculation. A wrong answer could give the impression that she wasn't fully committed to the internship. *This is the ultimate steppingstone for my 27-step plan.*

Horace sat back in his chair for a moment of contemplation, then leaned down to the bottom drawer of his desk. Pulling it open with a spine-tingling shriek, he grabbed a few papers. Before the three sheets were laid out in front of her, Liz knew exactly what they were. The first had a handful of riddles printed on it, the next had a dozen or so math and science questions, and the third was a simple "Spot the Difference" that looked like it had been poorly copied from a magazine or cereal box.

He reached over and grabbed his collection of pens and pushed it toward her, retreating into his chair carefully. Now that Liz had gotten a closer look at this explosion of craziness, she identified a few pens that were shaped like everyday objects, like a paintbrush and a rocket ship.

"Pick one, please," Horace gestured toward the cup, "These are some of my favorite problems. I'd really like to see how you do with them, Elizabeth."

She grabbed a pen with a small magnifying glass as the clicker as she felt it was very fitting to the situation and started on the problems.

ISAAC sat in his bedroom with only the light from his

computer illuminating the space. When he had started playing a few hours ago, it had been bright outside, and the natural sunlight was enough. The computer flashed with vibrant colors while Isaac tried to battle his way through a level he had been stuck on for a little while.

The ultimate objective was to reach the Wizard's Tower, but he was having trouble getting to the stage. It was the sequel to a game that Isaac and his older brother, Carter, would play when they were kids. It certainly would've been much easier with two players, but Carter was away at college and the only other person at home was his mom. No offense to her, but it wasn't much of an option at all.

Earlier in the day, he had sat reading a mystery book that he picked up at the library. This was not unlike Isaac, but there was a major difference. Normally, he didn't really get too many texts or phone calls from friends, nor did he really care too much about any social media. However, when he was reading his book, his phone rested on his chest. Isaac checked it every few minutes. In between those minutes that he checked, the novel certainly felt neglected just as much.

It really wasn't his fault though. All morning, he was awaiting a phone call or even an email from the famous detective, Horace Brown, to see if he had been accepted to his internship program. As the hours ticked by, he became more and more disinterested in the topic. Why wait for something that might never come? Disappointment was easy to avoid when it was denied power.

Just before noon, Isaac had seen that the first intern had been chosen through social media. A girl named Elizabeth had announced that she had been the first offered and accepted the opportunity. After a bit of snooping, it looked like she preferred to go by Liz and she was sort of a math and science prodigy. Isaac supposed that there were good reasons why Mr. Brown would choose such a brilliant mind. This acceptance was tough to swallow, but there was still some hope inside of him.

As he ventured out of his room for snacks or lunch, his mom asked him if there had been any news. He did not share his discouraged feelings on the topic, but he did alert her to the girl being accepted. She assured him that if he truly wanted it, it would work out. The truth was that he really wasn't sure. Summer after summer, and even while he was in school, Isaac kept to himself and either played video games or read books. There wasn't really too much else to life for him. His mom had pushed him to apply for the internship. At first, he was very nervous about the whole thing, but once he was able to come to terms with how much fun it could be, he knew it was something he wanted.

It was something he wanted, until the second announcement came through about half an hour after the first. A senior named Leo who appeared to be a baseball player was chosen and had accepted. It was not difficult to find, it looked like the original post came from Leo and was duplicated more than a hundred times on his follower's stories. Many were congratulatory or best wishes to him.

There was only one spot left in the internship program.

"Come on!" Isaac groaned, putting down his controller. Dying one last time, he turned off his computer and laid down on his bed, staring at the posters that wallpapered his room. For most of the day, he was trying to distract himself from the disappointment of not being chosen while also trying to push off hope that he could still be chosen. He was sure that the final intern had been chosen. They just hadn't make it known yet.

As if on cue, his phone dinged beside him. The news of the third and final intern came through.

If Leo's was shared a hundred times, this announcement must have been a hundred thousand. He recognized the third girl, Alura, as someone who went to school with him. They had never spoken but they had shared a few classes together. Both were going to be juniors when school started again. Although Isaac stayed far away from most people, it only made it easier to watch from a distance. Isaac didn't *know* Alura personally, but he knew that she was big into social media. Alura had close to fifty thousand followers for her makeup tutorials. She was also one of the most popular girls at his school.

Isaac sat quietly on his bed for a moment. A feeling of emptiness settled in his stomach, then disappeared like a coin into a vending machine.

Honestly, he wasn't even sure why he had hyped himself up so much. It wasn't something he wanted in the first place. Why did his mom get him so excited? He knew deep down that he wasn't going to get it. Besides, waking up early in the summer? That's not really something that he wanted anyway. It didn't seem *fun*. It was *work*. Why was he going to sell his summer to some detective? He wasn't even sure if he was getting paid for the work.

Isaac put his hands over his face and drifted into a trance.

His cat, Jasper, joined him on the bed and nestled up close. Suddenly, he felt a strange sensation on his back. He immediately sat up straight to find that he had been laying on his phone. Without a second thought, he knew exactly who it was. The phone number was the same as on the flyer for the internship. He quickly answered the call.

"Can you hear me? I'm looking for Isaac," a man's voice came through before he was able to get himself together. Why didn't he take a second before answering the phone? Isaac mentally facepalmed but pushed himself to answer the man.

"Yes, I'm here, sorry," he said as casually as he could. "I dropped my phone for a second. I am here though."

"Good!" the man exclaimed. It was Mr. Brown *himself!* Isaac shook off any premonitions and just tried to be present in the moment. "My son got me this strange *smart* phone for my birthday and honestly, it doesn't seem very smart at all. I never know if I'm doing something wrong. I think I might ask him for my old phone back. I wonder if he still has it."

Horace's voice trailed off and there was a moment of silence. Although Isaac couldn't be sure, he could picture the man writing himself a note as a reminder to ask. In his office yesterday afternoon, he had noticed hundreds of sticky notes around the man's workspace to ensure he would never forget anything.

"Anyway!" Horace returned with power after his short moment of silence, "I don't know if you've heard, but I have selected my interns for the program. I am still working with one, but as of right now, I have a full team." Isaac's heart sank a little bit at this confirmation. He let out a small sigh and put his free hand over his forehead. This rollercoaster of emotion was a bit too much for him. How did anyone ever apply for a job? The not-knowing was way too much for him, but the constant battle of accepting defeat and being hopeful was incredibly difficult.

"I just had a few questions for you if that would be alright," Horace started. "I really liked our interview, and I think you're a really intelligent individual." *Stop!* Isaac closed his eyes.

"Yes sir," he responded genuinely, "I really enjoyed our talk about mystery writers. I'm planning a trip to the bookstore soon to pick up some of the ones you suggested." There was a brief moment of silence. "Oh, and yes! I would be able to answer a few questions for you. Sorry about that, I'm a little nervous."

Why are we admitting that we're nervous? Isaac asked himself.

"So, my first question for you is," Horace paused for what seemed like an eternity, "I own a pet, true or false?"

"True," Isaac responded without a second thought. Although they hadn't discussed it, he had noticed two small dishes on the floor near the closet of his office.

"Alright, and what kind of animal is it?" Isaac wondered what this had to do with anything.

"It is a cat, sir," he responded, remembering the small fish printed on the bowl.

"Okay," he said. Isaac could've sworn he had heard a chuckle from the other end of the phone. "And what color is my cat, Mister Isaac?"

Isaac paused for a moment, trying to remember. He took a

deep breath and looked across the room at his computer chair. There were three chairs in Horace's office yesterday. One was his own behind the desk, and the other two faced him. Isaac occupied one, and to the left was the other. He chose the one on the right because the other had pet hair all over it. Could he be sure though?

"Isaac, I need you to tell me what color my cat is," Horace instructed. "If you don't know, that's alright. I really don't think that's the case though."

"It's…" Isaac paused, then with a burst of confidence, "grey. Your cat is grey."

"One final question, Isaac," Horace said, without any indication as to whether or not the previous answers were correct, "And I will admit that this one is going to be tough. My anniversary is coming up within the next few weeks…"

Isaac knew exactly what the question that followed would be, but he hardly knew how it held any significance. Had he fallen asleep when he laid down and this was a dream? Was the detective messing with him right now?

"What is the date of my anniversary?" Horace asked.

Isaac thought back to the calendar in his office. There was a large red mark on the calendar at the end of July. He tried to picture the exact placement of the circle to figure out what day of the week it would be.

"July 22nd is the date of your anniversary," Isaac said after taking a moment to think. He was willing to play the old man's game. What did he really have to lose?

"Thank you, Isaac," Horace said. "I would like to apologize for calling you so much later than the other three candidates, but I needed to make sure there was enough of an interval to test your memory. Over the last couple of days, I have interviewed dozens of kids, but I needed to make sure that your observational skills were truly as extraordinary as I hoped they were."

Isaac felt weak for a moment. *What is he saying?*

"Welcome to the team, Isaac," the detective said. "I would like you to meet me at my office on this upcoming Tuesday at noon. Come dressed professionally but bring a change of comfortable clothes. Please call me if there are any issues, and you cannot make the appointment."

"Thank, uh, thank you sir," Isaac said awkwardly. "I will be there at noon."

Mr. Brown hung up the phone, but it took a moment for Isaac to take the phone away from his ear. As he lowered the phone toward the bed, he fell backward with a huge smile stretching across his face.

2

HORACE placed the picture he was looking at back into the worn-out folder he had on his desk. Slowly, he closed it and stacked it with the others neatly off to the side of his workspace. The clock above the door showed about half an hour until the kids started showing up. He took a deep breath, unsure if any part of his old body would be knocked out of place when he rose from his chair. Luckily, he got to his feet without any further obstacles.

Shuffling around the furniture and toward the door, he started toward the front of the building to prepare for their arrival. As Horace walked down the narrow hallway, he noticed the peeling wallpaper. Fixing it would hardly be worth it as more and more would just start falling down. This time of year, it was always an issue. He assumed it was because of the summer heat and humidity, but who could really know for sure? The best solution, which Horace had already lazily done multiple times throughout his occupation of the building, was to put up pictures.

Out of the two dozen pictures on the wall, only three

of them didn't come with the frame. They included a picture of him with his wife, son, daughter-in-law, and their two grandchildren, one of a little boy and a little girl, and the final was a painting of the New York City skyline, which was an unconventional sort of a tip for excellent service. The others included lighthouses, valleys, boats, and the occasional random family. A person could find pictures cheap pretty much anywhere, and he got most of his at thrift stores and yard sales.

Horace continued his long journey up to the front of the building, passing the conference room, an empty office that doubled as a dump for all his random files, and the supply closet. He finally made it up to the desk and was greeted by Dot, his receptionist.

"Hello, sir," she said, fixing her glasses. "How is everything today?"

"It's alright," Horace said. "Any important calls before I start with our new interns?"

"Nothing to report," Dot said, looking down at her desk.

Dot started with Horace in 1978, just about five years after the agency opened. Back then, she was incredible and kept on top of everything. Over the years, Horace had seen her take three phone calls at a single time, never getting them twisted or mixed up. At some point, Horace started to consider her as one of his closest friends. He assumed she felt the same, but that conversation had never surfaced, which was fine with Horace.

"Did you finish your breakfast?" she asked.

"Yes," Horace responded with a faint smile. "While I am in the meeting, I'm going to ask you to hold everything, as if I was out of the office. Let them know that I will get back to them as soon as possible."

"Okay, that is doable," Dot said, looking for paper and a pen to make a note. "What would you like me to do when the kids arrive?"

"Well," Horace said, thinking deeply, "ask them to wait in the lobby, and I will be out to join them around noon. Elizabeth, the girl with the glasses, will be arriving soon. Then, my guess, Alura will come in about five minutes before noon, and Leo will rush in at noon or a few minutes after."

"Wait," Dot counted on her fingers, "isn't that only three? I thought you said you had chosen four. What about the other boy?"

"Isaac," Horace offered, "He won't be late." The detective bent down a little bit, so his eye level was closer to Dot's. He shakily pointed across the street to a bench where a young man with a backpack sat in a button-up shirt and tie.

ALURA received a ding from her phone while she stuffed her sweatpants and t-shirt into a reusable bag supplied by her aunt. Living with her aunt was great, but she had a few quirks, like how she needed to get a reusable bag from every place they went. This specific one was from an Egyptian exhibition at the Natural History Museum and had a cartoon mummy with the words "Who's your mummy" printed on it. Thankfully, it was one of the bigger ones so it could fit the requested change of clothes.

She leaned down to her bed to check the notification which informed her of comments and likes on her newest video that was posted this morning.

Most of the remaining replies wished her well and offered congratulations, but there were a handful that questioned why she had applied for the internship in the first place. While saying this to someone in real life might be considered rude, Alura was used to it. Most of her followers were complete strangers who didn't know her other than her makeup tutorials.

The truth was that Alura wasn't sure how much longer she really wanted to do them. She had made her accounts about a year ago, and she had close to 50,000 subscribers. While many users who posted similar content did it as a living and often took marketing companies up on paid partnerships, Alura had always turned them down. She really wasn't doing it for money. She just enjoyed doing it in general. Honestly, she had no idea why anyone even watched her videos.

Like so many adults, her aunt and uncle did not really understand how it worked either. They were incredibly supportive where they could be, but social media was a foreign concept for them. Alura hoped that, if and when she decided to stop, it wouldn't be disappointing to them. Becoming a junior in September was a big deal for any student. It was a signal for her and her classmates to start thinking about colleges and their futures. This was something Alura thought about often but rarely gained any ground on making a decision.

Alura took a deep breath and shoved her phone into her neatly packed purse, then grabbed the second bag. As she exited her room, she did a quick spin in front of the mirror to ensure that her hair was still in place and her shoes matched her dress.

Making her way down the hall, she was greeted by her Aunt Kate who stood over the counter making a sandwich for lunch.

"Hey," she said excitedly, putting down the bread, "ready for your first day?"

"I think so," Alura said. "I think I've got everything. Horace asked me to bring some extra stuff."

"Ooh, like what?" Aunt Kate asked. "Mysterious man making mysterious requests?"

"He asked me to bring a change of clothes. I don't know why," Alura pondered. "I guess it'll all be explained once I get there."

"Well, that *is* weird," Aunt Kate agreed. "I wouldn't think too much into it though, honey. He might have asked you just to throw you off a bit. He definitely knows you're sharp. He doesn't want you to outshine him in front of the other interns!"

She laughed and moved in for a hug and kiss on the top of the head. She was probably right. There was no reason why he would ask for the change of clothes. Either way though, the phone call that she had with him made her think that he was omitting something. She couldn't say he was lying or hiding anything, but there were definitely things that he wasn't sharing on purpose. It just made her even more ready for her first day on the job.

"Well, I'm going to get going," she said, breaking free of the embrace. "I've got about ten minutes to get over there and I

22

want to make sure I make a good first impression."

"Have a good first day and good luck!" Aunt Kate walked her toward the front door, kicking her Uncle Rick's recliner on her way by. "*Rick*, Alura is leaving for her first day. Wish her good luck!"

"Huh, oh," Uncle Rick sat up a little bit, obviously dazed and confused. "Good luck." He immediately dropped back down into the chair. Alura did not take it personally; she knew he had just worked an overnight shift. Being a security guard often had him working late hours. She waved to her aunt and in the general direction of her uncle and made her way out the door, closing it behind her.

As she stepped out onto the street, she took a deep breath. The entire situation was stressful, but she just kept reminding herself that it would be fun. She started her five-minute walk down the couple blocks to the detective agency. Her mind raced with the possibilities of what her first day would entail. Although most of the work would probably just be paperwork or making phone calls, she secretly hoped she would get the opportunity to crack a case. She tried her hardest not to get too excited, but her expectations were through the roof.

Her mind wandered away from the upcoming activities and shifted toward the other two candidates that she would be working alongside. With her social media expertise, she was able to get some information on them. As someone who had many people constantly watching her videos and checking out her posts, she knew that "snooping" was just a word that people who didn't want to seem strange used. *Everyone* did it. Just a week ago, a girl who made a point of being rude to Alura at school liked one of her videos and almost immediately retracted it.

Nevertheless, the internet was a public place and she used it as such. Leo seemed like a nice boy. It looked like he was a year older than Alura. They did not go to the same high school, but his was not far from the agency either. It seemed like he played all the sports his high school offered including baseball, basketball, and football. He had a large number of local followers which were clearly people he knew in real life. Alura made it a point to not judge a book by its cover. However, he seemed to have a good number of friends and attended parties often, leading her to believe that he was definitely one of the more popular kids in his school.

Liz was the other girl who had been accepted to the program and had a handful of posts on her ShutterSwift, mainly highlighting her academic achievements. There were a couple of pictures of her holding trophies at events and a few of her posing awkwardly at family events. Her pages were also sprinkled with pictures of her current and past projects, such as some sort of recycling machine she had invented herself. Liz was smart, there was no denying it. She was also a year older than Alura, and it looked like she attended the same school as Leo.

While Alura could snoop online until her phone battery died, there was only so much it could tell you. There was real value in meeting people for real and seeing their body language and the way they talked and dressed. She loved meeting new people for this reason.

ALURA loved the warmth of the sun in the summertime, peeking out from behind the skyscrapers. It made her feel invigorated and energized.

As she came up to the final crosswalk and Horace's building came into view, she spotted a boy standing off to the left of the big glass window, just out of view of the occupants inside.

He looked familiar to Alura, but it was difficult to place at this distance. All she could see was the back of his head and the wrinkle-free shirt that was tucked into his slacks. From across the street, she was also able to see his freshly shined dress shoes.

The boy was hunched over, looking at his phone. As she approached, she realized that he was scrolling through the home screen of his apps. It was immediately clear that the boy was either bored or nervous, or possibly both. He picked up his head when he realized that Alura was just a few feet away.

"Isaac?" Alura asked. "Hey!"

"Hi," he said, smiling shyly and putting his hand up in a half-wave. The other hand was carrying what appeared to be a plate of cookies in a zipper-seal bag. At this point, he had turned to fully face her, and it was obvious. He was nervous. The shaking hand and the glowing sweat were both indicators that solidified this fact.

"I don't know if you remember me," Alura started, "but we are in Math together. Sorry, we *were* in math together. I think you sat behind me, right?"

"Yes," he coughed, "I think you're right."

Alura didn't talk to Isaac much during their class together, but she knew he was smart. A couple of times, his test was passed back to her by mistake, and it was always a high grade. He didn't really talk to anyone if she remembered correctly. This was one of the first times he had used his voice in front of her.

"Wait," Alura processed, "are you an intern for Horace this summer?"

"Yeah," Isaac responded with a small smile, "I got a call a few hours after you guys."

"That's awesome!" she tried to get him a little more comfortable. It was odd, Alura thought there was only meant to be three interns. *Maybe one of the others backed out?* "Well, I'm just glad I know someone else here. The other two don't go to our school, and they're seniors."

Isaac nodded his head in agreement and took a deep breath. Alura could tell that he was still nervous, but she knew a friendly face would help him. She knew it would help her in that situation. Even though they weren't really *friends*, she knew that he was nice and just awkward.

Alura wondered if one of the other interns had backed out, or if Horace decided on a fourth team member instead. Her train of thought was broken when she zeroed in on what Isaac was holding.

"Did you make cookies?" Alura asked, taking a step closer to peek through the bag.

"Yeah, kind of," Isaac lifted the plate up higher, "My, um, my mom actually made them."

Although he was nervous, Alura knew that it was a lie. She believed that he had made them but was just too shy to take credit for it. Taking a closer look, the cookies were in the shape of little magnifying glasses.

"That is so cool!" Alura exclaimed, truly impressed with the craftsmanship. "They look just like the real thing!"

"Thanks," Isaac said, with a bright, prideful smile, confirming Alura's doubts. He looked down at the sidewalk.

"Well, I'm going to head inside," Alura tossed out. "Did you want to walk in together?"

Isaac nodded his head, and they moved toward the door of the detective's agency. Alura was surprised to see Isaac move a little faster than her to reach the entrance before she was able to reach for the handle. As he opened it and gestured for her to go inside, the feeling shifted from surprise that the shy boy wanted to enter first to a warmth at his kindness. She thanked him and smiled a little as she proceeded into the lobby.

Two people were inside, the girl named Liz and the receptionist that sat behind the counter. Alura and Isaac stood in the door for a moment before she looked up from her typing and waved them over.

"Hello everyone," she said with a weary smile. "I was just telling Liz, Horace will be out in a few minutes to grab you. It's Alura and Isaac, right? My name is Dot. I am Horace's secretary. It's really a pleasure to meet you all again. Our team has only been the two of us for the last few years. It's so nice to have some fresh faces around. You can have a seat if you'd like."

"Thank you, Dot," Alura shook her hand. "It's really nice to meet you too."

The two shook hands, and Isaac also leaned forward for a shake. Dot lowered herself back into the desk chair, pushed her small glasses up onto her nose, and began to type again. Alura was unsure what kind of work she was doing, but she sure was striking the keys furiously.

Dot reminded Alura of her first-grade teacher. They both shared similar facial features that highlighted their age but also their wisdom. Retirement was surely an option, but there was a certain sharpness in their eyes, showing how much they loved what they did. Although Alura had only had two interactions with the woman, a few things were very clear. Her loyalty to Horace was unmatched, she held a lot of knowledge and wisdom, and her innocent look did not match her personality.

As Alura moved toward Liz, Isaac followed behind, holding the paper plate of treats. As far as the pair noticed, Liz hadn't looked up from her phone since they walked in. Her attention was directed to the screen where a news article was pulled up. The girl pushed her hair out of her face as she scrolled.

"Hi, you must be Liz," Alura reached her hand out for a friendly shake. "My name is Alura, and this is Isaac. We are two of the other interns. It's nice to meet you."

"I knew about you, Alura," she said without looking up from her phone. "I was surprised to see *you*, though."

"Oh, yeah," Alura responded, awkwardly retreating her hand. "This is Isaac and I think the other intern's name is Leo. It looks like Horace changed his mind to *four* of us."

"I know Leo. We go to school together," Liz made a sour face. "I wouldn't be surprised if he isn't here after twelve thirty. He's been late to every class we've shared."

"That's awesome! Isaac and I go to school together too," Alura exclaimed, expertly avoiding the unpleasant conversation.

28

As Liz stood up, the time was visible. It was two minutes past noon, so it was true that Leo was a little late. Hopefully it wasn't too much longer, though. Alura was excited to get started and she would really hate to see Horace get upset with Leo on the first day. To break up the silence while also avoiding a staring contest, Alura moved toward the wall to take a look at some of the pictures. There was one that had a man and a woman with younger children. It looked like a family portrait. The husband had a strong resemblance to Horace, minus the frizzy white facial hair.

"That's Horace's son," Isaac said, leaning in to point at the man, "I think."

"I'd assume so as well," Liz said flatly. "The quality of the picture means that it's recent. I don't think it could be him. The photo would need to be older."

"Yeah," Isaac nodded his head, "he mentioned his son the other day on the phone."

Alura noticed that Isaac was shy about his thoughts but seemed to be unaffected by Liz's discouraging tone, which was interesting. The two presences seemed to be opposites. Both knew what they were talking about and were able to connect the dots easily enough, but Isaac was more reserved while Liz was very full speed ahead, fueled by her confidence.

She sidestepped to the next picture, which looked like a recent photo as well. The man was certainly Horace this time. He was gazing into the eyes of a woman with bright blue eyes and silver hair pulled back into a ponytail. The woman was looking back at him with a loving smile.

"Dot, is this Horace's wife?" Alura asked, pointing toward

the framed photo. She stood up and adjusted her glasses, squinting a bit.

"Yes," she said quietly, "That's Eleanor. She passed away a few months ago. It was a very tough time for everyone." She looked down at the floor for a moment, then sat back down and began working again. It seemed like a touchy situation, as any death would be. It must be difficult for anyone to lose their significant other. With Horace in the other room, she was sure that Dot didn't want to bring up any hard feelings.

Alura avoided eye contact with the other two teens for a bit and began to move toward the next frame, which appeared to be a painting. When she went in for her interview, she noticed more pictures on the wall in the hallway as well. She wondered what other secrets they held. Before she could start studying it, the door burst open, and Leo rushed into the room.

"Hey guys," he said, catching his breath. "Sorry that I'm late. I ran all the way here. Are those cookies?"

Without saying anything, Isaac held up the plate to the other boy. Alura quickly noticed that he was wearing basketball shorts and a T-shirt. She was fairly certain that Horace had asked them to wear professional clothing and bring a change of something comfortable, but she wasn't completely sure. It seemed that the others had the same understanding as Alura, since Isaac was dressed in his button-up, and Liz was wearing a sweater vest.

With Isaac still holding the plate, Leo unwrapped the end and grabbed a few cookies, shoveling them into his mouth like a conveyor belt.

"These are pretty good," Leo said, his mouth full of the treat.

"Thanks," Isaac said shyly. He looked toward the floor, awkwardly.

"Isaac actually made them himself," Alura said, calling him out on his lie. The reaction to Leo's compliment confirmed her theory that his mother hadn't made them. For a split second, he glared at her, but then his gaze returned toward the worn wood floors.

"Dude," Leo said between his chews, "these are epic. Definitely better than the ones my Gran makes."

"Thanks," Isaac smiled widely and used his free hand to return the thumbs up gesture from Leo.

"My name is Alura," she said, reaching out her hand. "This is Isaac. We go to school together. I think you already know Liz. She told us that you both go to the same school, too."

Leo crammed the final cookie into his mouth and quickly wiped the crumbs on his shorts, then shook Alura's hand. Afterwards, he gave Isaac a quick finger pistol.

"Yeah, I think Liz and I had a few classes together last year when we were juniors," Leo said, squinting a bit.

"Two," Liz confirmed. "We had Chemistry and History. Didn't Horace ask us to come dressed professionally?"

"Oh, I thought he said to bring a change of dress clothes but to come wearing something comfortable," Leo chuckled awkwardly. "I guess I didn't hear him right. Do you think I have time to change?"

Alura was surprised that Liz's eyes didn't disappear into the back of her head, she rolled them so hard. While Leo was in the wrong, it was like a trainwreck of awkwardness unfolding before her eyes. Alura herself didn't mind confrontation if it was called for, but it didn't seem like Liz knew where the brakes were.

"I wouldn't worry about it," Alura reassured him. "If he wants you to change, he'll probably ask though. I mean, as long as you have your clothes, I don't think he'll be upset or anything."

Leo nodded his head and reached for another cookie, his slightly nervous look disappearing into thin air.

During the couple of minutes they had, Alura took a moment to fully absorb the team. She wasn't sure what kind of work they'd be doing for Horace, but it was clear that the interns would probably need to work as a team. When it came to sociability and being talkative, Isaac was definitely an outlier. He didn't really say too much, whereas the other three seemed to fall into the extroverted category. However, he surely held other skills.

Leo seemed like a nice kid but very scatterbrained. His mannerisms and tardiness just highlighted this trait. Although she wasn't sure when it could come in handy for working at a detective's office, he was in better shape than anyone else here. She only lived two blocks away and she couldn't imagine *running* the entire way. Liz seemed to be incredibly bothered by his disorganized personality. Alura assumed that it was a combination of both Liz's experience with him before and a certain perfectionism when it came to how things should be, like punctuality.

Just like starting a new year in school, there seemed to be a bit of awkwardness in the air. Alura could make herself feel comfortable in most situations, especially involving new people, but the uncertainty about what this day would unfold into caused her to feel more out of place than she normally did. It wasn't just another year of school, this was her first job.

Her train of thought was broken when a door creaked open, and Horace appeared down the hallway. He began shuffling toward the waiting area. He looked a bit more relaxed than the first time they'd met him. His hair was still slicked back, the bifocals sat at the tip of his nose, and it looked like he was able to wrangle his beard today. He wore a wrinkled white dress shirt, tan slacks, suspenders, all accompanied with a striped bowtie. As he got nearer, his smile was evident through the crack in his moustache and beard as well as the highlighted wrinkles in the corners of his eyes.

"Hello, hello!" Horace greeted extravagantly, throwing up his hands. "I'm glad to see you all made it! Liz, Alura, Isaac, Leo, I hope you are all ready for a busy day of work."

The smile disappeared from his face as he addressed something more serious.

"Cookies?"

"Yes," Isaac held out the plate with a sliver more confidence than the first time. Horace took the entire plate and started launching them into his mouth. The resemblance between him and Leo was uncanny. Only a few decades of age separated the two.

"Before we get started, let me just check something with Miss Dot here," he turned toward her. "Anything important come through? I am going to be MIA for the next couple hours or so."

"Nothing at all sir," Dot informed him. "You still have your appointment Friday in the morning, though."

"Good, good," Horace nodded his head and began turning toward the hall. "If you'd all like to follow me, we can get started."

3

ISAAC was still internally smiling from Leo's compliment. At first, he was upset with Alura for outing him in front of the rest of the group, but he couldn't really be mad anymore. However, he was a bit bothered by how easily she was able to figure out that he had been lying.

People who can spot lies like that can be tricky, he thought to himself.

When he left his house this morning, he had a backup plan that depended purely on how comfortable he felt. Isaac didn't have many friends other than the ones he played video games with. Granted, he hadn't really *met* them in person. If he felt weird about bringing the cookies, he'd just say that his mother made them for the group.

While he was getting ready this morning, he thought more about meeting Leo and Liz. Isaac really didn't know what to expect. Alura made him nervous, of course. She was one of the prettiest, most popular girls in his school. Opting to go with the backup plan just made sense. However Alura knew that he was fibbing about the whole thing. He wasn't the best liar in

New York City, but he was surprised that she was able to identify it so quickly. Nonetheless, he was both impressed and a little grateful for the skill.

Mr. Brown led the bunch down the narrow hallway, his brown leather shoes reflecting the light from the front window. The hall was spotted with pictures on either side. He was followed by Liz, Alura, Leo, and then Isaac. As he was glancing at some of the pictures, he noticed the glossiness of the paper within the frames. It wasn't a normal shininess, almost like a magazine page. The group moved past two rooms across from each other. On the right, RECORDS was marked on the closed door. They could also see Horace's office. They made a right at the next set of doors.

In the room, there was a long table with four chairs on either side. At the end of the table was a whiteboard on wheels with numerous colors of dry-erase markers in the tray at the bottom. There were no windows, just discolored wallpaper. It seemed like a pretty average conference room to Isaac, except for the strange, lumpy object covered with a dusty tarp in the corner of the room.

"Have a seat anywhere, and we can get started," Mr. Brown instructed, assuming the position at the head of the table.

Liz sat toward the front of the table, taking a notebook and pen out of her bag and setting up her workspace neatly in front of her. Leo sat on the same side of the rectangular table but in the seat furthest from Mr. Brown. Alura sat a seat away from the front and Isaac pulled out the chair across from Leo.

"Welcome, interns. As I am sure you know, this is the first time that I have ever done anything like this," Mr. Brown said, stroking his beard. "I actually haven't hired anyone in close to fifteen years. For the majority of recent years, it has just been me and Dot as employees of the Horace Brown Detective Agency."

There was a brief moment of silence as he played with his moustache. Isaac wondered if he had missed something when he zeroed in on Liz furiously writing something in her notepad.

"Anyway, I will do a quick introduction," he continued, gesturing to each person as he spoke about them, "Leo, star athlete with several awards and honors for many sports. Alura, somewhat of an internet star as far as I understand. Liz, incredibly intelligent and knowledgeable about a number of subjects. Isaac, a boy with a very bright mind."

Mr. Brown shot Isaac a wink. Isaac recognized that most people would be bothered by the lackluster introduction compared to the other interns, but he was just happy that he wasn't the subject of a huge spectacle.

"My name is Horace Brown," he said, turning the figurative spotlight toward himself, "I started this business in 1973, long before you all were born. Probably before most of your parents were born, actually. I have always had an interest in helping people, especially those who cannot help themselves. I have worked both independently and paired with local police departments around the world that are in need of a *different* point of view."

It was no lie; Isaac had done a lot of research on the man before he signed up for the internship. The fan sites alone dedicated to this man and his company were overflowing with cases that he had solved across the United States, as well as Europe, Asia, and South America. The addition of his name to any investigation meant a solution was not far behind.

"Now, I'd like to give each of you the floor," he informed them, "but first, can you close the door, Isaac?"

Isaac nodded, completing the task and heading back toward his seat. Something was different, and he hesitated to sit down. A pair of piercing green eyes stared up at him. The small grey mass must be the detective's cat!

"Everything alright, sir?" Mr. Brown asked, looking in his direction. Isaac didn't think he was frozen for that long, but it was enough to get Mr. Brown's attention.

"I uh, um," Isaac struggled to put his problem into words and could've easily just sat in the next chair. Now, Mr. Brown had stopped the whole presentation because he didn't act quicker.

"Is it Alice?" he inquired. "I'd hate to say it, but your chair is gone, kiddo. There is no moving that cat once she has made up her mind. Come sit up here." He pulled out the chair closest to him, across from Liz and next to Alura. Isaac grabbed his stuff and moved to the front.

"Alright, now that that's settled," Mr. Brown cleared his throat. "What kind of responsibilities do you think you will have as an intern at the Horace Brown Detective Agency?" He grabbed a small notepad and pen from the breast pocket of his shirt, ready to take notes on their answers. The group was so silent, they could hear Alice purring. A few seconds passed, and then Alura broke the ice.

"Honestly, I know it's probably not going to happen," she

prefaced, "but I'm hoping we get to solve some mysteries. I'm up for anything, though."

"I agree," Liz said, "but I am expecting mainly organizing files and perhaps setting up appointments?"

Apparently, those two answers were not enough for Mr. Brown, because he wrote down both responses but still waited for more.

"Feed Alice?" Leo joked. Chuckling softly, Mr. Brown wrote down the answer.

"Maybe learning about the justice system? Um, like laws that need to be followed by private investigators?" Isaac responded shyly. It seemed that the detective just wanted an answer from everyone, because he then placed his notepad on the table.

Isaac had avoided thinking too much about what to expect from the internship for fear of being disappointed. Over the last couple days, he tried his hardest to distract his mind from wondering. He just hoped that it would be a fun summer.

"There are some great answers, but most of them are incorrect," Mr. Brown said, peering down at the small piece of paper. "I have brought you all here because I would like to share my knowledge with you. A fair warning, I put this program together myself and it will be difficult at times. You will need teamwork to push your skills further than you have ever before."

Mr. Brown paused once more, observing his four selected interns like a king looking over his bravest knights, preparing them for a quest.

"Tell me what you know about legends."

"Like mythology?" Leo asked with a smirk.

"Precisely!" the detective responded, his eyes lighting up and a smile drawn under his beard. Leo was taken back by his enthusiasm and his countenance shifted to confusion.

"Well, I know they aren't *real*," Liz expressed. "They are made-up stories that are created by people who either want to teach someone a lesson or make sense of something. Like the Greek gods, people only created them to explain phenomena that they couldn't figure out. For example, how Zeus *threw* lightning."

"Exactly," Mr. Brown responded, completely unphased by Liz's cynicism. "Can anyone think of any other examples? Just shout them out."

Isaac sat for a moment to absorb what was happening. So far, Mr. Brown had surprised him in ways that he was still having trouble figuring out. By Liz's explanation, Isaac felt like he needed to create a legend to explain the enigmas that existed in the old man's mind. He refocused on the conversation at hand and a few different examples popped into his head.

The Fountain of Youth?

"Aliens?" Alura asked skeptically, as if she wasn't sure if it was the answer he was looking for.

"Good one, good one," Mr. Brown began writing again, his notebook back in hand.

The Jersey Devil?

"I know what you are going for. Like El Dorado or mermaids," Leo said, staring at the ceiling, "but I'm seriously drawing a blank right now beyond that. Pass."

The room fell silent for a minute or so, leaving Isaac to internally panic as to whether or not he should share his thoughts. The choice was quickly taken off the table.

"Isaac? You've got something. I can tell."

"Like the Loch Ness Monster?" he offered.

The older man grabbed the whiteboard on wheels and brought it to the head of the table. He flipped it over, revealing the other side. Pinned to the edges were numerous newspaper articles and a picture of the Loch Ness Monster in the middle. Mr. Brown grabbed a marker and uncapped it.

"What do you know about the legend of the Loch Ness Monster?" he asked the group.

LIZ was willing to play along with the detective's antics. *Surely the most famous detective in the world isn't this ridiculous?*

"Loch Ness is in Scotland," Liz stated flatly. Her statement was quickly scribbled to the right of the picture. Mr. Brown returned his attention to the table.

"The first sightings were in the late 19th century, but most of the more substantial examples were in the 1930s," Leo stated. The three other interns looked at him in awe. He pulled his phone out from under the table and showed the group, who were suddenly less impressed with his encyclopedic knowledge.

Leave it to Leo to use the internet to solve his problems, Liz thought to herself.

"So, it was the United Kingdom during the Great Depression. They didn't have it as bad as we did in the United States, but they definitely felt the effects."

"Perfect, Leo," Horace said, trying to keep up with all the

facts he was spitting out. "It would be very difficult for someone to be in the right place at the right time to experience the creation of one of these legends. Generally speaking, they become well-known after the initial introduction. Correct?"

The group of teenagers nodded in agreement.

"I just wanted to make a quick disclaimer," Horace said sternly. "This conversation turns confidential from here on out. The secret I am about to share must stay between the five of us. No one else can know, not even your parents or Dot. If you think it will be difficult for you to keep any information to yourself, I ask you to speak up now."

Liz squinted at Horace. She was sure that this initial conversation was just some sort of transition to a more practical conversation. Detectives had to have some sort of dramatic flair, otherwise they wouldn't be interesting to read about.

"Good, then you are all on board," Horace continued. He pushed the whiteboard away from the table, brought over the cart and pulled off the sheet, revealing an old gramophone. A small shiny gold plaque that read EMIT was screwed into the base of the device.

Some people just don't age well, Liz thought to herself. *I wonder if they are still accepting students to robotics camp up state, or even the biology extracurricular at her school maybe?*

"Although this is something I had initially planned many years ago, Emit is an invention that I've brought to life in the last few months," he gestured toward the machine. "It is a music player that can take you back in time."

"Time travel is impossible," Liz said, trying not to roll her eyes out of respect for her new boss.

42

"Of that, I am unsure," Horace replied, brushing off the comment. "This device does not take you *physically* back, but you can transport your consciousness through time. Let me explain."

Liz took a moment to process what he was saying. While it seemed *possible* to create such a device, it was very unlikely that someone would be able to create such a machine. She thought back to a few nights ago, when Horace had trouble calling her with his smartphone. She held reservations that if *someone* was able to create such a thing, it couldn't possibly be Horace Brown.

"I have selected a handful of legends and compiled all known information on them. Sightings, expert testimonials, theories, you name it. From there, I have translated it into a tune that allows the listener to experience it in a different way than just reading it. These legends don't necessarily have a huge wealth of specifics, so there also needs to be something else. To fill in the gaps, I have also included thousands of articles that outline background information for the period."

The more he spoke, the more Liz believed it could work. Her mind began to race with the specifics of how the gramophone worked.

"The Loch Ness Monster, for example. News articles from a specific time all the way down to menus at restaurants in the area were included to create a genuine experience. Each record has tracks as well. Each time the Loch Ness Monster was spotted, there is a portion of the track dedicated to it."

There was a moment of silence as Horace appeared to be trying to read the room to see if they were comprehending what he was saying.

"How does it work?" Alura had wheeled her chair closer with squinted eyes, trying to fully grasp the concept.

"*Does* it work?" Liz asked with genuine interest. The others seemed to be surprised by her lack of raw skepticism, looking toward her as the question left her mouth.

"Great questions!" Horace raised a single finger upward. "Yes, it does work. I have tested it dozens of times before I had perfected the system. The mind must be in an incredibly peaceful state to accept the music and be transported to the selected date and place. The only way that I have discovered so far is to fall asleep listening to it."

"Ah, that's what the extra clothes are for," Leo muttered to himself.

"Precisely," he responded, and stroking his beard. "I must tell you that I have also placed myself in some scenarios that are not quite *ideal*. I can assure you that if you are injured or hurt, it will not carry over to the real world. It is safe in that regard."

"So essentially," Liz summarized, "you are *visiting* an artificial reality that is based on facts. That's incredible!"

Liz's mind continued to race with thoughts of how the device could be used. From creating accurate historical recreations to therapeutic uses for grief, this device was something that could change the world.

"But wait," Leo said, pausing for a moment to collect his thoughts, "doesn't going back in time mess with the timeline and all that? Won't we be changing the future?"

Liz was going to fly in with a snarky comment following her sigh of frustration. Her questions were far beyond any of the other interns who were still trying to wrap their head around what they were looking at. Before she could, Alura jumped in with a more delicate approach.

"I don't think that applies to this, Leo," Alura said, swiveling her chair to face him, "I think we are visiting a *fake* version of the time that our minds are able to create by listening to this special song. Right?"

Horace nodded his head slowly and Leo gave Alura a thumbs-up to thank her for her explanation.

ALURA felt like there was a pyramid of questions, but one sat on top of all the rest.

"But why are you showing it to us?" Alura asked.

"This summer, I would like to offer you the opportunity to use my invention to complete the tasks I will be giving you," Horace said. "You see, I'm an old man. As unfortunate as it is, that translates into the simulation."

"I'm sorry. I feel like I'm missing something," Leo said, running his hand through his hair. "I'm usually pretty lost, but this is really bad for me. What do you want us to use it for? What tasks are you giving us?"

"I apologize. I really have been jumping around, haven't I?" Horace responded. "I have solved hundreds of cases throughout the years. However, there are some that have been far beyond my abilities. I want you to use Emit to uncover the mysteries that have become legendary. Myths that have never been proven to be factual. What do you say?"

Silence filled the room. Isaac looked at his feet, deep in

thought. Leo looked toward the others, filled with confusion. Liz looked as though the gears in her mind were spinning so fast, she was unable to form a response.

Alura's gaze fell to Horace. He stood proudly next to Emit, like a father to his son, with a small smile on his face.

"If this is a secret project," Liz pondered, pushing the stillness from the room, "can we still use it on college applications?"

"I will write you whatever kind of letter of recommendation you'd like me to," Horace said calmly. It was clearly a question he had expected to be asked. "However, I wish to keep my invention a secret. Anything within reason, I will sign off on."

Liz nodded her head but continued to think to herself.

"I'm in," Leo said, throwing his hands up in surrender. "I've got to be honest. I have *no idea* what you guys are talking about, but this sounds awesome. Definitely more fun than any summer I can remember. What are you guys thinking?"

Alura took a moment to consider her own thoughts and feelings on the matter. It sounded like an incredible opportunity. It was better than anything she had expected from this internship and could give her a push toward a career or goal.

Of course, she did have some reservations with the idea that she needed to clarify before jumping on board.

"You know for sure that this thing is safe?" Alura asked. "If something goes wrong and one of us gets hurt, you need to promise that you'll do what you need to do, even if it means revealing this thing."

"I would never put anyone in danger," Horace said,

adjusting his bowtie. There was sincerity in his voice. "Your safety is more important to me than anything. If it comes down to it, you have my word. I will do whatever is within my power to fix it."

"And if any of us want out," she continued, "what happens?"

"Nothing. As long as you keep your promise of secrecy, I have no issue with any of you wanting to back out. Today, tomorrow, next week. Whatever you need, come speak to me."

"I'm in," Isaac blurted out. She could feel the excitement and nervousness radiating off of him. It was an odd pairing of feelings that were often intertwined.

"Me as well," Liz followed.

"Looks like we've got a full team," Alura said, smiling. "This sounds pretty awesome."

"Thank you," Horace clapped his hands. "Thank you for putting your trust in me. I promise it will not be for nothing. There is a bathroom at the end of the hall if you'd all like to take turns changing into your comfortable clothing. Afterwards, meet me directly across the hall and we can get started immediately."

The sightings of Bigfoot have spanned centuries, dating back to before written history. There are numerous Native American myths that are similar to the one we know today. Tales of "wild men" were first noted in the late 1800s, but Bigfoot really took shape in 1958 when supplies started going missing at a logging road in California. Giant footprints were discovered at the scene. Combined with popular movies, books, and other pop culture at the time, the hunt for Bigfoot kicked off. Something about the mystery of it all seemed to captivate the public.

LEO was already changed into his gear, but still walked with the group down to the bathroom so he didn't draw attention to the mix up. Honestly, he wasn't sure if he had misheard Horace or the man had misspoken. Leo had woken up this morning feeling nervous and worrying he was out of his element. His Gran had tried to make him feel better before he left the apartment with some reassuring words, but he was so unsure of what to expect.

Then, that conversation in the conference room just

happened, whatever it was.

The level of confusion was taken up a couple of notches, but for some reason, Leo felt better about the whole experience. Maybe it was because he felt more comfortable now that he knew what to expect or that the other interns were just as lost as he was. It was also possible that he felt like his nervousness was definitely warranted.

"You alright, Leo?" Alura asked. Apparently, his feelings were painted across his face.

"Yeah, I'm good," Leo responded. "I'm still trying to wrap my head around what's going on I guess."

"That definitely was a lot," Alura said with a smile. "Is there something that's confusing you?"

"Not really, I just can't believe *this* is the internship."

"Like in a good or bad way?" Isaac asked, turning to join the conversation.

"I really don't know," Leo said, laughing softly. "I really don't know what I was expecting. All I know is that this wasn't it."

"Agreed," Alura said, laughing along with Leo and Isaac.

Liz emerged from the bathroom wearing gray sweatpants and a pink t-shirt. While she was in there, she pulled her hair back. She grabbed her bag of professional clothes and began moving toward the room Horace asked them to meet in. Leo started walking with her.

Although they had gone to school together, Leo didn't know Liz well. They had shared a few classes throughout their years in high school, and she was well regarded as the most intelligent and best student within their grade, possibly the entire school. She was constantly excused from class for clubs that she had been a part of. Some were exclusive that required acceptance in order to attend. Leo normally kept to his friend group and rarely ventured outside it, and it seemed that characteristic was mutual between them. He was a social person in general and had a ton of friends including teammates but had a very small circle of best friends.

"So," Leo began as they entered the room, "this is a pretty cool twist, right? I mean, who could've expected it?"

"No one," Liz responded as if it were obvious, "I don't think anyone could've expected this to happen."

"Are you excited? This seems like it would be super interesting to you."

"And why is that?" Liz inquired defensively. She turned her attention away from her bag and turned to face him.

"Oh, I mean," Leo fumbled, "I just meant that it's a pretty unique invention that Horace has created. He must be really smart to have made it."

Liz had thrown him off balance with her pointed question. He really didn't mean any offense by the statement, just that it was impressive that she was able to understand Horace's creation right off the bat. It seemed that the other three interns had struggled at first to grasp the concept completely.

Some of his friends from school that knew Liz had warned him after they both got accepted to the internship that she was a bit condescending, and one had even used the word "ruthless" to describe her. So far, Leo really hadn't noticed it until this point, but he still didn't agree with any of the overlapping evaluations completely.

She turned her attention back to her bag. Leo pulled out his phone and scrolled through his notifications.

Missing you bro, one of his friends sent accompanied with a photo of a few of his friends at the baseball camp he attended every summer. Every summer except for this one.

Leo clenched his fists and could feel his face getting hot. He wondered if he had made the right decision to accept the internship. He felt like he was so far in the outfield that no one could even see him, feeding directly into the insecurities he felt earlier in the day.

You need to calm down, he told himself. *It's only the first hour of the first day!* He slid his phone into his pocket and turned attention to the room they were standing in while he waited for the others.

It was about the same size as the conference room but appeared smaller. The four corners were sealed off with light blue temporary walls that had doors built in. It reminded Leo of bathroom stalls, but they went from the floor to the ceiling and had small vents on the side without the door. Finally, Horace came in with his sheet-covered cart.

"Hello, hello," he said, pushing the cart into the center of the room. Although there were no windows to the outside, Horace seemed to be taking every precaution to avoid prying eyes and left the gramophone hidden under the cover.

Isaac and Alura walked in, both in their comfortable clothing. He wore basketball shorts and an old t-shirt, and she was wearing sweatpants and a hoodie. Isaac closed the door behind him, as per Horace's request.

"Alright," Horace began. "I am so excited that you all

decided to stay. I know I am asking a lot of you, both to take part in this experience and understand it. I know it probably wasn't what you were expecting. So, I have set up four, uh, *cubicles* we will call them. Each of you will have your own space to enter the world that Emit will create. From what I understand, some of you know each other, but I wanted to make sure that you all felt safe falling asleep here. It only felt right."

"Thanks," Alura said. "While I was changing, I was actually worried about that."

"They all lock from the inside," Horace explained, "And I do have an emergency key for each cubicle stashed away, just in case anything goes wrong. Now, any last-minute questions before we get started?"

"This might've been answered," Isaac began quietly, "But will we be together? Or alone?"

"Great question, Mr. Isaac!" Horace exclaimed. "If you all listen to the same track at the same time, you will be in the same, um…"

"Dreamscape?" Alura offered, seeing him struggle to find the right word.

"Yes!" Horace shouted out again, stroking his beard. "That's the perfect word. Up until this point, I have not had to explain the process to anyone, so the vocabulary is still coming to me. But 'dreamscape' sounds like the perfect terminology for what we are dealing with."

"And can we take anything with us?" Leo asked. The three interns looked at him with a strange look, as if they were trying to comprehend his question.

52

"It's a dream," Liz said scornfully. "You can't *take* things with you."

Condescending? Check. Ruthless? Yet to be seen.

"Actually, you can take things with you in a way," Horace explained. "Whatever you are thinking of when you fall asleep will be with you when you awake in the dreamscape. I have tried to limit myself to three or so items, otherwise my mind gets them all mixed up and nothing comes through properly. For example, if you are thinking about a flashlight when you are falling asleep, you will have one with you wherever you are going. Great question!"

"Can we talk to people in the dreamscape?" Leo followed up with after recovering his confidence from Liz's answer.

"Yes, you can completely interact with the entire world around you. You'll need to remain in character for them to respond accurately, though. Confidence is key, here. You'll need to be who they expect you to be in order to keep the dreamscape on its path," he said, turning to Alura. "Thank you again, great word."

"Anything else we should know?" Leo asked, realizing the more questions he asked, the more it made sense to him.

"Let me see, ah yes. Just remember, the information you are seeing might be different in the real world," Horace continued. "What you are seeing is a simulation of real events with filler information. For example, if an article mentioned that a person had a pet but did not specify what kind of animal it was, Emit will do his best to analyze data and figure out what option would be the most accurate. It may have been a cat in real life, but it will appear as a dog. The differences should be minimal and will not change anything. It's just something to note."

"The question that seems to be escaping everyone," Liz commented, "is where are we going? What legend are we investigating?"

Leo hadn't realized up until that point that the detective went into detail about pretty much everything besides where they were heading. She had a good point.

"I figured that you all could start off with an easier one where you won't need to go back too far in time," Horace began. "This legend was first *officially* recorded a few decades ago in the 1950s and then throughout the 1960s to the 1980s, it was spotted multiple times."

Leo had a feeling that he knew which legend had been selected for them to investigate first. Horace made a point to give a small pause after giving this information, maybe to see if anyone wanted to try their hand at identifying it before he did. After the previous blow to his ego, Leo decided to wait for a few more facts before he tried to throw a Hail Mary down the field.

"It has been reported to whistle but also shrieks and eerie howling has been associated with it," he looked at the four interns, and smiled when he got to Leo. "Leo? What are you thinking?"

"Northwestern United States?" Leo inquired.

Horace nodded his head slowly, prompting him to go on.

"Sasquatch, or as some know him, Bigfoot?" Leo guessed.

"Very good," Horace reached out and gave him a pat on the arm. "That was impressive. I have put together three tracks for you on this record. The first is from 1958 at a logging camp. Big names include the owner of the company, Howard Price, his right-hand man, Jim, and Bruce, the man who reportedly discovered the first tracks. I've chosen this dreamscape because it is the first incident that ended with a written account."

He took a deep breath, letting the interns process the information.

"Then, in 1972 there were several reports of him disturbing a kids' summer camp in Redwood National Forest, Northern California. This one particularly piqued by interest, as there were *multiple* sightings throughout the summer. Finally, in 2002, there were a few accounts of him near Silver Lake, Washington. These were the three most credible sources events that I could manufacture for you to investigate."

Horace began to prepare the device, grabbing a record from one of the cardboard sleeves under the cart.

"Remember, your goal is to solve the mystery of Bigfoot in these dreamscapes," he continued. "You are to look for three things. Who had the *means*, or who would have the tools and resources to commit the crime. *Motive*, which essentially means that the suspect needs to have a reason to do so. Finally, *opportunity* means that they had the chance to do so. You can stay organized by following these three principles. Any final thoughts or questions?"

The four teens shook their heads. Leo felt like he would have more questions teed up over time, but it was enough information for now.

"Alright then," Horace instructed, putting on a pair of headphones, "head toward a cubicle! Try to get comfortable, and I will get the first track started as soon as possible."

Leo made his way over to the corner that was closest to him and walked inside, locking the door behind him. It wasn't as cramped as it looked from the outside and had a nice bed off to one side, a dresser, and a couple of water bottles on top. Peeking through the dresser, each was filled with blankets and socks made of different materials. Grabbing one that felt like a cloud, he laid down on the bed and flicked the light switch that was conveniently within his reach so he could turn off the light from the bed.

Staring at the ceiling, he really wasn't sure if he was going to be able to fall asleep. He heard Horace outside the room getting the music set up. Leo wondered what kind of music it would be if any at all. It could even be a mixture of sounds. He closed his eyes and tried to relax his muscles. The day had certainly caused him some tension so far.

The music began but it was like nothing that Leo could describe. It sounded like various instruments, both familiar and unrecognizable to him, playing at once. It wasn't terrible, but he wouldn't add it to his playlist if he stumbled across it while working out. Then, the worst happened.

His stomach started grumbling, calling out for food. He had an early breakfast and had hoped that Horace would have some kind of refreshments for the day. Although his grandma had reminded him, he had forgotten to pack himself a snack as well. For about five minutes, Leo struggled to focus on the music playing and finally started to feel his eyelids get heavy.

A flash of purple flashed inside his eyelids.

ISAAC opened his eyes to see purple smoke dissipating around him. Huge tree stumps and grass surrounded him. The sound of loud machinery in the distance filled his ears and the smell of burning wood filled his nose. There was also something different about the air here. It felt clearer than back in New York City.

"Hey," a girl said from behind him, "Have you seen Leo?"

Isaac turned around to find Alura behind him and Liz standing a bit further back with her arms crossed, adjusting the straps of her backpack.

"Oh, hey," Isaac replied. "No, I haven't seen him."

Purple smoke suddenly filled the space between them. As it cleared, Leo was revealed standing between them. He held a small paper bag in his hand.

"Hey Leo!" Alura said. "We were just looking for you.

"Sorry about that," Leo apologized. "Had a hard time falling asleep."

"What's in the bag?" Liz asked pointedly.

"Nothing," he responded, putting it behind his back. It seemed that Leo knew exactly what was in the bag, though he had never opened it.

"What's wrong?" Alura said, giggling at his awkwardness. "Seriously, what's in the bag?"

"Fine, you really want to know?" Leo relinquished. He opened the bag and pulled out an exact replica of the paper plate that Isaac had brought with him to the office earlier that day, complete with magnifying glass cookies and plastic baggy. Alura and Isaac laughed at the reveal.

"*That's* what you brought?" Liz shook her head

disapprovingly. "Out of everything, you brought cookies?"

Isaac fought a smile. He was never good at accepting compliments, but he did appreciate them when they arose. A magnifying glass, a notepad, and a pen were the items that Isaac had chosen to bring into the dreamscape.

"They are pretty good cookies," Alura shrugged. "I wasn't sure what to bring so I have pen and paper, which it looks like Isaac had the same idea."

"Why, what did *you* bring Liz?" Leo inquired.

"Let's see," Liz took off her backpack and began listing items, "Rope, flashlights, tent, matches, first aid kit, soup, batteries, some cash, and my phone."

"Your *phone?*" Alura said, putting the palm of her hand on her forehead. "Why didn't I think of that?"

"Don't dwell on it too much, it doesn't seem to be working," Liz said, tapping and shaking the device. "I think it might be too much. Our brain can fathom writing on a notepad or zooming in with a magnifying glass but think of all the things a person could do with a phone."

"My brain can definitely fathom eating these cookies," Leo stated, slowing raising them up into his mouth. Liz ignored the comment, but Isaac and Alura giggled again.

"So, what's the plan?" Alura poised.

"Well, it looks like we're exactly where Horace said we'd be," Leo observed, "California, 1958, logging camp. That hill over there looks like a vantage point. It's also where all the noise is coming from. Maybe we could make our way over there and see what's over the ridge?"

The team nodded their heads and started to make their way

toward the elevated land. Isaac noticed that the ground was very soft with a chestnut color, like mulch. Surrounding the clearing were hundreds of trees and a tall chain link fence with swirls of barbed wire on top. Birds in the trees called out occasionally over the earsplitting grinding noise of the large equipment somewhere in the distance.

The air felt *different* around them, Isaac noticed again. It was peaceful, yet it felt as though there was a slight breeze moving around them.

The group got close to the top of the hill, slowing down with the steep incline. Slowly, buildings and trucks came into view in the distance. The fence stretched the entire way around a huge area, beyond what they were able to view. Yellow and green trucks seemed to be on a route in and out of the tree line, loaded with logs. Black smoke billowed from each vehicle, as well as a large warehouse-looking building situated to the left. On the right side of the encampment, there was a large gate and a smaller structure with proportional doors.

Liz shuffled through her bag and pulled out a pair of large binoculars. She began peering through them, moving from side to side slowly, observing the landscape.

"It looks like the building there is the office," Leo pointed out. "There are guys with ties going in right now, it looks like."

"Yes, it appears that way," Liz confirmed, then pointed at the larger structure with the metal siding. "The trucks are dropping off the trees there. That must be where they store the lumber."

Liz continued to stare through the binoculars while the other three turned to each other.

"What now?" Alura pondered, opening the floor to suggestions.

"Maybe we should go down and start interviewing people?" Isaac offered. "Like getting accounts from eyewitnesses?" He was thinking back to some of his favorite mystery books, wondering where they began. Although, this situation was a little different. They were teenagers *and* no one knew they were investigating a crime.

Confidence is key. Isaac remembered Mr. Brown's suggestion to keeping the dreamscape on track.

"I'm not sure," Leo said gently. "I think we might be better off just winging it..."

"Winging it?" Liz snorted. "What are you talking about? You can't just go down there and expect everything to fall into place."

"I think I'm going to agree with Leo," Alura said, following a moment of thought. "We should definitely have a plan, but no direct questions. Otherwise, people could get suspicious and confused. They'll be freaked out and things will change. If that happens, this will be super misleading."

Liz put her hand on her chin and stared at the ground, processing everything that Alura had said.

"I think Isaac is right though," Alura said diplomatically. "We need to get some eyewitness accounts, but I think *we* are going to be seeing it with our own eyes."

"So, we just go down and start talking to people?" Liz asked. Surprisingly, the question sounded more like confirmation without any contempt.

"I mean, we can walk in without any major issues. We just

want to avoid anyone thinking that we don't belong here. I think we should start with the office. What do you guys think?" Leo offered.

The four interns looked at each other for a moment, all of them were well outside their element. To keep a level head after everything that had transpired this morning, Isaac tried to think of this as one of his video games. It was designed to be linear with one way forward. He was starting to realize that it wasn't that simple.

"I think at this point," Alura volunteered, "we really just need to figure out how all this works. If the worst happens, we can just replay the track and see what happens. The biggest thing here is that we are able to recognize anything that could change from us being here. This isn't just a one-time thing, right Liz? We can redo it?"

The three of them turned to Liz, who still had a hand resting on her chin. Isaac wasn't sure if she would have an answer for the group, but she would know better than the rest of them. A few seconds went by, Liz hadn't moved, and Leo wondered if she had even heard Alura.

"Yes," Liz confirmed, breaking the silence. "From what I know about the device, it seems to be a safe bet that we could simply replay this simulation after we wake up. But I do have to agree with Alura, we need to be able to recognize if we altered the way that people act here. If anyone notices anything, you must remember and let the rest of us know. Even small changes can have huge consequences."

"So, it's settled," Leo said, pointing onwards. "Let's go down to the office and see what's going on. Nobody mention anything weird, alright? Let's just make some casual conversation."

The group nodded and started down the hill toward the office.

Leo led the way, with Liz just behind him and Isaac and Alura bringing up the rear. The summer sun kept the air hot, but a breeze went through every once in a while, breaking up any discomfort. The tree stumps that surrounded the group had to be more than two feet in diameter. They didn't have too many trees in New York City beyond Central Park, but Isaac started thinking about when he was younger.

A few times, Isaac remembered his mother taking him and his brother to the Jersey Shore for a weekend vacation in the summer. The trees in the area of New Jersey that they would visit were definitely big, but most were smaller than the ones out at this logging facility. As he started to think of it more, the color of the leaves seemed different, too. The tree line here was more of a dark green. He remembered the trees of New Jersey being more of a brighter, lime green.

Isaac's brother, Carter, had gone away to college two summers ago. Before that, his brother had been spending less and less time with him, and more time with his friends. Memories like the family vacations soured and became sad for Isaac, who wished that things could go back to the way things used to be.

As they got closer to the reddish-brown building, Isaac noticed a large metal gate blocking the path in and out of the compound, marked with a dirt road. Following it one way, it disappeared from view between the tree line. Looking at the path in the other direction, it went behind the building to a small parking lot, where a few vintage pickup trucks and cars were parked.

Not vintage, Isaac thought, *we are in the 1950s – those are probably brand new.*

"Hey!" a voiced bellowed from behind them.

 **5**

LEO turned to find a hulking man, close to seven feet tall, towering over them. He wore a red baseball cap backwards and a green canvas jumpsuit with worn out, dark brown boots covered in mud. It was difficult to say how old he was, even as he got closer. The wrinkles on his face were intertwined with a few unnatural marks and scruffy brown facial hair, and his skin reminded Leo of a football, just a few tones lighter. It was more than likely a hazard of working so many years in the sun.

"Yes sir?" Leo said, standing his ground at the head of the group.

"What are you doing out here? How did you get in here? You aren't one of those cow-handed birdwatchers, are you?" he rapidly fired at Leo.

"We were on a school trip," Leo explained. "The four of us stopped to take a look at some of the trees, but we couldn't find our group after that." He heard a quiet sigh of relief from his fellow interns.

"Is that so?" the man replied, looking them each up and down.

64

"Yes," Leo said confidently, remembering Horace's advice. "Is there any way you'd be able to point us to someone who could help us find our class?"

"Ah well," the man seemed to crumble in an instant, taking his hat off and scratching his head with his other hand. "Go see Mr. Price in the office down there. I'm Jim, by the way. I'm the manager over here at the storehouse. Wish I could help you myself, but there's been a lot going on these last few days."

After gesturing toward the large building standing behind him, he put his hand out toward Leo. He grabbed it, shaking it slowly. The man's hands were enormous and easily engulfed the entirety of Leo's. *After Bigfoot, maybe we can go hunting for giants,* Leo thought. *I'll know exactly where to begin.*

"Thank you, Jim," Leo said, bowing his head. "It's a pleasure to meet you. I'm Leo. This is Alura, Isaac, and Liz."

"Strange names," Jim said, squinting his eyes. Leo could feel the rest of the group holding their breath behind him. "Strange outfits, too. Where did you buy them?"

Leo looked down to realize that they were wearing the clothes that they had fallen asleep in. *I guess hoodies, basketball shorts, and sweatshirts don't fit in with this decade.*

"Oh these? My Gran got them for me for Christmas last year. Nice right?"

At this point, it was difficult to tell if the big man was truly questioning them or just curious, but Leo doubled down on his confidence. The easiest way to do that was simple: tell the truth. He was just happy Jim moved on from their names, he wasn't sure how he'd explain that.

"Ah, I understand," Jim responded with a chuckle. "Well, if

you want something more practical for the outdoors, there's a supply house down the road here, about 10 miles south. Just outside of town. They've got boots, jeans, and all sorts of flannel. It's going to start getting colder around here. You'll definitely want to bundle up."

"Thanks Jim," Leo said. "We'd better get back to finding our class. It was really nice meeting you. I'm sure we will see you around."

The two nodded their heads and turned away from each other. Jim started to make his way back toward the warehouse, disappearing around the corner of the building.

"Wow," Alura said quietly.

"What?" Leo asked, confused.

"That was amazing!" she exclaimed. "Great job. I thought we were found out for sure. That guy was ready to pick all four of us up and throw us over the fence. Probably at the same time."

"Oh," Leo said sheepishly. "It was nothing. I guess I'm just good at talking to people."

"So, can we consider him a suspect?"

The three of them once again turned toward Liz, confused.

"He had to be seven feet tall," Liz stated. "Did you see the size of his boots? I believe that falls under *means*."

"You definitely have a good point," Leo admitted, although he wasn't completely convinced. "We're going to need some more information before we really start to understand what this legend is all about. I don't really know too much about it other than it's about a tall, hairy creature that screams and whistles."

"Screams and whistles?" Isaac asked.

"Yeah, whenever the creature is 'spotted,'" Leo did air quotes, "there always seems to be a report of strange noises. Some people say whistling, some people say it's almost like a shriek."

"It's just a legend," Liz responded. The pace of her words quickened, as if she was annoyed that she had to explain it. "People are just copying what they know about it. If the first person who saw it heard a whistling bird, they would attribute it with the creature. Then everyone who plays out the legend, for whatever reason they have, needs to make it the same as before so it's believable."

Leo was slowly starting to see what his friends meant about Liz. *Brutality through bluntness*

"So, you don't think it's real? Not even a little bit?" Alura asked. Her curiosity seemed genuine, almost as if she hadn't decided herself. Funnily enough, Leo knew exactly what that felt like.

"No, of course not," Liz said, rolling her eyes. "How would that even be possible?"

"Couldn't it be the last of its kind?" Leo offered.

"In order for it to be the last of its kind, it would be near extinction," Liz explained. "Therefore, the species would need to be close to dying out, meaning that there were others in the past. Written history has never shown any kind of this creature, and this land has been explored for centuries. The oldest living animal, close to anything described by these so-called 'victims' or 'spotters' are turtles, which live to be less than 200 years old. There's no way it's possible."

"I guess you do make a good point," Leo admitted. Liz nodded her head, accepting his surrender. Quickly stealing a glance at the others, he noticed that Isaac seemed distracted by something in the distance and indifferent to the conversation while Alura was paused in thought. Leo evaluated the situation and assumed she must be thinking about the same thing.

Does anyone really have a strong opinion about Bigfoot? he wondered. The question of the creature's existence never really kept him up at night. That was for sure.

LEO and the rest of the group made their way toward the office. On their short journey, they didn't encounter any other employees of the lumberyard. The structure seemed temporary, almost like a headquarters that construction sites use.

As they turned the corner to the side with the door, they were met with a surprise. Along the wooden porch, hand-woven baskets that resembled birds' nests filled with colorful berries and fish of assorted sizes lined the walkway. In total, three baskets of varying spoilage and decay surrounded the entrance. There was a sign made of sheet metal hung next to the door, advertising Yosemite Lumber and Development.

As Leo reached for the door handle, he turned toward the others and locked eyes with Alura, who shared his confusion. Liz was kneeled down next to one of the baskets to get a closer look and Isaac seemed to be fixed on something outside the gate. He turned the knob and pushed the door open.

Inside, it seemed like a regular office. Two desks were strategically placed on either side. One was neat and organized with a single stack of folders, while the other was littered with hundreds of papers and pencils strewn about. Leo could appreciate the chaos of it. Other than the desks, there were few furnishings other than numerous filing cabinets lining the walls, all a bluish-green color that reminded him of the bathroom in his apartment, untouched by time.

While no one was in this room, it sounded like the next room was occupied. The teens made their way past the desks and toward the door on the other side of the room. As they got closer, the nature of the conversation seemed clearer. One of the men involved was clearly upset, while the other did not want to hear about it. Beyond this, Leo could not understand any part of the conversation. He reached his hand out to knock.

"Wait," Alura whispered. "Is knocking going to change the outcome of this?"

"Oh," Leo responded, "I didn't think about –"

He was quickly cut off by the door opening abruptly. A tall, thin man with a bushy mustache and glasses was being ushered out by another, much larger man. Leo immediately locked on to the large scar that ran the length of his entire face, from his forehead, through his left eye, all the way down to his chin.

"Yes, yes," the hulking man snarled as he was pushing the man over the threshold. "Have a nice day and all that. And please stop leaving baskets here, we don't want them."

"What baskets are you…" the thin man started, his voice trailing off. Both men stopped what they were doing when they realized there were four teenagers cluttering the small office. They had stepped to the side so Scar could continue his eviction, but their presence didn't go unnoticed.

Well, Leo thought, noticing they had clearly interrupted something, *sure hope this doesn't have consequences.*

"Who are you?" the large man said bluntly.

"The four of us are lost," Leo responded with a shaky voice. "We were out on a nature walk with our class. It was a school field trip." Somehow, this man made Jim look more like a normal size. It was like looking at a football player and then a normal person. Combined with the one-eyed stare, it shook Leo to his core.

"Ms. Jenny's class. Jim said you'd be able to help us find them," a voice piped up from behind the broad shoulders of the man, who turned to face away from Leo. He didn't know who saved him, but he certainly appreciated the lifeline. Leo took a moment to breathe after the impromptu interrogation.

"Oh, alright," the boss said with a sigh. He murmured for a moment and turned toward his office. His desk reminded Leo of New York, skyscrapers of stacked folders. "Let me just finish with Mr. Sanders here and I'll be right with you. I'm Howard, by the way. Howard Price."

"Thank you," Leo said with a small bow.

Although the man was never angry or upset, the sheer size of his build and his facial features made Leo uneasy. Howard began walking forward again, putting out his baseball mitt-sized hands and causing the man to begin backpedaling toward the front door. As Alura and Isaac came back into view, once hidden behind Howard, Leo realized it must have been Isaac who spoke up and took the heat off of him for a moment.

"Wait, wait," the man named Sanders pleaded, gripping a small pair of binoculars that were strapped around his neck,

"Just listen! I'm just asking for you to understand what I am trying to say."

"I do understand," Howard responded without slowing his step. "I cannot stop my operations simply because of the wildlife. I've told you this at least a dozen times. This is the last time I will be meeting with you. I don't know how you keep getting through the fence, but I'm going to call the police if I see you here again. Understand?"

Although the situation made Leo a bit uncomfortable, he was thankful that he was not being kicked out of the building. That thankfulness faded as soon as Liz audibly scoffed. Both men again stopped, turning toward Liz.

"Deforestation is a huge issue, it *does* hurt wildlife," Liz said, as if she was beginning a lecture. "It contributes to global warming, which is destroying everything, our very way of life."

"I'm getting really tired of this," Howard sighed, tilting his head downward and resting the bridge of his nose between his thumb and pointer finger. "How did you kids get over the fence? I can't stand these odd balls coming into my office and preaching to me."

Leo watched as Howard Price clenched his fists and had a small breakdown. He began to make short incoherent noises as he pointed to Sanders, then to his office, and back to Sanders. Leo's thoughts quickly transformed in his mind, like a basketball player passing the ball from one teammate to the next.

Why would she say that? he thought. His back tensed, first because of the unexpectedness, then anger. He closed his eyes for a second and took a deep breath. *We need to keep this dreamscape going, and we need to act. Fast.*

"We aren't odd balls," Leo took a step forward, channeling his courage. "She isn't talking about the same thing. She meant global warming as the way the globe is warming up to the idea of deforestation. People around the world *love* deforestation." The words stung slightly as they came off his tongue, but he needed to keep things going.

There was a slight chance that this would work, but Leo knew that it was a long shot. Howard slowly took his hand away from his face.

ALURA took a step back as the brawny man closed his eyes and put his palms together. The tension coming off Howard felt like it had raised the temperature in the room by at least ten degrees. Alura could feel sweat begin to form on her cheeks. He was like a stick of dynamite, and they were waiting to see if Leo was able to put the fuse out.

"Oh, thank goodness," Howard said, inhaling deeply. "I really don't know how much more of this I can take."

He turned to Sanders, who was still watching intently. Although he didn't seem frightened, Alura had been frightened *for* him. She wasn't sure if Howard was going to pick him up and send him through the roof of the building.

Sanders adjusted his baseball cap and attempted to form words but was quickly cut off as he was forced through the door by Howard "The Bulldozer" Price.

A large black box crackled to life on Howard's belt. He unclipped the walkie-talkie and held it up to his face.

"Repeat?" he requested.

"Sir," a voice came through the static. "You're going to want to get down here. We have a situation out on Redwing Bluff."

Another moment of frustration quickly came and went as Howard shook the radio, then stared down at it blankly.

"Sir?"

"I'll be right there," Howard said in defeat. "I apologize kids. This is something I need to take care of. Do you mind waiting here? As soon as I get back, we will get you to where you need to be."

"Mind if we tag along?" Alura asked innocently. "We might be able to find them on our way down. Then, you'll be able to get back to what you were doing."

He pondered for a moment, then nodded his head.

"If you don't mind walking a bit. The quickest path there gets a little dense with bushes. It isn't worth taking a truck."

"That's alright. We don't mind walking at all."

"Grab a hardhat from the bin over there," he said, gesturing toward a wooden crate in the corner. It was filled with construction helmets. "Can't have you kids getting hurt on my watch."

The group complied and each grabbed a safety helmet. Howard took three steps, and he was back in his office to grab his fedora-style hat and sunglasses. While the boss was out of view, Alura and the other teenagers watched Mr. Sanders sneak out the door of the office, quietly closing it behind him. The large man reemerged, ducking under the doorway.

"Alright, let's see what the issue is this time."

The five exited the building and Alura realized what Isaac

was looking at earlier. On the other side of the fence, there were about half a dozen protesters with signs and similar outfits to the man who had slipped out of the office to avoid being dropkicked back to the others. Many wore binoculars and baseball caps.

"Say, how did you kids end up all the way out here?" Howard asked. Now that they had seem him on the verge of an eruption, Alura was able to tell that this was the man making friendly conversation.

"It's a long story," Leo responded. He spoke fast without emphasizing any words. Alura assumed it was to quickly redirect the conversation to something that could help the conversation. "Our science teacher brought us out here to see the different types of trees. Pretty cool if you ask me. Have you been doing this for a long time?

"Well," he started with another sigh, "yes, I believe it's been about 25 years. But in the middle of that, I was called upon to fight overseas."

Things were starting to come together for Alura. *His posture, the commanding presence, the perfectly ironed shirt,* she thought, *it made sense that he was a military man.* Howard pulled a small silver chain out from under his shirt, revealing a set of dog tags from his military service.

Watching Howard tug on the chain that held the tags around his neck, Alura's hand drifted to her own. She felt a cool metal chain clasped. It was her mother's seashell necklace. She thought of her mother for a moment. This whole incredible world that Emit had created would've made her smile. It would've taken the Book Club for Two to a whole new level. She wiped a tear from the corner of her eye, and she suddenly realized something.

Alura hadn't been wearing the necklace today in the real world. *Where did this come from? Was it Emit?* she wondered. *Or was it because I was thinking about my mom?*

Alura decided that it was a thought for another time. She needed to focus.

"Oh, wow," Leo responded. "That must have been tough."

"There were times when it was, but also times when it wasn't," he explained. "I can say that I stand here a much stronger man than I was before I was deployed. There were plenty of scary times that I wouldn't wish upon anyone, but I knew what I had to do." He ran his thumb across the scar on his face. For some reason, both the gentle conversation and the revelation of the scar's origin seemed to put the team at ease. At least he wasn't a mafia hitman or something.

"So, what exactly are you guys doing here?" Liz chimed in.

"This is a logging operation," Howard explained, "We are processing the wood from these trees and selling it to different customers that want to make things like furniture. My company, Yosemite Lumber and Development, also builds new homes. After we are done clearing this area, we'll start on the new homes for families in the area. Sort of a win-win for both sides of the company."

Alura saw Leo staring deeply at Liz but couldn't seem to catch her gaze. He didn't want another comment that could disrupt the dreamscape. With what happened before, Alura was also afraid that Liz could be a loose cannon. For both their sakes and for the team, Alura hoped that Liz could avoid saying anything else controversial.

Horace's words echoed in Alura's thoughts. *You will need teamwork to push your skills further than you have ever before.*

"Hey," Isaac whispered to Leo, breaking her concentration on Liz. "How did that work earlier? With the global warming thing?"

"The environmentalism movement isn't going to be in full swing for another couple decades. It's pretty under-the-radar right now. No one really knows or cares about it yet," Leo shrugged.

"Oh, well that's pretty sad," Isaac pondered, "but I guess it worked for us. That's really cool that you knew that. It definitely saved us back there."

"What about you, bro?" Leo asked. "Who is *Miss Jenny*? That was an epic save back there."

"Oh," Isaac replied casually, "She was my first-grade teacher."

Leo grinned and reached out for a fist bump, making Isaac blush a little bit. The gesture turned into an awkward turkey-looking creation, which made Leo laugh.

Alura smiled.

LIZ tried her best to keep up with the group, but it felt like the muddy terrain was not slowing anyone down but her. The backpack she brought was filled to the brim with helpful stuff, but she had been a little unsensible with her selection of shoes. With every step, there was a quiet squelch as her flats sunk down into the mud. She was starting to feel it between her toes.

This was her first job, *ever*. She had no idea what to expect, but earlier today, the part of her that hated surprises attempted to create a few very feasible scenarios on how the day would go. For example, filing paperwork or answering phone calls came to mind. What didn't come to mind was a crazy detective tasking them to investigate legendary creatures or inventing a device that could transport your consciousness back in time.

Ever since *that* reveal, she couldn't get it out of her head. *How did he do it? It wasn't something that someone could just slap together. Horace was a smart man, but he didn't seem like an inventor.*

"Yes, these are actually all Douglas-fir trees," Howard explained, somewhat passionately, to Leo and Isaac. "They are pretty versatile when it comes to lumber. Great tree to work with."

"They're all *huge!*" Leo exclaimed. "How long does it take them to grow to this size?"

The conversation continued, but Liz was uninterested in the topic. She didn't want to be acquainted with someone who was contributing to global warming. The earlier conversation would've continued if Leo hadn't stepped in and stopped her. The comments weren't meant to throw the dreamscape off, but she understood why Leo needed to step in. Regardless, her feelings on the subject were solid and she wasn't afraid to voice them, even to men like Howard. People like him could make a person feel small, both mentally and physically.

The idea of having Leo here caused some conflicting feelings for her. He had been in a few of her classes, and he was always late, no matter what. It was just so disrespectful to the teachers and the other students in the class. His group of friends often fell into the "bully" category. Specifically, they would poke fun at the outfits she wore and how hard she worked at school.

So far, Leo seemed to be very different when he was away from his group of friends. To be fair, he personally had never really spoken to her. This included making fun of her clothes or demeanor. She continued to try her hardest to separate her dislike toward his friends and keep a neutral mindset when it came to Leo.

"Hey," a voice came from beside her, "did you want me to carry that for you?"

While she was daydreaming, it appeared that Isaac had

snuck up. He was gesturing toward the backpack she was constantly shifting back and forth.

"No," she responded, "I'm fine."

Isaac's shoulders slumped down and he retreated two steps back from Liz. Howard and Leo continued to lead the pack, while the others were behind them. Her entire body fit into the shadow of the large man.

What a waste of time, Liz thought, *talking about trees. We're not here to learn about forestry.*

"How are you guys doing?" Alura asked from the edge of the path.

"I'm doing alright," Liz responded. "I should've picked different shoes I guess."

"I've been walking closer to the trees. It seems like the mud isn't as bottomless over here." Both Liz and Isaac altered their course, making their way toward Alura.

"You're right," Isaac admitted. "This is so much easier. Pop quiz in math or Christmas morning?"

What in the world was he talking about?

"I couldn't have put it better myself," Alura said, seeming to know what he was asking. "On one hand, this is so cool. It just feels like it isn't real though."

"It isn't," Liz said, referring to the fact that it was a simulation. She tried her hardest to hold in a smirk but with both pairs of eyes directly on her, she gave in to it. Both looked very surprised by her display of emotion.

"I think that's the first time you've smiled all day," Alura said, looking to Isaac for confirmation. He nodded a few times in agreement.

The trio trudged through the mud for another few minutes until Isaac started acting strange. It seemed like he was coughing on something, as if he had swallowed a bug. He gained the attention of both Liz and Alura, who realized he was trying to gesture for them to look back. The two girls slowly turned their heads to realize they were being followed.

Sanders, the man from the office that was being escorted from the premises, was bringing up the rear. The noises that Isaac made to get their attention also caused Howard and Leo to stop and turn for a moment as well.

"Listen," Howard said, rubbing his temples, "I explained this to you many times, Mr. Sanders. Please go back to the front gate. I simply don't have the time."

"No, no," Sanders stuttered, "you've got it all wrong! I was making my way toward the exit when I overheard on one of the walkie talkies that some kind of monster had been spotted. I just wanted to see it for myself."

"This is a work site. I cannot authorize you to be here," Howard explained.

"If you let me tag along, I'll leave you alone," the slender man pleaded, nervously pulling at the collar on his shirt. Howard took a moment to reflect. "There are better places to protest anyway."

Howard seemed to be seriously considering the offer. *The chance to eliminate an annoyance from your life?* Liz recognized how rare an opportunity like that could be.

"Deal, but I don't want to see you ever again, you understand? On either side of the fence."

Sanders nodded his head in agreement. The two men joined

hands. Sanders cringed in pain for a moment, then grinned sheepishly.

"Good day," he greeted, joining the three interns in the back.

Now that the human-bulldozer was out of her way, Liz could finally get a good look at the man. He had small, round glasses that sat at the edge of his pointy nose with a brown mustache beneath it. He was especially tall and slender with slim pants and a vertically striped shirt with suspenders.

"My name is Theodore, Theodore Sanders," he continued. "It's nice to meet you all. Have you heard anything about this monster? Did he say anything about it?"

"No, actually," Liz said coolly. "We really don't know what is going on. We were just invited to tag along. What are you doing here, in the woods?"

"Well," Sanders responded, a little taken back by the bluntness of her question, "I'm part of the California Audubon Society. Whatever is happening here is really disrupting the bird migration patterns all over the area. It has been difficult for an enthusiast such as myself. My son and I used to come to this area all the time to camp out and see what kind of animals we could spot."

There was a pause in the conversation, when only the squelching of the mud and the chirps of the birds could be heard. Sanders uncapped his canteen and took a small swig, slightly wincing as it ran down his throat.

"I haven't seen him in some time, though," Sanders frowned, the edges of his mustache sagging below his lip. "We speak sometimes but his wife, my daughter-in-law, doesn't like me very much. Last time we talked, he told me I was going to be a grandfather. I hope I get to meet the little one soon."

"I understand that," Alura sympathized. "That has to be hard for you. I'm sure you'll get to meet with them soon."

Although the next leg of the conversation lay with Sanders, Liz couldn't look away from Alura. She seemed to be fixated on his facial expression. Her words were genuinely caring, but it looked like she was searching for something more from Sander's response.

"Yes, I suppose," he said with a slight sigh. "So, what do you think we are going to see?"

"Bigfoot?" Liz mumbled. As soon as it came out of her mouth, she realized her error.

"Huh?" Sanders asked, as all three turned to her.

Why is this so difficult for me? she berated herself. *It's really not that hard to stop saying stupid things.*

"She just said that her feet keep sinking in the mud," Alura responded to cover up anything that could disrupt the course of the dreamscape. She shot a slight nod in Liz's direction.

"Yes, sorry," Liz apologized to the three of them, but mostly Alura and Isaac.

They continued walking until the path got narrow enough that they had to walk in a single file. Howard called out from the front to let them know they were getting close. He was followed closely by Leo, then an empty space with the second group in the order of Alura, Isaac, Liz, and Sanders in the back. The path seemed to be drying up, which was much appreciated.

The group had only been walking for about fifteen minutes, but it felt like hours. Liz had only been outside of New York

82

City twice in her life, once when her family visited a theme park down south and another when their school took a trip to Niagara Falls. For obvious reasons, she was not equipped for this wilderness hike.

Although Liz was frustrated with the circumstances of the simulation, it often turned to inspiration. For example, the deep mud they were sinking into *wasn't real.* It was incredible, to say the least. Her thoughts fell back to wondering how the device had been created in the first place.

The path seemed to come to an end, where Howard and Leo pushed the branches out of the way so everyone else could get through.

Once through, Liz heard water running in the distance. She really hoped that it was the river that met Redwing Bluff. There was an open clearing where a few trucks were parked around an excavator with half a dozen workers in orange vests and jumpsuits gathered. They waited for Leo and Howard to get through the brush and then started walking toward the area that seemed to be a popular attraction.

"Careful, careful!" a man ran over, looking at the ground, as if avoiding explosive mines. "Don't come any closer. It looks like we have an issue, Mr. Price."

ISAAC stepped to the side, allowing Howard to come face to face with the worker who had ran over to warn them of the dangers. He was clean shaven with greasy, black hair hidden under his helmet. His feet filled a pair of muddy boots, partially covered by a pair of overalls that ran all the way up to his neck.

"As always," Howard sighed. "What is it, Bruce?"

It didn't really matter what the man said, Isaac felt as though Howard was some sort of an action-movie or video game villain. Based on his looks and demeanor alone, he was the type of character who would be the final boss or the mastermind who had seen everything go to plan. Isaac struggled to stay neutral and push this thought out of his mind. *He isn't a villain because he has a scar,* he reminded himself.

"Some kind of a monster tore out all the controls for the excavator," Bruce said, trying to catch his breath. "I went to turn it on this morning and realized they were missing. Take a look at the ground."

Scattered in the surrounding dirt were bare footprints imprinted in the mud, at least two or three times larger than Isaac's own. He crouched down and looked closer at the indentations that seemed to sink much further into the soft earth than any of the other boot prints. The heel in particular left a deep imprint. This could really only mean that whatever left them was running or weighed significantly more than any of the workers, who were all varying sizes of enormous.

"And what do you suppose did this, Bruce?" Howard asked skeptically.

"I saw something, something *hairy*, run into the woods right over there!" Bruce exclaimed, pointing toward the tree line.

"Oh, is that so?" Howard said quizzically, slowly crossing his arms.

"Yes, I swear it!" the man shouted confidently. "Ran right into the woods over there!"

"And this wouldn't have anything to do with you trying to

get out of work, *again?*" Howard said, taking a step toward Bruce, who matched him with a step backward.

"No sir, no," Bruce stammered. "It's really not like that…"

"Let's recap this week alone, shall we? Bad tuna sandwich, out Monday. Someone stole your car, out Tuesday. Someone stole your bike, out Wednesday. It's only Thursday, Bruce. I have just about had it with your games. You're *finished.* Go back to the office and get your things. You had better be gone by the time I get back."

Bruce looked like he had something he wanted to say to counter the order, but the behemoth of a man made his position on the subject very clear. Howard seemed like the type of man that did not put up with any kind of nonsense. However, Isaac noticed that he had never really raised his voice in any of the conversations he had witnessed.

With his head held high, Bruce started his trek back toward the office. The man was shaken by the interaction with Howard, but he was trying his hardest not to look affected. If what his boss said was true, this was probably not the first job he'd been fired from for laziness.

Motive, Isaac thought to himself. *Bruce had the motive to be Bigfoot to get out of work.*

Despite his large stature, Howard moved very swiftly through the field of muddy footprints. As the group made their way over to the broken-down excavator, Jim popped his head up from behind the machine.

"Hey there, Mr. Price," Jim said with a small grin.

"Hello, Jim," Howard said with a sigh. "What's the damage?"

"See for yourself," Jim said, climbing down from the cab of the excavator.

Everyone seemed to take a synchronized step forward for a better look. Inside, there was a seat facing a rather large hole. Isaac assumed that's where all the levers and buttons would be to drive it. The metal around the edges of the space was bent backwards with strange indents, almost as if someone had stuck their hands on either side to separate the rest of the dashboard from the controls and then rip out the middle.

"What the…" Howard said, his voice trailing off. "Any idea how this could happen?"

"Honestly, I don't think any human has that kind of strength. It's possible that someone could've taken it out with a crowbar, but that really doesn't explain the hand marks around it. Looks like fingers, doesn't it?"

"What about a bear? Didn't Bruce say he saw something hairy?"

"I mean, it's possible I suppose," Jim stated, scratching his head, "but the animals normally stay away from the vehicles. I think they're too loud. It scares 'em."

The two men stood side by side looking into the black space in the dashboard for a moment. Isaac surveyed the area and noticed Sanders had left the group. He could spot the man on the other side of the clearing, near the dense brush that Bruce had pointed to when speaking about the hairy creature.

Could it have been Bigfoot? Isaac wondered. As he wandered over to meet the tall man, another question began to roll around in his mind, which then led to another. *Are we supposed to be figuring out if Bigfoot is real, or are we supposed to assume he isn't? Does Mr. Brown believe Bigfoot is real.* He supposed these questions would be answered in time.

"See anything?" Isaac asked quietly, trying not to draw attention from the others.

"Doesn't look like anything's here," Sanders replied. He was trying to find a foothold to step through the bushes but struggled and stumbled backward. The man wasn't very graceful on his feet.

As Isaac was walking over, he identified the footprints in the mud. The toes of the final track pointed directly at a bush that had been crushed down in the center. Due to a tree trunk, the opening was hidden from the view of Sanders. Isaac made his way over and leaned in.

"Nice job, kid," Sanders voice came from behind him. "Easy access. What's back there?"

Isaac ignored his question as he took another step into the forest. The sunlight that lit up the clearing just a few feet behind him was almost completely useless. The interlaced branches above and his own shadow made it impossible to see anything but wet leaves and prickly bushes.

Holy cannoli, what is that? Isaac was able to see a small piece of paper under one of the bushes. He leaned down to get a better look, but the defense of the sharp leaves made it impossible to grab it.

It was about the size of a flash card, like the ones he had used to study for tests and quizzes. On it, there appeared to be four symbols: a cup, a coin, a sword, and an arrow.

It was different, but the art style printed on the card reminded him of an old fantasy card game called Lost

Journeyer. The cards represented everything from dragons to castles to magic wands. The more cards the player had, the more powerful they were in the game.

For a short time, Isaac and his brother, Carter, collected some of the cards before discovering that the game's creator had digitalized it into Lost Journey, a video game that was similar in the way it was played.

Why is this in the middle of the woods? Isaac wondered. Then, he remembered something that Mr. Brown had mentioned earlier about Emit and filler information. *Things in the dreamscapes may not be exact. This must just be a weird glitch in the simulation or something.*

LIZ and the others watched as Howard and Jim spoke about the issue with the excavator. More specifically, they discussed Bruce.

"Sir, if I may," Jim offered, "the guys here said they also saw something big and hairy moving around the site this morning but didn't think too much of it. I know Bruce has been known to make up stories before, but no one ever backs him up. They usually throw him to the wolves."

Howard rubbed his temples with his index fingers for a moment, then turned to the two men who nodded their heads to confirm what Jim said on their behalf.

"It doesn't much matter," Howard told Jim. "Bruce has been a thorn in my side for a while. Truth be told, I've fired him twice before this. The stories just keep flowing. He always shows up to work the next day and pretends like nothing happens. If he does or doesn't, I really don't care."

"Agreed," Jim said, nodding his head. "I suppose I'll try to get this up and running. It's going to take me a good bit of time though."

"Well, try to be as quick as you can," Howard said, looking up at the dark clouds rolling in above them. "Looks like it's going to be a wet one this afternoon."

Liz hadn't realized it, but dark storm clouds moved in overhead. With the removal of so many trees, mudslides were all but guaranteed with some significant rainfall. Looking around, she noticed that Isaac wasn't with the rest of the team near the excavator. Instead, he was over near the bushes where Bruce had said the creature broke through. Sanders was also over in that area, seemingly watching Isaac shuffling through the landscape.

Howard's deep voice recaptured her attention. He began commanding the workers that stood around the machine. "You, spread the word to the crew to get all vehicles back to the yard, then help Jim get this thing back up and running," Howard pointed toward the man on the left, then the right. "And you, grab the camera from my office and cement from the warehouse, I want you to make some casts of these footprints. They'll be washed away by morning, but we need to preserve what we can."

"Casts, sir?" the man questioned.

"Yes, oh my..." Howard took his head in his hands for a moment, "Like a mold of it."

The man squinted his eyes and scratched the back of his head.

"Alright," the large man took a deep breath, turning toward the other man, "you know what I'm talking about?"

"Yes, I know how to make a cast," the other man responded.

"Switch jobs then and get to it!" Howard said, and then turned back to Jim, who was back up on the excavator, seemingly making a parts list on a small notepad. "You'll oversee this and make sure it will get done?"

"Absolutely sir," Jim replied with a salute.

"Thank you. Between you and I, there's some weird things going on with this land. I'm starting to wonder if it's more headache than it's worth. Let me know if you have any issues. I'll send you an extra man once everything is back in the yard."

Following Howard, the three teenagers carefully moved their way out of the footprints. Isaac and Sanders started walking to join them.

"What other weird things are happening here?" Leo asked, trying to keep up with the large strides of the man, who seemed to be frustrated with the situation. He didn't turn his head to answer, keeping his gaze on the path ahead.

"You name it, it probably happened," Howard said. "A few of our machines wound up in the river after a good rain. Most of the men assumed it was just the mud, but it didn't really seem possible to me. Trees constantly falling on the roadways and trails, beartraps being set off without anything in them, materials constantly disappearing."

"Oh, gotcha," Leo said, taking a moment before asking his next question. "And what do you think is doing it?"

"That's the thing. I don't know," Howard shrugged. "A few of the men have said they've seen strange creatures moving around, but I've tried to keep it hushed up. More people find out about it, I'll have a mass exodus on my hands. Honestly, it's probably those nature protestors that have nothing better to do than stand outside the gate all day."

"Like me?" Sanders asked, "How do you think we can get into this compound? It's completely fenced off. Besides, how many of us do you think it would take to *push an excavator* into the river?"

"I mean there are a lot of you out there," Howard replied, his voice becoming louder. "All of you want houses to live in, but no one wants to disturb the wildlife. Tell me, how do you want it to get done?"

Don't say anything, Liz reminded herself. *This isn't your fight. It isn't real. It's a simulation.*

"There are other options," Sanders defended. Prior to his last word, Howard spun around to face the thin man, who had to look up at him.

"Tell me then," Howard demanded, raising his voice and taking a step toward Sanders. "Tell me how."

Sanders took a step back but fell backwards into the mud. He tried to get up, but the mud was too slippery. Liz could feel her face getting hot. *This oaf has no idea what he was talking about. Protecting the environment was no fool's errand, it was a matter to be taken seriously.*

"Deforestation is destroying the planet. Knowingly hurting wildlife will be a crime someday, and people like you will have to pay the price." Liz looked around and realized that everyone, including Sanders who was being helped up by Alura, was looking directly at her. As soon as the words left her mouth, she felt herself cool off. However, she instantly regretted her decision to speak up.

"You want to speak to me like that?" Howard said calmly. "Get out, all of you. Join your friends on the other side of the gate. Maybe they'll be able to help you find your teacher."

"Wait," Leo pleaded as he started walking toward the office.

"Let me be clear," Howard took a deep breath, then screamed loudly enough to disrupt the birds in the distance, "Get out!"

Purple smoke began to surround the group. Liz felt sleepy, closing her eyes slowly. When she reopened them, she sat up quickly in the bed she used to transport into the dreamscape. She buried her head in her hands for a moment, realizing that she had ended the simulation with her pointless interjection.

LEO sat straight up in his bed, his vision still fuzzy from exiting the dreamscape. The blood in his veins boiled. Frustration surged through him. *I fixed the dreamscape once,* Leo's mind played on repeat, *and you couldn't keep your mouth shut?*

He yanked the door open with such force that it made the plastic frame shimmy.

"Seriously?" Leo said, throwing his hands up. "*Why?* Why would you do that?"

Leo saw Isaac and Alura standing behind Liz, avoiding eye contact with anyone else in the room. Emit continued to play the random string of noises.

"She didn't mean to change things," Alura said quietly. "It was an accident."

"You're kidding, right?" Leo said, turning toward Alura. "You're going to *defend* her? That was the second time she did it, and it's the first day! We were so close to getting some real answers from Howard about what was going on!"

"I, um," Liz stuttered, suddenly unable to form words.

"You didn't need to say *anything,*" Leo continued. "It isn't even real! You don't need to defend your position to a fake person who lived more than 60 years ago!"

Now you don't have anything to say? Leo's thoughts were infected by his anger. He waited for her to say something back, but she never did.

Liz scurried from the room, pushing past Horace who stood in the doorway with a steaming mug of coffee.

"Why is she even here?" Leo blurted out defensively. "She's a *genius.* Some of us really need this internship." He stopped himself before his words could continue, but thoughts strew themselves throughout his mind inevitably, like a ball on its way to the outfield. All he could do was witness them.

Some of us need this internship to get into college. Some of us need to show the rest of the world they have something to offer. Some of us need this internship to have the opportunity to make something of themselves.

Leo threw himself down in Horace's chair that was positioned in the middle of the room, burying his face in his hands. The room grew silent, but he could feel the others looking at him as he tried to cool down.

LIZ felt an empty feeling hollowing out her stomach. She tried her hardest to hide it, but it was coming at her all at once. *Just get away,* she told herself. *You'll be alright if you can get away.*

She made a beeline for the bathroom and closed the door. She slowly sank down to the floor and could feel tears forming in the corner of her eyes.

This can't possibly be happening. The crazy detective. The

94

impossible invention. Hunting Bigfoot. Working with other people,
especially Leo. This was supposed to be an easy, sit-back-and-relax
part of her 27-step plan.

Liz wanted to turn the shame and sadness of throwing off
the dreamscape into anger for Leo for talking to her that way
or Howard or *anyone* else. *Leo saved me once, and I did it again.*
The Howard we met wasn't real. There was only one person left
on her list to feel anger toward. *I hate myself. This is all my fault.*

There was a rhythmic knock at the door.

"Hey, Liz? It's Alura. Can I come in? Or do you want to come
out? Horace said we could use his office if we wanted to talk
privately."

"That's alright," Liz sniffled. "I'm alright. I'll be out in one
second."

"Okay," Alura said gently. "Can I get you anything?"

"No," Liz answered, "I'll meet you in his office in a minute."

"Sounds perfect. I'll be waiting for you."

Liz stood up and made her way over to the sink where she
quickly washed her face and avoided looking in the mirror.
After making sure the coast was clear, she fully opened the door
and quietly slipped down the hall into Horace's office where
Alura was waiting in one of the chairs he used for the
interviews.

"Hey," Alura said, gesturing toward the other chair.

"Thanks," Liz whispered.

"Of course," Alura responded, reassuringly. "So, what's
going on? I always feel better after I talk it out, but that's totally
up to you."

"I know I messed up. Twice. But that was unnecessary to call me out in front of everyone. It was unfair of him to do."

"I couldn't agree more," Alura laughed. "I let him have it after you left the room. Honestly, so did Horace. Once he realized what had happened, he did one of those 'disappointed parent' looks. Finger wag and everything."

"No way," Liz held back a smile. "He did a finger wag?"

"Okay, so that part might have been embellished a little, but when I tell you that he is a master of the 'disappointed parent' look, I mean it. I didn't even do anything, and *I* could feel it from across the room."

"Alright," Liz shrugged. "That still makes me feel better."

"Can I be completely transparent with you?" Alura asked. "I really don't want to overstep though, so if you don't want to talk about it, that's fine."

Liz nodded, suddenly nervous. *Can a good conversation possibly follow that introduction?*

"Did something happen between you and Leo before this internship?"

That was about the caliber of what Liz was expecting to follow.

"Not exactly," Liz answered vaguely. "Him and his friends always make fun of me for being smart and dressing more formally than necessary for school, I guess. Why?"

"Well," Alura took a deep breath, "it's pretty obvious that you don't like him very much. It's just the way that you act around him and things you say."

The empty feeling returned. Hiding her feelings wasn't something she was good at, but was she that easy to read? Liz focused on a spot on the wall, quickly trying to replay the entire day's events to find what would make Alura assume that. *I guess I was kind of rude to him, but was it that obvious that I don't like him?*

"That's alright, we really don't have to go into it," Alura continued after waiting a moment. "But him and his friends bully you in school? I can set him straight if you want."

The offer was a truly sincere gesture, but Liz was never really upset with Leo prior to him yelling at her earlier. She couldn't recall a time that he specifically picked on her, but Liz didn't want to admit that to Alura. If only the chair she was sitting in was an ejection seat. She would give anything to get out of this conversation.

"No, no," Liz insisted, "that's alright. Don't worry about it. I suppose I just need to move forward."

Alura stood up and opened up her arms for a hug which Liz reluctantly accepted, but only for a split second.

"How are you doing?" Liz said awkwardly, hoping they could move the conversation along.

"I really *cannot* believe that Horace's invention actually worked. That was really incredible," Alura said through her smile. "I'm just really happy to be part of all of this."

Something about Alura made it easier for Liz to open up. She purposefully made a point of closing herself off at any junction. It didn't matter much anyway. People always seemed more interested in her ideas and knowledge, which was alright with her. In her eyes, there wasn't much logic in feelings.

"Me too, honestly," Liz admitted. "When he first pulled the sheet off that Emit device, I had a hard time believing it was going to do anything but set off the smoke detectors."

The two girls shared a quick laugh, and there was a knock at the door. There was a window to the hallway, but they couldn't see who was there through the frosted glass.

"Hey," Horace said, "it's me and Dot. Can we come in for a minute?"

"Sure," the two said in unison.

The door opened gently, and the two senior citizens shuffled inside, closing it behind them. Both of them took a few steps into the room and started leaning against the desk.

"Don't mind me, I'm just here for moral support," Dot said, winking. Horace shot her a quick look, as if she just let out one of Horace's deepest darkest secrets.

"Thanks Dot," Horace said, returning his attention to Alura and Liz. "I apologize, but it's true. I don't think I've talked to a teenage girl since the sixties. Wasn't good at it then either."

Horace stroked his beard for a moment while the others shared a collective laugh.

"Anyway," Horace continued, "I just wanted to apologize for Leo's behavior earlier. It was completely unacceptable. I have spoken to him privately and he understands that there will be consequences for his actions. I would like to hear what happened from your eyes, Elizabeth."

"Well, um," Liz began, "I may have made a few mistakes today. I wasn't exactly the best at the whole 'keep to the script' plan. I'm sorry."

Liz tried to keep things as vague as possible, remembering that Dot didn't know about the Emit device and Horace didn't want her to. Although, his secretary didn't seem to be too interested in the conversation anyway.

"That's alright! We all make mistakes. It's how we learn. Keeping the script is important for accuracy, so it is important to try your best. However, everything will turn out alright."

Horace's gaze wandered toward the floor. Liz understood that the next part of the conversation was going to be tough for him to get through, but she couldn't imagine why.

"Listen, I am not really great at this part. I've never really been the boss of anyone but myself," Horace explained, intertwining his fingers. "You tell me what you want me to do. I want you to understand that Leo is sorry for his actions, and nothing of that nature will come from him again. However, if you would feel more comfortable dismissing him from this program, I will do so."

Liz was very surprised by this offer. For a second, she made eye contact with Alura, who looked equally, if not more, stunned. Dot was staring at the side of Horace's head. Clearly, she hadn't been briefed before the meeting either. It really wasn't even a choice for Liz, especially after subconsciously being rude to Leo all day.

"No," Liz said confidently, "I would really like to move past this."

She would never admit it, but Leo was very important to the team. His raw confidence when it came to speaking to people in the dreamscape kept everything on track.

"You're sure?" Horace confirmed.

"Yes."

"Perfect. Well, I think we've had a good amount of action for the day. It almost two o'clock anyway, so I think I'm going to dismiss everyone for today, and we will reconvene here tomorrow morning. If you'd like to change, you can either use the bathroom or the…"

The old man snapped in the air, looking toward the ceiling to find the proper term.

"Cubicles?" Alura offered.

"You know," Horace said, "you're going to have to stay with me after the summer just to help me come up with the right words. It's got benefits. Dental's covered."

HORACE stood near the desk, waving to Isaac who was just heading out. He fell behind the others when Alice came into the lobby and demanded attention.

"Were you actually going to fire Leo from the internship?" Dot asked pointedly.

Horace knew the question was coming. In his office earlier, when he placed the offer on the table for Elizabeth, he knew Dot was surprised.

"Think about it. Do you think I would have?"

"I don't *know*," Dot said with a sigh, "That's why I asked you."

It was times like this that Horace realized he was a bit mysterious at times. His mind didn't quite match up to others.

"The wind can make a flower stand up," the detective said, staring through the window at the street outside, "but not without losing a few petals first."

He turned to face Dot, who appeared lost. The two had worked together for a long time. Even with all the time they had spent together, his metaphors were unappreciated by someone as straightforward as her.

"I knew what her answer would be," Horace admitted. "When you give someone the power to make a decision for themselves, it instantly becomes more valuable. It might take a little bit of time, but the four of them are going to be an unbeatable team. They are meant to be here."

 **8**

ALURA sat on her bed, reading through the abundance of comments on her newest post. It had been a long first day, and she was ready to unwind.

How was the big day? See any dead bodies?
Is it true Horace Brown is an alien? Or just a superhuman?
Did Horace say anything about future internships?

The internship itself had been rewarding enough, but since she had announced her acceptance, she often woke up to an influx of new followers.

She put her phone down on her nightstand and laid back against her pillows. Closing her eyes, she attempted to banish the negativity that sometimes inundated her in unfamiliar situations.

Alura started feeling this way at the beginning of the last school year, when she lost her parents. Her Aunt Kate and Uncle Rick were kind enough to take her in, giving her a place to feel she belonged when her world was turned upside down. It was a very tough time for everyone, but she was lucky enough to have someone so she didn't have to go through it alone.

In the beginning, she wondered whether or not it was something that other people experienced too. *After losing such a huge part of yourself, can you ever be whole again?* Regardless, the whirlwind of today left her feeling a bit overwhelmed. The entire experience was incredible, and she felt like she was in a movie or something.

Getting to work with a world-renowned detective? *Amazing.*

Using an old record player to travel back through time? *Glorious.*

Doing the above while also solving legendary mysteries throughout different time periods, all summer long? *Inconceivable.*

Alura placed her palms together, replaying the day in her mind to fully comprehend the events from the initial introduction of Emit all the way to experiencing the dreamscape. Her mind finally landed on the issue between Liz and Leo. Although it seemed impossible, Alura felt bad for both Leo and Liz simultaneously.

Liz had made *two* mistakes, but she immediately showed regret for her decision after the second time that interrupted the dreamscape. Leo had fixed her first mistake, even after Liz was rude to him all day. Similarly, after the anger left his body this afternoon and Leo saw Liz's face as she left the room, anyone could tell he was ashamed of his actions. Was there ever a time that two sets of shame and regret could cancel each other out?

If there was one thing that was obvious, it was that they needed to work together to solve this mystery and they hadn't done so yet.

Some of us really need this internship. Alura had thought about it on the way home, wondering why Leo *needed* the internship. It had also made her think about why she had applied for the internship. The truth was that she didn't really know. Alura didn't know what she wanted to do with the rest of her life. That answer was required to move forward, and it wasn't uploading makeup tutorials to ShutterSwift for the rest of her life.

Rolling over and looking at the clock on the wall, she decided it was time to eat. As she rose from the bed for the trek, her phone rapidly chimed twice. The first was to alert her to a new follower, while the second was a message.

Unlocking her phone, she clicked on the user who had both followed her and sent her a text, realizing it was Isaac. The profile picture was his cat, and he didn't have any posts on his profile. She stood in the hallway for a moment, opening the message.

IsaacDude0234 said: Hey sorry to bother you. Do you have a minute to talk?

Before she could respond, another message appeared.

IsaacDude0234 said: By talk I mean text. Like message on here.

There were still dots on the screen, indicating that he was still typing.

IsaacDude0234 said: Sorry.

She chuckled to herself, thinking of Isaac frantically fumbling with his phone to send another message.

You Replied: Sure, just text me though. It'll probably be easier

She tapped in her phone number and pressed the send button. The dots appeared two or three more times, disappearing after a moment. The phone vibrated in her hand, indicating she had gotten a text. When she looked, it was a number not in her contacts but was easily identifiable as Isaac from his first text. She laughed again, and slipped the phone in her pocket so she could grab her snack before returning to her room and the conversation.

Making her way down the stairs, Alura arrived in the kitchen. The fridge was decorated in a diverse array of magnets from all over the world, including countries in Europe and Asia. They were a mixture of places that her aunt and uncle had travelled to and gifts that friends and family had brought back for them, knowing that they had an assortment on their fridge.

As she was making her way into the kitchen, the door handle clicked and her Aunt Kate walked inside, setting down her purse and reusable bags with papers from work. Her glasses were askew and her button-up was half tucked in. Immediately, she zeroed in on Alura.

"Tell me all about it!" she begged. "How was it, your first day? Was it exciting?"

"Hey Aunt Kate," Alura said, moving in for a hug. "It was *amazing*. You wouldn't even believe what he's having us do..."

As soon as the words left her mouth, Horace's words swirled

around in her head. As painful as it was, she was sworn to secrecy.

"Oh yeah?" Aunt Kate prompted her to continue. "Tell me about it!"

"Yeah," Alura responded, choosing her words carefully to avoid any major lies. "He actually had a cubicle-type thing set up for each of us. The first half of the day was mostly introductions." To avoid any questions that she would have trouble answering, Alura shifted the subject. "I guess Horace added a fourth intern too. It's a boy named Isaac. He was in my math class last year."

"Math class this past year?" Aunt Kate inquired, trying to contain the brown strands of hair that had escaped her pony tail.

"Yeah, that's the one," Alura confirmed.

"Well," Aunt Kate said, "that's nice at least. Having a friendly face. I really don't feel like cooking tonight. You okay with heating over leftovers tonight?"

"Absolutely, that chicken last night was incredible. Let me know if you need me to do anything," Alura offered, realizing that she was just getting home from work now. "I'll heat up a plate now and I can put together one for you, too, if you want."

"That's alright, I don't know how long it'll be. I've got to get started on this paperwork here."

Alura went back upstairs after heating up her dinner in the microwave. It hurt her to have to keep a secret from her Aunt Kate. Not only that, she wanted to tell her about how unbelievable her first day had been, but Horace had been very clear about being able to share with anyone outside of their circle, even Dot. It was strange to Alura that Horace opted to keep Dot in the dark. The pair seemed to be very close.

She slipped her phone out of her pocket.

> Hey, sorry. I was talking to my aunt. What's up?

Isaac

> Nothing much. I just wanted to see how you were doing

She smiled to herself again, realizing that his shyness was translating into his message.

> Doing alright, I guess. Just kind of a crazy day. Not what I was expecting at all

> Couldn't agree more 😊
> I really can't believe that he brought us in to solve unsolved mysteries!

It seemed that Isaac was very much in the same boat as Alura. She realized that he was more than likely feeling the same way that she was and needed someone to talk to about it. With the secrecy and all, he was probably just reaching out because he needed help processing it, same as her.

> Can I ask you something?

> Sure, anything

There was a little bit of time that passed before he sent back another text, Alura noticed.

> Do you believe in these things?

Alura looked away from her phone for a moment, processing the question. It was a logical query, but it wasn't really the type of thing a person would have in their back pocket, like a favorite color or a go-to order at their favorite restaurant. The reason why they were legendary creatures was because no one really *knew*.

> Like legends or myths or whatever you call them

She began typing but struggled to form an answer. Before today, Alura had never really needed to think so deeply about it. It never affected her directly.

> Sort of. I'm not really sure. What about you?

> Same. I guess I believe in some supernatural stuff, but not most of it

Alura felt similarly. The belief of ghosts and other spiritual things seemed possible to her on some days, but not others. She also thought about lucky items, like her mother's necklace. Her thought process, combined with what happened today, brought her to one, well-rounded question.

Apparently, it was shared telepathically between her and Isaac, because that was the next thing he sent to her. Aside from the rest of the team, at least the two of them were able to be on the same page.

> Do you think Mr. Brown
> believes in them? Is he trying
> to prove they exist or not?

She continued to think deeply, pushing aside any stress that the day had caused. Some people may call it a gift, but Alura struggled with how deeply she connected with people sometimes. With Horace, though, it was very difficult to tell what his intentions were.

He was a detective, after all. He could just be very good at hiding his thoughts and emotions, not allowing them to translate into conversations or body language. It was also possible that what he was trying to do had no underlying meaning. He was simply curious.

> Maybe he's trying to answer that himself but I have no idea. Seems like Horace Brown is a mystery too

> Yeah right? How did he even think of inventing a time traveling gramophone?

> Honestly I have no idea. Did you see the look on Liz's face when he started explaining what it was?

> The fact that she was so impressed made it even more incredible for me. I still have no idea how it works

Alura found herself smiling again, agreeing with Isaac's take on the subject. Everyone had some amount of complexity to them, but some were easier to read. For example, Liz was easy. Horace was not.

Although Alura was surprised that Isaac had reached out, this conversation made her feel like he was a true ally and friend. Between the 'friends' she had online and the group she hung around with at school, genuine people were not easy to come by. Everyone had some kind of angle, which Alura had a hard time processing. She was truly herself, one hundred percent of the time. It seemed like Isaac was the same way.

> Hey, you feeling up
> for a challenge?

The frantic dots began again, appearing and sliding off the screen multiple times before she got a response.

> Like what?

> Since we're detectives now, I think
> we should sharpen our skills

> Oh yeah? What are you thinking?

> Rules are simple. First to find out
> if Horace believes in myths wins

> BUT you can't ask him
> any direct questions

There was a break of about two minutes between her last text and his response. During this time, Alura wondered if he had gotten distracted with something else or was considering the terms of the challenge.

> Depends. What does the winner get?

She snickered, thinking that her own response would've been the same thing.

> What were you thinking? Money?

> Unrelated question. Is this a paid internship?

Alura laughed out loud in her room. The truth was that she had no idea, but she was wondering the same thing at one point or another.

> I have no idea 😄 I was too afraid to ask. I was just going to see what happens

> Well maybe for our first faceoff, we could do a candy bar of the winner's choice. I think I can afford that

> Sounds good to me but I only go for King Size

 **9**

ISAAC arrived at the detective agency around nine o'clock, just about an hour before Mr. Brown had asked them to come in. For the first fifteen minutes, he sat in the conference room with his cat, Alice. Then, the detective joined him a short while after that with a small stack of papers.

The text conversation he had with Alura last night made him feel clearer about what was going on. It took him hours of talking himself up to send the first message, and he still felt like maybe he shouldn't have reached out. Putting himself out there made him feel nervous. It was never easy to take the first step. Sometimes it was better to let things play out without getting involved.

The fact that she didn't have much more of a handle on what was going on gave him some reassurance. As intimidating as Alura seemed, he knew that she was a kind person based on how she acted in school. Regardless, it was just comforting to have a connection with someone else who had been thrust into such a strange situation.

And now, it was time for the competition to begin. *Does the great Horace Brown believe in myths and legends?* Isaac was determined to find out.

"Have a good night, Isaac?" Mr. Brown asked.

"Yes, sir," Isaac said, nodding his head.

"Me too," the detective agreed, never looking up from his papers. "It's nice to have you all here. It feels much livelier."

For a moment, Isaac thought of the argument between Liz and Leo yesterday. It was a tough situation, but he was glad that he wasn't involved at all. Conflict was something that he avoided at all costs.

He was excited to get back to investigating today. They could check off the 1958 logging camp. Next up would be the California summer camp in 1972, followed up by a 2002 trip to Washington. His thoughts then shifted toward creating indirect questions to get Mr. Brown to talk about his view on what they were investigating.

"So," Isaac began, "do you think there are a lot of differences between these mysteries and the ones you've solved in the past?"

Try to get him talking, Isaac told himself. *Maybe he'll just spill the answer.*

"What do you mean?" Mr. Brown said, adjusting his glasses and looking up from the table.

"Well, I just feel like these are kind of different than your, um, average cases. Do you think so?"

"I suppose so," he responded with a gaze toward the ceiling, "but a mystery is a mystery. They all have the same elements, it seems. And all those elements go in a certain order. Then you have your solution."

Isaac processed what he said, then tried to find something that separated viewing them as a hoax that needed to be debunked or seeing them as possibly being true.

"But, like, motive," Isaac fumbled, "right? Do you think motives are different between the two?"

"Motives between my previous cases and the mysteries I'm handing to you all? I mean, motives can be tricky sometimes, in both instances," Mr. Brown explained thoughtfully.

Before Isaac could pose another question, a ringtone sharply filled the room. Mr. Brown slid slightly down his chair and reached into his pocket for his phone.

"This ridiculous thing," he muttered. "It's the size of a television. *Ridiculous.*"

For a man who invented something like Emit, Isaac thought, *he sure does hate modern technology.*

Mr. Brown looked at the screen, hit the lock button, then set it down on the table.

"Who was it?" Isaac asked.

"My son," Mr. Brown explained with a sigh, "He's been calling in to see how I'm doing. For some reason, he has this thought in his head that I should sell the agency and retire. Silly, isn't it?"

Isaac nodded his head in agreement. Mr. Brown was an older guy, but he seemed to be on top of things. A while back, Isaac's mother made the decision to put his grandmother in a nursing home in Connecticut. It was tough, but she couldn't take care of herself and there was no way that his mom would be able to travel to her and still hold a job.

"Wait," Mr. Brown shifted back to the conversation. "What

were we talking about?"

Isaac didn't have another question ready, but Liz walked into the room, setting her things down on the conference table.

"Good morning, Elizabeth," Mr. Brown said with a smile. "How was your evening?"

"It was alright," she responded, seemingly forcing a smile. "Good morning to you as well."

Isaac recognized her backpack from somewhere. It was electric blue in color but covered with assorted pins and patches. Although he couldn't be sure, he assumed that it was filled with books because of its squarish shape.

"Everything alright?" Liz asked. It took Isaac a moment, but he realized that she was speaking to him, staring quizzically at her bag.

"Oh yeah, sorry," he responded. "It took me a second to figure out where, but now I remember that your bag is the exact same one that you brought into the dreamscape yesterday."

"Oh," Liz said. "Yes, I just focused on it before I fell asleep, and it appeared exactly the same."

"Wait," Mr. Brown said, squinting his eyes. "You were able to take your exact backpack into the dreamscape? I've tried to bring in specific items before, but I suppose I couldn't focus enough on it to make it happen. That's impressive."

"Thanks," Liz said quietly.

The three of them sat quietly, with the squeaky fan spinning overhead. Then, Isaac could hear footsteps and floorboards creaking from down the hall. Alura appeared in the doorway, wishing everyone a good morning.

"Hello everyone," she said. "Anyone else notice it's like a

thousand degrees outside?"

"I think it was supposed to be almost a hundred today," Liz said. The delivery of her words felt smoother than yesterday and much less matter of fact.

"Well, that's not good for my wallpaper," Mr. Brown said defeatedly.

The three interns laughed, all noticing the problem with the peeling wallpaper in the hallway.

There was more creaking, and Leo snuck into the room, closing the door behind him at the request of Mr. Brown. It seemed that he may have planned better today, as he wasn't out of breath, and he donned his professional clothing.

"Good morning, everyone," Mr. Brown said, standing up from his chair. "I suppose we will get an early start today since we're all already here."

He wheeled over the clean whiteboard and uncapped a marker.

"Rule number one of being a detective: make sure you stop yourself every once in a while, to recap what you know. It's very important, otherwise you may forget some facts that could be helpful in solving the case. So, who are the players?"

"Howard Price owns the logging camp," Alura said slowly. "Jim's in charge of the warehouse. Bruce is the employee who spotted Bigfoot but is known for being unreliable."

Mr. Brown scribbled down the information, grateful that Alura was taking big pauses between the information to give him time to write. Once he was finished, he turned to face them.

"Don't forget about Sanders," Isaac offered.

"I don't think he's really important," Liz said. "I was thinking Bruce. He had opportunity *and* motive. As for means, I'm not sure if any human being would have the power to tear out the control box from an excavator."

"I'm going to write this Sanders fellow down anyway," Mr. Brown said. "He can't be ruled out if he was significant. Who was he?"

"Part of the Audubon Society," Leo said offered from the back of the room. "Like nature people, I think."

"Precisely, the Audubon Society was one of the first conservation groups in America, calling for the protection of birds," Mr. Brown assured them.

The five of them sat for a moment, looking at the four bubbles he drew on the board, one for each of the people they met in the dreamscape.

"I mean, I think it's pretty safe to say that we don't have enough information to come to a conclusion," Alura said, looking around to the others for confirmation. "Right?"

"I suppose that's true," Liz agreed quietly.

Isaac thought back to the dreamscape yesterday. While the others were talking with Mr. Price, Jim, and Bruce, he wandered over to the bushes where Bigfoot had been seen. *That card,* Isaac wondered. *How did it get there? It must've just been a glitch with Emit. It wouldn't have made much sense being there.*

He had considered bringing it up to Alura last night but opted to leave it out of the conversation. Isaac didn't want her to think he was weird. *Should I bring it up now?*

Before he could, the conversation took an unexpected turn.

"I'd like to volunteer to go back into the first lumber camp dreamscape this morning and see if we can find some more information that could have been missed," Leo said, standing up. His voice was oddly robotic, as if the statement had been rehearsed.

"No," Liz countered, "I'd like to volunteer instead. It was my mistake, and I will fix it."

There was a short awkward silence as both waited for someone to accept their offer.

"Kiddos," Mr. Brown sighed, "I appreciate your enthusiasm and responsibility. However, you must remember that I am showing you the skills to be detectives in *real life*. There are no second chances in the real world. Contrary to the popular phrase, I must not be kind and I cannot let you rewind."

Isaac understood what Mr. Brown was saying but was confused about the reference. *Do people actually say that?* Leo and Liz lowered themselves into their seats.

"That being said," Mr. Brown continued, "Work as a *team* in this next dreamscape. Remember, means, motive, and opportunity!"

"I don't think we really need to go back anyway," Alura piped up. "Let's set some goals for this next dreamscape. What do you think?"

Mr. Brown sprung up from his chair. "I think that is a *fantastic* idea, Alura!" Below the bubbles of suspects, he numbered one through three.

"Number one," Alura offered. "Get to know the people better. Anything we can learn can be helpful."

"Number two," Isaac jumped in. "Find clues and information that point to anything other than Bigfoot being a real creature.

There was a stale silence in the room. Mr. Brown looked to the side of the table where Liz and Leo sat, waiting for one of them to propose a number three.

"Number three," Liz said quietly. "Blend in with the dreamscape so well that it makes the other two goals as easy as simple addition."

"Perfect," Mr. Brown agreed. "Anything else you'd like to discuss, or should I get Emit set up for today's adventure?"

LEO was sure it would all blow over. It was just like the time a few months ago when he and his best friend, Cody had gotten into it about their baseball team. They co-captained the Bulldogs but couldn't agree on the batting order. After a while of arguing, it turned pretty ugly.

You're an idiot if you think putting our best batter up first is the right thing to do, Leo remembered saying, rather loudly. *Get rid of that stupid chap stick and go get a glue stick.*

I wish I had the patience and the crayons to explain this to you, Cody had fired back.

The following day, it was like the argument had never happened. Leo planned to employ the same strategy with the Liz situation. *Everything will be back to normal,* he thought. *Just avoid her for today.*

While Leo crossed his fingers, there was something deep in the pit of his stomach that told him this was not like a clash with Cody. He had tossed and turned all night, feeling horrible about the things he said to Liz.

The four interns got up from the table and started moving toward the door. Something was *definitely* different about Isaac today.

"Dude," Leo said, "What are you wearing?"

"Oh," Isaac answered, looking down at his less-than-conventional outfit choice today, "It's my old Squirrel Scout uniform. I thought it might help us avoid questions like 'why are you dressed that way' in the dreamscape. Like we did yesterday."

Leo looked him up and down thoughtfully, then smiled. Although the buttons looked like they were getting a real workout, it would likely make today's trip into the dreamscape easier for them. Specifically, the third goal that Liz had proposed. *Blend into the dreamscape.*

"That's a really good idea, I wish I would've thought of that."

"There's a matching hat, too," Isaac said. "But I thought that was overkill."

The others changed into comfortable clothes, then made their way into the cubicle room. Leo entered his cubicle, preparing to enter the dreamscape.

"Today, you'll be visiting 1972 to live through a Bigfoot sighting at Camp Tolowa," Mr. Brown's voice came from outside the cubicle. "The camp has been open since 1912 and operated by the Edwards family. You'll be meeting with the second-generation owner, Paul Edwards, and his daughter, Rosemary, who run the summer camp each year. Get to know the campers and others who are part of this story. Good luck!"

Outside, he heard the gramophone begin playing the

combination of instruments, everyday noises, and rhythmic beeps and clicks that created the dreamscape.

Leo closed his eyes, and a purple fog appeared in his mind. When he opened them, he stood beside Alura, Isaac, and Liz. They were surrounded by enormous trees and a narrow dirt path that was clearly built around the stumps of the trees that came before. Bushes lined either side, ensuring anyone following it would not lose their way.

"Glad to see everyone made it," Alura chuckled. "Which way should we go?"

Leo looked for a minute and noticed that one path seemed to have a slight incline, whereas the other side seemed to twist downward toward the bottom of the hill.

"Probably this way," Leo offered, pointing down the path that led upwards. "If we are looking for a camp, they'd probably build it high up. Less wind, drier, you know."

The group trekked up the hill. Leo's theory was confirmed by a sign in the shape of an arrow that advertised Camp Tolowa, followed by two large totem poles made up of animal busts carved from wood and a large banner that connected them at the top. Similar to the arrow sign, it advertised the name of the camp and a few doodles of small cartoonish children.

As the group entered, Leo took in the area and surrounding landscape. There were four buildings total, situated in a u-shape with the gate sitting at the open end. The first two that they passed on their left and right were identical. Looking closer, they looked like cabins for the boys and girls, both furnished with bunkbeds.

Straight ahead to the left, there was a smaller building that almost looked like a house. To the right, there was the largest building of the four which was easily identified as the meeting hall. As they entered the camp, a dozen or so kids were heading that way. As they walked, dust puffed and came alive at their feet before settling back down on the ground.

"What's going on?" Alura asked. Unfortunately, none of the others had any more clue than she did.

"It looks like everyone is heading over there," Leo suggested. "Maybe it's some kind of a meeting."

"Well," Liz said quietly, "if we want to blend in, we can't be late. Number three. Let's go."

The four again nodded in agreement and started off toward the building. The old wood of the porch creaked under their footsteps, and the door squeaked and banged as it was pushed open and closed every time another child entered.

In the front of the meeting hall stood an older man with poofy white hair, almost like a puff of whipped cream, flourished with *sick* sideburns. Despite the dirty outdoors, his black shoes shimmered. Beside him, there was a woman who was probably in her mid-thirties with curly red hair and piercing blue eyes that scanned the room. The two were the only adults in the room, waiting for kids to cease filing in, filling up the benches and tables. The older man seemed to radiate excitement, whereas the woman reminded Leo of a prison guard, vying for a promotion to warden or maybe even executioner.

"Yes, yes," he said, pointing to empty tables for anyone looking for a seat. "Come on in, everyone. We'll be getting started shortly."

As soon as everyone was seated, the older man pulled firmly on his suspenders, then tried to get everyone's attention by waving his hands over his head.

"*Quiet!*" the woman shouted.

"Thank you," the man said quietly, then turned back toward the crowd. "Good afternoon, everyone! It is time to start our second session for the 1972 Summer of Tolowa. My name is Mr. Edwards, and this is Rosemary, my daughter. If you love the great outdoors, you've come to the right place!"

Leo looked around and noticed food trays and iceboxes on the back wall. This building was more than likely used as a mess hall as well as an activity center. He looked around at the other kids at the tables. Most looked excited, but some looked as if they were dreading the entire experience, similar to Rosemary. Including themselves, there were probably around fifteen kids, most being boys. Ages seemed to range from eight years old all the way to teenagers.

"I see some familiar faces which is great! I also see we have a couple of campers from our first session who decided to stay for even more adventure," Mr. Edwards continued enthusiastically. "Now, unfortunately we do have some rules…"

While Mr. Edwards was fumbling to retrieve flashcards from his pocket, Rosemary stepped forward and abruptly took over the meeting.

"Listen up," she said sternly, crossing her arms. "You are to participate in at least two activities a day. We usually run five a day, so the choice is yours to what you want to do. You're late,

123

you don't get credit. Breakfast is at 7AM. Lunch is at 12PM. Dinner is at 6PM. All here in this building. I don't know how it is back home, but you will eat what is given to you. Period."

Mr. Edwards looked like he was trying to rerail his meeting. He put a finger up and opened his mouth to speak, but Rosemary continued with her lecture.

"You are to be in your cabin following dinner, no exceptions. Lights out is at 9PM, and there will be lanterns lit throughout the camp."

"We have to be in our cabin after dinner?" a boy asked from the crowd. "Last year, we could be out until 9 o'clock!"

There was an outburst of conversation between campers, mostly sharing their disappointment and a few groups banding together to revolt. Leo looked at the others who sat silently, shocked by the sudden rowdiness of the room. He turned toward the front of the room where Mr. Edwards looked like he was trying to get a handle of the conversation.

"*Quiet!*" Rosemary shouted over the children. This time, it felt like it shook the entire building.

"Thank you," Mr. Edwards repeated, turning toward the audience. "Listen, everyone. It's tough right now, and I can't have anyone out of their cabins after dark. There's been a lot…"

"Is it the monster?" a boy asked from somewhere on Leo's left. Once again, the room broke out into a fury of conversations, many of which expressed their confusion on the subject. Rosemary repeated her catchphrase, followed by another show of gratitude from Mr. Edwards.

"There is no cause for concern," he said with as much confidence as he could muster. "This camp is safe. However, being out after dark can be dangerous. Other than fictional monsters, there are bears, and roots that you could twist your ankle on."

"What are you talking about?" Leo asked politely. "There's a rumor of a monster?"

"Unfortunately, yes," the old man responded, looking to his daughter for backup. "Uh, there has been reports of a large hairy creature roaming the area. He only shows up after dark, though."

A collection of comments from throughout the room, suspectedly from campers who had been there for the first session, erupted.

"It leaves *huge* footprints!"

"I was sleeping one night, and I got woken up by a really loud roar! I almost fell out of bed."

"I *saw* it! It must be, like, ten feet tall!"

Jackpot, Leo thought to himself. *Easy home run. We'll be able to solve this one, no problem.*

"Listen up," Rosemary commanded. "The reason we want all of you in your cabins is because we know one of you little delinquents is doing it. More than safety, you need to stop. I don't want to hear any more on this subject, got it? If everyone is in their cabin after dinner, we can personally guarantee that the monster will not come back. Case closed."

The room fell silent for a moment.

"Okay," Mr. Edwards said. "Why doesn't everyone head to their cabins and get settled in? When you leave here, boys will be on the left and girls will be on the right. For anyone who is joining us for the first time, please feel free to come introduce yourself to both me and Rosemary. Dinner will be served shortly, so drop off your bags and pick a bunk. We'll see you back here soon!"

The kids throughout the room started getting up from the table. There was still a steady murmur of rumors and theories as they exited toward their cabins. As soon as the group got outside, they stepped out of the way of the door and huddled up.

"Okay, so what's the plan?" Alura asked, looking directly at Leo.

"Why are you looking at me?" Leo asked.

"Well," Alura paused to think for a moment. "Sorry, it just seemed like you knew what to do in the last dreamscape. I just thought…"

Leo looked around at the rest of the group. He had the solid gaze of Alura and Isaac, while Liz was looking toward the ground.

"Listen, guys," Alura continued. "I know it's hard because of what happened yesterday. I think we are stronger because of it, though. This is such a crazy thing that is happening to us. It's going to be stressful, and we're all going to make mistakes. Now, we need to work as a *team*. Can we just get past everything and move on?"

Alura scared Leo in a way. It was like she was able to pull back the imaginary curtain in his mind.

"Yeah," Liz said quietly. "What do you think, Leo? What's our first step?"

Everyone seemed a little surprised by Liz's lack of sarcasm. Leo was especially thrown off by this change in attitude. It was

126

a tough position to be in for Leo. *Can't she just be mad at me?* The defeated look on her face made him feel like he should crawl under a rock.

"Uh, yeah," Leo responded, running his hand through his hair. "Well, I think we should focus on our three goals, right? Get to know people and find out as much about Bigfoot as we can. Pay attention to anything that is *off* or points to him being anything but a legendary monster. Of course, we'll have to split up. Isaac and I will head over to the dude's cabin, you two head over to the girls' cabin. Meet the players but remember number three: play the part."

"I think it might be important to take note of who was here for the previous session," Liz suggested. "Anyone who just arrived won't have much information. We need campers who have been here for a while."

"You're right," Alura agreed. "Whoever was here before could know more."

"Or they could *be* the monster," Liz said. Her comment had brought something to the forefront of Leo's mind. It was something that had come up for him while reviewing yesterday's events.

Horace gave us the task to solve the mystery of Bigfoot, but are we asking ourselves if he is real, or are we assuming he isn't and it's some random dude in a costume? Liz had made her position on the subject clear yesterday, before Emit was even revealed to them. Regardless, they needed to keep an open mind, especially if they were going to split up.

"We don't all agree on what we're looking for in this investigation," Leo said flatly. "That's fine. Each and every one of us needs to keep in mind that we are either looking for proof of a real Bigfoot *or* proof that Bigfoot is not real. That would mean that someone is putting on a show."

"True," Alura agreed. "Whatever you believe, it doesn't matter. But clues go both ways, so don't rule anything out."

Leo put his fist in the center of the group and the others did the same, creating an ultimate fist bump. They turned to break away to their tasks when Isaac spoke up and called them back into a quick huddle.

"Just real quick," Isaac said timidly, "Why would Mr. Brown send us in the middle? Why wouldn't we be here from the, uh, beginning? You know what I mean?"

"I see what you're saying," Leo said thoughtfully.

The others shrugged, indicating that they didn't have an answer to the question either.

"Okay," Leo said. "Let's keep an eye out for that too. That is a really good point. Let's meet back here for dinner and we can go over what we find. Good luck."

 **10**

While Camp Tolowa and its campers are fictional, there have been numerous accounts of Bigfoot harassing camps and other wilderness institutions. In 1972, the Patterson-Gimlin films were released to the public. It is a low-quality video capture of an unidentified creature. Some scientists have claimed the video was staged with a man wearing a monkey suit. Others have noted specific movements of the creature, stating they could not be created by a human being.

LEO and Isaac made their way toward the boys' bunk along with five or six others.

"Hey," a boy that was a couple years younger than them started back-pedaling to get in front of them. "You guys are new, right? Me too."

"Nice to meet you, dude," Leo said, wincing every time the kid almost tripped backwards. "Yeah, we are new. This is my first time at camp. I'm Leo, this is Isaac."

"Radical, man," he responded, then started walking forward. "I'm Jeremy. I'll see you around."

Up until this point, Leo had completely forgotten they were

in the 1970s, fifty years in the past. There wasn't any technology, but that was pretty common for a summer camp. The outfits were also very standard for trekking in the wilderness, with Isaac and his boy scout uniform fitting right in.

When they arrived at the boys' cabin, they slowed their pace to allow all the other kids to funnel their way in before them. There were sixteen beds in total, with four bunks lining both outside walls and two rows in the middle. It looked like most of the top bunks had been claimed, but Leo rushed over to one that was completely open, tossing his bag up on top and gesturing for Isaac to take the bottom.

"Awesome," Isaac said with a breath of relief. It was clear that he was overwhelmed with the idea of picking a bed.

"So, we've got Jeremy," Leo recalled to Isaac. "He just got here. He could know something, but he probably isn't involved with any conspiracies."

"Agreed," Isaac nodded. "What's next?"

"Well, just go talk to anyone, I guess. But just remember, stay in character. We're in the 1970s so things that you know as normal are different."

Isaac stood still for a moment, looking as if he was creating a mental note in his brain.

Before Isaac could even break away, a little boy jumped down from the bunk on the opposite side of Leo's bed. He wore an outfit similar to Isaac, but it looked like it fit better. It included tan khaki shorts and a brown short-sleeved button up with a bright red neckerchief to tie it all together. Leo could hear a faint whistle that was synchronized with his breathing, more than likely from the air passing between his missing teeth.

"Are you guys on a secret mission?" he asked with eyes fully of wonder. "Can I join?"

"Uh, no," Isaac stuttered.

"Why would you think we were on a secret mission?" Leo deflected, crossing his arms.

"You're standing in the corner whispering," the little boy responded. "If you aren't on a secret mission, it's kind of weird."

"Fair enough," Leo admitted. "Did you just get here?"

The little boy's train of thought visibly changed when a smile appeared on his face, putting the symphonic gaps in his mouth on display.

"Nope," he responded. "My parents always send me here, every summer for the *whole entire* summer. It's the best part of the year. So many bugs, not enough time."

"Gotcha," Leo smirked. "I'm Leo, this is Isaac. What's your name?"

The little boy put his hand on his chin for a moment, as if he was deep in thought.

"Are those secret agent names, or your real names?" he asked. "Eh, it doesn't matter. My name's Scotty. I'm eight and a half."

"Well, it's nice to meet you, Scotty," Leo said with a playful salute.

There was a loud bell that sounded somewhere outside the cabin.

"Dinner time!" Scotty shouted. "Yes!"

Leo turned to Isaac, who shrugged. It was difficult to tell what time of day they arrived at the camp, but he thought he'd have at least a little more time to meet people. They made their way back over, then spotted Alura and Liz who were seated at a table by themselves.

"Hey guys," Alura greeted them.

"What's up?" Leo responded as the two of them sat down on the bench. "You get some good info from the girl's cabin? Not too much to report on the boys' cabin."

"We met every single person in the girl's cabin. Very anti-climactic, if I'm honest," Liz said flatly.

"You met everyone?" Isaac responded, blinking slowly in disbelief. "No way. It felt like thirty seconds."

For a moment, Leo was surprised that they had been able to move so quickly through their introductions. Then, after quickly scanning the room, he realized why.

"How many girls are there at this camp?"

"Including us?" Alura asked, holding back a smile, "Three. We met a girl named Isabella. She said her parents made her come here with her brother after some sort of *incident* involving spiders last summer. Normally, there are two boys' cabins, but this year they turned one into a girls' cabin just for her. Or so she thought, until we showed up."

"Oh," Isaac responded, "That makes more sense."

"We only met two of the boys," Leo said. "This kid named Jeremy and a little kid who thought we were on a secret mission."

An older teenage girl approached the table, putting her hand up to greet them. Leo assumed it must be Isabella, as there were a limited number of options. Her hair was pulled back in a ponytail, and she wore round glasses. She also wore bell-bottom pants that, once again, reminded Leo that they were in the past.

"Hey everyone," she said with a smile. "I hope you guys don't mind, but Alura and Liz told me I could sit with you guys. It's going to be a summer of loneliness and boredom, so I'll take whatever I can. Isaac and Leo, right?"

"That's us," Leo confirmed. "And you're Isabella?"

"And that's me," Isabella said with a thumbs up. "Other than that, not really too much to say."

Before she could sit down, Mr. Edwards made a quick announcement. He had also made a wardrobe change into a mustard-colored button up and a vibrant bowtie.

"Everyone, the food stations are now open over on the other side of the activity center," he informed the campers. "Please grab a tray and eat as much as you'd like!"

Leo noticed Isaac starting to rise from the table, then either realized that no one else was getting up, or that they didn't need to eat because they weren't really there.

"Good call," Isabella said. "I usually wait until the crowd dies down. These kids are ravenous."

Everyone at the table shared a quick laugh.

"So, you're here for the whole summer?" Leo asked casually.

"Yeah," Isabella replied, "with my brother. He loves coming up here, but my parents won't let him come alone anymore. I offered to come up with him, which I'm kind of regretting now. There's really nothing to do."

"I can see how that would be an issue," Alura chuckled. "At

least you had and will have the cabin to yourself."

"You all aren't staying too long, then?" Isabella asked, deflating with disappointment.

"We might," Alura said. "We just have to see how things go, I guess."

There was a brief silence, which was quickly broken up by an accusation slung at Leo and Isaac.

"You traitors," a squeaky voice came up from behind them. "I can't believe you would betray me like this. We were *brothers*. I should've made you swear the oath."

LIZ's body tensed as it filled with apprehension. The pointed accusation put her on edge.

It had been a tough night for her after everything that happened yesterday. When Liz was younger, her mother liked to remind her that successful women needed to know when to make their mark. *It isn't the bottom of the page,* Liz remembered her saying. *You need to stamp your name right in the middle. It's up in lights for all to see. Show them what you can do but pick your moment.*

"Hello, Scotty," Isabella said, rolling her eyes. "It's good to see you, too."

It took a moment to realize that Leo and Isaac knew the little boy. He must also be the trouble-prone brother that required supervision after the *spider incident* that Isabella described.

If this dreamscape is ruined, it won't be my fault this time, she thought to herself after taking a deep breath. *Remember, stay quiet and agreeable. You can solve this mystery if you focus. Quiet.*

134

Agreeable.

After the incident with Leo the day prior, specifically the part where Horace was willing to expel one of the interns from the program, Liz decided that she needed to be on her best behavior. *The plan: 27 Points,* she continued. *If Horace was willing to can Leo without a second thought, I need to be at the top of my game. Goal three, blend in.*

"So, we weren't really expecting a monster to be part of the things to avoid," Alura said nonchalantly, trying to steer the conversation towards something useful.

"Yes, what is up with that?" Liz followed robotically.

I sound like a Shakespeare play, Liz scolded herself. All eyes around the table turned to her. Liz put her head down immediately, staring at her lap.

"Honestly, I don't really believe it," Isabella said quietly, leaning in like it was gossip. "It just seems too weird. It's probably just one of the kids trying to play a prank on the camp."

Isabella looked skeptically toward Scotty, who put up his hands in innocence.

"If you think it's me, you don't even know me," Scotty said, "Giant hairy monkey man? No thanks. I'm a bug guy. Everyone knows that. If anything, it would be tarantula man or something to do with grasshoppers. They're cool, too. Come on, sis. You're ridiculous."

His sister sat back in her seat, looking convinced by his alibi. He nodded his head victoriously and continued to eat something that looked like mashed potatoes in one of the compartments of his plastic red tray.

"But like," Isaac started, "what is it?"

It frustrated Liz that the others were so good at formulating questions that kept the conversation going. Even Isaac, who spoke less than the others.

"Well, the camp has only been open for a few weeks this year. During the first couple days, there was nothing. Then, BAM!" Scotty banged his fist on the table.

"Campers are saying they see this weird hairy guy in the woods when it starts getting dark. He leaves these big footprints, too. One of my pals said they saw his glowing yellow eyes in the bushes. There was a loud roar," Scotty explained, imitating the sound. "Then, they got him."

The little boy continued to shovel through the food that was on his plate, often taking a spoonful of different items, mixing them together before slurping it off the spoon. With the various items on his tray, none really seemed to require chewing.

Although he was preoccupied with eating, Scotty still seemed unconcerned with the fact that one of his friends had supposedly been attacked by this creature.

"Wait, the monster took him? Who?" Leo asked.

"Oh no," Scotty said with his mouth full, shaking his hands. A pea shot out of his mouth and landed on the table. "His parents came and got him. The sheriff came up here to figure out what happened, and I guess he was too scared, so the cops called his parents, and they came and got him."

There was a sigh of relief from next to Liz. She looked over and realized that Isaac was relieved by the news that Bigfoot hadn't violently dragged a child into the woods.

Didn't Horace say that nothing could hurt us in the dreamscape?

"That's pretty much all we know," Isabella confirmed. "Some nights, there's a loud roar. Rosemary thinks it's the kids playing a prank or a bear or something, but Mr. Edwards seems pretty concerned about it. I don't know what to think. The monster thing only comes at night though, so you should be safe in your cabin. If it's real, that is."

Liz racked her brain a moment for more knowledge about Bigfoot. She had done some research last night. After filtering through her new knowledge, he remembered that Bigfoot was in the newspaper back in 1958, which means that it would be possible that they would know what he was talking about.

"Have you ever heard of Bigfoot?" Leo asked coolly. It seemed that his thoughts were aligned with hers.

Isaac and Alura looked toward him quickly, as if he had asked a question that could throw of the dreamscape. After a quick calculation, similar to Liz's, their faces returned to normal.

"Bigfoot?" Isabella repeated. "It sounds familiar, why?"

"Well, there was this weird thing that happened years back," Leo explained. "They found these big footprints, and a guy said there was a hairy-looking creature lurking in the bushes. It was a long time ago, though. In the newspaper."

"Like I said, I feel like I've heard it before, but I don't really know," Isabella admitted. "You think it could be him? Back again?"

"Awesome!" Scotty exclaimed. "They could interview me for the paper. That would be *wicked*!"

Everyone at the table laughed at his genuine excitement.

"Hey," Isaac said, pointing across the room. "Do you guys

know that kid?"

Liz turned her attention to a table near the corner of the room. While the rest of the room was busy with laughter and conversation, this spot seemed a little less bright. A boy, maybe around thirteen or fourteen years old, sat by himself. He wore grey pants and a dark brown button-up shirt, topped off with a baseball cap that covered most of his face.

"That's Third," Scotty said solemnly. "He's been here since the camp opened this year, like us. I've never heard him say a word though. Kind of gives me the creeps. I'm pretty sure he's an alien."

"He's not an alien, Scotty," Isabella said, rolling her eyes. "I've never heard him talk either. There are a bunch of rumors about him that went around with the first session of camp. I tried to talk to him once or twice during arts and crafts, but he just stays quiet." She shrugged, as if there was nothing else to say about the boy.

"Why do they call him Third?" Leo inquired.

"One of Scotty's friends told me it was because he played third base on his baseball team. Another of them said something about him having a third eye, but I believe that one less," Isabella said, shrugging again. "I'm going to get some food, any of you guys want anything?"

"No, thanks," Alura replied. "We all actually ate before we got here."

She nodded her head and went to join the line for a scoop of whatever food they were giving out.

Liz looked at the others, who clearly wanted to discuss what they had learned. There was the obstacle of Scotty, though.

They sat in silence for a few minutes, then Mr. Edwards made the announcement that everyone would be heading back to their cabin for some free time and then lights out.

The four of them took this opportunity to discuss a plan of action.

"So, what's next?" Alura asked.

"We have some more information on what's going on with Bigfoot," Leo analyzed. "I think we should try to stay up tonight and see if we notice anything strange going on. If this is a person who is playing the part of Bigfoot, then they could take advantage of the switchover from the first session to the second. Not even talking about motive, people take advantage of confusion."

He's right, she thought. *There's a special window of opportunity.*

"Agreed," Liz said. "We don't really need more sleep, that's for sure."

"Okay, what do you think, Leo?" Alura asked, smirking at Liz's unintentional joke.

"Isaac and I will sit near the front of the camp, somewhere between the cabins and the totem poles," Leo suggested.

"Wait, like outside?" Isaac asked.

The others turned to face Isaac, who was twisting his hands into one another. His face was as pale as a ghost.

"Yeah, outside. Is that okay with you?"

"I guess," Isaac said shakily, "but I don't want to get attacked."

"You won't get attacked because it isn't real," Liz explained.

"Liz is right. The dreamscape isn't a real place. If you get attacked, you just wake up in Horace's office. You'll be fine," Alura reassured him with a pat on the back.

Liz had been referring to the inexistence of Bigfoot, not the lack of reality within the dreamscape, but Isaac seemed to become slightly less unsettled.

"Can you two hang out over near the activity center and the office?" Leo asked, continuing his plan.

"You've got it," Alura confirmed, nodding her head. "Anything we should be on the lookout for?"

A giant hairy creature with glowing yellow eyes? Liz thought. *Shut up, Liz. Quiet. Agreeable.*

"No, I don't think so. I think you know what to look for," Leo concluded after a moment of contemplation. "Just remember goal three. Don't get caught or it could throw off the dreamscape. Observe only, try not to interact if you can help it."

The team broke in half and made their way toward their respective cabins.

ISAAC tried to keep his composure as they headed back to the cabin. He understood that no *physical* harm could come from a monster in the dreamscape, but what about psychological damage? *I don't like horror movies,* he thought to himself. *Particularly ones that are set in the middle of the woods at night.*

There was a slight breeze in the air, making the tall trees around them shake. The sun was going down now, and the camp would be dark soon. Leo and Isaac walked toward the cabin, feeling the hard dirt beneath their feet. Looking back toward the activity center, he saw Mr. Edwards and Rosemary setting up small, battery-powered lanterns throughout the railings of the building.

"So," Isaac said, "outside?"

"Yeah, sorry man," Leo said. "It's our best bet. We should head into the cabin and lay in our bunks for a bit. Then, we'll head out and find a place to hide."

Isaac's face uncontrollably contorted to show his discomfort.

"It's going to be alright," Leo reassured him, "If it does show up, I'll fight it so you can run."

Isaac smiled. *It's going to be alright*, he told himself. *This has been the coolest summer by far.*

While the whole thing was absolutely crazy, the dreamscape and solving mysteries reminded him of playing video games with his brother. After finding the card in the bushes yesterday, he couldn't stop thinking about Lost Journey. The objective of the game was to grow powerful enough to defeat the evil mastermind, Archibald Maledon, who sent creatures to stop the player. Carter had played as a knight, who was good in combat. Isaac chose the wizard, who was a supporting character that healed.

When Carter started hanging out with his friends more and eventually went away to college, Isaac tried his hardest to finish the game but could never do so. After all the years of building up his wizard, he still wasn't strong enough to defeat the monsters without Carter.

Horace's tasks along with the dreamscape crossed with Lost Journey. It almost made him feel like he had continued his quest in the game. It made him feel like a *hero*. Whatever the reason for the connection, he didn't want it to end. Maybe this time, he would be able to finish the challenge and capture Archibald.

The two teens went into the cabin, where they socialized for a bit to see if they could find some more information about the monster, which ultimately set off a group discussion on what they knew.

"It leaves really big footprints, just like my dad's!"

"If you see glowing yellow eyes, you'd better run."

"Last time it roared, I almost fell off my bed!"

As the conversation progressed on, more and more campers seemed to be fabricating experiences with the monster. Some included Bigfoot wearing a small hat that didn't fit on its head and the monster being so strong that it tore a school bus in half. Where the boy had seen both the monster and a school bus was beyond Isaac, but it probably wasn't worth pointing out.

During this group conversation, Scotty sat next to Leo on Isaac's bed. With every detail, he leaned forward further and further into the aisle. Leo could feel the boy's excitement bubbling up inside him.

Through the screen window, Isaac could see the light slowly starting to fade as his anxiety grew. One by one, the boys slowly made their way to the changing room on the side of the cabin, then to their bunks. Isaac and Leo did the same. *Goal three, blend in.*

Isaac was hoping that somehow Leo had fallen asleep and would forget about going outside. After a few minutes of silence, the bunk above him creaked and Leo dropped down next to him.

"You're sure we have to do this?" Isaac asked, rubbing his hands together to keep them from shaking.

"Yes," Leo confirmed. "Let's go catch ourselves a monster."

11

LIZ didn't particularly believe in luck, but it appeared they had some on their side. Isabella was an incredibly heavy sleeper, which made getting out of the cabin much easier. Liz had even slammed the door accidentally, and Isabella didn't stir.

Alura and Isabella had been talking about different fashions and makeup. It was interesting to see Alura partially fumble through the conversation, avoiding any words that would raise an alarm that they were not meant to be there. They were time travelers in a way, and needed to avoid saying certain things at risk of throwing off the dreamscape.

Liz and Alura snuck past the dark activity center, careful to avoid the illumination of the lanterns. Although there was no one else out, they stayed silent to keep anyone from raising an alarm. The entire camp was on red alert when it came to intruders, especially ones of the extra-large primate variety.

How could anyone believe that Bigfoot could be real? Liz asked herself. She did not consider herself well-versed on the topic, but there were certain holes in the theory that simply could not be explained. No one could change her mind. Of course, she kept these thoughts to herself. *Quiet. Agreeable. Goal three.* She needed to keep the dreamscape going in order to solve the mystery.

"How's it going back there?" Alura whispered in her direction.

"I'm alright," Liz grunted, pushing through the brush. They had to go around the back of the building to avoid being spotted by Mr. Edwards or Rosemary peeking from their window.

The problem with this plan was the inability to see. Liz could only see a blurry silhouette of Alura in front of her, and she was only a couple feet away.

"What do you think of this?" Alura asked. It was clear that she was gesturing to the surrounding area. It appeared that there were three trees that grew fairly close together, leaving a protected area in the middle.

I hate it. It's dark and dirty and gross, Liz held back, *and I'm pretty sure a mosquito just flew up my nose.*

"I think this is a good place to set up," Alura explained. "We are covered from multiple ways, and we can see the middle of the camp."

Liz could see enough of Alura's hand to turn her head in the direction she was pointing. The nest created by the trees was directly in between the activity center and the Edwards residence, making it possible to see the dirt courtyard perfectly.

"Alright, sounds good," Liz said, taking a deep breath before she lowered herself down on the trunk of one of the trees.

There were a few minutes of silence. Liz took the opportunity to close her eyes for a moment and try to take a

145

breath.

There was a distinct smell of dirt throughout the entire camp, even in the activity center. Here was no exception, but there was a hint of conifer trees in the air. Her ears were filled with the sound of numerous grasshoppers and crickets as well as the distant cries of an owl.

"Hey," Alura whispered, "are you alright?"

Liz wondered what she could mean by such a broad question.

"What do you mean?" Liz responded quietly.

"Just with everything going on," Alura said. "How have you been handling everything?"

Liz was still unsure what she was shooting for, but she hoped she wasn't going to ask about anything with Leo or her attempts to be better at the whole dreamscape thing. There was a brief pause in conversation, and Alura continued to explain herself.

"Like the internship and everything. It hasn't exactly been what I was expecting. What about you?"

"Oh," Liz said, pausing again to think. "Well, I guess I'm alright. I see what you mean. I was honestly surprised that Horace was able to invent such a *comprehensive* device like the Emit."

"Because of the difficulty," Alura inquired with a chuckle, "or because it's Horace?"

"Both," she answered before thinking.

That wasn't quiet or agreeable. Maybe I should just duct tape my mouth shut, Liz pondered. *Why do I speak?*

Alura tried to suppress her laughter to avoid drawing

attention to their hideaway. Liz wasn't sure why she thought it was so funny. Liz was embarrassed by her own words.

"I'm sorry," Liz floundered a bit. "Please don't tell him I said that."

"Don't worry about it," Alura said, still giggling. "It'll stay between us. I mean, I have to agree. It's pretty incredible to think that it was created at all."

"Horace seems like a really smart man," Liz said firmly, "but there are different types of intelligence. There's spatial, linguistic, musical… the list goes on forever."

"What does Horace strike you as," Alura continued, "intelligence-wise?"

"Well," Liz started, carefully choosing her words to avoid another mishap, "He doesn't strike me as an inventor. I think he's proven his emotional intelligence over the years. He understands people and how they think and act. That's why he's such a good detective."

"That's true, I suppose," Alura said, shifting her position along the tree stump. "What do you think I am? If any, I guess. You don't have to sugarcoat it for me either. Not that I think you would."

Liz could see Alura's teeth in the moonlight, revealing a smirk. Liz felt like she didn't know Alura well enough yet, but there were definitely a few ways that she could bend when it came to her strengths.

"I don't really know you that well yet, and honestly, I'm not the best at being able to identify it in other people," Liz responded, surprising herself with the amount of raw authenticity in her statement.

There was a brief moment of silence, which made Liz feel like her direct response had disappointed Alura.

"Do you want me to guess?" Liz offered. "You can't get mad though."

"Sure," Alura said excitedly. "I promise not to get mad, and I'll tell you if you're right."

Liz closed her eyes for a moment again, thinking of all of Alura's different actions throughout the two days that she had known her. It was a difficult task, but she had asked her for an honest answer. She paged through her memory, trying to remember all the different types of intelligence and settling on one that matched up.

"I'd say you definitely have some spatial intelligence," Liz said confidently.

"Oh, cool!" Alura responded. "What's that mean?"

"Spatial is like artistic, sort of," Liz explained. "It's like symmetry and design. It's hard to explain, but it's being able to picture things different ways."

"I guess that makes sense," Alura said thoughtfully. "What do you consider yourself?"

Liz had taken a test when she was younger, so she knew where she sat unless it had changed within the last couple of years.

"Mostly logical intelligence," Liz answered, "which is mathematics and science. Putting things together and understanding how they work."

"I could definitely see that," Alura said. "What about Isaac?"

The first thought that popped into Liz's head was that Alura was trying to bait her. *Why are you asking me about Isaac? Are you going to go back and tell him?* Liz wasn't really sure what Alura was doing, whether it be simply moving the conversation forward or something more.

"Oh," Liz said, "I'm really not sure. He really doesn't say much, so I'd say he's not linguistically intelligent."

Once again, Alura started laughing at Liz's unfortunate choice of words.

"I really didn't mean it like that," Liz stuttered. "Really, it's not what is sounds like."

"It's alright," Alura responded, quieting her laugh. "I know you didn't mean it the way you said it. What does that mean, though?"

"Linguistic intelligence just means that people have a really easy time putting their thoughts into words," Liz elaborated quickly. "Please don't tell him I said that, either. People who are better at public speaking are usually linguistically intelligent because their brain is able to translate it in such a way that other people's minds can understand it better."

"Can I ask you a question?"

"Okay," Liz said hesitantly.

"Do you consider yourself to be linguistically intelligent?" Alura asked, holding back another chuckle.

It took a moment for Liz to realize what Alura was suggesting, and then her face got hot. Although she had never really thought of herself as the best speaker, she felt like Alura was insulting her.

Quiet. Agreeable, Liz reminded herself. She took a moment to think about it. It was odd that Alura was being so direct, but there was no argument to be made. Liz was not linguistically intelligent.

"Obviously, I have proven that I am not linguistically intelligent from this conversation," Liz said, garnished with a slight smile.

Following their laughter, the two girls sat in silence for a few minutes. Liz had been nervous about sharing the night alone with Alura. The previous day, she felt like she was forced to open up to this girl she hardly knew. There were people who knew Liz for years that had never seen her cry before.

Liz suspected that she had gotten the trait from her parents. Her mom and dad often hid their feelings about pretty much everything. They seemed to avoid any kind of argument at all points of their lives, whether it be deciding on what to have for dinner to the time when Liz's dad moved the entire family to New York City on a whim.

Liz could feel her thoughts leading to upset feelings, so she stopped herself and began to take note of her surroundings again. The smell of dirt and the crickets chirping were consistent. She picked up a small twig from the ground and rolled it in her hand.

Suddenly, the noises of the forest ceased.

A scream came from the boys' cabin, followed by an incredibly loud roar that seemingly shook the surrounding area. It sounded like a mix between a gorilla's deep growl and a lion's powerful holler.

Liz jumped. Something had grabbed her wrist.

ISAAC had heard an owl somewhere in the distance earlier. He tried his hardest to focus on it's rhythmic call, aligning each inhale with the unseen bird.

"You okay, dude?" Leo asked.

Not really, Isaac thought, but kept to himself. The two had been talking earlier, but Leo had thought he heard a voice somewhere in the distance. The conversation had been cut off when he started scanning the tree line for anything out of the ordinary.

"Yeah," Isaac said, his voice shakier than he wanted it to sound. *Can't we go back to talking about comic books? Even sports. I'll pretend to know what you're talking about.*

His coping owl suddenly stopped and was replaced with a different bird call. It sounded more like a set of rapid *chirps* rather than a drawn out *hoo*.

The two were positioned on the side of the boys' cabin that backed up to the totem pole entrance. Leo's focus was toward the camp's entrance where he thought he had heard the noise. Isaac heard the creak of the cabin's back door and tugged on the bottom of Leo's shirt.

"*Leo,*" he whispered. Leo turned toward him, then followed his finger toward the back of the cabin. *Holy taquitos, is that Bigfoot?*

Two yellow orbs floated in the distance. Isaac interlocked his hands to keep them from trembling. The two boys sat silently as the lights got closer. As suspected, but not as requested, the glowing spheres were placed as eyes on the now-visible silhouette.

A shrill scream came from inside the cabin.

"Stay quiet," Leo instructed.

As if there was anything else I'd be doing right now? Isaac had started to bite his nails subconsciously. It was the first time in years that the nervous tick had taken over.

The creature was about twenty feet from the back door. It had stopped and seemed to take a moment to catalogue its surroundings. Then, it decided to act.

A loud roar filled the dark night air. Isaac could hear the thud of at least one camper falling from their bunk.

The creature turned away and hurried back into the woods. His eyes disappeared, but they continued to dimly illuminate the leaves as they crunched under his feet. Most importantly, the glow provided a clear outline of the monster's body.

Tall with long arms. Covered in hair. Enormous feet.
Bigfoot.

ALURA tugged Liz's wrist twice and she was able to calm down.

"Stay out of sight," Alura instructed, beginning to lead her around the back of the building to bring the boys' cabin into view.

The two of them kneeled behind a bush, just in time to see Mr. Edwards burst out of his cabin holding a lantern.

"Hang on," he shouted, "I'm coming boys!"

The scream or roar must've woken him from a deep sleep. He stumbled out of his cabin, narrowly avoid falling off the front porch.

They peeked over the bush to see into the tree line, but it looked like the creature was already gone. There was a rustle of leaves that slowly faded. It looked like two or three of the campers scrambled to get outside. They were also looking into the trees to see if there was anything to be seen.

"Yeah," one shouted, "don't come back here anymore!"

"Shh!" Mr. Edwards shushed, "You want it to come back?"

"Yeah," Rosemary scolded them, adjusting the curlers in her hair, "knock it off, brats!"

Alura spotted two familiar faces emerging from the other side of the cabin. Leo and Isaac probably saw it as an opportunity to remain accounted for and avoid prompting a search party. If they were out of the cabin, other campers would probably assume they were missing.

I hope they were able to find something, Alura said, crossing her fingers. *They won't be able to get out of the cabin again tonight.*

"Should we go back?" Alura asked.

"We should sneak back and check to make sure Isabella's still asleep," Liz agreed, "but I really don't think she's going to wake up for anything."

The two girls nodded their heads, then walked the perimeter of the camp behind all the buildings. Once they got to the other side, they peeked through the screen window to see that Isabella was still sound asleep. In fact, it didn't look like she had moved at all.

"What should we do now?" Liz asked.

"I mean," Alura said, planning in her mind, "I don't know if Leo and Isaac are going to be able to get out again tonight. Should we check out the area behind the boys' cabin?"

"Okay, that's a good idea," Liz said. Her tone made Alura feel like she knew they *needed* to pass through the bushes again, but she certainly didn't *want* to.

Alura led the way back toward the activity center with Liz following close behind silently.

When they passed by, Alura snuck a peak between the girls' cabin and the activity center, where it appeared Mr. Edwards and Rosemary were heading back to their cabin after confirming all the boys were there and safe. Alura stopped short and Liz ran into the back of her.

"Sorry," Liz apologized for running into her.

"Listen," Alura prompted.

There was a sound that was seemingly getting louder. *Something is coming.*

"It sounds like boots and keys jingling," Liz said, "coming from the camp entrance."

A man wearing a leather jacket and tan khakis came into view. Surely enough, his steps were synchronized with the noise they heard, and he had a large keyring attached to his belt. He also had a large hat, similar to one that cowboys wear but flatter on the sides.

"Who is that?" Liz whispered.

"It looks like a policeman or a park ranger," Alura suggested.

Alura was used to the police officers in New York City, who often wore blue suits and smaller hats. He looked exactly like some of the police officers that were in older television shows that her dad used to watch. Those movies and shows were considered older where they were from, but they were standard at this point in history.

Goal number one, Alura thought to herself. *Get to know the people involved.* Alura was sure they'd be able to solve the mystery if they worked together and followed their goals. Their investigation behind the boys' cabin could wait for now.

The pair carefully made their way over to Mr. Edwards and Rosemary's cabin, hiding out in a bush behind it. They were in place just in time for Mr. Edwards to invite the man into their cabin.

"Hello," he said, taking off his hat. "I'm Deputy John Aspen with the Humboldt County Sheriff's Department. The office received your radio broadcast a few minutes ago and they sent me over."

"Please, please," Mr. Edwards greeted the man, "come in, come in. My name is Paul, Paul Edwards. I run this camp with my daughter, Rosemary."

With the lanterns inside their house now lit, Liz and Alura had a perfect view directly into the living space of their cabin. There was a couch, a recliner, and a coffee table with numerous pictures and paintings framed on the walls.

Deputy Aspen had slicked-back dark brown hair and stubble around his mouth. He took off his jacket and set it on the arm of the couch with his hat. Liz estimated that he was in his mid-twenties. The deputy had very muscular arms that filled his sleeves and a shiny gold star pinned on the chest of his tan button-up.

"Would you like to sit?" Mr. Edwards offered. "Please, make yourself comfortable."

The deputy nodded a silent thank you and sat down on the edge of the cushion next to his hat and jacket.

"So," Aspen began, pulling out a small notepad and uncapping his pen, "can you tell me exactly what happened?"

"It's like I told them," Mr. Edwards said frantically. "There's something lurking out there in the bushes. This is the third time Camp Tolowa has been attacked this summer."

"You said third?" Aspen asked. "And you reported the other two incidents?"

"Yes," the older man confirmed, "Why?"

"Well," the deputy said with a slight sigh, "this is the first I'm hearing about it. I apologize."

It took Alura a moment to realize that Mr. Edwards had spoken to the police about this issue in the past, but it appears they didn't file any kind of report. This would match up with the fact that Aspen had no prior knowledge of the incidents.

Isaac pointed out that they hadn't started off at the beginning, Alura thought to herself. *This is why. There aren't any documents that Emit can use if no reports were filed before today.* According to written history, this was the first instance of Bigfoot at Camp Tolowa.

Mr. Edwards seemed to pause a moment, also processing this information.

"You're kidding," he said, dumbfounded. "You're telling me the other policemen that came didn't file a report or anything on the attacks?"

"It can be complicated, sir," Aspen explained. "Was there a crime committed? Was anything stolen, or anyone abducted?"

"No, but a lot of my campers are scared," Mr. Edwards exhaled defeatedly. "I can't run a summer camp without any campers. It just doesn't work."

Out of view of Liz and Alura, another person seemingly entered the room. Both Aspen and Mr. Edwards looked in the

156

corner of the room that was a blind spot for the two girls who were crouched behind the bush.

"Oh," an unfamiliar voice said, "hello there."

To their knowledge, the only other person in the cabin was Rosemary, but it didn't sound like her normal gravelly voice.

"Good evening, ma'am," Aspen greeted. Progressively, the stranger came into view.

It *was* Rosemary, with a much less raspy and aggressive voice. It became clear when she sashayed over to the police officer that she must've found him attractive, sitting down inches from him on the couch.

"*Eww*," Liz whispered.

"Agreed," Alura said.

The two girls shifted uncomfortably behind the bush, trying to push the idea out of their head.

"What brings you around here?" she continued in her slow, smooth voice.

"Well, uh," Aspen said, perplexed, "you two called me to come check out a disturbance?"

Alura watched Aspen squirm, trying to navigate the awkward situation. *She has absolutely no self-awareness*, Alura thought to herself.

"So," Mr. Edwards jumped in, "what can be done about this?"

"Honestly," the deputy started, "I can take down all the information and file a report. If anything does happen, we'll be ready. Do you mind if I ask you a few questions regarding the camp?"

"Anything for you, officer," Rosemary said with a wink.

"Alright, I appreciate it," Aspen cleared his throat. "Just keep in mind, I wouldn't be asking these questions if I didn't think they'd help us get to the bottom of it."

Rosemary sat down on the arm of the couch opposite Aspen, who tried to focus on the investigation.

The two men went through basic questions, like how many campers were currently there and how the different sessions ran throughout the summer. They also spoke briefly about the different activities offered. Rosemary chimed in every once in a while but spent most of her time batting eyelashes toward Aspen.

"Now," Aspen said quietly, "is there anyone that either of you have suspected? Anyone that would want to scare away campers or have the camp shut down?"

"I don't really understand where you are coming from, officer," Mr. Edwards said, tilting his head slightly.

"Well, if someone is doing this to your camp, they have to have a reason. Whether you have that answer or someone else does, people don't do this sort of thing without a purpose. A *motive*, if you will."

This guy is good, Alura thought to herself. *Horace would be proud.*

Mr. Edwards took a step back, as if he himself was accused of the crime. The slender man adjusted his collar before addressing the officer's suggestion.

"Deputy Aspen," he began, standing up straight, "I'll have you know that I have lived in Humboldt County for my entire life. Bigfoots, Sasquatches, whatever you'd like to call them, are part of our culture. They've been around for decades."

Alura could hear a grunt come from behind her and turned to find Liz rolling her eyes.

Rosemary put her head in her hands, embarrassed by her father's claim that the Bigfoot could be real.

"Dad…" she said.

Mr. Edwards took a small breath and relaxed his shoulders. Although he seemed to soften up following his statement, Aspen was surprised by his thoughts on the matter.

"All I am suggesting, officer," Mr. Edwards continued, "is that we should consider that this Bigfoot creature is real. Don't you think?"

Interesting, Alura noticed. *Mr. Edwards believes that Bigfoot is real. That could be useful later.* She made a mental note.

Deputy Aspen took a deep breath.

"Mr. Edwards, I can really only go on the facts," Aspen explained, speaking slowly as if to choose his words carefully to get the answers he needed to move forward with the case. "I'm not saying I don't believe in Bigfoot. I have also lived in the area all my life, and I agree. The legend has been a defining part of our community. Regardless of whether or not I believe, I can really only do something right now if it's someone trying to harm your camp, posing as Bigfoot."

The deputy paused for a moment to read the look on Mr. Edwards face, seemingly judging which way to move his position in to get Mr. Edwards to open up.

"Listen," Aspen sighed, "once we rule out that it isn't someone in a costume, we can take the necessary precautions and help you. Until then, there's nothing I can do."

LIZ was surprised that Mr. Edwards was a Bigfoot believer. He seemed like a well-educated man, so she wondered how he could believe such a ridiculous thing. As someone who took a huge interest in science, Liz could never be convinced that a creature like that existed. Even from a commonsense standpoint, things just didn't add up.

She had assumed that the rest of the team felt the same way. However, there was a moment earlier in the day that made her question whether or not that was true. The other three interns agreed to essentially investigate two different possibilities. One depended on Bigfoot being real, while the other was only if it was just a legend. *Quiet and agreeable.* It didn't make a difference to her if they wanted to waste their time investigating both possibilities.

While she was considering this, Mr. Edwards made his way over to the recliner, sitting down across from the deputy. It appeared that he accepted Aspen's explanation, as he returned back to the original question.

"Let me be frank with you officer," he said, "And I apologize if I come off as rude. There is no one who would want to hurt the camp. It's just a kid's summer camp. It doesn't make any sense."

"I really think it was one of those dirty brats," Rosemary blurted out. Her voice changed from flirtatious to the normal gruffness the others had witnessed before. Aspen's head swiveled, then his focus returned to Mr. Edwards.

When Rosemary broke her silence, Liz realized that she had slid closer to Aspen on the couch, and there was only about a foot between them now.

"What do you think," Aspen asked, gesturing toward Rosemary. "Is that something that could be happening?"

"It's impossible," Mr. Edwards said without any pause for thought. "They're all good kids. They like to play pranks, but they wouldn't do something like this."

"How can you be sure?" Aspen asked, gently pushing towards an answer.

"This is not something that one of the boys could do," Mr. Edwards said, adjusting his glasses. "It's much too elaborate. We've even found footprints on the nature trails we walk. The roar, the glowing yellow eyes. In my experience, most pranks are also targeted toward adults. If one of the campers was doing this, so many of the others kids wouldn't be so frightened."

Aspen nodded his head, retreating from that line of questioning.

"Dad," Rosemary offered, "what about that guy that came to us with the offer to buy the camp?"

"I don't think so, honey," Mr. Edwards said confidently.

"You had an offer from someone to purchase the camp?" Aspen asked, intrigued by the development.

There's the motive. Deputy Aspen was doing all the heavy lifting for the interns. All they had to do was sit back and watch. *Whoever offered to buy the camp instantly becomes a suspect.*

Mr. Edwards and Rosemary looked at each other for a moment.

"Yes, officer," Mr. Edwards confirmed, "Rosemary and I came up here about three months ago to get things set up for the first session. A gentleman came to me with an offer to purchase the land that the camp is on. He was a big guy who offered me a fair amount for it. It's not the first time that it's happened. Every couple of years, developers come to me with some kind of offer."

"Oh, I see," Aspen said, rubbing his cheek. "Well, Mr. Edwards, that can be a motive for this kind of behavior. You understand that if a person wanted to push you to sell your property, they could try to scare you into it."

Mr. Edwards shifted his feet, looking away from Aspen. The police officer was correct. In many fictional and nonfictional mysteries that Liz had come across, trying to push someone into doing something could always be a motive, regardless of what actions needed to be taken. Dressing up as a tall, hairy man with enormous feet was probably below some criminals, but not all.

"I understand where you are coming from," Mr. Edwards said, nodding his head slowly.

"What was this man's name?" Aspen inquired.

"He left his business card around here somewhere," Mr. Edwards said, setting off in frantic movements around his small living space. He pulled out the drawer to the end table and shuffled around for a few seconds, then set off into another room that was out of view to Liz and Alura.

"Dad, I think you pinned it to the calendar with the other cards," Rosemary shouted to him from her seat next to Aspen. There were a few clashing and clattering noises that came from the other room. Mr. Edwards returned with a small slip of paper, leaning out to hand it to Aspen.

"Ah, I see," Aspen said, copying down the information into his pad, "I know this name. His son took over the company a few years ago. They're a big name in this area. He's probably looking to buy the land for a new housing development or strip mall or something of the sort. Did you tell him that you weren't interested?"

"I did," Mr. Edwards said confidently, then remembered a bit more and corrected. "I told him I was not really interested in selling at this point, but I would keep his card in case I changed my mind."

Aspen scribbled something down on his notepad, then copied the information from the business card onto a separate page. Afterwards, he put the small slip of paper down on the end table next to him.

Liz felt an elbow nudge her. It seemed Alura had the same thought. *We need that card,* Liz thought. *Then, we can follow up with this developer guy and get to the bottom of it.*

"And how did he take it? Did he seem upset?"

"Well, no," Mr. Edwards said, trying to remember. "Please forgive me, this was a while back. He was a bigger guy. Intimidating, so I was expecting him to push a little bit. He didn't though. He explained that he was just a phone call away if I ever needed anything."

"And he went on his way?"

"Yes, sir. He seemed a bit disappointed, but it sounded like he had a lot of other projects going on throughout the state, so the loss of one wasn't really going to break him," Mr. Edwards recalled.

Continuing to take notes, the deputy nodded his head in acknowledgement as Mr. Edwards recounted the event.

"Well, Mr. Edwards," Aspen said, rising from his seat. "I

wish there was more I could do for you right now. Let me do some investigating along this line of clues, then I can follow up. Anything else you think of or if there's another issue, please request me directly. Here's a card with my information."

The officer pulled a similar card out of his shirt pocket and handed it to Mr. Edwards. The two men shook hands. Mr. Edwards thanked Aspen profusely for looking into the issue instead of just putting it off as the others had.

Alura nudged Liz again.

"We need to see that card," Alura whispered.

Agreed, Liz thought to herself. *Whatever name on that card becomes a prime suspect, but how are we going to get our hands on it?*

"Okay," Liz accepted. "So, what's the plan?"

"I'm going to wait until Aspen leaves, then I'll sneak up on the porch and stick my hand in the door. The card is within reaching distance."

Liz took a deep breath. *Show them what you can do but pick your moment.*

"You do know that we could mess this whole thing up if you get caught, right?" Liz asked.

"Yes," Alura said, "I know that. But one, I'm not going to get caught. Two, that business card has valuable information that could help us solve this case."

She was right and Liz knew it, but she was still risking a lot. After causing problems for the team yesterday, Liz was trying to find a way to make up for it. Either way, she would either help out the investigation or cause another issue which wouldn't really be too much of a change.

"I'll go," Liz said, already rising to her feet.

"No," Alura argued, but then softened. "Are you sure?"

"Yes," Liz confirmed, watching Mr. Edwards escort Deputy Aspen out the front door and toward the totem pole archway.

"Okay," Alura said confidently. She straightened up to improve her vantage point through the window. "I'll watch your back. Rosemary went into the other room, but I can't see too far in. Just be on guard."

Liz nodded, then moved slowly around the bush they were hiding behind toward the edge of the porch. Mr. Edwards and Aspen were still making their way toward the camp's exit.

Carefully, she put her foot down on the old wood planks that made up the porch, allowing them to creak softly. Liz knew the quieter the noise, the better. The crickets and grasshoppers were back in full force, covering up any kind of low, unnatural noise.

She got through the first two steps, and the door handle was within reach. *Open the door, reach backward toward the end table.*

Liz slowly reached out her hand to gently pull the door handle when she froze.

Inside the cabin, she could hear footsteps and a distinct, grating hum that belonged to Rosemary. It was a pleasant tune that sounded like it was being sung by a lawnmower. Peeking around through screen, she could see that the woman was making her way back into the main living room, preparing to sit down on the couch.

In a very tough spot, Liz tried to come up with a plan. *I can't reach into the room. She'll hear the door and see my hand. I can't wait here. If Aspen or Edwards turn around, even for a moment, they'll see me standing here.* The dim glow of the lanterns and the moonlight that peaked through the trees was enough to illuminate her.

Liz could feel her hands begin to shake and sweat form on her forehead. No matter what she chose, someone was going to catch her. *Number three, keep the dreamscape intact. There's only one option.* Slowly, she started backing off the porch.

Suddenly, Rosemary gasped softly. Liz took the opportunity to lean forward, seeing that Rosemary had turned toward the opposite side of the house. A small clinking noise came from somewhere, and she abandoned her seat on the couch to pursue it.

Without thinking too much about it, Liz took the opportunity to pull the door open and grab the card. She started her quick getaway off the side of the porch and back into the trees. As she stepped off the wood back into the dirt, the door closed a little bit harder than she had been expecting, making a sound. Both Mr. Edwards and Aspen turned to look toward their cabin, but Liz was already outside the area that was lit up by lanterns.

As quickly as she could without compromising her stealth, she returned to the bush where Alura was hiding.

"Did you get it?" Alura asked.

Out of breath, Liz held up the card. In return, Alura triumphantly gave her a small tap on the hand, which was the equivalent of a silent high-five.

"Thanks for the assist," Liz whispered, still trying to catch her breath. *I couldn't have done it without you.*

The two girls leaned in close toward the break between the

cabin and the activity center, using the light to look at the card. At first, Liz thought she misread the name. She pushed the hair from her eyes and pulled the card toward her face.

Is this real? The retrieval of the card won the battle, but the name on the card may have won the war. Liz couldn't help but feel excitement swell inside her. A smile stretched across her face.

"Let's get back to the cabin."

The two girls started to make their way back to the cabin when they were suddenly surrounded by a cloud of purple smoke. When Liz opened her eyes, she was back in the detective agency.

 **12**

ALURA sat up in her small bed, still riding the thrill of working with Liz to grab the business card. Like a kid on Christmas morning, she sprang out of bed and moved toward the door of the small room.

"Everyone," Liz said, beaming. Although Alura had only known her for a short time, she knew that this was a rare sight. Both Isaac and Leo were fixed on her countenance, concerned but excited to hear what she had to say.

"Yes, Elizabeth?" Horace said from center of the room. The needle on Emit was lifted, meaning that Horace probably paused the simulation at the perfect moment.

"You'll never guess what we found," Liz said. "Someone made an offer to buy the camp a few weeks before the first session."

Horace, Leo, and Isaac stood quietly, waiting for the big reveal.

"We were hiding behind the cabin after the attack," Alura elaborated. "A police officer showed up and started asking Mr. Edwards questions about anyone who would have a reason to dress up and try to scare the campers."

"Yes," Liz picked up, "and he said that someone made an offer on the camp just a few weeks ago. I snuck up onto the porch to see the business card of the person who made the offer. I was almost caught by Rosemary, but Alura distracted her while I grabbed it, and no one ever knew!"

Although it was probably just the adrenaline from the last couple minutes in the dreamscape, it was nice to see Liz so excited. Alura hadn't seen this side of her before. There was the couple of laughs and chuckles since they met yesterday, but she could feel Liz's positivity in her voice now.

"Yeah," Alura confirmed. "I just threw some pebbles at the window to get her away from the card, no big deal."

"Sounds like some mighty fine teamwork," Horace winked.

"Okay," Leo said, realizing what the development meant and joining in on the excitement, "So we have a motive. One of the first so far. Who is it?"

"So," Alura cleared her throat before continuing, "*Howard Price* made an offer on Camp Tolowa. More specifically, he wanted to buy the land for his development company."

"No way," Isaac muttered.

"You're kidding," Leo agreed. "We're...what? Fourteen years after the logging camp? So, Howard has to be pretty old."

Leo seemed to be calculating different ages in his mind to piece together a timeline.

"So, what now?" Liz asked, still smiling.

"Well," Leo said, rubbing the back of his head, "we've got to keep going."

"Seriously?" Liz asked. "Didn't we just solve the mystery?"

Alura had expected Horace to step in, but he stood idly by. He took a small cup of tea that had been on the table with Emit and sipped as he watched the interns discuss.

Leo does have a point, Alura thought to herself. *Betting against a character in a movie or story is proving they committed a crime in real life.*

"I agree with Leo," Alura said. "It's definitely a hunch worth following, but we can't really prove it was Howard Price without more information. Either way, we'll have to go back into the dreamscape to prove or not prove that he did it."

"It would've been difficult for the other dreamscapes, too," Isaac agreed. The others turned to him, confused. "Well, um, he didn't have any motive in the first dreamscape, right? Why would he destroy his own machine? And the third one that we haven't visited yet. It's set in 2002, and Howard Price would've been an extremely old man, no?" Alura watched as he shifted his feet uncomfortably.

Alura turned her attention to Liz. The edges of her mouth turned downwards, and she clenched her lips tightly together. She was disappointed and upset, but she held back from saying anything.

"Have we made any headway on our Goal Number Two?" Leo asked, shifting the subject. "When we saw him in the woods…"

"You *saw* him?" Alura asked. *Now, that was a development.*

"Yeah, but only for a second," Leo confirmed. "He was behind the boys' cabin. We could really only see his eyes and outline in the woods before he took off."

Alura leaned against her cubicle and thought back to Goal

Number Two. *Find anything that would point to Bigfoot being anything but real.*

"Nothing for goal number two from us," she replied, looking to Liz for confirmation. She nodded slightly.

"Seemed pretty real to me," Isaac whispered with a slight tremble in his voice. He seemed to be disturbed by the sighting.

"Alright," Leo said. "No proof that it's just some dude in a costume yet, but that's fine. I think we should amend the first goal to include looking for anything that connects Howard Price to the crime. It seems like a strong thread, but we want to make sure that all of us are on the hunt. Agreed?"

"Meet people, get to know them, but look for connections to Howard Price," Alura repeated. "Got it. Sounds like a strong plan."

"So, we are deciding that this is three separate investigations now?" Liz asked forcefully. The power behind her own words seem to catch her off guard. They seemed to be accusatory, but her sunken gaze indicated to Alura that it wasn't meant to be that way.

"What do you mean?" Alura asked gently.

"Well, you all just said that Howard Price wasn't Bigfoot in the first dreamscape and he would've been in a nursing home in 2002, right? So are we looking for three *separate* perpetrators?"

The four interns stood silent for a moment. Alura studied Horace's face, wondering if he would ever be willing to give them some sort of clue. *He wants us to solve this mystery together,* she noted. *He isn't going to help us.* She thought to the challenge she had created with Isaac the previous night and formed a question. *Does Horace Brown believe in the supernatural?* Unable to ask direct questions, she tried to get him talking.

"Horace," Alura started, "we were discussing this before. Is it possible that Bigfoot is real in these dreamscapes?"

Horace took a deep breath. "All mysteries have some sort of answer. I am very proud of your efforts so far," Horace replied. "But I must push you to continue. I think your goals are stupendous. Follow them, and you will surely get your answer. However, I can't help but notice there are three goals but four of you. Isn't that odd?"

Alura remembered back to the conversation earlier. Liz, Isaac, and herself had all proposed goals to meet while in the dreamscape. That only left one intern.

"Goal number four," Leo piped up, crossing his arms. "Look for any kind of connection between the dreamscapes. So far, we have Howard Price as a common thread in both the first and second dreamscapes."

"Goal number one," Alura repeated. "Get to know the people and understand the dreamscape. I guess this one is ongoing." The others smiled.

"Goal number two," Isaac said, "Try to find clues that Bigfoot is *not* real so we can confirm we are looking for some guy in a costume."

"Goal number three," Liz said, "Blend in so well with the dreamscape, all the other goals are as easy as possible."

Horace sipped his tea audibly and looked at his team. The wet ends of his mustache lifted into a smile.

We've got some leads, Alura thought to herself. *Let's see where they go.*

"You've got this, kiddos," he said. "Show me you can solve this one. You're on the right track, just follow your threads and work as a team. Let's get you back in there!"

ALURA and the other interns reentered the dreamscape. The sunrise poked through the screen window and illuminated their cabin. The songs of birds chattered in the distance along with one particularly noisy cicada singing backup.

Although she had never considered herself a nature person, Alura had always felt a connection to the world around her. Just about a year ago, she had been living in the small town in New Jersey where she had grown up with her mom and dad. They often went to the beach and went for nature walks.

After her parents died, it felt like that connection to the world had been severed. At times, Alura had felt like she was on the brink of closing herself off to everyone. Recognizing this, she often tried to pull herself out of the feeling by talking to people around her and trying to make friends. Before she lost her parents, it was always something Alura enjoyed doing. It still was, but it felt stained with the feeling of loneliness.

We're all humans, she remembered her mother telliing her. *The world is full of people. No one should ever have to feel alone.* She grasped the seashell necklace that Emit had provided her with once more. Alura smiled, wondering if her parents could see her now.

Snapping back to her surroundings, she saw Liz sitting on the edge of her bed, looking blankly at the floor.

"You alright?" Alura asked.

"Yeah," Liz responded, snapping back into consciousness, "I'm fine."

"What's going on?" Alura continued.

"Just thinking about how Howard Price could fit into this whole thing," she said thoughtfully. "It can't possibly be a coincidence."

Alura could see both sides of the situation, as she often could. *How could Howard Price be involved in two of the three dreamscapes, but not be involved?* The issue was that he didn't fit perfectly, though.

"I mean, it *could*," Alura said, shrugging. "It would be pretty surprising if it was, though. He's got to have something to do with it."

Isabella sat up in her bed as well, doing an extravagant stretch seasoned with a yawn. Alura was a little jealous. She looked just as good as when she laid down in bed last night. Her hair wasn't mashed to one side of her head and she didn't have bags under her eyes.

"Good morning," Isabella said, twisting her body to put her feet on the floor.

"Good morning, Isabella," Liz said. "I'm surprised you're up so early."

Although she didn't realize it until after Liz made the comment, she had to agree. Isabella didn't seem like the type of person to be an early riser. Especially because she was stuck at this camp, babysitting her brother.

"Why not?" Isabella asked, innocently.

"Oh," Liz responded. Alura watched as panic filled Liz's face. Alura wondered if it was because she was afraid of altering the dreamscape. It was also possible that she was making an effort to be nicer.

Before the conversation the two girls had last night, Alura would've assumed that preserving Isabella's feelings probably wouldn't be at the top of Liz's priorities. However, the way that she had asked Alura not to mention the potentially mean things to Horace and Isaac, it was a good possibility that she was trying her best, even with someone that, while based on a real person, wasn't a real person.

"She just means we went to bed kind of late last night," Alura jumped in.

Liz's shoulders sank, visibly releasing the stress the interaction had caused her.

"Oh," Isabella said, "yeah. Scotty and I live on our family's farm. A lot of our chores are early morning. Feeding chickens, brushing horses, that sort of thing."

"That's pretty neat," Alura said, trying to throw in some discreet seventies slang. She had been trying to come up with things that people from this time would say without drawing unwanted attention.

There wasn't too much to be done since Alura and Liz hadn't actually slept there and Isabella apparently woke up looking like a princess, so they were able to get ready quickly and started off toward the activity center. There were still some boys in the cabin, but most of them were heading to get breakfast as well, making a constant stream of campers heading into the building.

Many of the boys were whispering about the attack last night. Alura could only make out certain words, but some were stories of courage, like fighting off the monster, scaring it back into the woods.

Alura's attention was quickly pulled away from eavesdropping when Isabella became frustrated.

"Am I missing something?" she asked, clearly aggravated.

"I think there was an attack last night," Liz suggested nonchalantly.

"With the monster?" Isabella said, her eyes getting big with concern. "Is Scotty okay?"

"We saw Mr. Edwards and Rosemary check in on the boys' cabin," Alura recounted. "It seemed like everyone was there. No one was missing."

It was interesting to Alura that Isabella was not only able to sleep through the entire night, but she wasn't even awoken by the Earth-shaking roar of the monster or the bloodcurdling scream of the camper who spotted it. *What I would do for that kind of sleep*, Alura pondered. *Even just for one night.*

Scotty pushed through the door along with Leo and Isaac immediately after, allowing Isabella to relax. If he hadn't walked through at the moment, she probably would've abandoned her oatmeal and went to search for him.

"Scotty!" Isabella shouted, waving him over. "Thank goodness you are okay, did anything happen to you?"

"No, sis," Scotty responded, rolling his eyes, "although it would've been awesome if the monster grabbed me and took me back to his cave. Or cabin. Or treehouse. We'll just call it *his residence* for now. Either way, it would've been pretty cool."

Leo and Isaac stood behind him, snickering.

"That's really not funny," Isabella said flatly. "What would I tell mom and dad?"

"That their son is being raised by a hairy monkey man in the woods," he shrugged. "I'm sure they'd understand and respect my decision. I've got to go hang out with some of my other friends. See you around."

Leo and Isaac sat down around the table while Scotty made his way deeper into the activity center to find his other friends.

"Did you guys see anything? With the attack last night?" Isabella inquired.

"Not really, we were actually on the other side of camp," Isaac explained, seeming to forget that Isabella wasn't one of the interns. With a swift nudge from Leo and a whimper from Isaac, he tried to clear the air.

"He meant to say cabin," Leo corrected. "We were on the other side of the cabin, toward the front. The monster came up to the back door, facing the trees."

The screen door opened, with a well-put together Mr. Edwards and an average looking Rosemary coming inside and making their way to the front of the room. Although Mr. Edwards looked like he was calm, his walk and blank stare highlighted his discontent.

As the pair walked past tables, Mr. Edwards greeted many of the campers with a good morning. Many of them were focused on their food or antics with their friends, and the most he received in return were a handful of head nods and waves.

Once he reached the front of the room, he stopped, pulling a few index cards out of his shirt pocket.

"Hello everyone," he offered to the whole room. It did little to settle down the individual conversations at each table.

"Everyone, listen up!" Rosemary shouted from behind him. As if part of the routine, he turned to thank her, then began speaking to the silent room.

"As Rosemary and I have been working through some unexpected events in the camp," Mr. Edwards explained, pressing his hands together, "we will only have two different activities for today. Rosemary will be holding different arts and crafts here in the activity center while I will be taking anyone who wishes to join me on a nature walk."

"What?" someone shouted out. "What happened to the rest of the stuff we normally do?"

"Well," Mr. Edwards continued, "tomorrow we will begin on more of those involved activities. Today, I'm afraid, I just want to take it easy. I apologize for any disappointment."

"Is it because of the monster?" someone else asked, "I heard its Bigfoot! Like the monster that can rip the door off our cabin!"

The activity center erupted into numerous conversations throughout. Mr. Edwards attempted to start his next statement only to realize that no one was listening.

"Knock it off!" Rosemary instructed forcefully. The attention of the campers was again returned to Mr. Edwards, who thanked her again.

"I know it isn't the best thing right now," Mr. Edwards agreed, "but I need you boys to understand that this is a tough time for the camp. And girls, I apologize, I forgot we had ladies present this summer."

Alura wouldn't have even noticed their omission if he hadn't mentioned it.

"Let's all be safe and respectful," Mr. Edwards suggested. "Everyone, please line up and sign your name to this sheet of paper up in the front. The one column is for the nature walk, while the other is for the arts and crafts."

Leo and Isaac seemed to team up, bumping their fists together. The two jumped up and were the first two in line to sign up for their activity.

"What are you thinking?" Liz asked.

"I'm not sure," Alura responded. "A nature walk sounds nice, but that's probably what Isaac and Leo are doing. If we are going to gather as much information as we can, we should probably split up, teams of two."

"That's true," Liz nodded. "I don't think I can really go for another nature walk. I've had my fill for my entire life."

Isabella overheard Liz's comment and laughed.

"Me neither," Isabella agreed. "I don't know how Scotty is so interested in bugs, either. They're so gross, with all those legs and antennas. Bleh."

Leo and Isaac returned to the table, sitting down before Alura, Liz, and Isabella even had the opportunity to join the line.

"You guys are going on the hike?" Alura confirmed.

There were two conflicting answers that came out simultaneously.

"Yes," Isaac nodded.

"No," Leo responded.

The two boys looked at each other, as if they had both been betrayed.

"Wait, I thought we were going together," Leo said,

surprised.

"Me too," Isaac responded, scooting further down the bench to fully look at Leo.

"I picked the arts and crafts because I thought that's what *you* wanted to do," Leo offered.

"And I picked the nature walk because that's what I thought *you* were going to pick," Isaac countered.

Alura couldn't help but laugh at the tragedy.

LIZ could feel the tension rising in her body.

Another nature walk or I can spend the day stuck here with Leo, she pondered. *Both of them seem like cruel and unusual punishment.* On one hand, the nature walk was physically frustrating, while the arts and crafts seemed to be more psychologically taxing.

As much as she wanted to avoid Leo and, more importantly, another argument, the idea of going hiking filled her with dread.

Quiet and agreeable, she reminded herself. It was all she needed to get through this dreamscape. Once they did, they'd surely be able to prove that Howard Price was Bigfoot. There was no doubt in her mind. She looked over and noticed Alura studying her. After a moment, it seemed like she read Liz's mind.

"I'll go on the nature hike with Isaac," Alura offered.

"Are you sure?" Leo asked nervously, obviously realizing that he was in the same boat as Liz. Trying to avoid the other was certainly a tactic, but it wasn't going to solve the problem.

He looked to Isaac with desperation in his eyes. Liz would be offended, but she knew that Leo felt terrible about the things he said yesterday. It seemed he had the same tactic as her. Avoiding each other would prevent another issue.

"I can probably change my name, right?" Leo stammered. "You think it's too late? I'm sure Alura doesn't really want to go on the nature hike."

"Alright everyone who's with me, let's get going," Mr. Edwards announced near the door. It appeared there were only a handful of kids who wanted to go on the hike, whereas the rest stayed put. They rose from their tables to join the group.

"I think it might be too late to change," Alura responded, "but that's alright. You'll be able to get more information here. Try to talk to Rosemary if you can. Maybe she can give us some more information."

Alura and Isaac stood up from the table, leaving Leo and Liz, both with panic in their eyes. Prior to this moment, they spent the entire day on their best behavior. They weren't the best of friends, but that doesn't mean they couldn't get along. As they turned to leave, Isabella waved.

Liz watched as the door to the activity center creaked closed behind them. She turned back to the table and awkwardly made eye contact with Leo. Liz looked away abruptly, turning her focus to a small notch that was carved into the table.

Quiet and agreeable. It will be alright.

 **13**

ISAAC and Alura met the rest of the group outside, which consisted of Mr. Edwards, Scotty, and two other boys.

"Are you guys excited?" the older man asked, fitting a baseball cap on his head. It sat on awkwardly on top of his dollop of hair. He had opted to go with more comfortable shoes today, but they were still spotless. Isaac wondered how he was able to keep them protected from all the dirt and dust.

"Yes," Scotty said, rubbing his hands together maniacally, "I wonder what kind of bugs we will find."

"Scotty," Mr. Edwards said with a sigh, "remember what we talked about."

The little boy nodded with a bright smile which then turned into an evil laugh. Mr. Edwards rubbed his temples, turning toward the trees. The group of kids followed closely behind him as they made their way toward the totem poles.

"Can we go that way?" one of the other boys asked, pointing down the path that led behind the boys' cabin.

"Sure," Mr. Edwards shrugged, "I don't mind. Do you prefer this path over the others?"

"No," the boy responded, "it's just the way the monster ran last night. I thought we could go on the hunt for it."

The two unknown boys high-fived. *Do camp counselors need an extra lung for all the disappointed sighs?* Isaac wondered. Regardless, the group set off down the requested path.

It was a wider path, so they walked side by side. In the front, Mr. Edwards carefully walked, setting the pace for everyone else.

"Careful," he pointed at a root on the path, "tripping hazard." Throughout the hike, he did the same. Other than the roots, rocks and branches were often identified. Mr. Edwards reminded Isaac of his mom. She would also be incredibly cautious and protective when it came to activities like hiking.

Behind him, Isaac and Alura walked side by side, and the two other boys walked behind them, whispering and giggling with each other. Scotty was back and forth between either side of the path, turning over rocks to see what he could find, then hurrying back to the group so Mr. Edwards wouldn't notice he was falling behind.

"Any candy bars in your future?" Alura asked.

"No, not yet," Isaac shrugged. "What about you? Have you been able to find out if the great Horace Brown believes in the supernatural?"

"Nope," Alura replied. "I tried to get him talking earlier, but I couldn't get an answer from him. Although, he *did* say that all mysteries have an answer. Does that count?"

Isaac considered it for a moment. *It feels like part of an answer, I guess?*

"It isn't a *yes*," Isaac replied. "It also isn't a *no*, that he doesn't believe in the supernatural. I think we can count that as a win, right?"

"It's closer to an answer than we were before," Alura shrugged her shoulders. "We'll have to keep investigating though."

Their conversation was interrupted when Isaac felt a small body fall into him. Isaac stumbled but was able to stay on his feet.

"*Sorry*," Scotty apologized insincerely. He brushed himself off and scurried away. Isaac watched as he flipped over a large stone, revealing wet soil and a family of small beetles.

Isaac looked over at Alura, who smirked. The corners of her eyes crinkled.

"I guess you shouldn't get in between a man and his bugs," Alura teased. "Hey, can I ask you something?"

"Um," he replied nervously, "sure, I guess."

Isaac could see Alura examining him in the edge of his vision. She waited a moment before she asked her question.

"Do you think it's weird that Dot doesn't know about Emit?"

Isaac hadn't really thought about it, but he understood why she was asking. Dot did seem like a loyal sidekick to Mr. Brown. It *was* curious that he would keep her in the dark about everything, but it was even stranger that he was actively trying to keep it from her by instructing the interns to keep it to themselves.

"Yeah," Isaac agreed, thinking deeply about the question. "It is weird. I wonder why he doesn't want her to know about it."

"That's what I was wondering too," she said. The two of

them hopped over a pre-identified log with devilish intentions.

"If we can't get a clear answer from him about the supernatural," Isaac suggested, "maybe we move on to his relationship with Dot. What do you think?"

There were so many questions they were trying to answer, but Isaac felt comfortable keeping them ordered in his mind, especially when they assigned goals to them. It reminded him of a quest in a video game. If they were able to complete all their goals, they'd be rewarded. In this case, that would be solving the mystery of Bigfoot.

"Sounds like a plan," Alura agreed. She slipped into an English accent. "Thank you for your continued collaboration, detective."

"Of course, detective," Isaac tipped an imaginary hat, matching the accent. The pair laughed.

She's really cool, Isaac thought. *I don't know why I was so nervous before.* He thought back to the day prior, when all he knew about her was that she was one of the most popular girls in school and had a *huge* following on social media. Now, she just seemed like a normal person.

"Thank you, detective," Alura responded, still chuckling, "I look forward to our continued investigation."

As the group continued to hike, Isaac took note of the trees. The deeper into the forest they ventured, the larger the trees seemed to get. He knew that redwood trees were supposed to be huge, but they were incredible. The diameter of the stumps of the smallest ones were similar to car tires, while the larger ones in the distance were likely wider than Isaac if he was laying down.

They walked for about fifteen minutes when Mr. Edwards held out his hand, stopping them from moving any further. He crouched down and pointed up into one of the trees.

"Hear that?" Mr. Edwards asked.

Isaac heard nothing other than the slight breeze that was rustling the leaves above. Suddenly, a chirp echoed through the trees, allowing him to spot the small bundle of feathers it originated from.

"It's a Golden-crowned Kinglet," Mr. Edwards whispered, "Isn't that spectacular? These birds are normally found in coniferous forests. Their most distinct characteristic is, of course, their gold crown."

That sound, Isaac thought, *I've definitely heard it before, recently.*

"Hey," Isaac said softly, "do you recognize that noise?"

"You mean the birdsong?" Alura asked.

Isaac nodded.

"No, I don't think so," Alura said. She listened carefully to the song again. "Why, have you?"

"Yes, last night," Isaac said.

"You must be mistaken," Mr. Edwards said, overhearing their conversation. He adjusted his baseball cap and turned his attention away from the bird.

"Mistaken?" Alura asked. "What do you mean?"

"Well, that type of bird isn't nocturnal," Mr. Edwards explained. "It wouldn't be out during the nighttime, you see."

Maybe it wasn't the same bird noise? Isaac thought, doubting himself. There were so many birds that made so many different tunes.

186

"Wait," Isaac started, "so it couldn't have been that bird making that noise I heard last night?"

"No," Mr. Edwards confirmed. "There are other species that produce a similar song, but it couldn't have been that one. It could've been an owl or just something that sounded like it."

It's probably just a glitch with the dreamscape, Isaac thought. Mr. Brown *had* said that things wouldn't be perfect. He didn't want to keep pushing Mr. Edwards and potentially throw off the dreamscape.

ALURA and Isaac continued to bring up the rear of the hiking team. The path had become more of an incline as it narrowed, forcing everyone to walk in a single file and slow their pace. After another few minutes, the group came upon a clearing that was outlined with berry bushes.

The largest redwood tree that they had seen so far was situated in the middle. It had grown directly upwards without yielding to any other conifers around it. The light was able to sneak through the branches and illuminate this area better than the rest of the forest.

"Let's pause for a minute," Mr. Edwards said, lowering himself onto the log. "Okay team?"

"Sure," Scotty said excitedly. He ran around the open area, pushing flat stones over with a stick he had found. His exclamations of wonder drew the attention of the other two boys, who made their way over to check it out. After a couple seconds, the three of them were oohing in unison.

Mr. Edwards had removed one of his shoes, rubbing the

bottom of his feet. Alura noticed that Isaac was staring straight at him, probably unintentionally.

"This is what happens when you get old," Mr. Edwards laughed. "I love the outdoors, but it starts taking a toll on me after a while." Alura and Isaac smiled.

This is a great opportunity to build goal number one, Alura thought to herself. *Let's get to know Mr. Edwards.* He seemed harmless enough, but maybe he knew something that could help them.

"I didn't realize how different walks and hiking were," Alura agreed. "How long have you been doing this? Running the camp, I mean?"

Mr. Edwards seemed a bit surprised by the question. He took off his glasses which revealed soft, tired eyes and more wrinkles around his cheeks. While Mr. Edwards thought about the question, he rubbed the bridge of his nose with his thumb and pointer finger.

"None of my campers ever really take an interest in that sort of thing," he responded. "We've been open every summer since 1912, when my father started the camp. When he passed away about ten years ago, Rosemary and I took over the camp full time." Mr. Edwards looked like he might tear up at the idea that one of his campers was interested in his personal life and history of the camp.

As he spoke, Alura tried to keep track of ages. From a distance, she would suspect he had been in his fifties. However, the creases in his face were more prominent when up close, adding at least ten years onto any estimate made from further away.

188

"That's cool," Alura said. "Is it open all year round, or just the summer?"

"Just the summer," Mr. Edwards explained. "I was a teacher, until I retired a few years ago."

"And you don't get sick of the kids?" Isaac blurted out. The three of them shared another laugh.

"No, no. Of course not," he said through a smile, waving his hands, "although some are more difficult than others."

Mr. Edwards returned his glasses to his face, giving a subtle head nod toward the three boys who were currently using the stick to draw houses for the bugs they found in the dirt.

"This is your first summer here, right? Are you guys enjoying it so far?" Mr. Edwards asked. His voice was relaxed and smooth.

Alura prided herself on being able to read people and their true intentions, but it didn't seem like Mr. Edwards had anything to hide. He just seemed like a genuine, kind old man with a *ton* of patience. Since Isaac and Leo had seen Bigfoot behind the boys' cabin last night and Mr. Edwards had come running out shortly after, he didn't have the opportunity to play the part. All of this was only relevant *if* they were pursuing a person posing as Bigfoot, of course.

Mr. Edwards was just a man who had found his calling and dedicated his life to teaching, even in retirement. *I wonder if I'll ever be able to feel that motivated about an occupation,* she wondered.

"Honestly, yeah," Isaac said, "it's awesome. I never really thought I'd enjoy camp."

"Ah yes," he said. "I remember many years ago, when I was

younger. I'd spend a lot of time with my brother, TJ, running in the woods. We actually used to sit under this tree quite often." He gestured gently to the behemoth redwood in the center of the clearing. "The two of us called it the Singing Tree, because of all the birds that would sit among its branches. When my father heard the name from the two of us, he made it the official name. What I would do to go back to those summers with TJ."

Alura had always wondered what it would've been like to have a sibling. Her family had always been very close. She remembered her summers with her mom and dad, often filled with ice cream from the boardwalk and family barbeques with her Aunt Kate and Uncle Rick.

Focus, she reminded herself. *Goal number one. We need to get as much information as we can if we are going to show Horace we can do this.*

"Are you and your brother still close?"

"No," he explained, resting his hands on his knees. "We went our separate ways when we were younger. Not in a bad way, but it was difficult to keep in touch. I actually met with him a couple of months ago for the first time in many years."

Mr. Edwards seemed like so many teachers that Alura had met over the years. Many loved teaching but were worn out by the constant antics of her classmates. It always made her feel horrible that kids could be so cruel to someone who gave up so much to ensure they have a good future.

The twinkle in his eye showed how much he cared about what they were discussing. It was tough to think about him being pushed to sell the land to a man like Howard Price who would just level it and build more houses. Of course, there was a need for people like that, and the development of land was necessary to continue moving forward, but Mr. Edwards was invested in his campers making happy memories and exploring nature.

"That's a pretty cool bowtie," Isaac commented, interrupting Alura's thoughts.

The bowtie was forest emerald green in color, with small black polka dots evenly space throughout it.

"Oh, this?" Mr. Edwards said, tugging on the sides. "It's actually one of the only ones I own that isn't too colorful. Sometimes, bright clothes can scare off birds and other wildlife. It's not easy, dressing vibrantly during the year and then digging out my neutral colors for these nature walks."

"Hey, guys," Scotty shouted from the other side of the clearing, "you've got to check this out!"

ISAAC was intrigued by Scotty's call for assistance but hung back to take advantage of the distance between the two groups. Mr. Edwards smiled, then groaned as he got up from the makeshift bench to see what the little boy was shouting about.

"Should we ask him about Bigfoot?"

"I don't know," Alura whispered. "I feel like he trusts us. Do you think asking him about it would make him suspicious of us?"

"I don't know, either," Isaac shrugged. "I was worried about that too."

"Hang on, I have an idea," Alura responded.

She quickly polished the wording in her head, then made her way over to the rest of the group. If this worked, it would open the door to the conversation without changing their relationship with Mr. Edwards. It wasn't perfect, but it didn't need to be anything spectacular.

"What kind of bug is that?" Alura said, crouching slightly in the dirt to see it closer. Truthfully, she wasn't the fondest of bugs, but she was willing to take one for the team. Luckily, it wasn't anything too creepy or crawly, just a small beetle with a shiny purple shell.

"It looks like an ultra-beetle," Scotty responded confidently, with some quiet exclamations from the other two boys. "Isn't it cool?"

"It really is," Alura confirmed. "Didn't you say this morning that you wanted to move into the woods?"

Without taking half a second to think about it, Scotty started smiling from ear to ear. *I see,* Isaac realized. *She's trying to bring up the topic without causing any ripples.*

"Yeah, I would," he blushed, "but I don't think I said that this morning, did I?" He scrunched his face in thought. "Oh, wait. No, I said that if the monster grabbed me and dragged me into the forest, I would happily live out my days with him. He seems like a pretty cool guy, after all."

Mr. Edwards was quiet for a moment, then posed a question to the group. While it was on topic with what Alura was hoping, it was less in line with a perfect scenario that would've led to more answers.

"How are you all doing with everything going on?" Mr. Edwards asked. "I know it's a little crazy right now."

192

Mission complete, Isaac thought, shooting a nod in Alura's direction. She smiled slightly, but was trying to pay attention to the rest of the conversation.

"I think it's really cool," Scotty said, nodding his head vigorously. The other two boys agreed, making similar comments.

Mr. Edwards took a breath of relief, but the subject still seemed to cause him stress. Alura could see the conversation dying out, so they had to think of something to keep it going.

"Have you ever seen it, Mr. Edwards?" Isaac asked, one step ahead of Alura.

On the spot, he couldn't think of a better question, as it fit into the conversation and would give them further insight to their impromptu interrogation.

"Me? Oh, no," Mr. Edwards said, taking a step back while shaking his head. "There was a time in my life when such things interested me, but not so much anymore. I do have friends that have searched for the creature before. Or creatures, depending on what you believe."

"What do you mean?" Alura asked, playing dumb to get him to speak more about it. "You think there could be more than one?"

"Well," Mr. Edwards sighed, realizing he had backed himself into a corner, "when I was a child, there were always talks of *wild men* living in the forest. Some believed them to be escaped gorillas from a zoo, others thought they were men who chose to live in the wilderness. Over the years, the idea evolved, and people needed an explanation to connect the dots."

Alura quickly glanced over to see that Scotty and the other

two boys appeared to be in a trance, fixed on the story that Mr. Edwards was telling.

"There were so many different accounts, it became very jumbled as to what was truly going on. Certain encounters could be explained, others could not. Keep in mind, also, that there were no video cameras back when I was a kid, and cameras were bulky and produced blurry images if they weren't held completely still."

He held out his hand and asked Scotty for his stick. The little boy was hesitant but eventually handed it to him.

Mr. Edwards drew three circles in the dirt, all that shared space by overlapping. Isaac recognized it as a Venn diagram.

"See, here?" Mr. Edwards asked, pointing at the rightmost circle, "This is a circle for people who don't think there can possibly be a Bigfoot or Sasquatch, whichever you'd like to call it. Whatever the reason, they believe that it cannot possibly exist."

Liz's comments about Bigfoot rang in his mind. *She definitely doesn't believe.* He mentally threw her in that category.

Moving the stick to the middle circle, Mr. Edwards drew a stick figure inside.

"This circle is for the people who believe it's *possible.* That's where I stand on the matter," Mr. Edwards explained, then pointed to the final circle on the left. "This circle is for the true believers, not a doubt in their mind that the creature exists. These are the people that plan treks for weeks to capture some kind of evidence. To me, that sort of commitment is borderline ridiculous and unnecessary."

"What do you think most people believe?" Isaac asked.

Mr. Edwards paused for a minute, scratching the side of his head.

"I'd like to say in the middle, thinking it's possible," he responded, "but I cannot say for sure. Ironically enough, the more information that comes out makes the facts less and less clear."

He indicated the shared space between the two groups by using his pointer.

"There are also these areas, where some people have an opinion," Mr. Edwards explained, "but they don't care enough to prove it. I've lived in Northern California my whole life, and I can say that I do believe it exists, but I don't think seeing is believing, if that makes sense."

He quickly scribbled out his stick figure with his writing utensil, then redrew him in the space between the "absolutely without a doubt" and the "no way" categories.

"Do you think it's really Bigfoot, Mr. Edwards? That's been visiting us?" Scotty asked, his eyes still glazed with wonder.

Thank you, Scotty, Isaac thought, providing silent gratitude.

"Well," Mr. Edwards started, taking a deep breath, "honestly, up until last night when I spoke to someone, I did believe it was really Bigfoot. Now, I'm not so sure. History shows them being harmless, benevolent creatures. There have even been reports of them helping humans that are hurt from animal attacks, bringing them home. They don't normally behave like this. That's why no one has been able to prove their existence. They keep to themselves."

Isaac was trying to absorb as much information as he could. He had read a bunch of articles the night before, but it was *nothing* like meeting someone like Mr. Edwards in person.

"No need to dwell on it, though," Mr. Edwards said in a peppier tone. "Why don't we continue our hike?"

 **14**

One of the biggest reasons against the existence of Bigfoot is the fact that no one has ever discovered a body or bones. However, there have been numerous enthusiasts who have noted there could be reasons for that. For example, most national parks have a general number of certain animals that live within its borders. Hikers who travel the path regularly mention they have never seen a member of species that have populations in the hundreds or lower.

If this creature or species is intelligent, it is very possible that they are able to avoid contact with humans. They may also bury their dead. One researcher has also noted that bones have never been discovered because it is a natural instinct to hide when close to death. Some animals, like porcupines, also use bones to sharpen their teeth which accelerates the breakdown.

LEO wasn't happy about Isaac leaving him behind, but there wasn't too much he could've done to prevent it. The hiking group was already heading out by the time they realized the mix up.

Don't worry about it, dude, Leo thought to himself. *You've got this. All you have to do is avoid talking to her.*

There were also worse things to be stuck in than Arts and Crafts. Math class, walking lunges, having to explain how emailing works to Gran, to name a few. The only thing that made the situation less than pleasant was Rosemary.

The woman seemed to hate her life on the most fundamental level. Leo had yet to see her smile or laugh. She was completely miserable working at the camp. Not to mention, it was obvious that she hated kids. *Why is she even here if she was so unhappy?*

Other than Leo and Liz, Isabella stayed behind. The three of them sat together at the same table where they had eaten breakfast. Jeremy, the clumsy kid that almost fell when he introduced himself the other day was also present, along with the weird kid, Third.

What are the chances that a mysterious person wouldn't *have some connection to the case they were working on? No one even knows where his name comes from, let alone anything else about him.*

Learning more about the people in this dreamscape was one of their goals. Leo was determined to follow his hunch just as Horace had suggested.

His plan involved the table that Rosemary had set up with all the different options to fill the criteria of Arts and Crafts. There were coloring pages, suncatchers, small birdhouses to paint, and white t-shirts with fabric markers. Currently, Leo was working tirelessly on coloring a horse and pig posing in front of a barn.

Third also appeared to be coloring. As soon as he got up to

get a new sheet from the table, Leo would *conveniently* need a new page as well. That would give him the opportunity to get up at bat. He'd be able to make some kind of comment or ask a question that could open up a conversation.

Simple, Leo thought. *Easy to execute.*

"How's it going over there?" Isabella asked.

Leo broke off his surveillance, turning to face her. She appeared to be taking a break from her bracelet project. Leo could hardly even look at the tiny beads she needed to feed through the string without becoming anxious. *Who has patience for that?*

"Good, good," Leo said, nodding his head.

"I wonder how Third is doing," Isabella pondered.

"Why?" Leo asked.

Leo thought he had been fairly under-the-radar with his plan, but Isabella's questioning look, complete with squinted eyes, made him realize that he was being a bit too obvious.

"What do you want me to say?" Leo shrugged. "He seems like a nice kid."

Isabella crossed her arms and sat back on the bench.

"Alright, okay, gosh," Leo gave in. "I'm just really curious why everyone calls him Third."

"Why don't you just go *ask him?*" Liz suggested. She was also coloring with crayons. She had a particularly difficult picture of a landscape. There were small flowers all over the ground, and numerous birds throughout the trees. It appeared she had it well in hand, though. All the colors she chose fell perfectly within the lines.

Leo ignored the suggestion, thinking it might be too

obvious. Since Arts and Crafts started, no one had really gotten up from their seats, other than to grab more supplies from the table.

I just need to be patient, Leo reminded himself.

He continued his masterpiece when the doors to the activity center were pulled open violently. Leo's eyes began to water as a putrid odor filled the room.

LIZ looked up from her coloring page when the screen doors clattered. A stout man wearing tan khaki shorts and a sleeveless fishing vest stepped inside.

That smell can't be him, she thought to herself. *There's no way that a human being can smell that bad.* Liz held back a gag.

Rosemary jumped up from her table on the other side of the activity center. Before making her way over, she placed her romance novel, featuring a bare-chested man on the cover, facedown on the table.

"No, no," she shook her head, stomping over to the grimy man. "You leave right now before my father comes back. He doesn't want you here, you lunatic."

"Rosemary!" the man exclaimed, completely avoiding the rudeness displayed toward him. "I hardly recognized you. You've gotten *old.*"

Although she was nasty to pretty much everyone around her, Liz felt the comment was unfairly hurtful. Even she recoiled for a moment, before firing back at him.

"You smell," she responded, pinching her nose. "What do you want, Reid? There's no reason for you to be here."

The man she called Reid took off his hat, revealing a large bald spot surrounded by short stubble. He scratched it, as if trying to remember why he had chosen to visit the camp.

"Of course there is, dear," Reid mocked in a stuck-up tone. "I am here because I hear you have a problem with a certain *monster.*"

"Is my father expecting you?" Rosemary asked.

"What do you think, hon? We ain't spoken in ten years! It's also tough to reach you, being that you live in the woods and all."

"We don't *live* in the woods," Rosemary corrected him. "We run the camp in the summertime. You could call us any other time of year."

Reid put his hand up in retreat, indicating that he no longer cared to carry on the conversation.

"Where's Edwards?" Reid asked.

"He's not here, but I'll tell him you stopped by," Rosemary said. "Now, get out."

The chubby man put a hand over his heart, as if he was suddenly wounded by her words.

"Don't play that game," Rosemary scolded. "You dragged my father deep into that hole, believing in that idiotic legend."

"I'm not going to spend time talking to a non-believer," Reid responded, rolling his eyes. "Your father knew the truth, and he backed away from it all. No part of his involvement is my fault."

Rosemary turned toward the table that Liz, Leo, and Isabella were sitting at.

"Isabella, right?" she asked, pointing. "You're in charge. I have to run to my cabin quickly. Just make sure nothing burns down, alright?"

Isabella nodded, her ponytail bobbing up and down. Rosemary purposefully bumped into Reid, pushing him out of the path to the door. She gagged, which seemed to be in general disgust at first, but then the reason became clear when another wave of the strong odor floated over to the table. The abrupt movement must've disturbed his scent, dispersing it into the air.

Liz studied the man, who was now picking at his teeth with his pinky finger. By the look of him, he must've slept in a dirt pile last night. Both his skin and clothing were smeared with mud, with small sticks and leaves stuck in the large patches. His skin was also glistening with sweat, a sight that Leo had seen and experienced many times at sports practices. Of course, it was normally followed by a thorough shower.

Reid stopped picking at his teeth and began scanning the room, meeting eyes with Leo. He seemed to turn away, avoiding eye contact. *Too late.*

"Hey, dude," he greeted Leo. "What's your deal? Aren't you a little old to be going to summer camp?"

Liz was instantly more impressed by Rosemary's ability to hold down her breakfast.

"Not really," Leo answered. "Aren't *you* a little old to be going to summer camp?"

Don't you dare throw off this dreamscape, Liz said, then reminded herself that it wasn't her problem. She could only be responsible for herself. *Quiet and agreeable. Don't get involved. Eventually, we'll be able to prove Howard Price was behind this whole thing.*

There was a brief "ooh" from the surrounding tables that heard Leo's comeback. Reid took a step back, clearly shocked by the comment, then embarrassed by Leo's backing.

"I'm not *going* here," he stuttered. "I'm… I'm here to see Mr. Edwards. We go way back. I'll have you know, I'm the president of Lodge Four's Bigfoot Hunter's Club."

Bigfoot Hunter's club? What in the world did that *mean?*

LEO paused for a moment. This smelly man was a Bigfoot hunter, meaning that he was probably here to talk to Mr. Edwards regarding the monster terrorizing the camp. Leo decided to see if he could get more information about Reid.

"How do you know Mr. Edwards?" he asked.

"Buzz off, kid," Reid responded. "I've got no interest in talking."

Leo partially regretted the comeback because now he wasn't sure where to go from here.

"You actually started talking to *him*," Liz piped up from the other side of the table.

While Leo was surprised by the interjection from Liz, he appreciated her help.

"Yeah, well," Reid started, "whatever, you brats. When Edwards gets back, he'll put you in your place."

"Oh, yeah?" Leo prompted. "Why is that?"

"We go way back," Reid repeated. "He was a Bigfoot hunter, too. One of our most active members, actually. One day, though, he walked away."

Leo hated to admit it, but the tag team maneuver between himself and Liz kept this conversation going. Reid definitely held more information, and they needed to get it out of him. Leo continued the questioning by carefully building another small insult.

"Was it when you became president?" Leo suggested, rolling his eyes.

"No," Reid scorned. "It was because he lost his dad and had to run the camp by himself. Wait a minute."

Reid's eyes got wide when he realized that he had just given Leo the answer to his original question. He crossed his arms and huffed, stepping toward the door.

"I'm done talking to you, brats," he pouted. "I'm going to wait outside."

Pushing the door open, Reid made his way outside and sat down on the small porch of the activity center.

Leo was trying his best to follow the goals they had set out. Learn more about the players, try to find clues that confirm Bigfoot is a dude in a costume, preserve the dreamscape, and figure out if they were connected at all. He had crossed his fingers that following that game plan would lead them to the truth.

We need to solve this mystery, Leo said. He hoped that the others were just as confused as he was, but he doubted it. He started thinking of his guidance counselor suggesting he pick a different college. *I need to solve this mystery. Get as much information as you can, maybe there will be a nugget in there that points in the right direction?*

He thought of their leads so far. There were really only two possibilities right now. Howard Price was a *very* large man who had the means, motive, and opportunity to terrorize the camp. The other, of course, was that Bigfoot was real. Leo knew how ridiculous it sounded and, through his dedication to preventing another problem with Liz, he wasn't going to suggest it any time soon.

Returning to his original mission, Leo turned his attention back to Third. The boy was still sitting by himself. It appeared he hadn't gotten up for another coloring sheet, either.

"Hey," Liz said quietly. "Want some help?"

"Sure," Leo responded, sliding down the bench to sit across from her. "What's up?"

Leo was surprised that Liz was talking directly to him. He was fairly certain she was using the same tactic as he was to avoid any further complications.

"You're waiting for him to go get another coloring page?" she asked, not looking up from her coloring page.

Leo nodded slowly, wondering what kind of help she could offer him.

"People don't color with pencils," she suggested, gesturing toward him with her green crayon.

As he looked over, he immediately understood what she meant. Third was never going to get up from his table to get another sheet, because he wasn't coloring. A long, yellow writing instrument made its way across the page, which was part of a bound book. Third was drawing, not coloring.

Leo was going to have to tweak his plan a bit.

"Thanks," Leo whispered, sliding back toward the other end of the table.

I can't believe I didn't notice that, Leo scolded himself. *At least she pointed it out and didn't keep it to herself. Who knows how long I would've been waiting here.*

The best way to get information in this situation might be a direct approach.

"I'll be right back," Leo announced to the table.

He got up from the bench, making his way toward the folding table that was set up with all the different craft options. As Leo shifted his target to Third's table, he felt a tap on his shoulder.

"Hey," a familiar voice whispered from behind him.

Leo turned to find Jeremy standing behind him. He was able to get a better look at the boy, with his large glasses and dark brown hair. He wore a tie-dye t-shirt with a colorful spiral in the middle. Leo estimated that he was probably finishing up middle school and starting high school. Ages were tough for Leo to figure, but it was easier when he determined how they compared to other kids at his school.

Although it wasn't necessarily important, Leo also remembered that Jeremy arrived at camp for the second session, meaning he arrived *after* the attacks started on the camp.

"Hey, what's up?" Leo asked, half turning away from Third.

"Remember me? Jeremy?" the boy asked.

"Yeah, man," Leo confirmed with a nod, "of course I remember you. We met yesterday, walking to the cabins."

Jeremy smiled, obviously pleased with the fact that Leo remembered him. Although he wasn't the best with names and faces, Leo had just met him less than 24 hours ago. Less than eight hours, actually, outside of the dreamscape.

"I was just wondering," Jeremy said, looking down at his feet. "Your friend - she's really pretty. Would you be able to see if she'd be interested in, maybe, hanging out with me?"

"Alura?" Leo asked, "I don't think she'd really be too interested in dating anyone at this, uh, time, I guess."

Leo chuckled internally at his unintentional joke. He was somewhat surprised that Jeremy was asking about her. Alura seemed to be a really cool girl, but definitely not a good fit for Jeremy.

"No, no," Jeremy said, gesturing toward the table, "Her."

"Isabella?"

There was no harm in setting the two of them up, although it wouldn't amount to anything, being a simulation and all.

"No," Jeremy repeated, "The other girl."

"*Liz?*" Leo blurted out, louder than he intended.

Jeremy took a step back and nervously fumbled with his hands, then nodded his head to confirm.

Leo quickly took a look around and realized that most of the activity center was staring at the two of them, including Liz. They met eyes for a split second, and then she coolly turned back to her color sheet, pretending like she hadn't heard her name.

Obviously, there was no need for Leo to come up with a reason for Jeremy to lose interest. The only thing he really needed was the fact that they were basically time travelers. Once the four of them woke up, this reality would no longer exist. All he really needed was some sort of reason to get out of this conversation so he could get back to his investigation into

Third.

He went through a couple of excuses in his mind, then decided it really wasn't worth the effort.

"Why don't you just go talk to her?" Leo suggested. *He could know something, and he'd be more likely to share it with Liz.*

"Oh, well," Jeremy stuttered, "I was really hoping you'd be able to talk to her for me. Like, as my friend. Try to see if she might be interested."

"Just go talk to her, man," Leo said, giving him a pat on the back for a confidence boost. "You've got nothing to be afraid of. She can come off as a little intense, but I think she's alright. Just go for it. You've got this."

Before Jeremy could object, Leo continued toward the table that Third sat at alone. The boy didn't even look up from his drawing to notice that Leo had sat down across from him.

"Hey, dude," Leo greeted him. "My name's Leo. I just saw you over here and I wanted to say hey."

Third continued to ignore Leo completely, continuing to draw with his pencil. *Does he even know I'm here?* Leo wondered.

The boy looked thirteen or fourteen, probably starting high school soon. He wore a jean jacket with a couple of squares that seemed to be getting weak, as the white thread showed through. The outfit was accompanied by a plain blue baseball cap that covered his eyes while he was looking down at his drawing.

"What are you working on?" Leo inquired, leaning in closer to see what was on his drawing pad.

Third shaded a corner of the page near Leo, with his wrist blocking most of the picture. As far as he could tell, it was an incredibly detailed drawing that almost looked as if it had been printed. From what he could see, it looked like a picture of a boy holding a spear.

"Is that you?" Leo asked, trying to get him to say something. Maybe Third was deaf and he really didn't know Leo was there? Based on what other campers had said, he didn't talk much, but maybe it was something else.

Leo sat silently for a moment, hoping that he might open up to him if he was patient. He watched as Third's pencil swept back and forth across the page, adding depth to a portion of the boy's torso.

Suddenly, he felt something hit him in the shoulder. Leo looked down and saw a crayon laying on the floor under the bench he was sitting on. *Is it raining crayons now?* Turning it over in his hand, he looked up at the ceiling.

Another crayon bounced off of his arm. He scanned the room and found Liz looking directly at him. *Is she pointing at me? What's her problem? Whatever.*

Leo turned back to face Third when he noticed a presence lurking behind him.

 **15**

ISAAC normally didn't enjoy taking nature walks, but he had to admit that he was having a good time. Mr. Edwards pointed out different animals and birds as they walked, as well as rattled off some facts about the forest itself. The experience reminded him of the time his mom convinced him to join the Squirrel Scouts when he was in elementary school, especially since he was wearing part of his old uniform.

Gathering badges by learning and accomplishing new things was cool, but the constant nature trips weren't something he was interested in. He believed that his mother had only signed him up to introduce him to other kids, but he was content spending time with classmates and school and family at home.

Summer had become more difficult for him over time. He didn't mind playing video games and reading books, but Isaac couldn't forget all the times that he and his brother would spend together. He didn't want to leave them behind.

"Hey," Alura said, pulling him out of his trance, "You alright?"

"Oh, yeah," Isaac said, pulling himself out of his trip down memory lane. "Sorry."

"What are you sorry for?" Alura asked, looking at him as they walked. The question came out more compassionate than accusatory.

I don't know, Isaac thought. *Better to apologize for nothing than to not apologize for something, right?* He knew the others were trying their hardest to conserve the dreamscape, but his mind kept pushing him to protect the team and keep them together. He shrugged at Alura's previous question.

"Good info, right?" Alura continued. "I feel like I *understand* Mr. Edwards now. He seems like a nice guy."

Isaac nodded. While he agreed with the first part about getting information, he didn't really know what Alura meant when she said she understood Mr. Edwards better. He did notice that the bowtie the man was wearing was pretty awesome though, with round little beetles spread across it in a pattern. It was very fitting of the nature walk, especially when Scotty discovered the secret society of purple beetles under the rock.

The six of them continued walking, coming to a few crossroads. In these situations, the procedure was the same. Mr. Edwards left it up to a vote, Scotty and the two other boys asked which one was more dangerous, the camp leader took a deep breath or rubbed his temples, then the three boys voted on whichever way he said was the most dangerous.

Isaac and Alura hadn't been able to vote yet, as they were outnumbered by the others. It didn't matter much to them, though. Whichever trail they decided on seemed to be smooth with limited roots and inclines.

Is Mr. Edwards just picking the easier path? Isaac wondered. It was certainly not a problem with him, but he couldn't help but wonder.

The landscape was incredible, with enormous trees surrounding the group as they walked. Mr. Edwards had mentioned they could have started growing 1,500 years ago, which was a thought that Isaac had trouble fully processing.

Isaac also noticed the sounds of leaves rustling and various birdsongs echoing through the trees. Isaac thought of the birdsong he had heard last night. *Mr. Edwards is probably right,* he confirmed. *It's probably just a scratch on the record or Emit made a mistake.*

"Woah," Scotty whispered quietly from behind them.

The expression wasn't new from Scotty, but the hushed volume was a cause for concern. Mr. Edwards, Alura, and Isaac turned to face the boy, whose mouth was hanging wide open.

Imprinted in the mud on the side of the trail, there was a large pawprint.

"Could that be from the monster?" Scotty asked in awe. "I mean, Bigfoot?"

"What a find! That appears to be a bear footprint," Mr. Edwards identified. "See the claw marks?" He pointed to the small, triangular indentations above the pads.

Isaac leaned in to see it better. If Mr. Edwards hadn't pointed out the claw marks, it could've easily been mistaken for a human footprint missing the elongated sole.

"Why aren't there any others?" Alura asked, referencing that the direction the bear was traveling was onto the trail, which was made up of dirt.

"Bears walk on the bottoms of their feet, like humans. Their weight is evenly distributed over their four legs," Mr. Edwards explained, "which means they don't leave indents in anything that isn't soft enough for them to sink in. This dirt is pretty well packed down, but the mud is soft, meaning he or she sank a little when passing through."

Isaac was convinced, and it wasn't large enough to be considered unusually big, ruling out that it could belong to a creature called "Bigfoot."

"What about this one?" one of the boys asked. He was bent down near a different footprint. The others hurried over to check it out.

"Woah," Scotty gawked.

Holy banana split! Isaac could see that this footprint was different. It very clearly belonged to a human. There were no claw marks and the entire foot, from toes to heel, were perfectly pressed into the malleable dirt.

Alura nudged him. "That looks like the one from the logging camp," she whispered.

It does, Isaac agreed based on shape and size. *But it's different. The footprint seemed to have an even depth throughout. The toes had sunk into the mud just as much as the heel did. The other footprint wasn't like that. Maybe it was in a hurry before, but not now?*

Isaac turned to Alura to mention it, but Mr. Edwards interrupted his plan.

ALURA studied Mr. Edwards reaction to the development.

Work as a team, Horace's voice echoed. *Use your strengths.* Alura was confident that Isaac would be able to gather any information on the footprint, and she wasn't willing to miss out on anything his reaction could tell them.

"Well," Mr. Edwards said, wiping his brow with a small red handkerchief, "I think we'd better continue our walk."

He's nervous, Alura noted. *But why? It could be because he's afraid of the creature, or he knows something more than he's letting on.*

"Is everything alright, Mr. Edwards?" Alura asked sympathetically.

"Yes," he replied, scanning the trees around them. Mr. Edwards seemed to snap out of his skittish state before continuing his thought. "I'm sure it's nothing. Let's keep moving. Don't want to miss lunch!"

The group started down the path again. Alura grabbed Isaac's arm, holding him back from joining right away.

"What do you think?" Alura asked. "That's weird, isn't it?"

"I mean, yeah," Isaac admitted. He stared down at the footprint in the mud. "We don't want to get lost. We should keep going."

Alura didn't push the subject for two reasons. *Goal number three, don't throw off the dreamscape. If everyone else was acting nonchalant about the footprint, we need to follow their lead.* The second reason was the look in Isaac's eyes. Alura knew they hid the fear of the monster in the woods.

"It's going to be alright, Isaac," Alura whispered. The two of them started walking in the direction of Mr. Edwards and the other campers.

"Yeah," Isaac replied quietly. "I know. Just nervous, I guess." He seemed to have pulled himself out of full shutdown mode.

"Was there something you were going to say about the footprint?" Alura asked.

Isaac slowed his pace for a moment. He was either trying to remember what he was going to say or was debating on whether or not to share it.

"I'll tell you later," he promised.

"Alright," Alura smiled. "When the team is back together, I think we'll all have to compare notes."

Alura couldn't help but feel concerned about Isaac. He had already been nervous about the whole thing. The encounter last night must've really shaken him up. Sometimes it was a blessing and other times it was a curse, but she always had to look out for the people around her.

Especially when they were a team.

 **16**

LEO recognized the figure behind him without fully turning around.

"Oh, hi, Rosemary," Leo said through a sheepish smile. "How's it going?"

"Get up, Leo," she said sternly. "Come on, let's go."

Rosemary grabbed him by the shoulder, leading him past the other tables through the double doors.

"What is going on?" Leo asked. "Am I in trouble? What did I do?"

Rosemary stayed silent, walking him around the building toward their private cabin. *I'm pretty sure this is how death row inmates feel after their final meal,* Leo pondered. *Or maybe children before the evil witch puts them in the oven?* One thing was for sure, he was going to figure out why Rosemary was protecting Third.

Once they were out of view of the other campers in the cabin, Rosemary released her hold on his shoulder and sat down on the step leading up to their porch, gesturing for him to do the same.

216

Confidence, Leo reminded himself. He had to get her talking without throwing off the dreamscape. Leo was no stranger to talking his way out of trouble, like the time he and his friends put sticky notes all over a teacher's car or bubble wrapped an entire hallway.

"Listen, kid," Rosemary said quietly, "don't bother Third. Alright?" Her voice was softer and her words sounded more like a favor than a command. *I don't like this version of Rosemary,* Leo decided immediately. He couldn't help but wonder why she was being so nice. The best place to start was by paying back the respect she was giving him.

"Sorry, Miss Rosemary," he said innocently, "he just looked so lonely. I thought I would try to see if he wanted someone to talk to."

With a deep sigh, Rosemary put her hand on his shoulder again. Her face seemed to soften, with her permanent frown becoming slightly more neutral.

"I understand, and I appreciate it," Rosemary said. "You don't need to worry about him though. He's going through a tough time right now. My father and I agreed to look after him this summer."

Mr. Edwards and Rosemary are taking care of him? Leo just assumed that he was another camper, same as all the other kids. Leo nodded his head thoughtfully as he thought about the wording of his next question to keep the balance between being respectful and pushing for more.

"Is he alright though?" Leo asked. "He doesn't really talk to anyone. I feel sorry for him."

"You really don't need to worry about him, Leo," Rosemary

reassured him. "Just let it be. You seem like a nice kid with good intentions, but I'm afraid that having friends around isn't going to help. He just needs time to process what happened."

"What happened to him?" he continued, pushing gently.

Rosemary sighed deeply and looked into Leo's eyes. It was like she was a different woman.

"Keep this between us, alright?" She made him promise. "He lost his parents a few months ago. Poor kid was all alone, until one of his other family members took him in."

Other family members, Leo analyzed. *That means that Rosemary and Mr. Edwards are somehow connected to him, right?*

"It didn't really work out though," Rosemary explained. "Some kind of legal issue or something. Third ended up with us, and my father and I were happy to have him."

Leo didn't want to push any harder. The only parental figure he had ever known was his Gran, and he couldn't imagine losing her so suddenly. With the new development, it seemed that the Third lead wasn't going anywhere. All the mystery that intrigued Leo was warranted. Although, there was one last thing he wanted to know.

"Why does everyone call him Third?" Leo asked.

Rosemary's mouth twisted further upward, becoming even less of a scowl. In fact, it was progressively becoming closer to a grin.

"Is that why you were talking to him?" Rosemary asked, then continued before he could respond. "Third is a nickname that his mother gave to him. Now, that's what he wants to be called."

Leo was good at talking himself out of tough spots, but he

was new to the soft interrogation game. He never really understood people like Isaac, who chose not to speak up. For some people, it was just easier to talk to others, and Leo knew he excelled in that department. It came naturally to him.

Live to fight another day, Leo decided. He needed to continue to preserve the dreamscape, and it seemed that he had followed the thread to the end with the mystery of Third.

"Alright," Leo said. "Thanks, Rosemary. I'm sorry for causing any problems."

"I appreciate it, Leo," she responded, the corners of her lips curling into a very slight smile. "You seem like a good kid, better than most of those troublemakers."

She rose to her feet and began to walk back toward the activity center. Leo sat for a moment to let everything sink in.

Maybe Liz is right, Leo wondered. *Maybe Howard Price is the link between the three dreamscapes and the culprit.* He supposed they would need to wait and see how things played out.

LIZ was coloring her landscape, trying to keep to herself to avoid any hiccups in the dreamscape. On top of that, there wasn't much left to be done with this dreamscape.

It has to be Howard Price, she concluded. He was built like a freight train, which gave him the means. His motive was to scare away the campers. And, of course, he had the opportunity to commit the crime. The final cog in the machine was the *inspiration.* It couldn't have possibly been a coincidence that he made an appearance in both dreamscapes. It was an easy open-and-shut case, like from one of her mystery novels.

Liz was pulled back to reality when the activity center doors swung open to Rosemary and a familiar face, although he looked slightly different since Liz wasn't peeking through branches.

"Thank you, ma'am," Officer Aspen said, taking off his hat as he entered the activity center.

"My pleasure," Rosemary gushed.

She ushered him toward the table in the corner where they would be able to have a private conversation. The table was perfectly situated so that Liz could eavesdrop on what they were saying by going over to find a new craft.

Although she was confident that Howard Price was the perpetrator, it couldn't hurt to hear what Rosemary and Aspen were talking about. She also craved that adrenaline rush she got when she was spying on them earlier.

Liz rose from the bench and started walking casually toward the folding table littered with different projects. Once she reached the table, she picked up one of the coloring books and began flipping through the pages.

"So," Aspen started, "what was it you needed, Rosemary?"

The police officer was in an awkward situation, trying his hardest to stay professional. Liz was not a people whisperer by any means, but there was nothing more obvious than Aspen not being interested in Rosemary whatsoever.

"There's a man here." Rosemary said. "His name is Reid. He was a friend of my father a long time ago."

Liz had returned her gaze back to the activity table to avoid looking suspicious, but she could see that Aspen was scanning the room, trying to find the man she was describing.

"Oh, he's not here officer. No need to be jealous," Rosemary said, grabbing the officer's hand reassuringly. He immediately pulled away, clearing his throat.

"This man is trespassing, then?" Aspen asked, sitting up even straighter than before. He seemed excited that he hadn't been called back for another ridiculous monster hunt. The enthusiasm was taken the wrong way by Rosemary.

"Yes, sir," Rosemary responded, still oblivious to the fact that the police officer couldn't be any less interested in her personally.

Liz was startled by a tap on her shoulder. She turned in the direction of their table to try to steal another glance. Behind her, there was a young boy with greasy hair and a polo shirt.

"Uh, hi," he stuttered awkwardly.

"Hello," Liz greeted him. "Can I help you with something?"

The boy was a couple of years younger than her, probably a freshman in high school. Liz was sure that she had seen him before, but she couldn't place it.

"I'm, uh," he continued, "I'm Jeremy."

He reached out his hand for a handshake, but Liz was slow to accept it. Both his hands were a much darker shade than the rest of his body, which she quickly realized was because they were covered in dirt. Liz didn't consider herself a germophobe or a clean freak, but there was something about dirt under fingernails that made her gag.

On top of that, she was trying to focus on the conversation between Aspen and Rosemary. *Could you possibly take a hike?*

"Hey, um," Jeremy started again.

Liz put up her pointer finger to ask Jeremy to stop speaking for a moment, then took a step back toward the table where Aspen and Rosemary were sitting. If he was going to try to talk to her, she was going to use it as a cover to get closer to them.

"You see, Reid and my father used to be part of this silly cult," Rosemary explained. "They worshipped that *thing...*"

"Sorry, I can go," Jeremy offered. Liz shushed him and continued eavesdropping.

"It was unhealthy," Rosemary continued. "I didn't speak to my father for years."

Although she had her back to them, Rosemary's voice indicated that she was concerned about her father. Liz tried to tune back in to see what they would talk about next.

"I really need you to..." Rosemary continued.

"I just wanted to ask you a question," Jeremy said, shuffling his feet.

How can you possibly be so oblivious? It was clear that Liz was trying to do something. She tried her best to stay calm, but this Jeremy kid was really testing her patience.

"What?" Liz said, gritting her teeth together. "What could you possibly want from me?"

After a moment, she realized that her question had come out a little more aggressively than she had expected. Then, Liz remembered where she had seen the boy before. Leo was speaking to Jeremy earlier, right in this same area of the activity hall.

The entire room was focused on the two of them, including Aspen and Rosemary, who looked annoyed. Although this wasn't much different than her normal expression, it was enough for her to suggest to Aspen that they take their conversation outside and start to look around for Reid. The two rose from the table and started making their way toward the door.

As Liz's gaze followed them, she realized that Leo was entering through the screen doors.

Great, Liz thought. *Just in time for him to see me screwing up the dreamscape. Again.*

She was expecting him to march over and give her another reprimand about the importance of discretion. Instead, he returned to his seat near Isabella. The two of them returned to their coloring pages. The rest of the room had returned to their rowdy selves.

"I, um," Jeremy stuttered, "I'm sorry. I just thought you were, um, really beautiful and I just wanted to tell you that."

This sticky kid is trying to tell me he's interested in me? Could this nonsense come at a worse time? She could feel her face get hot and her heart start racing. To keep her hands from shaking, she put them together in a knot behind her back.

Overwhelmed with everything that had just transpired in the last fifteen seconds, Liz needed to get some air. There was so much going on, and she just needed to get away from it.

Quiet and agreeable, her mother's voice resonated inside her brain. *Remove yourself if you need to.*

Without another word, she walked briskly toward the door, pushing them both open. The fresh air immediately felt nice on her face, but she still needed to find a place to be alone. The back porch of the girl's cabin seemed like a good place to collect her thoughts.

 **17**

ISAAC's palms started to sweat as the panic set in, and he knew Alura could sense it. He did his best to manage it, but every twig cracking or leaf crunching made the hair on his neck stand on end. Isaac hid his trembling hands in the tight pockets of his Squirrel Scouts uniform.

It's going to be alright, Isaac reminded himself. *Be strong. Don't be afraid. Nothing bad is going to happen. If it does, just wake up.*

Although Isaac estimated they must have been walking for more than an hour at this point, they couldn't have been more than two miles away from camp. The twists and turns of the trail and the number of Scotty's pitstops to check out insects had kept them from getting too far away.

They reached another crossroad, this one next to a stream. Going left was downhill, following the flow of the water. Going right was an incline, going against the flow of the water.

"Can we go this way," one of the boys asked, pointing to the right. *The direction that footprint was pointed. Great.*

"I don't think so guys. It could be dangerous."

As soon as the word left Mr. Edwards' mouth, his face filled with regret. Admitting to these kids that one way was dangerous might have been the biggest mistake of his career, both as a camp instructor and a teacher. Immediately, the three boys started begging to go that way.

Mr. Edwards stood silent for a moment, being bombarded by the questions. Then, Isaac was surprised by the sternness that powered his presence.

"We cannot go that way," Mr. Edwards said unyieldingly. "We will go this way, down the stream, or we will go back to camp. That's final."

The three boys sighed in unison, disappointed by the decision.

"That was weird," Alura whispered.

The group stood there in silence for a moment, with the boys looking at Mr. Edwards with big eyes, hoping that he would reconsider his position on the subject.

Isaac noticed that the birdsongs had stopped, and the only noises in the forest now were the scraping of the leaves as the breeze pushed them along the ground and the trickle of water in the stream.

Suddenly, a loud roar echoed through the trees, followed by the sound of bird wings flapping away. *Not again,* Isaac thought disappointedly. *I hate this. Hate hate hate it.*

Mr. Edwards began shouting something incoherent to the others, then gathered the three boys and pushed them toward the way they had come. Isaac turned to follow, but Alura grabbed his shoulder, pulling him behind one of the trunks of the redwood trees. She put a finger against her lips.

Mr. Edwards and the three boys ran down the path, the clomping of their shoes slowly drifting into the distance.

"Can you get us back to the camp?" Alura asked.

Isaac nodded his head confidently. He remembered every twist and turn they had chosen. Reverse it, and they'd be on their way back to the camp.

"Good," she whispered. "Let's go see what's going on at the mouth of the stream."

"Wait," Isaac said. "What about Bigfoot?"

Translation, Isaac thought, *can we not come face to face with an eight-feet tall, hairy, terrifying monster?*

"You don't need to be scared," Alura said reassuringly. "If it's actually here, we'll be careful. Keep our eyes and ears open. But we need to find out why Mr. Edwards was so protective of that path."

Was Mr. Edwards really trying to hide something? To Isaac, it just seemed like he didn't want to go uphill again, for the sake of his feet. Had he missed something so obvious?

"You think there's something up there?" Isaac asked.

"Did you see the way that Mr. Edwards snapped at Scotty and the other two?" Alura said, "People like Mr. Edwards don't get *that* snippy unless there is something else, too. It's just a hunch, I guess, but what's the harm in checking it out?"

"The Harm in Checking it Out," by Isaac, Isaac thought to himself. *Number one, getting attacked by Bigfoot.* Regardless, he nodded, accepting there was probably something that he had missed, or Alura was just a better detective than him. Only time would tell if it was worth investigating the mysterious path. Or in Mr. Edwards' own words, the *dangerous* path.

Alura peeked out from behind the tree to ensure the coast was clear, then waved to Isaac. The two of them started off on their trek uphill. The path seemingly ran next to the stream the entire way, although it did loop around different obstacles like trees and rocks, varying the amount of space between the trail and the water.

Isaac checked behind him every minute or so, just to make sure they weren't being followed.

"You alright?" Alura asked.

"Yeah," Isaac said, taking a deep breath. "Just a lot going on, I guess."

"You don't have to worry about Bigfoot," Alura said. "If he shows himself, just wake yourself up. You don't need to put yourself through that." Leo had said something similar last night, but that was *before* Bigfoot actually made his first appearance.

They continued walking, closely monitoring the ground to potentially spot more footprints, bear, Bigfoot, or otherwise. The trail started to get much steeper, then flattened out into another clearing.

Similar to the Singing Tree, the edges of the area were lined with bushes. Although, it was much smaller and had the stream on the one side with only one path, leading in or out. The pair were forced to stop their trek.

Isaac made his way over to the stream, listening to the water as it hit the rocks on the way down. He scanned the area, trying to find anything that could be a clue. Although he had been looking all day for anything that could've been considered helpful in proving that Bigfoot was just a guy in a costume, he hadn't come up with much.

Alura seemed to do the same on the opposite side, along where the trees and bushes met the clearing.

"See anything?" Alura asked.

"No," Isaac shrugged. "There's not much here. See anything over there?"

Isaac's eyes focused on something shiny in the water. He crouched down and reached out carefully to avoid falling into the stream. He grabbed the stone, pulling it out. For a moment, he flipped it in his hand, turning it over and over to see all sides.

Holy mashed potatoes, Isaac thought. *Is this a gold nugget?*

"Nothing," Alura said. "Wait a minute…"

Isaac turned to find Alura pushing through a bush. Once she was far enough, she grabbed something from behind one of the enormous tree stumps. As she pulled it out, Isaac couldn't help but be surprised.

Someone had hidden a shovel behind the tree stump, away from prying eyes.

"Why would someone have this out here?" Alura wondered.

The two of them studied it in silence, but there wasn't anything out of the ordinary in terms of appearance. It was just an everyday metal shovel with a worn wooden handle.

ALURA looked at the shovel, hoping that an answer as to *why* someone would leave it out here might pop into her mind.

"This was also in the water," Isaac offered, dropping a rock into her palm.

"Is this gold?"

"I think so. I've never seen a gold nugget before," Isaac admitted.

Mr. Edwards seems like such a good-hearted person, Alura thought. *Was there really any way that he could have some sort of nefarious intentions?* It almost hurt to think that someone so kind and dedicated to others could be hiding something like this. Before she fell down a well of conspiracy theories, she stopped herself and looked toward Isaac.

"What are you thinking?" Alura asked.

"It doesn't really make much sense," Isaac said, "but Mr. Edwards could know about the gold, right? He could be protecting it? Greed is a motive, right?" He was thinking the same thing as Alura.

"I guess it could be but it couldn't have been him anyway. We've been with him all morning. And he was in his cabin last night during the attack," Alura shook her head. "Mr. Edwards genuinely loves this camp. I don't think he would do something like that. To scare away his campers, why would he do that?" Alura made good points, but Isaac needed to follow the theory to the end.

"Well, money? He could also be working *with* someone," Isaac suggested. "But I don't think so either. It doesn't make any sense, really. Who would use a shovel to get gold out of the creek?"

Isaac set to work, scanning the ground near the tree line. He seemed to be looking for something specific.

He's right, Alura thought. *Why would he use a shovel?* Isaac did make a good point, though. If he was a fantastic actor, they could make a case for means, motive, and opportunity if Mr.

Edwards was working with someone else.

Alura watched as Isaac stopped abruptly over a pile of dirt that appeared darker than the surrounding area, as if it had been turned over recently. Alura handed him the shovel and he started digging.

Just a few inches from the surface, a worn-down metal box appeared. The red paint was chipped around the edges of the lid. It looked like some sort of repurposed toolbox or tacklebox for fishing. The name *Paul Edwards* was written on the front in black ink.

This belongs to Mr. Edwards, Alura thought to herself. *I was right, there was something hiding up here!* The two of them crouched down as Isaac undid the latches of the box. The lid creaked as he opened it, revealing the contents inside.

Directly on top was an old black and white photo of a man in front of the familiar Camp Tolowa sign, totem poles and all. Although the picture was old and grainy, the sign was new or close to it.

There were other photos as well, but the one on top appeared to be the oldest. Many of them were of the man, and some included two boys. Isaac and Alura looked closely at each photo as he shuffled through the stack.

"Is that Mr. Edwards?" Alura asked, pointing to a photo that included two men in front of the Camp Tolowa sign.

"It looks like it," Isaac confirmed, then pointed to the other man. "Do you think that could be his dad?".

"Looks like a good possibility," Alura shrugged. The two men shared a similar facial structure, but one was clearly older than the other.

Alura checked the back of some of the photos. Most were blank, but there was an older photo of a man with two boys that had words scrawled across the back in red ink. *Me, Paul, and TJ – June 1920.*

"What is this?" Alura asked, grabbing a small figurine that was similar to a chess piece. It was a chunk of wood that had been carved into a familiar figure.

"Is this supposed to be Bigfoot?" Alura said, holding it out flat in her palm for Isaac to get a better look at.

The wood had been whittled in such a way that it appeared to bear a striking resemblance to the mythical creature. Alura shuffled through the box. Hidden under more pictures and a few outdated pamphlets for the camp were more figures, similar to the craftsmanship of the Bigfoot. Rather than a large, monkey-like figure, the others were in the shapes of birds, deer, bears, and other woodland creatures.

"He's into woodcarving, I guess," Isaac suggested.

"It just feels like there is something else going on here, doesn't it?" Alura asked.

All the clues they had just discovered only made Alura feel more confused. *If only there were cleaner lines to create a reason why someone would be attacking the camp as Bigfoot. Even if something here was able to prove that it wasn't a real monster.* She was frustrated.

"None of it gives a clear answer," Isaac agreed. "Who would use a shovel to extract gold from a creek? Why is there a toolbox of Mr. Edwards' things out in the middle of the woods? Why does he have a carving of Bigfoot?" He paused for a moment, deep in thought. "Do you think there's any way that we could ask Mr. Edwards about this?"

"That could throw off the dreamscape, though," Alura said.

It was true, if the four kids that didn't fit in with the camp started questioning Mr. Edwards, he might become suspicious and closed off. So far, they had gained his trust, and it wasn't worth risking it.

Alura watched as Isaac opened his mouth to speak but tensed up and turned his attention to the forest that surrounded them. He carefully surveyed the areas.

"We have to go," Isaac whispered, quickly closing the lid and pushing the box back into the hole. He used the side of his foot to push the dirt back over it.

"What were you going to say, though?" Alura asked, still crouching over the area where the box was.

Isaac picked up the shovel from behind her and carelessly tossed it back behind the tree in a panic. Looking directly at Alura, he repeated his demand.

"We have to go," Isaac said, looking directly into her face. The seriousness in his eyes meant more than his words. Alura jumped to her feet.

Suddenly, there was a familiar roar. This time, though, it was much louder, and it was accompanied by the sound of crunching leaves, indicating that whatever made the noise was *much* closer than before.

Alura grabbed Isaac's hand, and they started running down the path, heading toward camp.

 **18**

LIZ sat down on the dusty wood platform that faced the woods. Closing her eyes, she laid back slowly. Although it wasn't the most comfortable thing, it did make her feel at peace. Liz could feel her face return to its normal temperature as she controlled her breathing.

She began to think about what she had learned by snooping on Rosemary and Aspen.

That dirty man, Reid, was a friend of Mr. Edwards. They were both part of, Liz assumed, a Bigfoot hunting group. *How can a single person believe such a silly thing, let alone an entire group?*

This was the first time Liz had experienced a boy telling her that he liked her. Jeremy wasn't so bad, other than the fact that he was close to seventy years old. It was silly to even think about it.

But why did Rosemary call Aspen? Liz assumed it was to have Reid removed from Camp Tolowa for trespassing so that her father didn't have to face him again.

There was also the fact that Jeremy was repulsive, with his

gross hands. For some reason, that didn't really matter to her right now, though. *It could never work anyway.*

Reid was such a bad influence on Mr. Edwards that he hadn't spoken to his daughter for years. She was probably just protecting him from falling back in with the group. Although Rosemary seemed to be miserable, she did care for her father. *She's willing to run a camp with kids. It couldn't go much further than that, especially for a woman like her.*

She and Jeremy were both, literally, from different times. And technically, he didn't exist. He was just a recreation of a person who lived years ago.

Liz sighed deeply in frustration. It was like there were two different things going on in her head at the same time. Thoughts bounced around in her mind like a puck on an air hockey table. Her brain wanted to think about Rosemary and Aspen, but the rest of her kept defaulting to what Jeremy had told her earlier.

Obviously, there had been some difficulties with the internship so far. Working as a team and talking to people were two things that worried Liz after Horace had explained what they would be doing over the summer. Both were warranted, as they led to a massive Nuke-Leo explosion halfway through their first day.

The current predicament was a little less connected to the entire thing. So far, the internship had caused her to step out of her comfort zone, but this was expected. However, this level of "outside her comfort zone" might even be on a different planet. This whole experience was so *chaotic.*

Liz found herself wishing Alura was with her. *She's probably had a ton of boys confess their love for her.*

For a brief moment, she thought her wish had been granted. There was a soft crunching of leaves growing louder as someone emerged from around the cabin wall.

"Hey," a small voice greeted her.

Although she would've been disappointed, the sight of Jeremy wasn't the worst thing she could imagine.

"I just wanted to say that I'm sorry, uh," he continued, "I didn't mean to make you uncomfortable. I hope you're alright."

Liz sat up and slid down on the step, making room for him to sit next to her.

"Are you sure?"

She nodded her head in confirmation and patted the bench. Now that she wasn't blindsided, Liz felt like she could actually have a conversation with the boy.

"Are you alright?" Jeremy asked.

"Yeah," Liz replied, "I'm alright. It was just a lot all at once."

Although she never really knew the right words, Liz was very rarely to the point where she didn't know what to say. There was always something floating around in her mind. Sometimes that was better, but other times it came out like a sandwich where the bread was in the middle.

Right now though, she couldn't come up with anything to say to Jeremy. The two of them sat in silence for a couple of minutes. This would normally make her anxious, but it was nice watching the tree branches sway back and forth in the breeze. Although she wasn't the biggest fan of nature, it seemed like the perfect thing for her right now.

"Hey, can I ask you something?" Jeremy asked.

This dreamscape is really crossing into nightmare territory. What could he possibly need to ask me? Regardless of her apprehension, she reluctantly nodded her head.

"Are you afraid?"

"What do you mean?" Liz asked.

He looked nervous for a moment, turning his hands into each other. Liz was more curious than anything. There were so many things he could be referring to.

"Of the monster thing," Jeremy said, gazing down at his feet. "People are saying it's Bigfoot, you know."

"Oh," Liz responded, relieved that it wasn't anything more serious, "no, I'm not scared. It's probably just some guy in a suit. There's no such thing as Bigfoot."

"How can you be sure?" Jeremy asked.

Why was it such an easy concept to believe that there was a possibility that this mythical creature existed yet no one was willing to believe it didn't exist? It just doesn't make sense. Wouldn't it be easier to think it wasn't real?

"There's really no way there could be a creature, or entire species, for that matter, to be wandering the forests of the Pacific Northwest without anyone ever seeing them. It just isn't plausible."

Jeremy blinked.

"What I'm trying to say is," Liz said, taking a deep breath, "Bigfoot is a legend. There's just too much evidence pointing to the fact that he doesn't exist."

The boy nodded slowly, and his gaze returned toward the tree line. While they sat quietly for a moment, Liz was thankful that Jeremy had started with such an easy topic of conversation. Talking about a fake creature was much easier than having a discussion about their feelings or anything of that nature.

"So, you think it's just someone in a costume?" Jeremy asked. "You aren't afraid at all?"

"Nope," Liz confirmed. "No reason to be. Not even a little bit."

Although she was confident that there wasn't any kind of monster lurking in the woods, it probably didn't hurt that she was in a simulation and couldn't actually be harmed.

"A lot of the boys in our cabin are pretty shaken up," he said, puffing out his chest, "but not me. I think it's pretty neat."

Liz couldn't help but chuckle at his display of strength. Crossing his arms, Jeremy frowned in her direction.

"What?" he said, his voice shrinking. "I'm not. I'm not scared."

"I believe you," Liz said, still chuckling. "It's alright if you are, though."

Jeremy uncrossed his arms and let out a huge sigh of relief.

"Oh, thank goodness. I'm *terrified*," Jeremy admitted.

The two of them shared a laugh. Liz tucked her legs up, resting her head on her knees.

"I'm glad I took Leo's advice," Jeremy said.

Leo's advice? The situation suddenly came into view for Liz. Jeremy had likely asked Leo about her, and that's why he shouted her name randomly in the activity hall earlier.

"About telling me how you felt?" Liz asked.

"Yeah," Jeremy admitted, "And…"

His head suddenly swiveled back toward the forest, avoiding

eye contact.

"Never mind."

"No," Liz said. She could feel her face getting hot again. "What else? What else did Leo tell you?"

Jeremy lowered his head into his hands, still looking away from her. *What could Leo have possibly said to him? Probably something about low standards or something mean, like what his friends would say to her at school.*

"I promised I wouldn't say," Jeremy said, throwing his hands up.

"Tell me," Liz demanded.

"Well," Jeremy started, rubbing his hands together, "after you left the activity hall, I was a little sad about everything, I guess. He came over and told me I should come find you. He said that even if you didn't like me, that you might need a friend right now. Just someone to talk to."

Leo didn't say that ... did he?

He took a deep breath. "So, I came to find you. I hope that's alright," Jeremy continued. "But please don't tell Leo, he scares me more than Bigfoot. He could probably break me in half."

On one hand, Liz felt like she should be upset with Leo. There was no reason for him to go out of his way to make her feel better. On top of that, why would anyone want to talk to the person they just rejected, even if it was unintentional?

Liz wanted to hate Leo, like she hated his friends who picked on her. She wanted to be upset and angry about everything that unfolded yesterday. As hard as she tried, Liz didn't feel annoyed or upset. She felt grateful, in a way. This was one of the nicest conversations she'd had with a teenage boy.

"Your secret is safe with me," Liz said, smiling awkwardly.

"Thanks," Jeremy said. "You have no idea how much I appreciate that."

He turned his entire body toward her, crossing his legs on the patio.

"Hey, listen," he started nervously, "I just wanted to tell you. I don't know if you are leaving tonight, but whoever is left from the boys' cabin is going to stay up to see if we can see the monster. You think you might want to join us?"

Liz was surprised by the question, but she supposed the next logical thing for a boy to do after admitting his feelings for a girl was asking her out on a date, regardless of how boring and gross it sounded.

"What do you mean, leaving tonight?" Liz inquired, pushing past the invitation portion of the question.

"Oh, well, a lot of parents are coming to pick up their kids tonight," Jeremy shrugged, "because they either want to go home or their parents don't think it's safe. I'm staying though because my parents are on vacation and they're *definitely* not coming to get me until next week."

Campers are going home following the Bigfoot attacks on the camp? It sounded like the gears of Price's plan to purchase the camp's property were in motion. Without any campers, Mr. Edwards would have no choice but to shut down the operation.

Every fact that she came across solidified the fact that it was Howard Price in that abnormal gorilla suit.

"I was just thinking it might be fun," Jeremy babbled on. "It was actually Third's idea. He did it last night, waiting out on the porch. It would be cool to hang out with you if you want. It's totally up to you though."

"I'll think about it," Liz offered.

Although she would love to stick around and spend a little bit of time with this imaginary boy, she would have to see if she'd still be around.

Suddenly, a fury of screams and shouts filled the camp.

LIZ and Jeremy came out from behind the cabin, trying to catch a glimpse of what was going on.

Mr. Edwards was leading the pack, red-faced and out of breath with three boys trailing behind. She recognized one as Isabella's brother, Scotty. Whatever happened, he looked thrilled to be a part of it.

Although most of the words coming out of Mr. Edwards mouth were gibberish, Liz could make out "help" and "Bigfoot" within the exclamations. Rosemary and Officer Aspen appeared from somewhere on the other side of the camp, rushing toward them to see what the commotion was about.

"Perfect," Mr. Edwards said, leaning down on his knees to catch his breath. "You're here officer. It's out there, right now. It's out there, in the trees."

"Woah, woah," Aspen said, kneeling down to meet his face. "What's out there? *Bigfoot?* You saw it?"

Mr. Edwards, still out of breath, put up his pointer finger to indicate he needed a moment to respond.

"We sure did!" Scotty piped up. "We were walking along the

creek, and we heard a *huge* roar, then Mr. Edwards told us to run back toward camp!"

The police officer stood back up, looking over Mr. Edwards to speak to Scotty.

"Just to confirm," Aspen said sharply. "You *saw* it? With your own eyes?"

Mr. Edwards shook his head, responding to the question before Scotty and the other boys could spin some kind of tale of heroism. Based on their disappointed looks, this was their plan to look cool in front of the rest of the camp.

Liz shifted her view by taking a step out from behind the cabin, followed closely by Jeremy. Everyone who was in the activity hall had filed through the screen doors and were now standing on the porch. *Why do Leo and Isabella look so concerned?*

Then, Liz realized. *Where are Alura and Isaac?* They hadn't returned with the group. It wasn't a huge loss, as it was a dreamscape. They couldn't get hurt here. If anything, they would just be able to wake up and return to the detective agency.

"Figures," came a voice from the other side of the camp, near the totem pole sign. A slight breeze sent a smelly indication of who it could be.

Everyone who wasn't facing that direction, including Mr. Edwards, the three boys, and Rosemary, turned to find a particularly grubby man strolling toward the group.

"Reid," Mr. Edwards said, seemingly surprised, "what are you doing here?"

"Well, my old pal," he said, "I heard you had lured Bigfoot to this place. Bringing kids here every summer must've finally paid off. Congratulations."

Rosemary stepped forward, putting herself between her father and Reid.

"I think it's time you go," she scolded. "You've done nothing but cause problems for this family. We don't want to see you around here anymore. Understand?"

"I don't make problems, I fix them," Reid defended himself. "I came back because we need you back, Paul. Your brother stepped away and we need an expert tracker. You're the best of the best."

Rosemary seemed to be revved up and ready to continue, but Mr. Edwards put a hand on her shoulder.

"Reid, I will not be returning to the group," he said sternly. "Understand?"

"Come on," Reid pleaded. "We *need* you. Please?"

"Officer Aspen, would you be kind enough to remove this man from the camp?" Rosemary requested.

The officer placed the hat back on his head, then turned back toward Mr. Edwards, looking for confirmation that he agreed with his daughter's stance. It was his property, after all.

He nodded, then turned away from Reid.

"I get it, I get it," Reid admitted defeated as Aspen started toward him. "I would've tried to get your brother back in the group, but no one has seen him in weeks. It's like he gone and fell off the face of the Earth."

Mr. Edwards didn't seem too distraught by the fact that his brother was unreachable, or he was too busy worrying about the current dilemma to process it.

Aspen escorted Reid under the totem pole archway, where

he started down the path away from the camp. The police officer then returned to the group.

"We've got a problem, sir," Mr. Edwards said. "Two of my campers are still out there. I could've sworn they were still behind me. When I turned back, though, it was just the four of us."

Realizing that the eyes of more than a dozen campers were fixed on them, Rosemary pulled on her father's shirt, indicating that they should take it somewhere a little more private. After making a quick announcement that all campers should convene in the activity center and stay there until further notice, the three adults made their way to their private cabin.

Liz and Jeremy made their way over in silence, pushing the doors open. Once inside, they sat down at the table with Leo and Isabella.

"What do you think happened to them?" Isabella wondered aloud.

Both of their faces, along with Jeremy's, held genuine concern about the others.

"I'm sure they'll be fine," Leo reassured her.

Liz thought back to what Horace had said about the dreamscape. If someone gets hurt in the simulation, it won't carry over to the real world. Was Leo not paying attention for that part of the explanation?

"Nothing bad can happen to them anyway," Liz said matter-of-factly. "They're actually…"

"Yeah," Leo said, speaking over her, "they're really resourceful."

I almost did it again, Liz admonished herself. *Why can't I just keep my mouth shut? This mystery will be over soon if I can just stop being an idiot.*

Leo avoided her gaze, which she appreciated. Although, she much rather would've preferred a look of anger or disappointment than the blunt shun. The least he could do was be annoyed with her.

Liz was drawn out of her thoughts by the doors abruptly squeaking open once more. Red faced and out of breath, Alura and Isaac tumbled in.

 **19**

ALURA had never run so fast in her life, and she assumed that Isaac wasn't any kind of track star either. Isaac led the way as they sprinted down the winding dirt paths, kicking up dirt as they ran back to Camp Tolowa.

As soon as they got back to the camp, they ran directly to the activity center, collapsing on the floor in an attempt to catch their breath. Alura put her hands over her eyes to try and relax. After a moment, she realized every camper had created a circle around the two of them.

"Did you see it?"

"Was it trying to eat you?"

"How did you get away from it?"

Alura tried to answer, but no words came out of her mouth.

"Hey, hey," Leo said, pushing through the crowd. "Give them some space, alright?"

He helped Isaac to his feet, propping him up on one of the benches. Then, he came back over and did the same for Alura, helping her get to a seat.

The other campers had taken a step back, but their

excitement could hardly be contained. Leo, Liz, and Isabella stood in front of them.

"Are you guys okay?" Leo asked, kneeling down in front of them.

The two of them nodded. Alura turned to Isaac, who was still shaking from the encounter. She felt terrified, too, but her exhaustion made it difficult to focus on anything else.

Isaac was right to be scared, Alura thought. She remembered the feeling of something in the forest *watching* them, and then the thunderous roar.

"Did you see it?" Leo whispered.

Alura remembered back to the forest near the creek, where Isaac had somehow known that Bigfoot was going to show up. The two had turned to run, but Alura caught a glimpse behind them of the creature. It was tall, hairy, and had these glowing yellow eyes. It roared one final time before the two of them bolted into the trees.

I never thought it would be like that. She imagined herself being brave and reminding herself that it was just a dreamscape. As soon as that first roar echoed through the trees, it was like everything but fear exited her body.

"Yes," she managed, still trying to catch her breath.

All the campers erupted into conversations. Suddenly the world around them was swept away in a purple cloud of smoke.

Alura blinked. When she opened her eyes, she realized she was back in the cubicle at the office. She sat up in her bed for a moment, still trying to catch her breath.

The tiredness had transitioned into more of an emotional feeling than a physical one. It felt like waking up from a nightmare. Alura just needed to let her mind catch up with everything.

There was a light knock on the door.

"Hey, kiddo," Horace said, "are you alright in there?"

She got up from the bed and made her way to the door, opening it. The other three had also woken up and already joined Horace in the center of the room near Emit.

"Yeah, sorry," Alura said. "What happened?"

"I stopped the track," Horace explained. "It pulled you out of the dreamscape. I heard you and Isaac struggling. I just wanted to make sure everything was alright. You can return if you'd like though, it'll put you back in right where you were."

"I think," Alura said, looking toward the others, especially Isaac, "I think we could use a minute to regroup. What do you guys think?"

Isaac gave her a thumbs up, while Liz and Leo nodded in agreement.

"Why don't we have a quick meeting in the conference room?" Horace suggested. "It's always good to review the facts of a case."

ALURA and the others sat in the same chairs they had the previous day and that morning. Horace distributed cold cans of General Ginger Ale to everyone.

Of course, Alura and Isaac started with a full debrief of being chased by Bigfoot.

"Are you guys alright?" Leo asked. "You saw Bigfoot?"

Horace wheeled his chair closer to the table.

"Is that what happened? You saw it?" Horace asked.

"Yes," Isaac responded. "It chased us in the woods."

"Are you sure it wasn't a bear or something?" Liz asked skeptically.

Alura remembered back to the half-second glance she got of it. In a word, it felt *unnatural*, like something that wasn't supposed to exist. A tall, hairy creature that didn't move like a bear.

"No," Alura confirmed, "it couldn't have been a bear."

"Maybe like a mutant monkey or something," Isaac suggested, "but not a bear."

"Why don't we review some clues," Horace said, getting up from his chair and pulling over the whiteboard.

He uncapped his green marker, ready to start writing.

"Goal number one, meet the people in the dreamscape. Let's start with suspects," he started. "Shout them out."

"Howard Price," Liz said, wasting no time. "He had the motive to do it because he wanted to buy the land for a housing development. He also had the inspiration."

Horace scribbled down the information in the form of bullet points, then prompted them for more.

"Reid," Leo said. "Motive would be to bring Mr. Edwards back into the Bigfoot hunting group. He also disappeared during the time that you guys saw Bigfoot in the woods, only to show up a few minutes before you got back to the camp. That's opportunity and motive."

Leo also included a small review of who Reid was, to keep Alura and Isaac up to speed with what they missed. The marker squeaked as Horace picked out important points from the recap.

"Would that be possible?" Liz asked. "Wouldn't it be difficult for him to be near them, then get back to the camp before them? He didn't look like the type of guy that ran. *Ever.*"

"Well," Alura suggested, "we followed pathways back so we would know where we were going, but he could've cut directly through the woods. It's possible that his way was quicker."

"We'll keep him for now," Horace said. "Who else?"

"Mr. Edwards," Isaac said.

Alura noticed that Liz and Leo were surprised, with good reason. This was the first time they had heard about their suspicions.

"There's gold in the creek," Isaac continued. "We saw it. There was also a box with old pictures of the Camp Tolowa totem poles. We couldn't figure out what it meant."

"So, you think Edwards was protecting the gold? Trying to scare people away?" Leo asked. "You really think he'd terrorize his own camp for money?"

Alura remembered talking to Mr. Edwards in the dreamscape. He was tired, but she could feel the passion he had for the camp and the kids. *I feel horrible even thinking that it's possible, but it's worth mentioning, isn't it? Even if it's not the perfect scenario?*

"The thing is," Alura said, taking a deep breath, "we know there is something more to Mr. Edwards. We don't know what it is, though. There has to be something, and it would add up, don't you think?"

"It's possible," Leo replied. "When we go back in, we should try to get more information from him." Horace wrote it as a sub-line under goal number one. "I did some digging into Third, too. Rosemary told me that he lost his parents a few months before the dreamscape."

Wow, Alura thought. She remembered the menagerie of feelings, ranging from grief to guilt, after her parents died. Alura wanted to shut out the world, too, but her Aunt Kate and Uncle Rick kept her from closing herself off.

"*That's* why he is so quiet and mysterious," Leo continued. "I thought he might have some kind of connection to Bigfoot, but I guess not."

The room fell silent for a moment. Alura could still feel a certain amount of awkwardness between the four of them, regardless of having the opportunity to work with each other more closely. Between Liz and Leo, there was still a fair amount of tension.

"Mr. Brown," Isaac said, clearing his throat, "Can I ask you something?"

Alura looked back at Isaac, who was sitting behind her. He met her eyes for half a second, then returned his gaze toward the front of the room.

"Do you think it's possible that Bigfoot is real?"

"I've actually been wondering the same thing," Leo joined in. "What if he's real? Wouldn't this whole thing be a wild goose chase?"

Horace looked like he was preparing to answer the question but was interrupted by a scoff from Liz.

"Do you have something to add, Elizabeth?" he asked.

Immediately, she turned red, a look of panic spreading across her face as she slid down her chair.

Why can't the two of them just act like normal human beings? Alura wondered. *Just talk to each other. We need to be working together, not avoiding each other.*

"No," Liz responded. "Sorry."

Horace stood at the head of the table and placed his hand over his forehead. Alura could feel his frustration. He stayed like that for a moment while the four interns watched him closely.

"Guys," Alura said, taking the floor. "We need to be working together. We hit a snag yesterday, yes, but a team doesn't *work* if two of its members are avoiding each other."

Horace smiled in Alura's direction.

LIZ crossed her arms and rubbed her elbows.

"Elizabeth, say what's on your mind, please."

Liz took a deep breath. *Can't you just leave me alone? The last time I said what was on my mind, it just caused problems.* The others continued to look in her direction, forcing her to reveal her thoughts on the matter.

"I think it's utterly ridiculous to think that Bigfoot could be real," she said so quickly, Alura almost missed it.

"Why?" Horace inquired without missing a beat.

"Because there is no way that a single creature or entire species could exist for this long and no one has ever seen one. There have never been any clear pictures taken or bones discovered."

Horace seemed content with this answer, turning his attention to a different member of the group.

"Leo," Horace asked calmly, "do you feel offended?"

"No," Leo said, "but…"

"Attacked?"

"No…"

"Upset?"

Leo shook his head.

"Good," Horace said, "but I'd assume you have a rebuttal for Elizabeth?"

Liz felt a wave of anxiety begin to rise, starting in her toes.

"Yes," Leo said, sitting up in his chair. He looked professional, as if he was going to give a speech on the subject. "I was actually doing a lot of research on the subject last night. There are certain animals that are really hard to get pictures of. Like, borderline *impossible.* Bigfoot could just be an extreme example of that. Also, did you know that porcupines and other animals chew on bones to sharpen their teeth? It breaks down the bones into smaller pieces, which means they'd disappear quicker."

That wasn't so bad, Liz thought. She could feel the tension flush out through her fingertips. *He* does *have some good points, but they're still not convincing enough.* The issue with this argument was that there weren't two clear sides. The position that Bigfoot was not real was definite, but the argument that Bigfoot *could* be real was not.

Horace lowered himself into the chair near the whiteboard, capping the green marker.

"Alura, Isaac, anything to add?"

ISAAC and Alura shook their heads. For one, he didn't have anything to add. For another, he didn't want to get himself involved with the conflict that brewed on the other side of the table.

The detective closed his eyes and stood in silence for a moment, running his fingers through his hair.

"Kids," he took a deep breath, "I picked the four of you for a reason. I want you all to succeed *together*. I've been in this business for a very long time, and you need to understand that there will always be someone who doesn't agree with you."

His gaze fell to the floor as he let out a chuckle, possibly remembering an old memory.

"Those are the times you will be at your best. If no one challenges you, there is nowhere for you to go. You need to embrace the differences of opinion. They'll push you toward the truth."

"But we don't even know what we are looking for," Leo argued. "What exactly are we investigating?"

Mr. Brown stayed silent for a moment, sitting in his chair and studying the faces around the room.

"My advice is, use your resources," he suggested. He stepped aside and gave a clear view of the whiteboard. Using a bright red marker, he drew an arrow to the second goal they had set for themselves.

Find clues and information that point to anything other than Bigfoot being a real creature.

"Someone in this room has the answer you are looking for, whether or not they know it," he continued. "Alura, what do you believe?"

"Honestly," she shrugged, "I don't know what to believe. I didn't have an opinion before we started investigating, and I really don't have one now. I'm sorry, team."

"Well said," Mr. Brown responded, looking anything but disappointed. "Elizabeth."

Isaac quickly realized that Mr. Brown was going to ask everyone and started to rack his brain, cataloguing the day's activities. *Introductions, then the stakeout, then breakfast, and then the nature walk.* He went through each part of the day with a fine-tooth comb, trying to recall anything that could help them.

"I am under the impression that you are not convinced that this creature could be real. You feel certain that it is someone dressed up, causing chaos for the camp. Is this correct?"

She nodded her head in agreement.

"Any dreamscape-specific evidence to support this stance, or just the outside knowledge?" he asked, flattening his moustache.

"No, that sums it up," Liz said, crossing her arms and sitting back in her chair.

The old detective shuffled his feet, then turned his attention toward Leo.

There's nothing, Isaac thought. *But there has to be something. I can't let the team down like this.*

"Leo," he started, "From my understanding, you don't know whether or not the creature is a charade or the actual Bigfoot, correct?"

"Yeah," Leo said in agreement, "and I feel like that's making it hard to solve it. It's like we are trying to solve more than one mystery."

The dreaded moment was upon him. A smile spready across Mr. Brown's face when he turned toward Isaac.

"And what do you think, kiddo?"

"I don't know," Isaac said, pondering. "He could be real, I guess."

The room fell silent. After a moment, Isaac glanced around the room and realized that everyone was still looking at him. Mr. Brown sat at the end of the table, still smiling.

Alura swiveled her chair to face Isaac and cupped her hands around his ear to protect their conversation.

"You *do* know something," she whispered. "More than the rest of us. How *did* you know Bigfoot was watching us by the creek?"

Isaac realized that she was right. They had a solid ten second head start before the first roar came. *How did I know it was coming?* he asked himself. *Come on, stupid brain. Just think!*

The rhythmic squeak of the fan overhead felt like his brain playing the same track again and again to no avail. That whole memory was clouded by panic, but there was a moment when it wasn't. The moment when he knew they were in trouble.

"Might I provide a clue of my own?" Mr. Brown offered.

Isaac nodded in response. He was fighting both the fear of being put on the spot by the others *and* reliving the Bigfoot attack, trying to forcibly rewind his mind to the perfect moment.

"You may not be looking for something that exists."

What the heck does that mean? That's not a clue at all, Isaac thought, even more confused than before. Then, the loading screen in his mind instantly turned into the answer he was looking for. *Holy pepperoni pizza!*

"The wildlife!" Isaac exclaimed. Mr. Brown looked upon him, like a proud parent. The other interns looked confused by the response. "Before both attacks, behind the cabin and in the woods, everything went silent."

"Like the birds and cicadas?" Leo asked. His face began to light up, realizing that Isaac was right. When they had spent the night hiding next to the cabin, anything from owls to crickets ceased their respective sounds.

"Birds only stop making noise when there are predators around," Liz explained. "More specifically, other animals that are dangerous to *them*. If it was actually Bigfoot, the birds wouldn't be threatened because—"

"They are not part of his supposed diet. Some say that he is an herbivore. Other sources say that he is a carnivore but eats either large animals, fish, or bugs. They don't say anything about small birds," Leo said, snapping his finger at the realization.

"You know what would cause birds to stop chirping?" Liz said. "A human running through the woods in a giant monkey suit."

"I knew you'd get it," Horace said, winking.

LIZ smiled. It was nice to have a win for once. She was still confident that Howard Price was the culprit, but at least they were gaining some ground and checking off boxes. If Horace needed them to provide solid facts, then that's what they would do.

"But wait," Alura said. "I hate to be Devil's Advocate, but I feel like someone needs to point out that no one *actually* knows what Bigfoot eats, so how can we be sure?"

It would be a fair point, Liz thought. *If Bigfoot really existed.*

"There is something else," Isaac said quietly. It seemed he was debating whether or not to continue. "The footprint."

"The footprint?" Leo asked. "What do you mean?"

"The two footprints were different," Isaac fumbled. "Alura and I saw one on the nature walk, but it was different than at the logging camp."

Liz was intrigued by Isaac's description. She sat closer to the table.

"Different? Different how?" she asked.

"Well," Isaac tried to explain, "The ones at Camp Tolowa were flatter. The ones at the logging camp were more uneven, I guess?"

She unzipped her bag and grabbed a notebook. After scribbling a crude footprint, she slid it over toward Isaac.

"What parts were pushed further in the mud at the logging camp?" she asked. "Do you remember?"

Isaac closed his eyes and rubbed his temples, trying to get the picture to come into view.

"The heel was deeper than the rest of the foot at the logging camp," he recalled, pointing to the part of the diagram.

Well, that's odd, Liz thought. There were two things that Isaac's observation confirmed for the investigation.

"If the footprints don't match up," Leo concluded before Liz could say anything, "then it *can't* be the same culprit for both dreamscapes. Right?"

"Agreed," Liz replied. The others nodded their heads. "But more importantly than that, if Bigfoot was *real,* then the impression *wouldn't* be even all the way around. The footprints must've been made with something large, flat, and stiff. That means the Bigfoot of Camp Tolowa is *fake.*"

The others gasped at the realization.

LEO was relieved that they were making progress, but there was something they were missing.

"What does that mean for the footprints at the logging camp, though?" he asked.

I could be wrong, but it sounds like she just said that Camp Bigfoot isn't real because the footprints aren't as correct as the ones from Logging Bigfoot?

"You're on to something," Horace said, clearing his throat. "I suggest you follow the thread you have and focus on the Camp Tolowa Bigfoot. Keep it up with your goals. They seem to be working!"

"I think our best move right now is to find out as much about Mr. Edwards as we can," Alura agreed.

"That sounds like a fantastic plan," Horace said, tugging his bowtie.

The old detective lifted himself from the chair followed by the interns.

"I think we have at least an hour or so before you should start getting on home," Horace said, twirling his moustache. "If you feel up to it, there's only a little bit more of the campground dreamscape to experience."

The four interns looked at each other. One at a time, starting with Leo, they nodded their heads in agreement. With that, they were off to Camp Tolowa.

 **20**

ISAAC felt like he was getting more comfortable with falling asleep in the small cubicles. Mr. Brown turned on Emit, and he was back in California before he knew it.

It seemed that they were back in the same spot of the simulation, as Isaac remembered the light from the sun slowly fading. The four of them sat around one of the tables, still surrounded by numerous other campers who were inquiring about what had happened with Bigfoot.

One camper in particular was trying to get Isaac's attention.

"If only Edwards hadn't pulled me away," Scotty said, punching the air. "I could've protected you guys. Knocked that monster's socks off."

The group began to fade away after the doors to the activity center squeaked open.

"Excuse me," a small voice could be heard within the overlapping conversations.

"*Move it,* you brats," Rosemary shouted, using her arms to push through the crowd.

A police officer that Isaac didn't recognize was joined by Mr.

Edwards and Rosemary. He wore a large cowboyish hat, similar to the hats that park rangers wear. Isaac assumed that this must be Deputy Aspen. Earlier in the day, he had learned the name from Alura.

With a jingle of keys, the officer took off his hat and knelt down near Isaac and Alura.

"Hey there," Deputy Aspen said with a soothing voice, "do you mind if I talk to you two privately? I understand you've been through a lot in the past hour or so."

Isaac had almost forgotten the feeling of panic and exhaustion he felt before they paused everything to take a breather.

"Sure," Alura said, nodding her head.

The two of them stood up and followed Mr. Edwards, Rosemary, and the police officer. They immediately made a left, turning toward the Edwards Cabin.

"Make yourselves comfortable," Mr. Edwards gestured toward the couch. "Please. I just wanted to apologize for what happened earlier."

"We know it isn't your fault," Alura said empathetically. To Isaac, she almost sounded sorrier than Mr. Edwards did.

They both lowered themselves onto the couch. It was soft but had misshapen cushions. Isaac felt as though he was sliding toward the middle. He did his best to stay contained to his side.

Rosemary and Aspen stood near the front door and Mr. Edwards stood near the entrance to the kitchen. There was a large display cabinet with trinkets scattered on shelves surrounded by glass. The whole setup brought back memories of Isaac and his brother sitting on the couch when they were younger, ready to receive a talking-to from their mom for something they had done.

"So firstly," Deputy Aspen said, clearing his throat, "I just want to ensure the two of you are okay."

They both nodded, confirming that they were alright.

"Good, good," he continued. "Now, you *saw* the creature?"

"Yes," Alura said.

"Can you describe it for me?"

Isaac hesitated for a moment but realized that Deputy Aspen was searching for the same answers they were. *Maybe his investigation can help us with ours?* They both offered the best description they could.

"It was like a big monkey," Alura explained.

"And glowing yellow eyes," Isaac added. "It was hairy with big teeth. And no clothes."

Deputy Aspen pulled out a small notepad from his shirt pocket and uncapped his pen. From what Alura had said, the policeman had seemed skeptical of what Mr. Edwards and Rosemary were saying. Now, though, there were actual witnesses.

"And it chased you through the forest?" Deputy Aspen asked. "How did you get back to the camp?"

"We just followed the pathways," Alura explained. "Isaac remembered the way we came from."

He continued to scribble notes on the small sheet of paper.

There were other questions, like asking them to recount events leading up to the spotting. With each question, Aspen wrote extensively. It seemed that there were more words on the page than either of them had spoken, perhaps theories he had on the subject.

While they were questioned, Isaac couldn't help but notice different things around the room. Near the door they came in through there were pictures hanging on the wall. While there were many of them, one was familiar. The picture they had seen, with the two boys and an older man standing in front of the Camp Tolowa totem poles was framed. It must've been a second copy.

"You two are good to return to the activity center," Aspen said, completing his line of questioning.

"Head over and Rosemary and I will be over shortly with dinner," Mr. Edwards instructed. "We're having a campfire tonight, so save room for marshmallows."

Isaac struggled to get up for a moment, with the lumpy cushions being no help whatsoever. The pair made their way toward the door when Isaac tapped Alura on the shoulder.

She turned, and Isaac gestured for her to open her hand. She obliged, and he dropped the piece of gold that had been hiding in his pocket. They met eyes for a moment, and it seemed like she understood what he was trying to communicate.

ALURA twisted the lump of gold in her hand. Isaac's awareness was refreshing. Just from the look he gave her, Alura could feel that he was uncomfortable bringing up the subject to Mr. Edwards. They both knew that she was the better candidate to do so.

Now, if only Liz and Leo could get on board, maybe we'll be an actual team.

"Hey, Mr. Edwards," Alura said, turning back toward the center of the room.

"Yes?"

"I don't know if it matters," she started innocently, "but we found this in the creek by where we saw Bigfoot. We thought it may be a reason why someone is doing this."

Deputy Aspen leaned forward to take the nugget from her hand. Bringing it closer to his face, he held it between himself and Mr. Edwards. The two men inspected it for a moment.

Looking at each other, they both smiled.

"That would've been an interesting turn," Deputy Aspen said. "I can see the headline now. 'Man dresses up like Bigfoot to steal gold from camp.'"

"Yes," Mr. Edwards grinned.

Are we missing the joke? They had just given them a gold nugget, yet the two men were joking about it being a motive for the crime.

"Kids," Mr. Edwards explained, "unfortunately, this isn't gold. It's pyrite, or Fool's Gold. Here, smell it."

Mr. Edwards took a step forward, placing the rock under their nose. Alura thought it resembled the smell of hard-boiled eggs. Alura was once again surprised by how thorough Emit was at creating dreamscapes.

"It's made of sulfur," Deputy Aspen said. "This area is lousy with it. There's no real gold left out here, I'm afraid."

Dead end. It wasn't the strongest theory they had, but at least it was something to investigate. Now, they were back to the Howard Price theory being at the top of their list. *Liz is so dedicated to it. Maybe she's right and we're just wasting our time?*

Although he hid it well, Alura could feel her disappointment was shared by Isaac. She wondered if she should bring up the box they had found near the creek but decided it wouldn't be a great time to bring it up. *We don't want him to think we're accusing him of anything.*

The pair made their way back to the activity center with no suspects that had a solid means, motive, or opportunity.

There are three time periods and places, but how did they fit together? Why were these the three that Mr. Brown wanted them to investigate? There had to be something that links them all together, but what is it?

ALURA pulled open the screen door to the activity center. The two of them made their way back over to the table where Leo, Liz, and Isabella were sitting.

"Any news?" Leo whispered, trying to keep Isabella out of the conversation.

"Yeah," Isaac said, "Mr. Edwards is a bust."

"The gold wasn't real," Alura elaborated. "There's no motive there. Unless he wanted to shut down his own camp for some other reason."

"So, Howard Price is our top suspect?" Liz asked.

"Right now," Leo admitted, "yeah. But I feel like there's something we're missing. There's got to be something else."

The five of them sat quietly, coloring with crayons. As they waited for dinner, Rosemary came in a few times to grab different campers from their tables. When she returned, they were no longer with her.

"What exactly is happening?" Alura asked, noticing the mass exodus of campers.

"Rosemary is making dinner," Isabella explained. "Camper stew, she calls it."

Leo laughed, but Alura and Isaac were still confused.

"Sorry," Isabella said, smiling softly, "I thought it was funny. Seriously though, a lot of parents are coming to pick up their kids. They're scared, with Bigfoot lurking around and everything."

"Are you staying?" Alura asked.

"Yes," Isabella said, rolling her eyes, "Scotty would chain himself to the cabin before he let our parents take him away. He literally has a countdown to summer every year."

The whole table laughed. Although Isaac had never been that interested in anything, he could very easily imagine Scotty waking up each morning, being disappointed that it wasn't summer yet.

"Do you know who else is staying?" Alura wondered.

"Actually, funny you should ask," Leo said. "While you were gone, we did a little reconnaissance."

"The five of us, Scotty, and that boy Jeremy that was talking to Liz, I think," Isabella said, "That's all."

Maybe it is Howard Price after all. His supposed plan seemed to be working. The camp would have to close in no time.

"And Third," Leo added. "Rosemary said that they were looking after him this summer. So, I guess if the camp is still open, he'll be here too."

Alura glanced over and saw Third, sitting quietly at his own table. His notepad was tilted, the pencil drifting from one side to another. *He must be in so much pain*, she thought, recalling how she felt a few months ago, after her parents had just passed away. Alura just wanted to go over there and speak to him. It was irrelevant to the investigation, though, and she couldn't risk throwing off the dreamscape.

She grounded herself and found the others listening to stories from Isabella. Although she appeared to be the same age as the interns, Isabella reminded Alura of her mother, probably because they were born around the same time. It felt like she was able to speak to one of her mother's friends, lost to history.

Stop, Alura reprimanded herself. *You need to focus. We need to solve this mystery. I need to stay on track for the team.*

As the four interns carefully asked her questions to avoid giving away that they were from a different decade, Mr. Edwards joined them in the activity center with food. He had also made a wardrobe change into a bright yellow shirt with puffy sleeves and a red ascot.

"Hello, everyone!" Mr. Edwards said from the front of the room, "I just wanted to thank you all for being here. I believe this will be our group for the next few days, until we get some new campers."

Isaac looked around, and it appeared that Leo and Isabella were correct. It was only the five of them, Scotty, Jeremy, and Third.

"If you'd all like to grab something to eat, feel free," he instructed. "With everything going on, I just wanted to get the campfire going. If you'd like, come and join us outside. We have enough seating for everyone. We won't be traveling for the campfire tonight. It'll just be right outside."

LEO was less uncomfortable around Liz, but there was still a staleness to their interactions. In other instances of fighting among friends, things had already gone back to normal by now. He appreciated Alura and Horace pushing them to speak to each other, but he couldn't help feeling that their relationship was irreparable.

Regardless, he was going to try his hardest to push through the awkwardness and hoped that Liz would, too. *Imagine if half the baseball team didn't communicate with each other? That's not a team at all.*

"Hey, boys," Mr. Edwards said, calling over Leo and Isaac, "would you be able to roll over the logs that are next to the boys' cabin? They work great for benches. We'll probably only need three of them, there's not many campers left."

He frowned, then went back to placing the stones in a circle around the twigs and grass he had in the middle.

Leo and Isaac followed his instructions, finding the logs exactly where he said they would be. The makeshift seats had some dirt and leaves scattered over the top like a layer of dust. The boys took a moment to brush them off. Each of them took a side and rolled the large logs into the clearing, boxing in the campfire that Mr. Edwards was creating.

As soon as they started placing them, the three girls thanked them and sat down. They were deep in a conversation, leaning in closely to avoid any eavesdropping. The two boys walked back and picked out another log that didn't have too much moss on it.

"Hey," Isaac said.

"Yeah?" Leo said, leaning over to pull out the log.

"What do you think they're talking about?" Isaac asked, pointing toward the three girls who were still huddled on the first log.

Leo looked at the group of girls. Isabella and Alura were sandwiching Liz, who sat uncomfortably in the middle.

"Probably Jeremy," Leo shrugged. He addressed Isaac's look of confusion by explaining the events that happened while they were gone, starting with Jeremy approaching Leo and ending with him pushing him to go find her after Liz ran off. Isaac still looked lost but seemed to accept defeat. "Just girl stuff, bro. You don't want to be a part of that conversation, trust me."

Ever since he had hunkered down next to the cabin with Isaac, staking out Bigfoot for the night, Leo had felt he understood him better. Before he really got to know him, Leo thought Isaac was just a quiet kid because he didn't have much to say. It turned out that Isaac *did* have things to say, he just didn't think they were important enough.

Through his gift of observation, combined with a push to share it, the team had experienced their first solid lead. *Bigfoot is just a dude in a costume.* Leo had a feeling that Horace wouldn't be sending them out here on some crazy mission, but Liz's unwavering denial had backed him into a corner. *Someone* needed to play the other side and point out that Bigfoot could be real.

 **21**

LIZ sat on the log opposite Mr. Edwards and Rosemary. To her left, Scotty, Leo, and Isaac occupied their conifer chairs, and to the right sat Jeremy and Third. The fire crackled and danced in the center and got brighter as the sun disappeared through the base of the trees.

Can we get another log? Liz wondered. *Just a log for one.* After Isabella had shared the story of Jeremy with Alura, the two were relentlessly asking questions. It made Liz feel oddly warm inside, which made her *very* uncomfortable. She would've even preferred to sit with Leo, but his log was full. And she *definitely* wasn't going to jump ship to sit near Jeremy.

"So, campers," Mr. Edwards said, clearing his throat, "we've got some marshmallows here. Grab a stick and start roasting if you're interested. Chocolate and crackers are on the side over here."

Liz rose from the log with the others to grab a marshmallow. *Something else to focus on, thank you!*

"Fun fact, s'mores were actually invented by the Girl Scouts, back in the 1920s," Mr. Edwards narrated as campers grabbed their supplies.

"Back when you were a kid, right?" Scotty suggested.

Liz suspected that Scotty was making a joke but quickly realized that Mr. Edwards was likely born in the early 1900s, based on his age.

"So, I was thinking some campfire songs," Mr. Edwards said, pulling a guitar out from behind his foldable chair. "Everyone in?"

"Boring!" Scotty shouted, rolling his eyes.

There was a muffle to his voice, probably because he had already shoveled in two marshmallows.

"And what were you thinking, Scotty?" Mr. Edwards asked.

"Scary stories!" Scotty replied, hardly giving Mr. Edwards enough time to ask for his input.

Mr. Edwards adjusted his collar, as if he was apprehensive about the suggestion.

"There's a monster terrorizing our camp," Rosemary said with her hands on her hips, "and you want to hear scary stories?"

Scotty nodded his head vehemently, indicating that he would like nothing more.

Liz hadn't even gotten the marshmallow on her stick yet, but Scotty's hands were coated in a mixture of marshmallow, chocolate, and graham cracker pieces. There was also a splatter around his mouth.

"Very well," Mr. Edwards said, giving up, "any stories in particular you'd like to hear, campers?"

Scotty sprung up with his hand in the air, ready to share his opinion. Before he could shout it out, though, there was another idea proposed.

"Can you tell us about Bigfoot, Mr. Edwards?" Alura asked.

"Ah," Mr. Edwards paused, swallowing hard, "I don't know if that would be the best idea. Will you all be able to sleep tonight?"

"It doesn't need to be a story," Liz said. "We just want to know more about it."

All the other campers seemed to be in agreement, except for one sticky-handed boy. While a scary story about a giant grasshopper or a killer worm would've been interesting, it wouldn't have helped them figure out what was going on with Bigfoot.

To prevent his counterattack, Leo gently rolled back on the log, knocking Scotty off balance for a moment.

"I think that's a great idea," Leo said. "Let's do that."

Before Scotty could get reorientated, Mr. Edwards reluctantly agreed to tell the group what he knew about the monkey-like creature.

The camp was quiet for a moment, with only the sound of the crackling fire and the distant chirp of crickets filling the space. Rosemary watched her father closely. Although he had already agreed to share the information he had about Bigfoot, she seemed curious as to what he would say.

"Well," Mr. Edwards started, "I do actually know quite a bit about Bigfoot. Some people call him Sasquatch, which comes from the Halkomelem tribe. Depending on what you believe, there is either one single Bigfoot, or it's a species."

"Like dogs and cats?" Jeremy asked proudly.

"Yes," Mr. Edwards confirmed, "like dogs or cats."

Jeremy looked over and shot Liz a wink. Alura and Isabella must've noticed too, because there was a slight giggle from either side of the log. *This* was why she didn't get involved with boys.

"Anyway," Mr. Edwards continued, rolling up the sleeves on his button-up shirt, "legend has it, they have lived in these woods for hundreds of years, but anyone who has seen one couldn't get any kind of proof. The closest thing to hard evidence we've ever gotten are fuzzy photos and casts of footprints."

Those are probably the casts that Howard Price had his employees make. Liz was still positive that the culprit had to be Howard Price.

"About ten years ago, I was actually part of a Bigfoot hunting group," Mr. Edwards explained. "We did our best to chase after and try to find him, or one of him, depending on what you believe. We did all kinds of interviews, also. Early reports referred to him as a 'wild man' rather than Bigfoot. There are some accounts dating all the way back to the 1800s, which was a *long* time ago."

"Do you believe the legend is real?" Liz asked pointedly.

"Yes," Mr. Edwards said, "and no. I do believe there's something, but I don't think it is what people expect. From what I've seen and heard, he's harmless. He's somewhat of a *protector* of the forest. Even if he doesn't exist physically, I think that the spirit of Bigfoot is something that we can all believe in. Nature working together is beautiful and he is just a character to represent it."

Classic, Liz thought, trying to stop herself from rolling her eyes. *Another yahoo who can't take a solid stance either way.* Like all of her teachers, Liz wanted to show Mr. Edwards her respect, regardless of his opinion of ridiculous theories.

"Was that group where you met Reid?" Leo asked.

"Yes," Mr. Edwards said awkwardly, "unfortunately. He joined the group after I did."

"And your brother? Was he part of it, too?" Leo attempted to steer the conversation.

Liz cringed as Rosemary stood from her chair, the glow from the campfire illuminating her face. Leo was like a surgeon, trying to carefully extract information about Mr. Edwards like the team agreed upon. He may have nicked an artery by going too far. *Let's hope it's not too far gone.*

"That's enough," she commanded, then whispered something inaudible to Mr. Edwards.

The older man stared blankly into the flickering flames. There was complete silence from all the campers. They had seen Rosemary give stern instructions many times, but this one felt slightly less forceful.

Streams of purple smoke leaked from the fire, encircling the group of campers and their counselors. Liz held her breath and made eye contact with Leo, who was doing the same.

ALURA could feel the space around the fire getting hotter. The campers all averted their focus away from Mr. Edwards, but she kept a close eye on his demeanor.

He's pulling up some seriously difficult memories, Alura thought to herself. There was sadness in his eyes that glistened through the flames. There was a big reveal coming.

Alura held her breath as she waited to see if Mr. Edwards would continue.

"No, no," Mr. Edwards said, his voice becoming distorted, "it's alright. You see, the full truth is a little less clear cut, but I'll explain quickly. I think, perhaps, I owe you all an explanation. With everything going on, you deserve that much."

The campfire seemed to shine brighter but illuminated the space around them less. Alura could no longer see the buildings that outlined the area and could just see faint silhouettes of the campers around them, almost as if they were within the limits of a framed photo.

"I'll have to start in the beginning," Mr. Edwards explained. "Years ago, when I was a child, my father built Camp Tolowa. Back then, it was only meant to be for our family. We had our cabin that the three of us would stay in, my father, my mother, and myself."

The voice of Mr. Edwards sounded both further away but also all around them. As he spoke, three basic figures, almost like cave paintings, appeared in the fire. Alura watched as the two taller ones leaned down and hugged the smaller one.

"As I got older," the disembodied voice of Mr. Edwards continued, "my father realized how much I loved nature. The two of us came up to the cabin more often. The grass, the dirt, the fresh air. There was something that could never be replaced. One day, he had an idea."

The lines of the original image morphed together for a moment, and then became a cabin with the two characters, likely Mr. Edwards and his father, standing in front of it. They were animated slightly by the dancing flames.

Alura was pulled from her trance when something touched her arm. She turned to find an excited Liz. Looking past her, it appeared that Isabella was unbothered by the eerie purple smoke around them and the images in the fire.

"What is *happening?*" Alura whispered.

"I think this is a dreamscape *inside* the dreamscape," Liz proposed excitedly. "I thought this might be possible. The machine must have us in some kind of flashback within Mr. Edwards' mind!"

Thought this might be possible? Although shocked by the theory, those words made Alura wonder. *How well does Liz understand Emit?*

"Why not open a summer camp?" Mr. Edwards continued, mimicking his father. "And he did. My father gathered up some of his friends, and they built a bunk cabin. It was so exciting! He let me help where I could, but there was only so much an eight-year-old could do when it came to construction."

Alura wondered if Mr. Edwards did have a brother, and when he'd be showing up in the story. *How had he not come up in the story yet?*

"My father opened up the camp that summer, and there were a dozen kids who had already signed up. We did all sorts of things, like hiking, birdwatching, you name it. Most of the boys stayed for a week or so, but one of my best friends ended up staying the entire summer."

One of the shadows from the log to her right came into view. As it leaned closer, Alura realized it was Scotty, reaching out with a bag of marshmallows. She calmly took it and passed it on to Liz. Alura didn't want to disrupt the sketches that lived in the fire.

"His name was TJ," Mr. Edwards explained, "and, while he wasn't my actual brother, my father and I loved him just as much. At the end of the first summer, no one ever came to pick him up. My father did some digging and found out that he was an orphan from San Francisco. TJ had asked his home if he'd be able to come spend some time outside of the orphanage, and they agreed."

The Golden Gate Bridge, portrayed by the small lines, appeared in the red and yellow flames.

"I don't remember exactly what happened," Mr. Edwards said, "but I remember the feeling I had, thinking about the kind of person I'd be if I had lost my parents. Regardless, my father called the orphanage back and told them to forget sending someone to pick TJ up. He would be staying with us."

His voice broke at the end. Although she couldn't see him, Alura knew that Mr. Edwards was getting worked up recalling old memories. A tear welled up in the corner of her eye. It was such a heartwarming story.

ISAAC turned to Leo when the purple smoke began to rise from the campfire. Neither one of them knew what was going on, but at least they weren't alone.

He listened intently to the story Mr. Edwards had shared about the first summer of Camp Tolowa, his attention captivated by the images in the flames. The adoption of his brother struck Isaac as interesting.

The world must've been such a different place, he thought to himself. *To be able to pick up the phone and say, 'this kid isn't coming back to the orphanage.' No paperwork, no background checks.*

"Anyway," Mr. Edwards continued after a brief pause, "we spent our childhoods growing up together, it was fantastic. We were inseparable, going to school together, playing games together. There were so many times when we would take a trip to the library and each check out a book, then switch and read the other. The two of us were interested in the same things, like fantasy and science."

Isaac could feel a small amount of sadness poisoning his mind for a moment. The two stick figures that lived their childhood in the fire could've easily been him and his brother, years ago. *Inseparable.*

"Years went by, and we both started our families. I married and had a daughter," Mr. Edwards said, "while TJ married and had a son. Unfortunately, they moved several times. While I wanted to keep in contact with him, it wasn't as easy as it is today."

Imagine what Mr. Edwards would think of the Twenty-First Century. Cellphones or even email would be mind blowing.

"We lost touch," he explained, "but it didn't matter. For some reason, I still felt our connection, even though we hadn't talked. I knew that we would always be there for each other, and that was enough. Years go by, though, and suddenly there was a sighting of this wild, hairy creature with enormous feet that had attacked a logging camp, not too far from here, actually."

Leo nudged Isaac. "That must be the Yosemite Logging Camp. From yesterday's dreamscape?"

Isaac nodded in agreement.

"Now," Mr. Edwards admitted, "I'll be honest with you all. This was not the first time that the creature had been spotted, but for some reason, it caused some kind of an explosion of interest in the subject. It became more and more *intriguing*. So, about fifteen or so years ago, I took it upon myself to do my own research. Rosemary had just moved out, and Mrs. Edwards had her own hobbies. I was often left by myself quite frequently."

For the first time, a Bigfoot-shaped creature lumbered into the campfire, blocked slightly by Scotty's skewered marshmallows.

"So, I decided to take advantage of this fascinating new topic that fell right into my lap. As a nature lover myself, I couldn't even imagine discovering a new creature."

The Bigfoot stick figure became an image within a book, studied by a larger, human-shape peering down at it.

"A few years in," he continued, "I really had nothing to show for all my hard work, but that was okay. I was working my job and getting older. It was just something to pass the time. If nothing ever came of it, at least I enjoyed doing it. Then, I discovered that I wasn't the only one who was doing this. There were *hundreds* of explorers and expeditioners out there who had groups dedicated to searching. In fact, there was one nearby, right in the city of Klamath, only a short drive from this camp."

The voice of Mr. Edwards' seemed to direct itself toward

Leo, addressing his earlier question.

LEO had to admit, he was fully panicked that he had ruined the dreamscape when the purple fog had began to form a wall around them. Now, he just sat quietly and listened to the voice of Mr. Edwards.

This is huge, Leo concluded, thinking about their goals set for the dreamscape. *We wanted more information about Mr. Edwards and we're getting his full life story. It's like we're inside his mind.*

Although he was disappointed with the debunk of the gold-in-the-creek theory earlier, it was exciting to have one of their suspects completely open up. They didn't need to pry or calculate their words, like with Rosemary earlier.

"At this point," Mr. Edwards explained, "I met Reid. He was the leader of this small group, only about a dozen or so men who were interested in the topic of Bigfoot. They all had fancy cameras and notebooks filled with information and data."

The lines formed a comical figure with small flies buzzing around him. *That must be Reid,* Leo thought. *I wonder if that's how Mr. Edwards sees him or just how I imagine him?* The Emit thing that set up the dreamscapes was a bigger mystery to Leo than Bigfoot.

"I'm not proud to say," Mr. Edwards explained sheepishly, "that I fell down a sort of *rabbit hole* when I retired. I had so much more time on my hands, I spent a lot more time with the Sasquatch Seekers and met other groups, too. Whether you'd like to call it a coincidence or fate, I came back in contact with my brother, TJ, after almost twenty years. He was leader of a group further north of here, up in Oregon, I think? Regardless, it was funny that we had both taken such an interest in the same thing: *Bigfoot.*"

"Can I have another –" Scotty started.

"Here, take mine," Leo talked over him. He handed the little boy his marshmallow, toasted to perfection over the fire.

Leo felt like he needed to keep this flashback sequence going as long as he can, for the others. They had proven they were able to find things that were important to the investigation, like Liz and the business card, or Alura and Isaac with the box in the woods. *Maybe they've already gotten clues from this conversation,* he hoped.

"However, his group was a little different than the Sasquatch Seekers," he elaborated. "They believed that Bigfoot was violent and needed to be stopped. They headed into the woods often, seeking to hunt it, rather than document it for science. Not only was the group something odd, but it felt like my brother had *changed.*"

A small stick figure, representing a little boy, grew into a tall, dark figure with the flames as Mr. Edwards spoke.

"I quickly learned that he had lost his wife and had picked up some nasty habits. After his son graduated from high school, he walked away from TJ as well, which only made things worse," Mr. Edwards continued, his voice becoming gravelly. "I suppose all the grief filled him with hatred and turned him into someone I didn't recognize."

Mr. Edwards took a deep breath, but Rosemary stepped in for a moment.

"That *moron*, Reid," Rosemary's voice said, filling the interval, "did the same with their group. He convinced everyone that Bigfoot needed to be stopped."

"Yes," Mr. Edwards said, "and before I knew it, I was in the Redwood Forest with a rifle, searching for a legendary creature. Up until that point, all my time and efforts had been harmless. All I wanted to do was see Bigfoot with my own eyes. I thought it would be incredible. But Reid changed the mission to something that was dark and warped. Both my wife and my daughter helped me see that it wasn't what I was meant to do."

The lines that illustrated the story dissipated into the night sky and the purple smoke began to dissolve around them. *I guess that's the end of the story.*

"After that moment," Mr. Edwards explained, "I left Bigfoot behind. I tucked away all my research and decided it best to leave it be. I poured myself into Camp Tolowa and built the extra cabin and activity center a few years ago."

Leo could now see Mr. Edwards and Rosemary, still in the same position as before. He quickly glanced around at the other campers. He met eyes with Alura and Liz, who both confirmed they had witnessed whatever *that* was with a head nod.

"Do you believe that Bigfoot is actually attacking the camp?" Leo asked, trying to keep the conversation from dying out.

"Well, it's tough to say," Mr. Edwards said. "I spent most of my life documenting that he was peaceful; just a creature that lived in the woods and wanted nothing to do with humans. But, as I've said, others believe that he is a ravenous monster that can destroy. I suppose it's all up to what you believe."

ALURA sat quietly throughout the presentation, but followed Leo's lead to keep Mr. Edwards talking. He had just opened up to the campers about so many heart-felt things. It felt like it was a good time to ask about what they had found in the woods.

"Mr. Edwards," Alura said quietly, "when Isaac and I were out in the forest, running from Bigfoot, we found something. Other than that rock."

He put a palm against his cheek and directed his attention toward her.

"It was a small container, like a box," she explained.

He chuckled, seemingly knowing exactly what she was talking about.

"Out by the creek, correct?"

"Yes," Alura confirmed.

"When my father passed away years ago, I placed some of his things in a box and buried it out there, sort of as a memorial," he said. "I've always felt he would want to be close to Camp Tolowa. He loved it so much."

Alura was torn. It was yet another logical explanation that ended one of their threads, but at least she was right about Mr. Edwards. He *was* a good man, and it didn't seem like he was hiding any secrets.

Isaac stood suddenly from the log. He pointed into the tree line, garnering the attention of all campers and adults. It seemed he was trying to say something, but no words came out.

As she turned, Alura saw what had frightened him.

Two bright yellow eyes appeared between the tree trunks.

For a moment, everything went silent. Then, an incredibly

loud roar shook the ground, and all the campers scattered. Just like that, the dreamscape was swallowed up into a puff of purple smoke.

 **22**

Most Bigfoot followers believe that Bigfoot is a species, meaning there are more than one. When referring to a single Bigfoot, many think of the creature that represents conservation in the United States. There is also a split belief that Bigfoot is a vicious carnivore with a bad temper, while others tend to lean toward a docile creature that eats berries and bugs.

LEO said goodbye to the others, then started making his way home. He only lived a few blocks from the detective agency, but it was still a walk. At this time of year, the sun was still up around dinnertime, bouncing off the numerous glass windows of the skyscrapers.

There hadn't been enough time following the Camp Tolowa dreamscape for the group to reconvene and compare notes, so they gathered their things and headed out. Prior to doing so, he watched as Liz and Horace had a conversation about *Inner Dreamscapes*, which were basically flashbacks of the characters who had been written into the record Emit played.

It was incredible to watch the two of them speak about the

device, as Leo had no idea how Emit worked or how Horace was able to create it. He crossed his fingers that the final dreamscape they visited tomorrow might be more fruitful than the two they had already visited.

Checking his phone, Leo discovered that he had a handful of unanswered texts from friends. There had been a number of summer sports camps that started alongside the internship, including basketball, football, and, of course, the one Leo had attended each year for baseball.

> Dude didn't see you at camp today. You sick?

> Missin out on a great year bro

That one came with a group selfie of some of his teammates.

Leo regretted looking at the messages. He wondered if he had made the right decision to ditch the summer camp and join the internship. *It doesn't feel right,* he thought to himself. *How does joining an internship that taught him to be a detective give him more traction for a baseball scholarship than an actual baseball camp?*

The pedestrian signal blinked from the stopped hand to the walking figure and he crossed the street, coming up on his apartment building. His grandma lived on the fourth floor in Apartment 4E, and there wasn't an elevator, unfortunately. Not that it mattered too much. If he left the house, he was guaranteed at least eight sets of stairs for his fitness watch. After climbing the stairs, he fished his keys from his pocket.

"Leo," his grandma's voice came from the kitchen, "is that you, honey?"

"Yeah, Gran," he responded, kicking his shoes off and placing his backpack into the closet behind the door. "Just me."

He made his way further into their apartment and found her making dinner. It smelled delicious and looked like some kind of stir fry with chicken and rice.

"That smells amazing," Leo said, reaching into the pan to grab a chunk of the chicken.

"Yes," Gran responded, smacking his hand away. "Well, set the table and you can have some."

Leo didn't mind living with his Gran. It was all he had ever known. They split up chores, with her doing most of the cooking and cleaning. She didn't move around too well, so she rarely left the apartment. For this reason, Leo made his grocery store run on Saturdays, mostly.

The plates and utensils clinked and clattered as he grabbed them to set the table.

Gran placed a potholder on the table, then brought over the large pan of stir fry. Luckily, she also grabbed a huge serving spoon. Running through different time periods was tiresome work, and he was ready for a feast.

Their apartment was small, so the couch was only a few feet from the dining room table. On Wednesday nights, it also made it possible for them to watch their favorite game show on the television.

It was called Trivia Touchdown. Each team was made up of two members. One had to answer random trivia questions which fueled the other team member in their challenge. Last week, for example, for each trivia question the team got right, they would get one football. Then, the other member of the team had to throw the football through a tire swing. Whichever team got the most balls through the tire won the game.

After finding the remote in between the couch cushions, Leo changed to the right channel. The theme this week was romance movies. For every question correct, the team would be awarded another person on their side of a tug-of-war.

The two of them always joked that they would be the perfect team. Gran rarely got a question wrong, and Leo would be able to handle all the physical challenges.

"How was your day?" Gran asked during the first commercial break.

"Oh," Leo said, swallowing his mouth full of food, "it was good. Nothing crazy, we're still looking at those cold cases that Horace found in his records."

He didn't like lying to her, but the specific instructions were to avoid mentioning specifics to *anyone*. Besides, he wasn't really lying. It was just a vague answer. Gran had been very supportive of his decision to join the internship, even if she didn't really understand what it meant for him.

She nodded her head, then went back to eating. After a moment, the show came back on.

They didn't talk much during the episode, other than Gran calling out every answer and Leo cheering on his weekly favorite team. After it ended, Leo got up from the table and grabbed the dishes, making his way into the kitchen. He rinsed them off and placed them neatly into the dishwasher. While he was taking care of the dishes, Gran put the leftovers into plastic containers, stacking them on the bottom shelf of the fridge.

Gran sat down on the couch, but Leo was feeling especially exhausted. Although he'd technically been sleeping all day, he was completely worn out. It wasn't the same type of sleep.

"Leo," Gran said, putting her feet up on the ottoman, "can I talk to you for a minute?"

Turning around in the hallway, he was nervous about what this conversation could consist of. There were discussions that started with that question and ended with a swift punishment. There were also ones that ended with a thank you for something he had forgotten about. With Gran, there was no way to tell until she started talking.

"Sure, Gran," Leo said, sitting on the arm of the couch. "Everything okay?"

"Yes, yes," she assured him, "everything is great. I just wanted to let you know if you can't make it to the food store this weekend, I can figure out some way to get there. Don't worry yourself if you need to work."

"Oh, no," Leo said, "it's alright. I don't think I'm working this weekend, Gran. And if I do, I'll go before or after. We'll figure something out."

"But if you can't..."

"Don't worry," he said, putting a hand on her shoulder. "We'll be fine."

It was really the least of his worries. Running errands was two hours each week, maximum. Leo wasn't concerned at all.

"It is summer, Leo," Gran said. "I want you to be able to rest, too. And spend some time with your friends. This is the last full summer before you go off to college, you know."

Thank you very much for the reminder, Leo thought sarcastically.

"I don't want you to worry about it," Leo said. He appreciated the sentiment, but it wasn't anything to get worked up about. "Just keep making good food and it'll power me up."

They both laughed as Leo flexed his arms.

"I'd hate to do this to you, Gran," Leo apologized, "but I think I'm going to head off to bed. I'm exhausted and I have to be back at work pretty early tomorrow."

"That's alright," Gran said. "Thank you for watching our show with me. Good night, Leo."

He wished her a good night and shuffled down the hall into his room. Before flopping down on his bed, he pushed the door closed and threw his phone on the bed.

It was a small room, but it had all the necessities. He had a bed, a dresser with a mess of things on top of it, and a desk that he used for homework. To make it his own, there was also a large pile of dirty laundry in the corner. In the closet, his shoes were neatly lined up beneath his shirts. There were also a few posters advertising his favorite sports' teams.

The screen of his phone lit up. It was a message from his friend, Cody. This one was difficult to ignore, both because it was his best friend and the content.

Cody

Bad news dude

Coach says if you can't come to camp this summer then you can't play on the varsity team this year

Leo gripped his phone in anger. He could feel his face get hot as his vision blurred. The room felt like it was spinning. *I'm doing all of this, the internship, so I can play baseball. For the rest of my life. Can the coach even do that?* He sat down on the edge of the bed and took his head in his hands.

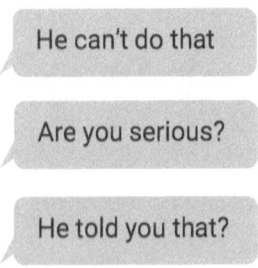

He can't do that

Are you serious?

He told you that?

A couple of minutes, which felt like a century to Leo, passed before Cody sent another message.

Nah dude I'm just playing. He didn't say anything like that

Lighten up

Leo could feel himself calming down, but it felt like the world was packing up all the frustration it could find and mailing it right on his doorstep. The first delivery was when every *single* one of his friends questioned his decision to join the internship, which he was nervous about to begin with.

Then, this crazy old man pulled a sheet off of a gramophone that can somehow take them back in time, and *everyone* else seemed to understand it except for him. Not to mention all the guilt he felt for the way he treated Liz, which was a bond he wasn't sure he would ever be able to rebuild.

Did I make a mistake in accepting the internship? Did Horace make a mistake by offering me a spot? He couldn't help but wonder why the detective, who seemed to have all the answers, picked *him* for the team. Maybe everyone else was right and he was out of his element.

> Haha you're hilarious

> Don't text me again

Leo knew Cody would think he was kidding, but part of him really meant it. He pulled up the menu on his phone and turned to Do Not Disturb.

Although he was tired, Leo knew it was going to be difficult to fall asleep, especially after getting fired up with Cody. He began scrolling through his phone, searching for terms they had found during their investigation into Bigfoot. He located a ton of modern-day photos of Camp Tolowa, which seemed to still be open in California.

His eyelids started to get heavy, until an article caught his attention. Leo shot up in bed. When he clicked on it, a photocopy of an old, worn-out newspaper popped up on his screen.

Summer Camp Tragedy: California Boy, 14, Reported Missing

Everything matched up. The year, the dates, Camp Tolowa, and even the involvement of Bigfoot were noted in the summary of article. The issue was that it was only the front-page article with limited details. Leo continued to search but couldn't find any more information on the supposed kidnapping.

It was a while ago, Leo thought. *Maybe the records were lost?*

After searching for a bit longer, he decided to call it quits. Somehow, this was the only article that referenced this event. He hoped that Horace would be able to shine some light on the subject.

He pulled up the alarm app on his phone and picked the one he was looking for, sliding to activate it. Leo glanced one last time at the messages from his friends, including the one from Cody.

You're going to spend the summer with some nerds in an office over baseball camp?

You should have a backup plan, just in case things don't work out.

Students with a similar grade point average would choose a different college.

The last thought that rounded Leo's mind was a wish that someone, *anyone*, could understand how he was feeling.

Alone.

23

LIZ, Alura, and Isaac sat quietly as the ceiling fan above creaked overhead. Horace had just entered, followed closely by his small gray companion. Alice jumped up onto the table and flopped over in front of Isaac.

The team was waiting on Leo, who still had a few minutes before he was officially late. While it wasn't surprising, Liz found that it didn't bother her quite as much as it did on the first day. With Horace's push for them to respectfully speak to each other yesterday, Liz felt more comfortable both with Leo and the rest of the team. It was difficult to explain, but it felt like she was among friends rather than strangers, or even rivals.

Isaac leaned forward to give the feline a long stroke from head to tail. Alura placed a candy bar down on the table and did the same.

Liz's parents were very strict when it came to pets. She remembered a time when she was younger, and her parents had a saltwater fish tank. The colorful fish used to twist and swirl around. It was more entertaining than TV in Liz's opinion.

"Good morning, all," Horace said as he slowly made his way

to the head of the table.

He held a bright yellow folder in his hand with papers sticking out in every direction. Liz wanted nothing more than to tap them on the table to get them all in a neat row.

"No Leo, yet?" Horace noticed. "No problem, we'll wait a little longer for him. Then, we'll get started."

As if on cue, the door to the conference room slammed open.

"Sorry, guys," Leo apologized. "I set an alarm, but I accidentally did it for 7 o'clock tonight instead of this morning."

"No bother," Horace said. "My understanding is that someone has something they'd like to share?"

Liz mentally recapped the day yesterday, including the inner dreamscape of Mr. Edwards and the final attack of Bigfoot.

"Actually..." Leo started.

"Yeah..." Isaac said at the same time.

The two boys looked at each other and smiled.

LEO wondered if Isaac had stumbled across the same information, or if he had noticed something in the dreamscape. While Leo's information wasn't a homerun itself, maybe their combined knowledge would amount to something.

"You first," Isaac offered.

"You sure? Alright," Leo shrugged. "I came across this article last night. It says that a boy disappeared from Camp Tolowa right after the campfire Bigfoot sighting."

"Ah, yes," Horace said with a smile. He put a finger up, as if he remembered something about it.

Awesome, Leo thought. *If he knows about it, maybe he can give us more information.*

"So?" Alura asked. "Who was it?"

"That's the thing," Leo explained. "This old newspaper is the only reference I can find to it. I don't think it was ever solved. There's *nothing* else. I was hoping that Horace could help us maybe?"

Horace sat up in his chair.

"You want my help?" he asked. "With what, exactly?" The surprised tone of his voice made Leo feel as though he wasn't going to be as helpful as Leo hoped.

"Well," Leo proposed, "if you know about it, can't you tell us more?"

Horace brought his hands to the table and twiddled his fingers. The room was so quiet, Leo could hear Dot striking her keyboard in the lobby. *If Horace isn't willing to help us, how are we going to figure out who was kidnapped? There's no other information.*

"I must admit," Horace said, finally breaking the silence, "I told myself that I would not help you kids under any circumstances. For that reason, I must decline the request."

"But how are we supposed to solve a mystery if we don't have all the parts?" Leo replied, a little more forcefully than he had intended.

How are we supposed to show you that we can do it if you don't give us the proper tools?

"All the information you need," Horace said casually, "is right here in this room. I won't give you a ladder, but I will give you a step stool. Read the headline again, kiddo."

"It says *Summer Camp Tragedy: California Boy, 14, Reported Missing*," Leo recited. Even after rereading it, it didn't give him the identity of the boy who went missing.

"Well," Alura said, "That narrows it down, right?"

Isaac nodded his head. "There's only two campers who fit that description."

Leo felt like an idiot. He had forgotten that most of the campers had gone home before the final campfire. They were right. There were only two kids it could've been.

"Jeremy or Third," Leo said, finishing their thoughts.

"I know it isn't a perfect answer," Horace explained, "but you will very rarely have all the pieces of the puzzle."

ISAAC sat in his chair, pinned by the detective's cat, Alice. He listened as the others talked about possible reasons why Jeremy or Third would've been kidnapped, but there weren't any solid clues that pointed to *why* either of them would've been taken.

Oddly enough, Isaac took some solace in the fact that someone had been taken. *At least there was a reason to be scared.*

After the fruitless discussion came to an end, Leo turned to him.

"Isaac," he said, "what did you want to talk about? Did you find something?"

He was hesitant to share the photos he had found on the internet last night, especially after Leo's clue was only able to provide more questions.

"Uh," Isaac started. "That's alright. It probably isn't

important."

"Come on, bro," Leo said. "You've got to tell us what you found."

Liz is going to hate me for this one, Isaac thought. *I just know it.*

Isaac unzipped his backpack and pulled out a handful of grainy pictures he had printed last night, securely fastened together with a paperclip.

"I had trouble falling asleep last night," Isaac explained. "So, I started looking stuff up. I guess Leo did the same thing. I found these."

He pushed the pile of papers into the middle of the table. Leo, Alura, and Liz all pulled one to look at. The subject of each was the same, with one similarity.

"These just look like pictures of old men," Liz observed.

"Uh, yeah…" Isaac tried to explain.

"Why are they military uniforms?" Leo said, speaking over him.

Isaac looked to Alura, who sat up squarely in her chair.

"Is that…?" she started.

"Yes," Isaac explained. "The one guy in the picture, off to the left in all the copies, is Howard Price."

Isaac shuffled through the remaining papers to find the article he had printed. The other interns continued to study the pictures.

"The thing is," Isaac said uncomfortably, "this is a conference for World War II Veterans in France." He pointed at the article. "Howard Price couldn't have been our Bigfoot because he was out of the country at the same time as the second dream…"

ALURA stared at the photo in her hand. A well of emotions swirled inside her. She was frustrated that Howard Price was ruled out but also impressed that Isaac had been able to find all of this information.

Better make today's dreamscape count.

"How can we *know*, though?" Liz asked with desperation in her voice. Alura knew that she had been clinging to the idea of Howard Price ever since she had heroically grabbed the business card.

"Well, that's the thing…" Isaac continued, only to be cut off.

"Howard Price was the best option we had," Liz argued. "He would make offers on land and then scare away the occupants." She gestured to the whiteboard behind Horace. "See? Means, motive, and opportunity. He even had the *inspiration.*"

Alura looked over Isaac's shoulder to the article he was referencing.

"It says here," Alura paraphrased, "that Howard Price was given an award, the Medal of Courage, for his actions during the war." She slid over the photo of the plaque that came with the honor. "It looks like it even has the date printed on it. It was July 20th, 1972, the same day that we were visiting Camp Tolowa."

Liz stared blankly down at the paper.

"Sorry for the bad news guys," Isaac apologized.

LIZ watched as the checkmark in Howard Price's opportunity box was erased, leaving just a smudge of dry-erase marker. She hadn't realized how dedicated she was to the theory until it had been ruled out.

Now we're stuck with nothing, Liz thought. The others discussed the possibility of Mr. Edwards, Rosemary, and even Deputy Aspen, but there were no clear breakthroughs. It seemed that the closest thing they had to a true suspect was Reid, who *sort of* fit the profile of the perpetrator.

She felt stupid. Liz had expected the answer to be clear and concise, like one of mystery novels she read often. *Maybe real life is messier than a story.*

"So," Horace said as the interns made their way to the cubicles, "the final dreamscape takes place in 2002, in Silver Lake, Washington. There isn't much to discover, I'm afraid. There's only a gas station with a convenience store and a small rest stop where people used to park their campers. Beautiful views, great walking trails. I've actually been back once or twice just to take a lap around the lake."

Liz imagined the old man sitting back in his recliner, enjoying the nature of the forest without having to travel from New York City. *Imagine all the good that this device could do if it was shared with the world*, she thought. *Psychology, entertainment, history.*

When she was younger, Liz always had trouble falling asleep. Even now, her mind would constantly be running with ideas and thoughts about the day. Her mother had helped her with a trick that she still used. Liz began counting down from fifty, letting her eyelids get heavy.

When she opened them, the purple smoke began to dissolve around her. It was similar to the other two dreamscapes they had experienced. There were large trees all around them, although they weren't nearly as large as the Redwood trees they had seen near Camp Tolowa. She stood on the side of a windy one-laned road that was only visible for a short while before disappearing behind a large rock or over a hill in either direction.

Turning around, Liz found a large sign made of wood that had the words *Welcome to Silver Lake* carved into it. Although the sign, the name, and Horace himself had advertised this lake, she had yet to see it.

"Hey," Alura said, waving her arms from the other side of the street. She looked both ways to make sure there weren't any cars coming, then jogged across to where Liz was standing.

"Hey," Liz said. "Have you seen the other two?"

As if on cue, they turned around to the sound of crunching leaves to find Leo and Isaac emerging from trees.

"So," Leo said, rubbing his hands together, "game plan?"

Liz had to admit, she liked that Leo was getting right down to business. It certainly made it easier to shake off the earlier defeat. It almost felt like the time in middle school when she had misread the essay prompt and wrote an entire essay on the wrong subject. With only fifteen minutes left of class, she was able to plan and execute a paper that actually answered the question that was asked.

Crunch time, Liz thought to herself. *Focus. You're starting from scratch but that's alright. There's no time to think. Just do.*

"I mean," Alura shrugged, "it doesn't work in horror

movies, but splitting up seems to work for us. We've been getting a lot of information."

"Yeah," Leo laughed, "a lot of information that we don't know what to do with."

Liz frowned while Isaac and Alura laughed.

We have no leads, Liz thought, *and all our threads have run out. Is it really a time to be making jokes?* Liz knew that her college applications and the internship itself could be collateral damage if the four of them couldn't solve this mystery.

"Want to do me and Isaac," Leo suggested, "you and Liz?"

"Sounds perfect," Alura said.

Isaac nodded in agreement.

Liz appreciated the matchup. Although she was on better terms with Leo, she wasn't sure she could trust herself not to make any kind of unintentional rude or hurtful comments. On the other hand, Alura wasn't her first pick either at the moment. Yesterday, at the campfire before the inner dreamscape, Isabella had brought up that Jeremy had been talking to her. Alura and Isabella tag-teamed Liz into talking about everything. Liz hated the topic, but liked talking about it in a way, which made her hate the situation even more.

Does that mean Isaac would be my top pick? Liz considered. *He's really quiet, which was nice, and doesn't seem easily offended.*

"Alright," Leo said, "one group looks into the rest stop, the other goes to the gas station?"

The four of them nodded in agreement.

"We actually saw the gas station," Leo said. "It's a little way down the road, over the hill. The rest stop is closer if you two want to go to that one, less walking. It should be right down the road behind the rock."

It seemed like splitting up was the best option, since they were in opposite directions. Liz wasn't going to thank him, but she was happy that he offered that they go to the one that was further away. She wasn't sure how much more of this wilderness stuff she could handle.

"Should we do a huddle?" Alura suggested, with a laugh.

"What?" Liz said, looking for clarification.

"You know, when we all reach into the middle and put our hands up as a team," Alura explained. "Like in movies. Am I crazy?"

According to the looks that everyone else was giving her, it appeared so. Suddenly, Isaac leaned in, placing his hand out flat. Then Alura placed her hand over his. Leo laughed, then put his hand on top of hers. Liz groaned, then did the same.

They all shot their hands up in the air, mumbling different things. In the cacophony, Liz heard the words mystery, intern, and Horace's name.

Well, Liz thought. *That was really sad.*

"We'll work on it," Alura promised joyfully.

ALURA reminded herself of what they were looking for. *Meet the people. Find clues about Bigfoot. Keep the dreamscape intact. Look for anything that can connect the three time periods.*

After wishing the others luck, Alura and Liz began walking toward the large rock that cut off visibility to the rest of the roadway. They hadn't seen any cars yet, but they listened mindfully to avoid any accidents.

Alura decided to wear something a little more colorful today. Yesterday, with the combination of gray sweatpants and gray hoodie, she felt more like a prisoner of Camp Tolowa. It seemed that Liz had picked out a new outfit as well, which included hiking boots. Alura hadn't noticed if she'd been wearing them before or if it was an item she had brought into the dreamscape. She wondered if Liz had taken the idea from Isaac, with his Squirrel Scout uniform yesterday.

She hoped that Isaac would be up for another challenge. He had brought her a candy bar earlier that morning because he had broken the rules and asked Horace outright if he believed in the supernatural. In a way, he had taken one for the team, trying to propel their investigation in the right direction, but it felt like a fake win to Alura.

"So," Alura said, drawing out the word, "how was your night?"

"It was alright," Liz paused for a moment, then blurted out, "And how was yours?"

"Oh, you know," Alura said, shrugging, "it was good. Nothing really to report."

Alura could feel Liz bottling something up, and she theorized it was likely the whole Howard Price issue. It could've also had to do with Jeremy. Liz didn't seem like the type of person who was comfortable sharing her feelings, but she was almost excited to talk about Jeremy yesterday, after cutting through the awkwardness.

"Hey," Alura said, "are you alright?"

"I'm fine," Liz offered.

"Okay, that was sad," Alura said with a sympathetic smile.

"You expect me to believe that you're *fine* when you say it like that? Talk to me, what's going on?"

In a way, a conversation with Liz was exhausting. Alura always felt like it was an uphill battle in getting her to talk. *We're a team*, Alura thought. *Teammates are always there for each other.*

Alura watched Liz's facial expressions closely as they walked. She wasn't able to tell if she was trying to figure it out for herself and formulate the words, or if Liz was trying to find a way to exit the conversation entirely.

"It's just," Liz groaned, "this whole Howard Price thing, I guess. I really thought I had the solution, and then Isaac goes and tells us that it couldn't be him."

"You aren't really upset with Isaac, are you?" Alura asked. The last part of her statement almost seemed accusatory, as if it was Isaac's fault. *She does know that Isaac didn't invent an actual time machine and take those photos just to kill her theory, right?*

"Of course not," Liz continued. "I guess I'm just annoyed with the whole thing. We have no other leads to follow. Mr. Edwards seems to be a dead end. That disgusting guy that smells like burnt popcorn in a sweaty sock doesn't seem viable. Not to mention, I have *no idea* who Bigfoot in the first dreamscape is."

She's right, Alura thought. The four of them didn't have much to go on and Horace wanted them to prove that they were able to figure it out for themselves. *We need to stay optimistic, though.*

"Sorry," Liz apologized, "I didn't mean to…"

"Liz," Alura cut her off, "it's alright. You do realize that no one else knows anything more than you do? I promise you that *everyone* is in the same boat. I will personally guarantee that Isaac and Leo are no closer to a solution than we are. Otherwise, we wouldn't be so stuck."

"I know," Liz said, trying to collect her thoughts. "I just wanted to be…"

Liz was a difficult person to read at times, but Alura knew exactly how she was going to finish that sentence. *She's used to being the smartest person in the room.*

"Right?"

"Yes, I guess so," Liz admitted.

"Well, you can still be right, but not without all the facts," Alura offered. "I think we're going to crack this case, but it's going to take all four of us. Just like Horace said, we need to be acting as a team."

"I know, I know," Liz said. "The whole thing just makes me want to scream."

Am I finally cracking Liz? There was a difference between understanding a person and having them open up, and Alura felt like she was on the very edge.

"Then do it," Alura prompted.

"Do what?"

"Scream," she reinforced, "as loud as you possibly can."

Liz hesitated for a moment, then threw back her head. The scream came out like the roar of a lion.

That wasn't Liz, Alura thought. She recognized that sound. *Bigfoot.*

The two girls looked at each other and quickened their pace, heading right toward the gravel parking lot.

 **24**

LIZ tried to step on the grassy patches, which seemed the most promising. Her boots didn't sink into the wet mud quite as much. The moisture of the air fell gently against her face as she walked.

Liz and Alura hurried toward the open lot that must've been the Silver Lake rest stop Horace spoke of. In the parking lot, there was only one RV. A large white box stuck out over the cab, which looked like a box truck.

The pair quickly but casually approached the motor home. There was a loud ruckus coming from the other side, where the door to the living area faced. They popped their heads around the side to find a tall man with rubber overalls and a baseball cap advertising a fish. There was also a folding table and chair.

When the man saw the two of them out of the corner of his eye, he nearly jumped ten feet in the air. He stopped frantically collapsing all the furniture to issue them with a warning.

"You need to get out of here," he instructed. "There's something out there, in these woods, it's a monster."

"Like a bear?" Alura asked innocently.

Liz assumed that Alura was poking the man to see if he'd tell them more before he took off. There was no way that she would've thought the man was describing a bear.

"No," the man said, his face growing dark with fear. "It's *Bigfoot!*"

Great. This guy isn't going to be able to help us, Liz thought. *Just another moron who believes in the supernatural.*

As if whatever he saw could hear him, there was a loud roar somewhere in the bushes, but it sounded far away. He turned back to his task of packing up all his stuff, slammed the door, and ran around to the other side of the camper. After flinging open the driver door, he must've had some amount of clarity wash over him, if only for a moment.

"You girls need a ride?" he offered, realizing that he was about to leave two teenage girls in the woods with some kind of creature that made him nearly wet his pants. *Good thing they're made of rubber, at least.*

"I think we're alright," Alura said calmly.

"Suit yourselves," the man said, throwing it in reverse, then drive, and then the camper flew out of the parking lot. The tires kicked up a lot of the mud and some small stones that made up the lot. Once it cleared, it was only the two of them standing there, not really sure what to do next.

"Well," Alura said, "I was hoping we'd have some people to talk to. What do you think we should do now?"

Liz took a moment to consider the options. There weren't many. The best thing that could've happened was that there were people to interview. Now, there seemed to be one that stood out among the rest.

308

"The roar came from that direction," she suggested, pointing into the tree line.

"Want to go check it out?" Alura confirmed, shrugging.

The two of them nodded in agreement, then made their way across the lot. They found a narrow path that appeared to be beaten down by other hikers who had used it. Soon, they disappeared into the bushes.

ALURA took the lead down the narrow trail with Liz following her footsteps. Her brand-new shoes were covered in mud and she could feel the moisture soaking inside to her socks.

This Emit thing is incredible. She had to remind herself that her shoes weren't *actually* ruined.

Although they were following the sound of the roar, the two girls weren't really sure what they were looking for, not to mention that the loud noise wasn't anywhere close to the rest stop. Regardless, they trekked on. Alura had taken a note from Isaac, trying to remember which way they had come. There was really only one main path, but she was afraid that it might look different if it was backwards.

As they walked, Alura's thoughts fell to Horace. He seemed tired this morning. She couldn't help but wonder if he was disappointed with them. The four handpicked interns were now in the final dreamscape he prepared, and they hardly had anything to show for it.

We're grasping at straws, trying to pin the impersonation on someone we met, Alura thought. She remembered her mother, reminding her to always stay positive. *Just one clue, that's all we need. Something to tie everything else together. We need to solve this to show Horace that we can do it.*

Alura didn't want the internship to end as quickly as it started. For the first time in a long time, she felt like she was working toward something that mattered. Whatever was at the end, whether it be a true sense of purpose or just a feeling of satisfaction, Alura wanted to make it there.

As the two of them walked through the woods, they pushed through thick bushes. There was a mist-like rain starting. It was just enough to get their clothes wet, but not quite enough to be hindering. On the way back, though, she hoped the trail wouldn't be any muddier than it already was. Any wrong step and Alura felt herself beginning to sink.

"Do you think we should head back?" Liz suggested.

"I don't know," Alura shrugged, still pushing forward. "There's got to be something out here, don't you think?"

"Not necessarily," Liz said flatly. "That guy didn't seem too coherent. Maybe there isn't anything out here at all."

Alura felt the urge to meet Liz's negativity with positivity, but she knew better. The tactic wasn't effective with people like Liz. When Alura radiated encouragement, Liz sunk deeper into her pessimism.

She's just in a bad mood, Alura reminded herself. Liz was used to being the smartest person in the room, but Horace's challenge was different than anything they had ever experienced. It wasn't like school, where studying harder means better grades.

It was hard for Alura to watch the frustration, even pain, that Liz experienced by not being able to find a solution to the puzzle. It was like she *needed* to be right, but not in an entitled or annoying way. In the worlds that Emit created, the only way to *win,* so to speak, was by being observant, open-minded, and able to connect the dots. The way that Liz couldn't see past the primary thought in her mind, like the Howard Price theory, seemed to be a major hinderance for her.

"Hey," Alura asked, trying to drum up some small talk. "Do you have an opinion about the disappearance? Any thoughts on whether it was Jeremy or Third who went missing?"

"Not sure," Liz grunted, the squish of her shoes becoming louder with each step. "I wish we knew more, like whether or not they were found."

"I hadn't really thought of that," Alura said. She had been so deep in thinking about who it was to see beyond.

The thought of either of the teenage boys, lost in the woods, left Alura with a hollow feeling in the pit of her stomach. *They must've been so scared.*

Clenching her hand into a fist, she refocused herself and remembered that they all had to be at the top of their game to find clues that could help solve this case. The two girls continued to walk in silence, with only the occasional pinecone crunch under their shoes.

Finally, they caught a glimpse of something that gave them hope. There was a brick wall that came up to their waists running alongside one edge of the pathway they were following. Not only did it widen the path and make it easier to walk, but it meant there was something out there.

They continued to follow it for another minute or so, as it followed the trail's twists and turns. Eventually they discovered a break in the wall, where there was another path, sprouting off from the first. On the other side, the wall continued, making it appear as a gateway of some kind.

"What do you think?" Alura asked.

"I think it's something," Liz said. "I'd vote it's worth checking out."

LIZ made her way up the hill, following closely behind Alura. She tried to keep her footing as the ground became steeper and slipperier with the falling rain.

A small house with a wooden wrap-around porch came into view. It was older and seemed to be in less-than-perfect condition. Shutters hung askew, and the color of the siding had faded with time. There was also a shed off to the left that looked like it was large enough to fit a car inside. A wide gravel path looped the home and led over to the shed in a P shape.

As the two girls reached the flattened area at the top of the hill, they scanned the property to see if anyone was around.

"What should we do?" Liz whispered.

"Well," Alura said, considering the options, "we could either go knock on the door or sneak around and see if we can find something."

"Let's check out the shed," Liz suggested, pointing over to the old wooden structure.

They crouched, then snuck over to the shed. As they approached, Liz noticed the double door on the front was closed and padlocked, which meant they weren't going to get inside to take a look around.

Liz continued around the other side of the shed, where there was a small, dusty window that would allow them to get inside. She snapped her fingers to get Alura's attention.

As Alura approached, Liz attempted to gently open the window, but it was no use. It was a very old structure, so it was possible that the window wasn't meant to open or it had been closed for such a long time that it was stuck.

"Hang on," Alura whispered. She moved in front of Liz, who took a step back. Alura pulled the sleeve of her shirt over her palm and tried to wipe away some of the dust and grime. It appeared that most of it was on the inside of the window, but she had been able to brush away enough that they could now see inside.

The two girls pressed their faces against the glass to see if they could get a look as to what was in the shed. It wasn't a crystal-clear viewing experience, but it appeared to be a workshop of some kind. There were tools hanging on the walls as well as a large wooden workbench against the back wall.

Liz shuddered. The house in the woods and the old workshop reminded her of a horror movie she saw when she was younger.

The sound of a car engine and the crackling of gravel rocks under tires startled her.

"Someone's coming," Liz said, pulling on Alura's sleeve. "We have to hide."

 **25**

ISAAC had given it some thought this morning and decided to go with a t-shirt. There wasn't too much risk involved with it, especially since they were only travelling back about twenty years or so. He knew that fashion choices weren't that much different than modern times.

The two boys walked along the side of the road, following it until they made it to the gas station and convenience store combination that Mr. Brown had spoken of in his summary of what this dreamscape would include.

It wasn't a perilous journey by any means. They walked on the paved shoulder when they could, and in the grassy patch next to it when it disappeared. Isaac noticed that Leo wasn't talking much, maybe because he was tired with everything going on.

Oh no. Is it because of the pictures? Isaac worried silently. Not that he was a professional mind reader by any means, but Isaac felt Leo was especially hard to get a feel for. He was chatty at times but seemed to fall silent in an instant. Neither version bothered Isaac in the slightest. Either way, it meant that *he* didn't have to fill any empty spaces.

Isaac hoped that the photos that ruled out Howard Price weren't driving a wedge between himself and Leo. So far, he felt like the two got along well. Isaac also felt like a unit with Alura but hadn't had the chance to really work with Liz yet, who seemed the most damaged by the thrown away theory.

Sometimes, heroes make sacrifices, Isaac reminded himself. He wasn't risking his life or anything, but he did have to forfeit the exciting competition between himself and Alura and prompt the team to throw out their top suspect. *We need to solve this mystery, and Howard Price wasn't the guy. Right?*

As they quietly followed the route ahead of them, the cloudy weather turned to misty rain around them. The landscape was very similar to what they had witnessed at Camp Tolowa. They were surrounded by uncountable trees, most with diameters that were similar to the largest trees in Central Park.

Isaac remembered back to past summers, when his mother would take him and his brother to the park to play. It was like an oasis of color in the middle of a colorless city. Their trips into the dreamscape reminded him of how bright the world outside the city was, even when it was raining.

After walking a bit further, it looked like there was a neon glow through the trees. By the time they rounded the next bend, the gas station came into view. There was a tall sign that advertised their prices per gallon with a single pump in the center of the paved lot. Isaac recognized the owl logo of the Night Owl Convenience Store, built behind the gas pump.

"I didn't know that they had Night Owl stores this far back in time," Leo said, smiling back at Isaac.

Isaac also smiled, both because Leo didn't seem upset with him and he recognized the store from back in modern day New York City. It was difficult to walk more than a couple blocks without seeing one. The yellow and blue logo seemed to be slightly different, which was neat. It was cool to be able to see what had morphed into the current company's sign. The word *retro* came to mind when he saw it.

ALURA peeked through the window after cleaning it off. On the opposite side, there was assorted fishing equipment hung. When she had first moved in with her aunt and uncle, Uncle Rick had taken her fishing a few times. There were numerous white and red bobbers that had their own shelf in the workshop, which were often used for freshwater fishing.

Maybe this guy spends some time down at Silver Lake fishing? Alura wondered. *I guess we can count that toward our first goal.* The goals the team had set earlier on seemed so much more helpful when they had more dreamscapes to explore. Now, every small, insignificant detail felt like another jab at their investigation.

When the sound of an engine came into earshot, Liz started to pull Alura back toward the side of the shed that wasn't visible from the driveway.

Just as they did, an old, rusty pickup truck pulled up from the other side of the house. Now that it parked on the crunchy gravel, it was clear to Alura that they had approached from *behind* the house.

Hopefully there's an easier way to get back to the main road,

Alura thought. Her shoes were soaked from the mud and rain, and the narrow path was likely muddier than the first time they had traveled it.

A bearded man, probably in his forties or early fifties, got out of the truck and pushed the door closed with a squeak. He was wearing a pair of the rubber overalls just like the man they had seen at the rest stop. The truck bed fell open when he pulled the handle, revealing a large blue cooler with wheels.

Alura and Liz continued to quietly peek from the corner of the shed. They stayed as still as statues to avoid capturing the man's attention. He sat in a rocking chair on the porch to take off his wet overalls, then draped them over the railing, presumably to dry. After a brief skirmish with his keyring, he unlocked the door, brought the cooler inside, and pushed the door closed with his foot.

"Should we leave?" Liz asked. "We can probably go without being seen."

"I don't think we're going to find anything else," Alura said, "but I think he might've been at the lake with the other guy. They were both wearing fishing gear. Maybe Mr. Cabin-in-the-woods has seen something."

"Okay," Liz said cooly, "so we're going to knock on his door then?" Her tone was steady, but Alura could tell she was nervous.

Alura nodded, indicating that they should sneak over closer to the truck, so it didn't appear like they had just come out from hiding behind his shed.

As far as she was concerned, they were still empty-handed. They came for clues, evidence, *anything*. If they had the opportunity to talk to someone who may have seen the attack, they should definitely take it.

The two returned to their normal stature after getting over by the truck, to make it look like they had just walked up the driveway. The gravel crunched under their feet as they made their way toward the front porch. The rain was also starting to pick up a bit.

"Follow my lead," Alura whispered.

As her foot hit the first step, it creaked loudly. Without another sound, the front door to the house swung open, with the bearded man standing there with an angry look on his face. His mouth was hidden under his bushy mustache, but Alura could identify the scowl lying underneath.

"What do ya want?" he said angrily. "Can't read the sign? It says no trespassin'. Now get on out of here."

"Sir," Alura said politely, "we've gotten lost in the woods. It's been hours and we can't find our family."

The man took another look at the girls, and his face seemed to soften. The wrinkles that defined his face faded away as he relaxed.

"Alright," he said, stepping to the side. "Get in here, where it's dry."

"Thank you, thank you," Alura said, bowing as she walked past him into the house.

Going into a stranger's cabin in the middle of the woods? Guess I can check that *off my bucket list.* She felt apprehensive, even if they couldn't be physically harmed in the dreamscape. *It's a necessary risk,* she reminded herself.

"Living room's right here," he directed. "You can have a seat on the couch. I'll get ya some towels to dry off with."

Alura and Liz sat down on the edge of the couch. They both looked at each other but didn't speak. Although the man had gone into the other room, he might still be able to hear them, and they didn't want to give away their cover.

The room was decorated with wood paneling and a fireplace in the corner. On the mantle, there were a few framed photos. Along with the couch, the chair, and a lamp, there weren't any other furniture items. The walls were cluttered with a number of paintings. With the lighting, it was difficult to tell what they depicted, but they looked like landscapes.

They all look like the same style, Alura noticed. *I wonder if they were all painted by the same person.*

The man returned with two bath towels. Around his ankles was a very old golden retriever. The fur around his face was much lighter than the rest of his body.

"Here ya go," he said as he distributed them. They reeked of cigarette smoke and dust, just like the rest of the house.

The dog may have been old, but his tail was wagging. With the initial greeting Alura and Liz received, it was safe to assume they didn't get many visitors. The dog made his way over, sitting between the two of them.

"This is Rusty," the man said with a cough. "He's fragile, so don't pet him too hard."

Alura expected him to at least crack a smile, but it never came. For that reason, she only gave Rusty very gentle strokes from the top of his head all the way down to his tail. His fur was soft and smooth, leading Alura to believe that he was well taken care of.

"Thank you again for helping us," Alura said. "My name is Alura and this is my sister, Liz."

"Never leave a man behind, that's what they say. Name's Theo," he introduced himself. "Say, how did you girls get lost up here, anyhow?"

"Well, it's a long story," Alura started. "We were camping, then we had to stop for gas which I thought was somewhere around here. There was a really loud roar, and everyone scattered."

"Ah," he smiled, "you heard it, too?"

"Yeah," Liz said nonchalantly. "What was that?"

Theo moved a painting and sat down in the recliner across from them, then cleared his throat.

"Well, there's a legend around here, see," he explained, stroking his beard, "the legend of Bigfoot. Apparently, he exists in these woods."

"Have you ever seen him?" Alura asked.

"Nope," Theo replied with a slight twinkle in his eye.

"Even living out here, you've never seen it?"

"Nope," Theo said with a smile, "because it isn't real. It's all just a bunch of malarkey. Met a lot of people in my day that were interested in that sort of thing, but none of them could ever prove either way."

He rose from his chair, asking either of them if they'd like tea. After listing off the different packets he had, Theo disappeared back into the kitchen.

Alura looked over to find a wide-eyed Liz staring her down. At first, Alura thought something might be wrong, but then Liz clarified.

"He knows what he's talking about," she mouthed, referring to him telling them that Bigfoot wasn't real.

Theo came back into the room with a silver tray occupied by three small teacups of varying designs and shapes. From the outside, Alura wouldn't have assumed that there were any teacups in this house. Actually, from the inside, too.

"What was that roar, then?" Liz asked pointedly.

"A bear, perhaps?" Theo suggested. "I'm sure it's nothing to be afraid of."

Concerned that this topic might push Liz to be even more aggressive in her line of questioning, Alura made an executive decision to alter the course of the conversation.

"How long have you lived here?" she asked kindly, sipping her tea.

"Ah," Theo squinted while he thought. "At least thirty years, I suppose. I moved here with my grandfather some time back."

While the man had started off unpleasant and rigid, Theo seemed enjoyable to be around. Through the light of the lamp, Alura could see the corners of his eyes sagged. This, combined with the hint of softness in his hoarse voice, led her to believe that he had been through a lot in his life.

"Does anyone else live around here?" Liz asked.

Alura winced but realized that the question was less hostile than the previous one. *Maybe she realized that she sounded like a police interrogator.*

"Not that I know of," Theo shrugged, "but I'm not sure. Up until a few years ago, mine was the only house. Then, they built that gas station. Guy who owns it lives behind it, I think."

Theo leaned back into his recliner and frowned.

"Don't much like that little dirt lot they call a rest stop, though. This past summer, the road became more travelled after they paved it and people started camping out there," he explained. His words seemed to be muffled by his beard. "More than one occasion, I've found hooligans on my property. Progress, I guess, but I liked being able to keep to myself out here."

The words that came from his mouth seemed unfriendly, but his tone seemed to portray sadness. *I guess there really are people who like to be alone in the woods.*

"Why do you think it's getting busier?" Alura asked.

"I'd ask you the same question," Theo smiled gently. "Your family decided to drive by Silver Lake, I think that gives you reason enough. I suppose it's just a shortcut for most folks, though."

Alura pursed her lips. Mentally, she took note that she had almost blown their cover. *Definitely a question I should've had the answer to.*

"Well," Theo said, rising from his chair once more, "I suppose I should be getting you back to your family. Let me drive you back down to the gas station, and we can see if we can find your family. Sound good?"

No, Alura thought. *There's still so much to talk about!* She didn't want to call it quits yet.

"That sounds fantastic," Liz replied, likely fueled by her desire to avoid walking in mud again.

Alura closed her eyes and took a deep breath. A ride back was certainly better than walking in the rain. She crossed her fingers that Isaac and Leo had found something worthwhile.

322

 **26**

LEO and Isaac made their way across the parking lot. There was a single dented sedan parked on the side of the building, probably to keep parking open for customers who just hadn't arrived yet. So far, they hadn't met, or even *seen*, a single person in this dreamscape.

Hard to investigate when there's nothing out here, Leo thought to himself.

As the boys walked toward the front door, a familiar roar echoed through the trees and into the open area.

"That sounded like it came from the direction Liz and Alura went in," Isaac noted.

Leo paused for a moment. "I'm sure it'll be fine," he reassured. "If something happens, they'll just wake up. It also gives us something to talk about."

He watched as Isaac relaxed his shoulders. He knew that Isaac was in no rush to face Bigfoot again after what happened yesterday.

As they entered the store, a small bell dinged overhead.

"Good afternoon, boys," an older woman behind the

counter greeted them. "You looking for anything in particular today?"

A small name tag was pinned near the pocket on her shirt, identifying her as Betty. She had silvery hair and a small set of glasses that sat on the tip of her nose that reminded Isaac of Mr. Brown. Betty also wore a striped button-up shirt, similar to the vest that Night Owl workers wore back in New York City.

Other than the changes in the marketing posters and colors of the store, it was basically the same as a modern-day convenience store. There was a candy aisle and a bunch of reach in fridges and freezers lining the outside walls. Water bottles, sports drinks, and sodas sat inside, waiting for someone to purchase them.

Based on the number of people they had seen on their way to the store, which had been zero, most of the items in the well-stocked store had to be expired or close to it. Isaac and Leo hadn't even seen a car on the road the entire time they were walking up here.

"No, nothing specific," Leo started, then artfully used the abnormal noise outside to cut to the chase. "We heard this really loud noise outside. Any idea what it was?"

"Oh," Betty said, looking puzzled, "I didn't hear it. What did it sound like?"

Although it was an incredibly loud noise and anyone within a mile would've been able to hear it, Leo believed that she was telling the truth. Just like most convenience stores, there was a rhythmic hum that overpowered most other noises, probably originating from the refrigerators. On top of that, there was music playing over the speakers.

324

"It was like a bear," Leo said, trying to describe it without leading her. "I'm not sure."

She seemed to realize what they were talking about with that brief description, as the baffled look she first displayed melted into a look of disappointment.

"Ah, that kind of noise," Betty said, the corners of her mouth curling into a frown. "It's a long story. It's also the reason we don't have many customers."

"So, it's a bear?" Isaac asked, trying to take Leo's lead.

"No, it isn't a bear I'm afraid," she said, leaning over the counter and beckoning them closer with her pointer finger.

The two boys stepped off the mat in the doorway and made their way over to register. She perched herself over the counter to get even closer.

"It's a legend," she whispered. Betty continued, but Leo could only make out a single word through the mumbled speech.

"Bigfoot?" Leo repeated at full volume.

Suddenly, the curtain that was behind the counter tore open and an older, bald man was standing in the doorway. He scoffed in disdain, then told Betty to wait in the back.

Perfect. Just another screwed up play by Leo the Great. He hoped that the angry man wouldn't be enough to send the dreamscape into a tailspin.

"Betty," he said bitterly, "you've got to stop with this. If you keep telling our customers that Bigfoot is around, we will *never* make any money. Who would want to come to a place if they knew there was a *murderous, ferocious beast* waiting for them?"

Betty looked down, muttering something before making

her way into the back of the store.

"You two," he said, getting closer, "what do you want? Either buy something or get out. Slurpees are two-for-one for a limited time. How did you even get here anyway? Where are your parents?"

Although the full width of the counter and then some stood between himself and the man, Leo could see a large, bulging vein in his forehead that was as red as a tomato. *Can someone's head actually explode from anger?* Leo wondered.

"We walked," Leo said coolly. "We heard a roar in the woods, is that what it was? Bigfoot?"

"Why is *everyone* so interested with this ridiculousness of Bigfoot?" the man shouted. "Buy something or *get out!*"

He came around the counter, using his hands to shoo the two of them toward the door. Leo put his hands up in retreat, and they exited with another ding of the bell. The man waited for the door to close behind them, then stood inches from the glass, waiting for them to walk away.

"What should we do now?" Isaac asked.

"Well, two things," Leo said, holding up corresponding fingers. "One, people know about the Bigfoot legend, and think that he's here in this forest. Two, we aren't going to get any information from that store. The question is: where can we get more information?"

As if on cue, a camper squealed into the parking lot and up to the gas pump. The driver side door swung open, and a thin man almost fell out. He was completely out of breath and wore what appeared to be rubber pants.

Well, Leo thought, *at least one thing has gone right today.*

326

ISAAC watched as the driver of the camper jumped out and quickly made his way to the other side of the vehicle. Completely out of breath and donning rubber pants, he unscrewed the gas cap and placed the nozzle inside.

Isaac and Leo looked on as this man appeared to be having some kind of mental breakdown.

"Hey," Leo said, making his way over to him, "are you alright?"

Isaac followed him, peeking over his shoulder to see if the angry store manager was still standing in the doorway. Luckily, he was not. Otherwise, he might come stomping out and yell at them once more for annoying his customers.

That outfit choice, Silver Lake, fishing, Isaac thought, connecting the dots. The rubber pants started as boots on his feet and made their way all the way up to his shoulders in the form of straps.

"You need to run," he said between short breaths. "It's all true. It's out there. *Bigfoot!*"

"You saw it?" Leo asked calmly. "Where?"

"I was parked in the rest stop down the road here," he said, pointing in the direction that Alura and Liz had headed off. "I was fishing, up at the lake. Then, I saw it across the lake. Glowing yellow eyes. It was *huge!*"

Isaac's stomach churned as the man recalled his recent encounter.

"Is that what that noise was?" Leo continued.

"No, no," the man said, recounting his story, "it didn't even *need* to roar. I was out of there real quick. Left behind my rod and my cooler and *everything!*"

The door behind them let out another ding, signaling that either someone was going in or someone was coming out. Since Isaac hadn't seen anyone pass them, he could only assume it was someone coming out. Silently hoping that it wasn't the man coming out to berate them further, Isaac slowly turned around.

Instead of seeing the angry man charging toward them, it was Betty. She took small but quick strides toward them to avoid getting too wet in the rain.

"Hey there," Betty greeted the man. "Getting gas?"

"Yes," the man said, "I've got to get out of here. I'm filling it up."

"Are you alright?" she asked. "Looks like you've seen a ghost."

The man looked like he was about ready to cry. He leaned back against his camper and slid down the side, his rubber attire squealing until he hit the wet pavement.

"My friend," Betty said, leaning down and patting him on the shoulder, "it's alright. What happened?"

The man buried his face in his hands.

"He saw Bigfoot," Leo offered.

Betty stood up straight, looking shocked. For someone who had mentioned it just minutes before, the topic of Bigfoot seemed to throw her off guard.

"I really shouldn't be talking about this," she said to all of them, then turned toward the two boys. "I apologize for my husband. The sightings have been a detriment to our business.

When we first opened, business was good. Travelers from all over. Then, when that rest stop opened, Bigfoot seemed to come with it. He spooks anyone who takes this route."

"That's okay. We get it," Leo said. "It only started when the rest stop opened?"

"Yes," Betty confirmed.

"That's interesting," Leo replied.

An event that caused Bigfoot to suddenly start showing up? Holy hoagies, that's huge!

While Isaac had to agree with Leo, he was having trouble seeing how it fit into the bigger picture. It didn't make much sense, but an event that caused Bigfoot to suddenly start showing up was a key piece of evidence.

"Is this your father?" Betty asked.

The man shook his head in response to the question directed toward them

"No," he replied, "I've never seen them before in my life."

"Where are your parents, boys?" Betty asked.

Before the cogs in Isaac's brain could start turning to come up with a story, Leo had a fully baked, three-tier story with a beginning, middle, and end.

"We passed this place a few minutes ago," Leo explained. "My dad can't turn around the camper. It's too big for the small roads. He was afraid he might get wedged between a tree or something. So, we offered to walk back and get some snacks."

"As long as you don't talk about *you-know-who*," Betty offered. "You can come back in the store to get out of the rain. It's really starting to come down out here."

She turned to the man who had been slumped against the

side of his camper.

"Why don't you come inside, too," she suggested. "You're going to catch a cold out here."

"I think I should get going," he said, tapping the gas nozzle, then handing Betty a wad of crumpled bills. "Keep the change. Thank you."

Within five seconds, the man was back in his camper and peeling away from the gas pump. The three of them stood there for a moment dumbfounded as the vehicle made its way into the distance and out of sight.

"We'll take you up on that offer," Leo accepted for both of them. "Sorry if we got you in trouble."

"Oh, don't be silly," Betty said with a smile. "My husband's just very stressed out with everything going on."

The three of them made their way back toward the store, using their arms to shield themselves from the rain. Once they made it back inside, their shoes squeaked on the smooth tile floor. The two boys carefully dried their feet on the door mat decorated with the owl.

The curtain once again flung back, but before the man could continue his tirade, his wife cut him off.

"It's raining, and I will not have them walk in the rain," Betty said sternly. "No more Bigfoot talk, I promise."

Without breaking direct eye contact with the two boys, he disappeared as he pulled the red curtain back over the door space.

For the next few minutes, Isaac and Leo walked around the store. They looked at the different drinks and snacks available. The selection was almost identical to the Night Owl stores in

New York, but things were slightly different. Some had different colored packing, while others seemed to have larger portions. They laughed with each other as they held up items on different aisles.

Isaac picked up a Mallow Out candy bar, the one with marshmallow and caramel coated in chocolate, and turned it over in his hand. It was the one Alura had chosen as her prize. He wasn't surprised. It was one of the best out there in Isaac's opinion.

The decision to ask Mr. Brown if he believed in Bigfoot and other legends had been impulsive, but he felt that the detective's answer to the question could be the key to solving the mystery. The answer the team had received was just as cryptic as Bigfoot himself, providing no traction to the investigation. He had been disappointed by both the lack of clarity *and* the end of the competition between himself and Alura. However, they both promised to start another contest as soon as they could.

Isaac felt guilty. He thought about Alura and Liz traveling through the rain, trying to find clues to fill their goals and ultimately solve the mystery, while he and Leo were nice and sheltered in a convenience store, reading the nutritional facts on the back of candy bars and chip bags.

The rain was starting to slow down just as another vehicle pulled into the parking lot. This time, it was a rusty, old pickup truck. It parked in one of the spots in the front of the building. Then the driver and passenger doors opened.

A middle-aged man with a bushy beard and a baseball cap hopped out of the driver side, while two familiar faces exited from the other side.

"Leo," Isaac said, trying to get his attention, "look."

He was looking at one of the shelves but popped back up when Isaac said his name.

With Leo taking the lead, the two of them walked outside to meet up with the girls, hopefully to see what they had found. Isaac had to admit, he probably wouldn't have taken a ride from a bearded man in a beat up pickup truck. Instead, he would've opted to walk in the rain. It wasn't like they were actually getting wet, anyway.

"Hey guys," Alura said. "What's up?"

"Nothing," Leo said, then whispered. "You guys find anything?"

Alura started walking toward the side of the building to get out of earshot. It looked like the driver was going into the convenience store anyway, but it was a good plan, just in case.

"Who is that?" Isaac asked. *And where in the world did you find him?*

"That's Theo," Liz explained. "He lives in a house near the lake. We found it by accident. Supposedly, he and the owners of this convenience store are the only ones who live around here."

They stopped walking for a moment, standing on the side of the building next to the dumpster.

"Do you guys have anything else you want to look into?" Alura asked, pinching her nose. "I think we should get out of here and talk about it somewhere nicer. Like a detective agency, maybe in New York City. With comfy chairs."

"Agreed," Leo said.

With that, Isaac and the others closed their eyes inside the dreamscape, filling their vision with purple fog.

 **27**

LEO woke up feeling good this morning but once he started moving, his energy quickly drained. He could feel himself quickly slipping into autopilot. It wasn't a common feeling for him, and he *hated* every time it took over.

His newfound dedication to getting to work on time had already been thrown off on day two by his alarm mistake this morning. While he impressed himself by only being five minutes late, it still made him feel bad for making the others wait.

Leo was only ever late for his first classes, where he would normally get detention from teachers for the first month or so. After that, they realized that it was more of a punishment for themselves because they had to stay with him after class. After that, most ignored his tardiness until the cycle repeated the following year.

The four interns had reconvened in the conference room after returning from the dreamscape.

"Find anything interesting in that one?" Horace asked.

Nope, Leo thought to himself. He looked at the rest of the

334

team. Alura and Liz stared at the whiteboard in the front of the room, their eyes glazed over. Isaac was sitting quietly with the detective's cat on his lap. The lifeless room portrayed a feeling similar to what Leo was feeling. *Yet another dead end.*

They had visited three separate dreamscapes, scattered throughout a timeline, to solve a mystery no one could. *And we have nothing to show for it.* Leo had hoped that the final dreamscape would be the finale that would tie everything together.

Leo hated feeling pessimistic. He had tried to pull himself out of the funk, but the team just kept hitting foul balls. He was also used to his body being tired, but now his brain felt completely drained as well. Leo hoped that no one else noticed how beat up he felt and that the feeling would just fade with time. He pushed the thoughts out of his mind and tried to focus on what was happening around him. Maybe Isaac had another trick up his sleeve, like noticing the birdcall before each of the attacks.

They could only hope, because there really was no other solution.

"Okay," Alura started, "Isaac, can you write again?"

Isaac nodded and made his way up to the board, grabbing the marker from Horace on the way by.

"We can start," Alura offered, gesturing toward Liz. "We met this frazzled guy who was scared senseless. It looked like he was fishing before he saw Bigfoot across the water."

They went into more detail, explaining that they had found him at the rest stop in a frenzy, trying to get all of his stuff packed up.

"We saw him too," Leo said. "He was getting gas."

"There's also this nice guy named Theo," Liz continued. "He lives up on a hill, somewhere off the main road. He offered to drive us back to meet our family."

"Family?" Horace asked.

It was an understandable confusion. The two of them were probably presented with the same question. *Why are there two random teenagers wandering through the woods?*

"We did the same thing," Isaac said. "Well, Leo did."

"Yeah," Leo said, explaining the situation to Horace. Alura took the time to explain their cover story as well.

While Leo had to admit it was a solid move, he did have some pointers. Alura and Liz had decided to go the *lost* route when they were asked why they were in the woods. It could be a tricky situation, though. *What if the stranger cares enough to help you find your family? Then you're really stuck.*

Leo decided to keep his recommendations to himself for now. He was afraid his exhaustion might make it come out as rude rather than constructive, which was a very fine line.

Alura and Liz continued recounting their story to the end, and then it was Isaac and Leo's turn to go through all their clues. There weren't many, though. They walked to the Night Owl store, which was familiar yet oddly different.

Isaac didn't add anything specific, other than the fact that there were no other customers at the Night Owl. He also chimed in to mention the man's odd choice in overalls, which Alura was able to confirm was proper fishing attire.

They continued a round-table discussion to go over the facts of the past three dreamscapes. The four of them got nowhere, and eventually the conversation just went in circles. The same points and suggestions were brought up time and time again.

Leo checked his watch and could hardly believe they had been at this for *hours*. Actually, it did feel like they had been sitting around the table for a while. He could feel his eyelids growing heavy. As he closed them for a moment, he leaned back in his chair.

"Why don't we break for lunch?" Horace suggested. He had been quiet since they started the deliberations and this was one of the first times he spoke up.

Everyone got up from the table. Leo stretched, putting his hands in a knot and drawing them back over his head. Isaac and Liz sat back down. Liz leaned down and pulled a purple lunchbox from her backpack. Isaac did the same, but it appeared his was packed in a brown bag.

Alura and Leo made their way out of the room and down the hall. Horace had a minifridge in his office, underneath his desk. He had told them if they wanted to bring anything cold for lunch, they could use it.

After Leo grabbed his sandwich that he had slapped together before sprinting to the detective agency, both he and Alura reentered the hallway and began to walk back toward the conference room.

"You go ahead," Leo said, stepping aside for Alura. He knew that he couldn't sit back down in that chair without falling asleep.

"Everything alright?" Alura asked.

A question I wish I had the answer to, Leo thought to himself.

Alura had stopped and waited for a response. He looked into

her bright eyes. It seemed that she genuinely cared about his response.

"Yeah," Leo mumbled, "I think I just need to get some air."

"Mind if I join you?"

I just want to be alone. He knew the feeling well. The stress and frustration of the past few days still simmer inside, turning him into a ticking time bomb. It was just a matter of time before he let his anger out on someone.

On the other hand, Leo hadn't taken the time to get to know Alura. So far, Leo had only partnered up with Liz and Isaac. He had done some research about her before the internship to potentially avoid some of the awkwardness. Leo's initial evaluation of Alura couldn't have been further from the truth, though. After watching some of her videos, he had expected her to be stuck up, bratty, and even oblivious. He had only known her for a few days, but she seemed very kind, caring, and friendly.

"Sure," Leo agreed after a moment of consideration.

The two made their way out to the lobby, where Dot was sitting at her computer. Before she could click out of it, Leo caught a glimpse of her Solitaire game on the screen.

"Hello, guys," she said awkwardly. "Horace letting you out early?"

"No," Alura explained, "we were just going to sit outside for a moment, get some fresh air."

"Ah," Dot said, adjusting her glasses, "enjoy!"

Leo and Alura made their way outside and sat on the bench in silence, chomping away at their sandwiches. On any other day, he would try to fill the air with some kind of small talk.

Anything from new movies to sports to animals. Leo could hold a conversation on pretty much any topic. Today just felt different, though.

Leo could sense that Alura knew something was wrong. Based on what he learned about her over the last few days, he knew that she was inevitably going to try to make him feel better.

"I know we really don't *know* each other," Alura started, "but I feel like something is wrong. You don't seem like yourself."

"Yeah," Leo sighed. "Honestly, there isn't anything wrong. Nothing happened. I just feel completely wiped. You ever feel that way?"

Alura suppressed her laugh into a smirk. She turned away, looking down at her shoes.

"What's so funny?" Leo asked defensively.

"I know exactly what you mean," Alura said. "I've felt that way for the last year of my life. At least since my parents passed away."

Leo didn't realize that her parents had passed. For some reason, though, it made sense. It always seemed like the kindest, most understanding people had some tragedy in their past.

"Sorry," Leo fumbled. "I had no idea."

"It's alright," Alura replied, adjusting the chain on her necklace. They watched as a bus across the street dropped off a few passengers. "It was tough at first, moving in with my aunt and uncle and starting at a new school. Now, it just seems like the little things hurt the most, you know?"

Leo nodded. He did know exactly what she was talking about. His Gran loved him very much, and it was the only thing he had ever known.

"I never really knew my parents. It's always just been me and my Gran," Leo explained. He wasn't really sure *why* but there was one instance he felt he needed to share with Alura. "What you were saying about little things, they're like little poison darts that really hit you hard. There was this one time, in second grade, and it was Career Day at my school. We were told to bring a parent so they could talk about their job."

Leo could feel a tear forming in the corner of his eye.

"No one even said anything mean or upsetting to me," Leo continued, "but I remember looking at that handout and all the other kids talking about their *moms* and *dads* and what they did. I went home and cried. I couldn't even find the courage to tell my Gran. I was afraid it would've torn her apart."

"I think moments like that," Alura placed a hand on his back, "they make us *powerful.*"

Leo felt warm inside. Somehow, a girl that he had just met a few days ago made him feel comfortable enough to open up about something that had happened *ten years* ago.

He *was* proud of the person he had grown up to be, but he had always wondered how different life would've been if they had been around. *They could've come to all my games,* Leo thought. *We could've looked at colleges together.*

Meeting people like Alura always made him feel like he wasn't alone, because there were people in similar situations that came out stronger on the other side.

"Hey," Alura said, "can I ask you something? You don't have

to answer it if you don't want to."

"Anything," Leo replied. He worried for a moment that he would come to regret his response.

"Do you ever think," Alura said, pausing for a moment to collect her thoughts. "Do you ever think that it was all *meant* to happen this way?"

It was a question that occasionally prevented him from sleeping some nights. *If things weren't predestined to be this way, how could anyone be sure they were making the right decision?* Leo thought. *But if things are set in stone, then nothing really matters, right?* It was cruel either way.

"I wasn't sure about this whole internship thing," Leo admitted. "My friends thought I was crazy to do this over baseball camp, but my guidance counselor told me I needed to *diversify my extracurricular activities,* whatever that means."

The two of them laughed as they finished their sandwiches.

"I like to think," Alura said, "that everything in my life, the good and the bad, led me to this moment. All the decisions I've made, and even the things I couldn't control, have put me right here, on this bench. When I get up from this bench, I hope that I will continue to be *exactly* where I am supposed to be."

ALURA thought that maybe saying the words aloud would make her feel like they held more truth, but they tasted bitter. She had hoped her father's wisdom would be able to help Leo with whatever he was battling. It was clear that he was struggling with something beyond the internship.

There was some truth in what she said. Alura *wanted* to

believe that the universe was nudging her in the right direction. To believe that the cosmic power of the universe was trying to provide her with purpose was difficult for Alura, as it had already taken so much away.

She chose to be optimistic. The four of them existed and were chosen by Horace, which had to count for something. Now, they were all together with a clear goal in mind. Alura knew they could do it.

"During our lunch break," Horace proposed, "I came up with an offer for the four of you."

The four interns settled back into their unofficial assigned seats.

"You're stuck," Horace acknowledged. "Any good detective can appreciate that. My offer is that I will answer *one* binary question about the investigation. If I don't know the answer, I will find out."

One question? Alura thought to herself. *That's a gamechanger.*

"*But,*" he continued, "there are two stipulations. The four of you must unanimously agree on the question you are going to ask me *and* I challenge you to find the culprit of both the second and third dreamscapes by tomorrow afternoon. Talk amongst yourselves, kiddos."

Alura wasn't sure if it was the refuel from lunch or the excitement of the proposal, but the other interns seemed to gain a considerable amount of enthusiasm. Even Liz flipped frantically through her notebook.

"Well," Leo started, "I think we should ask who went missing from Camp Tolowa. That's just my opinion." He threw up his hands.

"That's not a *binary* question," Liz snapped. "That has more than two answers."

"We could ask if Jeremy went missing," Alura chimed in. "If the answer is *no*, then we know it must've been Third, right?"

Leo and Isaac nodded, agreeing with the logic.

"I think we should ask if the dreamscapes are connected," Liz said, crossing her arms stubbornly.

"What does that prove?" Leo argued.

"How does knowing who went missing help?" Liz fired back.

Alura tried to think about both questions, but Leo and Liz continued to bicker. It was difficult to have a coherent thought about *anything*.

It's nice that they're finally talking to each other, but this is getting us nowhere.

"There are so many questions we could ask," Isaac whispered to Alura.

"I know," Alura replied, then addressed Leo and Liz. "*Guys.* Can we focus?"

Leo and Liz ceased their squabbling.

"Sorry," Leo said. "How about this? We all write down our best questions on a piece of paper. We'll write them up on the whiteboard and vote."

"That won't work because everyone will just vote for their..." Liz started.

"But you can't vote for your *own*," Leo concluded, speaking over her.

The four nodded in agreement and Horace passed out sheets of copy paper for everyone to use. Even in silence, Alura struggled to come up with a question that would propel the investigation but was finally able to jot something down.

Isaac approached the whiteboard and wrote them as neatly as he could. When he was finished, he took a step back and it read:

Was Jeremy the boy who went missing from Camp Tolowa in the summer of 1972?
Are the dreamscapes connected to one another?
Is Bigfoot in Silver Lake the same person as Camp Tolowa?

And finally, Alura's question:

Was the boy who went missing from Camp Tolowa ever found?

Alura suspected the Silver Lake Bigfoot versus Camp Tolowa Bigfoot question must've been Isaac's as the other two interns had already verbalized their opinions. They had already proven that the first two dreamscapes were not the same culprit but had yet to determine whether or not the Camp Tolowa Bigfoot and Silver Lake Bigfoot were different people.

Isaac returned the pages they wrote their questions out on. Each intern flipped it over and wrote their vote on the back.

"I'll start," Leo said, "I voted for Alura's question. I think knowing whether or not the missing kid was found would be helpful."

"I voted for Isaac's question," Liz declared. Of the three available questions on the board, Isaac's question seemed to be closest to her own.

"I voted for Leo's question," Alura said.

Everyone turned to Isaac, who seemed to be coming to the realization that he had the deciding vote. It was also possible that this whole idea could end in a stalemate, if he were to vote for Liz's question to be asked.

"I voted for Alura's question," Isaac said. "Sorry."

"So, you'd like to ask me whether or not the missing boy was found?" Horace asked. He went around the room and confirmed with each of the interns. When he got to Liz, she sat quietly. "Elizabeth? We need a unanimous decision. Do you agree that this is the question you'd like me to answer?"

The other interns watched Liz. She seemed angry or upset with the decision. *Please just agree,* Alura pleaded. It didn't even matter whether the question helped them at this point. Alura just wanted to avoid another argument.

"Yes," Liz mumbled.

"Well," Horace said, fixing his bowtie, "that's an easy one. I still wish to see *you* four solve this mystery, so I am going to make my answer as brief as possible."

He paused. *If this is for dramatic effect,* Alura thought, *it's working.*

"The boy who went missing from Camp Tolowa in 1972 was never officially found by police."

 **28**

LIZ wanted to feel like Horace's internship was a challenge, but it just felt more like a sick joke. The day felt heavier and heavier with every moment that passed after Isaac pulling the photos from his bag.

Not a single suspect, Liz thought, seething in her own incompetence. *No one has the means, motivation and opportunity. How can I not see the answer to this puzzle?*

The four interns recapped the three dreamscapes for hours, up until lunchtime. Isaac was quiet, Alura had been bringing up clues that had no bearing on the investigation, and Leo continuously asked stupid questions. After Horace had provided the answer to the question they had *all* agreed on asking, he recommended they go home and get some rest.

Liz had cleared the variety of machine parts off her desk that she had been using to tinker with her recycling machine. She sat with her laptop open, scrolling through articles about the most famous Horace Brown cases. Every few minutes, Liz would come across another case that she hadn't heard of, and she had been researching him for hours.

Maybe if I'm able to think like Horace, she had thought earlier, *I'll be able to see an angle that the others can't. Then we'll be able to solve this.*

The part that frustrated her the most was the so-called offer that Horace had dangled in front of them earlier. The old detective had made it seem like he was doing them a true favor by answering a question for them, but there was no *single* question that they could ask that would provide any kind of insight.

Liz groaned and got up from her desk. She flopped down on her bed, which was neatly made and pushed to one side of the room with her dresser to make more space for her assorted parts. It looked like a mess, but everything was organized.

She pulled the notebook out from under her pillow and uncapped the pen on her nightstand, flipping to the last page she had visited the night before.

The greatest mystery, as far as Liz was concerned, was the Emit device.

Horace Brown is a genius, she admitted, *but he doesn't seem like a inventor kind of genius.*

The night prior, Liz had been stuck on a very basic question before she had drifted off to sleep. *Does the disc power the machine, or does the machine power the disc?* She understood that the gramophone effectively *played* the music, but how does that music create a dreamscape?

This was the kind of machine that won awards and could change lives. However, she had to keep her own promise and was unable to discuss the machine with the scientific community. For curiosity's sake, she just wanted to understand how the machine worked.

Tonight though, she laid on her bed, her thoughts were a pinball being bounced between the Bigfoot mystery and the device. As much as she knew that letting it consume her would only lead to overthinking, there wasn't much else to do.

Her parents were out of town again, and her younger siblings were with the babysitter downstairs. Liz was expected to take care of herself and help out with them while her mother and father were at some conference across the globe. However, the babysitter had assured her that he had it well within hand and would call her if she needed anything.

They were all fairly low maintenance, anyway. Junior enjoyed his building blocks while Kelly and Emily played with dolls in their room. If this internship went sideways and Liz needed to go into babysitting, she hoped that her charges would be as easygoing as her brother and sisters.

Her phone vibrated in her pocket. When she pulled it out, she saw that she had been added to a new group chat, title *Horace's Heroes.* It included Alura and two other numbers she didn't have saved in her phone. However, she could easily guess who they belonged to.

Alura P.

> Hey, anyone want to get together tonight? I hate the way we left things this afternoon

Liz glanced at the time bannered at the top of her screen. It was almost seven o'clock.

> Where at?

Alura P.

Can't get in contact with
Horace so we can't use
the office I guess

(917)-555-6970
I'll be there. Just let
me know where

She tried to rack her brain, thinking of a quiet place they could meet to discuss the case. She would invite them to her house, but she wasn't comfortable having people over. All the libraries were closed now.

(646)-555-2224
I know just the place 😊

A moment later, an address popped up on Liz's screen. She grabbed her keys from the nightstand and pulled the door closed behind her.

ALURA got home and immediately started thinking about the investigation. She wasn't able to shake the feeling that they were missing something.

Now, she stood with Liz and Isaac outside a pizza parlor that looked like it was getting ready to close, waiting for Leo to arrive. The summer air was warm and calm, even as the sun was disappearing between the buildings.

"Where is he?" Liz asked, "I thought this place was *his* idea."

"It was." Leo voice came from the alley between the restaurant and the apartment building next door. "Uncle

Basil's. Best pizza in town, of course."

"You live here?" Alura asked.

Leo turned to face the building. "Yeah, up on the fourth floor."

Alura smiled. *Even when the meetup is the building next door, he's still the last one to arrive.*

Isaac pulled the door to the pizza place open, and everyone shuffled inside. There were booths on the right side and brick ovens on the left, separated by a glass counter.

"Sorry kids," the man behind the counter said in a heavy Italian accent. "I was just closing up, stop by tomorrow."

"Hey, Uncle Basil," Leo greeted.

"Leo!" the man exclaimed. "I miss you this summer, where have you been?"

"I've got a different job," Leo explained, rubbing the back of his head timidly. "I've been working with the detective across town."

Based on his expression, Uncle Basil was impressed. It seemed he even knew *which* detective that Leo was talking about. Maybe he had heard about the internship. It was in newspapers and even on television for a brief time.

"Wow," Uncle Basil said. "Congratulations, my friend. You deserve it."

He reached under the counter and threw Leo a silver key.

"Stay as long as you like," he explained. "You know the drill. Lock up when you're done. And make sure you take the pizza from the bottom shelf. It goes bad first. Make sure you take a slice home for Gran, will you? I haven't seen her in a while."

"I would," Leo said, "but she doesn't like frozen pizza, bro."

"Fro – *Frozen?*" Uncle Basil said, holding his heart. "You offend me, Leo."

Leo smirked and gave him an audible slap on the back.

"I'm just kidding," Leo said. "Best pizza in town. No contest."

With that, the man hung up his apron and grabbed his sweatshirt from the hook in the corner, then disappeared into the back of the restaurant.

The group decided on a booth that was against the back wall, hoping that no one would see them from the street and think the store was open.

"So," Alura started. "There's something I was thinking about. Something that Theo said to me and Liz in the third dreamscape. I wanted to see what you guys think?"

"Hit me," Leo said. He was behind the counter, watching his slice of pizza spin in the microwave. "I mean us. Hit us. With the theory, I mean."

"Theo didn't really like the fact that there were campers in the woods," Alura explained. "Right Liz?"

"That's true," Liz built upon it. "He was also pretty reassuring that there was no Bigfoot in the woods."

After offering the others pizza, Leo hopped over the counter and joined the booth, sliding in next to Isaac.

"That's motivation," Leo said, chewing with his mouth open. Crumbs fell from his mouth onto the table.

"Can you not do that?" Liz asked politely. "It's kind of disgusting."

"*Sorry,*" Leo replied. "Just hungry. It does taste like it's a few days old though."

Liz rolled her eyes at Leo's obliviousness. *I don't think she was talking about the pizza itself,* Alura noted.

"So, building a case for Theo as Bigfoot," Alura said. "*Go!*"

"With what you two just said about him, it's pretty obvious," Isaac concluded.

The other interns looked at him.

"Well," he continued, "it's hard to say I guess for sure. With opportunity, you said he was just getting home after you heard the roar, right?"

"Correct," Liz said. "That checks that box." She gestured into the air metaphorically.

"Betty, the cashier at the Night Owl," Leo contributed, "very nice lady, by the way. She said that the attacks didn't start until after the campground started. That goes towards motivation, right?"

Now we're getting somewhere, Alura thought excitedly. The booth was silent for a moment while all the interns thought of other clues they could put forth toward Theo being Bigfoot in their final dreamscape.

"Now that we're talking about it," Isaac suggested, "what about the cooler?"

"What cooler?" Leo asked.

"Alura and Liz said something about Theo bringing in a cooler," Isaac said. Alura agreed, quickly repeating the part of their encounter when Theo was unloading a cooler and bringing it into his house. "Leo, remember what the guy at the gas pump said?"

Leo scratched his head in confusion, then happily took another bite of his pepperoni pizza.

"The camper guy, with the rubber pants," Isaac recalled, "he said that he had to leave all of his stuff behind. I can't remember everything he said, but he did say that when he ran, his cooler was still at the scene of the crime."

"That sounds like the nail in the coffin," Alura concluded. "Doesn't it?"

"We'll have to do some digging," Liz said, stroking her chin. "To confirm everything, I mean."

LEO leaned over the counter at Isaac's request, grabbing him a notepad they used to write down large orders. He used the pen to scribble the conclusions they had just come to, including all of the evidence.

Did we just solve part of the mystery? Leo felt invigorated.

"Awesome," Leo said. "One down, two to go."

Liz cleared her throat. "Yes, but we still have to confirm the Theo theory don't forget."

With the thrown away Howard Price idea, Leo suspected that she didn't want to get too attached to another idea, even if it was as rock solid as it was going to get.

"Why don't we try to work on the second dreamscape now?" Alura suggested. "Camp Tolowa?"

It felt like someone had turned on a vacuum and sucked all of the excitement from the room. Leo sat in silence, hoping someone would start and they'd be able to bounce off each other again.

"I guess I can start," Alura said. "I was thinking about that question we were able to ask today."

The one that revealed that the missing kid, Third or Jeremy, was never found, Leo remembered.

"It got me thinking. How, or *why* were the police never able to find him?"

"Bigfoot could've dragged him into the woods," Isaac suggested.

"That's what I was thinking!" Alura said, a little too excitedly.

ISAAC sat in horror as a dark joke he made was suggested to be a reality.

Bigfoot dragged a kid into the woods? Isaac wondered. *Maybe Earth wasn't the place for me anymore. Are they still taking volunteers for colonizers of Mars?*

"Well, sort of," Alura expanded. "If the Bigfoot of Camp Tolowa wasn't a real person, which we can all agree upon, what if he was looking to *kidnap* one of the campers? That would be a motive, right?"

"Yes," Leo said skeptically, "but that would mean someone would want to kidnap Third or Jeremy, right? Those are the only two options."

Wait a minute...

"Correct," Liz confirmed. "Strictly speaking of motive for the time being, we would need to find someone who had a reason to take a camper. Why would someone want to steal a camper? What would that really accomplish?"

It doesn't have to be a kidnapping.

"What if he wasn't taken?" Isaac blurted out. The other

interns were pulled from their deep thoughts.

"I think that's what we're focusing on right now, bro," Leo said. "Can we stick to one thing at a time? I'm on the edge of the Confusion Canyon here."

"No, no," Isaac clarified. "Along the same lines as what Alura is saying. Except he isn't *taken,* the camper goes *willingly.*"

"Okay, I'm hearing you," Alura said. "Keep going."

"The birdcalls," Isaac started.

"The ones that stopped when Bigfoot was around?" Leo asked.

"No, but yes," Isaac said. He was faced with looks of confusion.

Come on, stupid brain, he thought. *Just put the words together. You can do it.*

"I thought I was imagining it or Emit had made a mistake, but Mr. Edwards said that the Golden-crowned Kinglet only sang its song in the morning," Isaac explained. "That birdsong happened *right before* the overnight attack and the one at the campfire. Almost like a signal."

LIZ had first thought that the theory they were discussing was completely circumstantial. It felt like the other interns were trying to cram puzzle pieces in places that didn't belong to create a picture that didn't exist until a clue flashed in her mind.

What did Jeremy say, she thought, trying to remember. Liz had written it off as unimportant at the time because Howard Price seemed like the only candidate with means, motive, and opportunity. There was something in the private conversation she shared with Jeremy that was trying to surface.

"Hang on," Liz said, holding up a hand. "*If* everything that has been proposed so far is true, then Third would be the one who was kidnapped."

Leo rubbed his hands together. "Now we're getting somewhere!" He hopped over the counter again and started heating up another slice of pizza.

"Can you stop eating?" Liz groaned. "This is serious."

"Come back," Alura said. "Why would it be Third?"

"I hadn't really thought about it until right now," Liz explained, "but Jeremy said that Third was waiting out on the porch the night that Bigfoot came up behind the boys' cabin."

Isaac snapped his finger, then started to recall what happened in those moments prior to the attack. "First, the crickets and the owls stopped. Then the Golden-crowned Kinglet. After that, the back door to the cabin *did* open before we saw the yellow eyes in the trees."

LEO tried to follow their logic as best he could, but there seemed to be quite a few moving pieces to the theory. The foundation of a kidnapping or runaway situation was clear, but the evidence they were using to back it up made him feel lost. He listened to the others as his pizza heated up in the microwave with a low hum.

"If it's Third," Alura said, "we need to think about him specifically. Who would Third want to go with?"

The booth looked to Leo, who was standing behind the

counter.

"I told you everything I figured out," Leo said, putting up his hands in surrender. "Third lost his parents and Rosemary and Edwards took him in for the summer."

"What do we know about Third?" Isaac asked, flipping to a clean page in the small notebook. He jotted down basic information, like a physical description and his age.

"You said his nickname came from his mother, right?" Liz asked Leo, who nodded in response. "My mother started calling my brother *junior* because he has the same name as my father. Is it possible that Third could be a nickname like that?"

"Like *something* the third?" Alura clarified.

"Yes," Liz confirmed. "Exactly like that."

The sound of distant honks and cars driving by filled the air of the restaurant while the interns were deep in thought. Leo racked his brain, trying to think of anything that he could contribute to this idea the others were working on.

I wish I would've paid more attention, Leo thought. *There's nothing that I remember that could help us here.* There was only one thing that wasn't on the list that popped into his mind.

"He likes drawing," Leo offered.

"Great," Liz said sarcastically. "We have something for the letter D in his acrostic poem."

ALURA tried to focus as Leo and Liz started arguing again. Their voices seemed to melt into the background as she closed her eyes and took a deep breath.

The dreamscapes are *connected,* Alura realized.

"Third likes to draw," she whispered to herself. "*Guys!*"

The pair paused their bickering and turned to her.

"You know who else liked art?" Alura asked, looking toward Liz. She could picture the dusty wallpaper, covered by dozens of framed paintings.

"I don't know," Liz admitted. "Who?"

Alura couldn't help but pull a Horace Brown and pause for dramatic effect.

"*Theo.*"

The silence that filled the room this time was different. It wasn't laced with cold frustration, but warm revelations.

"Bro," Leo's jaw dropped.

"It would make sense," Liz said. "He would be the correct age. He also said that he lived with his *grandfather.*"

A rush of emotions came over Alura. The four of them had gone most of the morning and part of the afternoon bouncing ideas off each other, and now they had a surplus of clues to build their investigation to its end.

"Okay," Leo said, "but who is Third's grandfather? Or Theo I guess, whatever he prefers."

"There's someone we hadn't met in the dreamscape," Alura explained, putting the pieces together as she spoke. "Mr. Edwards' brother, TJ."

"TJ could be short for Theodore," Liz shrugged. "But why would his grandfather want to kidnap him?"

"Rosemary told me that Third had been taken in by another family member and it hadn't worked out," Leo recalled. "Maybe it wasn't *his* choice. Maybe the person he ended up with wasn't who he wanted to be with."

Alura felt they were so close to completely solving this mystery. It felt like she was around the table with her mother again, holding off on the final chapter to see if they could solve the mystery before the story ended. *Just a little further. We need to keep working together as a team.* She couldn't let the silence defeat them. Alura desperately tried to find where the thread was headed.

"It wasn't," Isaac piped up. "It wasn't Third's choice or his grandfather's."

"What do you mean?" Leo asked.

"Using birdcalls as a signal," Isaac started. "Does that remind you of anyone?"

Alura tried to think of everyone they had met, and even the people they had only heard about, like TJ.

"We *did* meet TJ," Isaac said. "The birdwatcher from the logging camp. Remember?"

"Dude," Leo said, grabbing Isaac and shaking him. "This is absolutely *blowing my mind right now.*"

Alura thought back to the first dreamscape, where they had met the man who was saddened by his family situation. She remembered the words that carried so much grief.

We speak sometimes but his wife, my daughter-in-law, doesn't like me very much, Theodore Sanders had said. *Last time we talked, he told me I was going to be a grandfather.*

"So, just to recap," Liz said. "Theodore Sanders was outcasted by his own family. He said so himself in 1958 and his adopted brother, Mr. Edwards, said so again at the campfire."

"Yes," Isaac confirmed. "After Third's parents passed, his grandfather took him in."

"*Except,*" Leo said, "it didn't work out. But the question is *why* wouldn't it have worked out? Sanders was willing to dress up as Bigfoot and Third went with him willingly, right? You said they lived in the woods together."

Alura frowned. It was a concept that she had become close with in the past twelve months. When her parents passed away, she was thrust into this strange new world where the courts decided who would receive custody. There wasn't really much of an option, and ultimately she went to live with her Aunt Kate and Uncle Rick who were happy to have her.

LEO watched as Alura attempted to fight off her emotions. She was trying to share something with the team that would answer the final question of how everything fit together.

"It's tricky," Alura explained, biting her lower lip. "After you lose your parents, they take a look at the entire situation. The courts look at the family you have left and if they'll be able to take care of you."

Leo watched as Alura struggled through the conversation. He thumbed through his mind, trying to find a way to complete the thought so she didn't have to relive the pain of losing her parents. *I can't even imagine having my life torn away from me like that.*

"In the first dreamscape, Sanders told us that his daughter-in-law didn't like him very much, remember?" Alura asked.

"You think that it could've stopped him from getting custody of Third, even though he was the closest family he had left?" Leo proposed.

"Yes," Liz confirmed. "If there had been a formal will or something similar. Even if Third's parents had made it known that they didn't like Theodore Sanders to a friend or neighbor, that would be considered in a cookie-cutter custody case. Or they could've asked Mr. Edwards at some point to take in Third, if something were to ever happen to them. There are a lot of variables."

Leo studied Alura's face from the corner of his eye. She seemed to be alright but had grown quiet.

"Alright," Leo said. "So, Sanders and Third want to be together, but there's only one way for them to do it. They both have to disappear, so they move to a remote cabin in the woods up in Washington state?"

"Precisely," Liz said, nodding in agreement.

"So, we have an answer for the second and third dreamscape," Isaac analyzed. "What about the first one, though?"

That's a good point, Leo thought. *It couldn't have been Sanders. Any one of our suspects seems like a stretch.*

"Well," Alura said, "Horace said to only worry about the second and third dreamscape for now, right? Let's see what he says about our theory."

LIZ held back a smile. The theory they had come up with was far-fetched and included so many obscure details from the dreamscape.

But how can everything fit so perfectly, Liz thought, *if it isn't the solution?*

She silently hoped the interns had figured it out, but there was only one way to know for sure.

Leo's phone sat on the table in front of them. Liz could see Horace's distorted phone number through the cracked screen. It hummed as it tried to connect with the detective.

"Hello?" Horace's voice came through after a moment of rustling.

"Hey, Horace," Leo started. "It's Leo."

"*Who?*"

While Leo had been stuffing his face with pizza all night, this time it was Horace's hearing to blame.

"Leo," he repeated. "One of the interns you hired?"

"Oh," Horace said excitedly, "*Leo!* How's it going kiddo?"

"Pretty good!" Leo said. "I'm here with Liz, Alura, and Isaac. We think we have a solution to the Bigfoot mystery."

One at a time, they each chimed in to share specific details of the case. Starting from the beginning, each of the interns built the story in chronological order, like a perfectly arranged orchestra.

"So," Leo concluded, "what do you think?"

The phone sat silently on the table. *Did Horace fall asleep? Just tell us if it's the right answer!*

"I knew you'd get it," Horace's voice congratulated them warmly.

 **29**

ALURA was tired from a difficult night's sleep. She headed home after meeting up with the others at Uncle Basil's, replied to some of her messages on ShutterSwift, then fell asleep immediately afterwards.

Some nights, she had a difficult time staying asleep. On occasion, nightmares invaded her mind and filled her with feelings of dread, sadness, and even anger. More frequently than that, though, she was awoken by dreams that *challenged* her. In these dreams, there was always some kind of never-ending mission that Alura was tasked to complete, ranging from finding her favorite makeup brush all the way to saving her Uncle Rick, who was dangling over an active volcano.

My mind really knows how to mess with me, Alura realized. The dreams had really ramped up when her parents had passed away but had mellowed out since. *Or maybe I'm just getting used to them?*

After an hour or so, Alura pulled together enough energy to get out of bed. She ventured downstairs to get something for breakfast after hearing her aunt and uncle moving around the house.

"Morning, Alura," Uncle Rick said with a sour face. It was nothing personal, he was just the furthest thing from a morning person someone could be.

"Morning, Uncle Rick."

"How's it going? Solve any mysteries lately?" He held a bowl of cereal in one hand and adjusted his bathrobe with the other.

"We did actually, yeah," Alura replied with a slight smile.

For the first time in the conversation, Uncle Rick made direct eye contact with Alura, rather than staring blankly at the wall behind her.

"You don't seem very happy about it," he commented.

"Just a rough night, I guess." Sometimes it was difficult to hide how she was really feeling. It must've been pretty obvious if Uncle Rick noticed. Not to mention, it was before sunrise.

"Hey, kid," he said sympathetically, "if you're feeling down in the dumps, I can get your Aunt Kate. I'm not really good with the feelings stuff. Hang on…" He turned toward the stairs and inhaled, ready to send out an SOS.

"Thanks, Uncle Rick," she said, stopping him from releasing his summons, "but I'm fine. Really."

He shrugged and started heading for his favorite recliner. Alura made her way back to her room upstairs. She tried to push the dream and the feelings it had brought up out of her mind.

I should be happy about the Bigfoot mystery, she told herself. The four interns had finally banded together and solved their first case as detectives. Just as Horace had promised, they *did* have all the information they needed.

As individuals, they needed to share the clues they had collected. As a team, they were able to put all the information in order so it fit properly.

While the rough night still plagued her mind, she was excited to see what the internship had in store for them next.

ALURA had been itching to get back to work but was quickly disappointed when she received a text from Horace.

Horace Brown

Forgot brake fest plans this morning, please come 2 office late @ noon. Thank

The message had come in about an hour before she had to leave to make it there on time, but now Alura had hours before she had to depart. She sat on her bed, thinking about what she wanted to do. She brushed off multiple ideas, including going through her closet and recording a new video. Instead, she pulled a sketchpad from the bottom drawer of her dresser and a pencil from her desk.

Alura had always loved art. She used to draw and paint sometimes, especially when she was feeling inspired. It had been some time since her inspiration had visited, though.

She used her pencil to draw some mismatched lines. The scratch of the tip gliding across the page felt freeing, even though the picture had yet to be developed into anything recognizable. Her thoughts stuck to a specific part of their investigation.

Theo ended up with his grandfather, she thought, *even though his parents didn't want him to. The two of them were all alone. Theodore Sanders poured himself into his research, sometimes going further than he should.* Alura wondered if Theodore Sanders had ever met Third before his parents passed away, or if that moment was the first time.

There were certain things that people couldn't understand through no fault of their own. For anyone who hadn't experienced loss, the caliber of loneliness could not be explained. For Alura, that feeling could fill a hundred swimming pools.

She couldn't help but notice that when they met Theo in 2002, that feeling didn't seem to have a hold on him. He lived by himself in the woods, but he wasn't bitter or sad.

How was he able to move past all the pain? she wondered.

An idea began to come into focus, like a polaroid picture. She remembered that Theo wasn't a fictional character and could still be alive. A quick search on her phone brought up the only phone number of Theodore Sanders in Silver Lake, Washington. Impulsively, Alura typed the ten digits into the keypad.

Her brain began to play tennis with her thoughts.

Is this a moment of weakness, she asked herself, *or a moment of strength?* It was difficult to believe that those two seemingly opposite sentiments could be the only two options.

She placed her phone face down on the bed beside her and drew a deep breath. In one swift motion, she grabbed the device and hit the send button.

Buzzzzzz.

I should hang up.

Buzzzzzzz.

What was I thinking?

Buzzzzzzz.

Alura started to take the phone away from her ear when a voice crackled through on the other side.

"Hello?" It sounded older and weaker than it had when they met Theo in the dreamscape, but it was definitely the same man.

"Hi," Alura greeted him, "You don't really know me, but…"

"You aren't one of those telemarketers, are ya?"

"No, no," Alura fumbled, afraid that he might hang up on her. She had finally worked up enough courage to call. She needed to come up with a way to explain herself. "My name is Alura. I actually work for a detective agency in New York City."

Alura's hands shook as she rose and began to pace back and forth in her room.

"Oh, ah," Theo said, suddenly less combative, "you work with that fella Horace Brown?"

Out of all the things Alura expected Theo to say, she didn't expect him to ask her *that.* Horace Brown was certainly the most famous detective in New York City. *But how would a man living out in rural Washington know his name?*

"Yes," she confirmed. "Do you know him?" It was the gentlest way for her to get more information.

"Truth be told," he admitted, "I don't know him well. A couple of months ago, he reached out to me to buy one of my paintings. Was asking me about a playing card, you know the one."

Playing card?

"Yes," Alura fibbed, "of course I do."

"Yeah, well," Theo continued, "I don't normally sell my paintings, and the card had sentimental value, but for $50,000? I'd dig a hole to China if that's what he wanted me to do."

The original reason Alura called Theo immediately took a back seat. She closed her eyes and tried to process what Theo had just told her. With every word that Theo said, Alura had another ten questions.

Where did Horace get $50,000? Why is he spending it on a painting and a playing card? Why didn't he tell us that he had spoken to Theo before?

"I was afraid that he wouldn't want the card," Theo continued. "You know how collectors are. Horace had said that it was a limited edition or some nonsense. Had a print of a boy with a pointy stick on one side. There was a funky pattern on the other side with a stick, a circle, a cup, and a knife. This one had a bent corner and some creases. My grandfather gave it to me before we were separated."

"Separated?" Alura had a feeling she knew what separation he was talking about, but she wanted to keep him talking.

"Yeah," he said, "When I was younger, I lost both my parents. My grandfather took me in, but they came and took me away to stay with my Great Uncle Paul at his summer camp. It was alright, but I just wanted to be with Grandpa. He really understood me better than anyone else. Knew just what to say most of the time."

Alura smiled. During a tragic time of his life, he was able to find happiness.

"I actually just lost my parents recently, too," Alura said, trying to get back to the original reason why she called. While she hoped to get back to the information about the painting and the card later, it was an easy transition.

"Oh, I'm so sorry," Theo said, clearing his throat. "You sound young. I wish there was something I could say to make the pain go away, but truthfully there isn't."

She could feel her heart wilt like a rose, the petals falling into her stomach.

"I can tell you though," he said in a cheery tone, "that things will get better." Alura felt as though he could sense her disappointment through the phone.

"How?"

"Well," Theo said, pausing and clearing his throat again. Alura expected some sort of mountain man wisdom. "You will never be the same person again. You will never be rid of the grief. In fact, you will add to it over time. You just need to remember that you lost something, yes, but I'm sure you gained something as well?"

Aunt Kate, Uncle Rick, Alura listed mentally. *The internship, my friends.* Without losing her parents, she would've never moved to New York City. For just a moment, she felt *whole,* like all the puzzle pieces had been returned to her box.

Suddenly, a dog's bark overtook the other end of the phone. *Rusty couldn't still be around, could he?*

"Do you have a dog?" Alura asked innocently.

"Uh huh," Theo replied. "Seems like he's got to go out and do his business too. I call him Crumb. Spends a lot of time in the kitchen, waiting for scraps. I've got Patches here too. She's

369

on my lap. Found her quite a few years ago down at the Night Owl."

Alura wanted to ask more questions about the painting and the playing card but had decided against it. There wasn't much else that Theo would be able to tell her. Besides that, she had gotten the answer that she was looking for. *Theo is happy.*

"Wow," Alura said. "I'm sure they keep you busy."

"Sure do," he chuckled.

The two of them wished each other well, then hung up. Alura thought of Theo for a moment. In a way, she had experienced some of the most influential parts of his life.

After closing out that train of thought in her mind, she circled back to the issue at hand. *A painting? A playing card?* She wondered if Horace would bring up the subject, now that they had solved the first mystery.

She scrolled through her phone and quickly found the *Horace's Heroes* group chat. She sent a message to see if they would be available for a meeting after work.

If Horace is keeping secrets, we're going to have to figure out what's really going on.

Horace Brown
D E T E C T I V E ~~A G E N C Y~~ *Academy*

Follow us

online!

www.DetectiveHoraceBrown.com

@DetectiveHoraceBrown

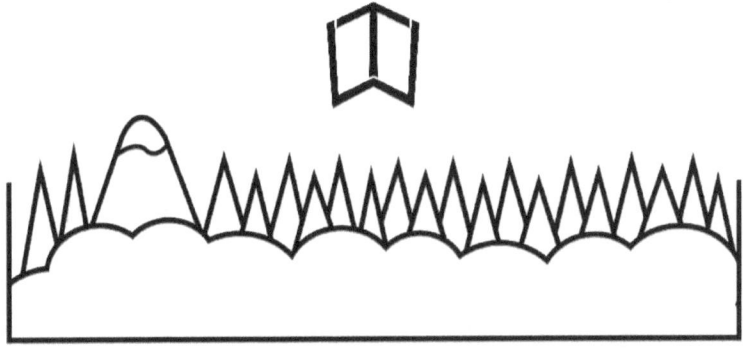